DEVILS...

Man's voice screaming as the dragon lifted and tossed him and caught him in its mouth. Man's voice shrieking as the dragon shook him as a dog shakes a rat. Man's voice babbling witlessly as the dragon released him. Man's voice gibbering as man's feet tottered and ran. Man's voice screaming as the dragon came after him again.

There seemed no end to it.

They had formed a circle, the Devils had —Kar-Chee on the inside, dragons on the outside. The man ran blindly, stumbling, drooling and piddling in terror. The Kar-Chee cuffed him back. He fell, he crawled, he got up, he ran. . . . Blood ran down his naked sides. And suddenly the dragon, as though tired of the sport, closed his jaws with a crunching, mashing sound. The man's voice continued for another second, still, high and thin, like an insect's screech; then it stopped. The dragon tossed the mangled body aside.

DEATH TO THE KAR-CHEE

The author wishes to acknowledge, grate-
fully, the suggestions made for ROGUE
DRAGON by Grania Davidson, Theodore
R. Cogswell, and Damon Knight.

AVRAM DAVIDSON has been a re-
spected figure in both science fiction and
mystery circles for many years. He has
won both the Hugo award for best science
fiction short story of the year, and the
Edgar award for the best mystery story,
and was editor of *The Magazine of Fantasy
and Science Fiction* before turning to full-
time writing. His other books for Ace are
THE PHOENIX AND THE MIRROR
and PEREGRINE: PRIMUS.

The Kar-Chee Reign

Rogue Dragon

Avram Davidson

SF

ace books

A Division of Charter Communications Inc.
A GROSSET & DUNLAP COMPANY
360 Park Avenue South
New York, New York 10010

An ACE Book

Cover art by Olivia

This Ace printing: March 1979

The Kar-Chee Reign

I

THE BIG PLACE on the old Rowan homesite had just been freshly thatched—and what a disturbance of birds, snakes, lizards, mice and spiders the removal of the previous thatch had caused—but its thick walls had stood there for generations; scarred and chipped and streaked with smoke and smeared with grease, but in all, still sturdy. The first Rowan had built well; he had not come here with his wives and children and his flocks and herds after the sinking of California, for he had had none of those. He had in fact landed with one small boat and one small dog and a determined mind and a hopeful heart, marrying a daughter of the land (that is to say, he had concluded a major treaty by the terms of which he granted use of his infinitely precious cold chisel for half a year of every year and in return was granted use for the whole of every year of an area of land for building and farming and hunting and fishing, plus a girl who had been captured almost casually from a far-off people years back and was of an age to be manned), and had put up his house according to a plan existing in his own head only—then, unprecedented; since, the standard model.

He had left behind more than a set of walls

1

and a style in housing. His long head and long bones and wide, smiling mouth were now part of the common fabric of the people; his casual, personal turns of speech had become the way one spoke. If a problem was regarded calmly as something capable of solution instead of occasion to retreat into dreams and resigned surrender, this, too, was part of the long legacy of Rowan the first settler.

The present head of the homesite, old father and artificer, was one Ren Rowan, six generations descended from the settler on one side and seven generations removed on another; his wife's lineage was similar, though of distant cousinship. He was all seamed and grizzled now, she—though slightly younger—only now beginning to show gray in her long hair. Her hands were deft at many tasks. It was her way to offer advice to her husband quietly and in private, it was his—usually—to take it.

"Well, we needn't thatch this roof again for a while," he said to her, she coming to join him on the bench more to treat him with her company than because she particularly needed rest from directing the work of feeding those who had helped with the work.

"Might think of cutting some house timbers," she said, in her soft, slow voice. Meat sizzled and spat. There was a burst of laughter. A child stumbled and wailed, was righted and comforted with a grilled bone that filled the small mouth.

"Might," Ren agreed. "Always might . . . why now?"

His eyes followed hers to where his youngest son stood in conversation with a girl on whose hip his hand rested so lightly that one might almost assume neither of them to know it was there at all. Almost; but not quite. "Mmm. . . . That seems a flighty girl to me. I suppose she's twitched her rump at him and now he doesn't know whether to build a house or drag her off into the bushes. . . . Of course, one needn't preclude the other. Still. Flighty."

Moma said, "Babies make good ballast. You were on the flighty side, too, recollect."

"That was before the Devils came," he said mildly.

"Not so long ago as that. . . . Well. House timbers. Might think about it. . . ."

A comfortable silence fell between them. He, his work being officially over, might have put on the loose shirt and kilt, both decoratively worked in dyed threads, which she had laid out for the purpose in their room. She, her work being officially still on, would not yet slip into the equally loose dress (only the unmarried women need endure the discomfort of tight ones), equally brightly embroidered, which hung in her corner. Both, then, were girded briefly around the waist, and wore no other clothing. The afternoon's sun was still warm.

The moma and popa of Home Rowan looked on and about quietly and contentedly. The large, sturdy old house with its rounded ends was well- and newly-thatched; let the rains fall in due season as they surely would (forfend a drought!), it would not let by a drop. The walling palisade and gate were solid and well-set, the pens held fat stock and poultry, fields and garden were in good tilth, and the storehouses

were as full as any homesite's should be that was
not niggard with its help. Neighbors, kinsmen,
and even those not so allied had come to help
with the work and were feeding and—depending
on age—frolicking or enjoying a peaceful visit. A
potbellied pupdog, descended out of the lean
loins of the Settler Rowan's home companion on
the long voyage hither, nosed along for scraps,
followed by an equally potbellied grandchild.
The pupdog paused, spread its legs, piddled.
The child did the immediate same. . . . Startled
by the sudden laughter, he looked up, ready for
tears. Seeing only Moma and Popa, he smiled
proudly, and gurgled vigorously as he tottered
off in pursuit of the pupdog.

It hadn't always been a goodly scene. There
had been famine, preceded by droughts; plagues
of beasts and plagues of men; there was once
something mightily like a little war; wild beasts
had raided and attacked, and—rarely, rarely—
wild men. Floods had lapped almost to the
doorsills; retreating, they had left behind mud
and wreckage and bloated bodies. A favored
daughter had suffered of a long and painfully
wasting illness before dying, and a less favored
son (perhaps because of that, or for another reason none could think of) had one day walked
down into the ocean and not come out. Nor had
Old Ren, as he was beginning to be called, in-
herited the homesite peacefully. His years of en-
during the usurpatous tenure of his wicked and
godless uncle, Arno Half-Devil, and how he had
finally wrested all away from him and sent him
to die in the caves, formed the integuments of a
legend which was still in formation.

And now, when the minor festivity of the thatch party ordinarily would be beginning to slow down, it received fresh life. In past the carven blue gate posts came another party of guests, their cries and gestures as they saw the new roof firmly in place already expressing a mixture of dismay and self-reproach and rueful good humor.

Old Ren said, "Jow's people . . . late because they started late . . . started late because they didn't think to come at all. Only coming now because Jow's got something on his mind that came up on a sudden. Well. Got to feed them." He rose and prepared to welcome them.

His wife said, "Won't be enough meat. Kill or hunt?"

But he had already gestured his decision to his two younger sons, and was now waiting for Jow to bring his people and his unhappy face up to the bench to be welcomed.

Lors, Duro, four or five of young nephews and cousins to beat and help bear, and one of the just-arrived guests—uninvited, but not thereby unwelcome—trotted off, huntbound. Duro was still young enough to love hunting next to eating. Lors would much rather have stayed with his hand on Mia's hip . . . he would much, *much* rather have gone with her where he could put his hand somewhere else . . . but his father's expression and gesture were alike unmistakable and undeniable. Guests had to be fed, there was no ignoring it, and it was up to the popa to decide if stock were to be killed or if the huntsmen were to go out. The alternatives were equally honorable to the guests. The fields lay, for the most part, up and away from the sea. There were deer in the rainier lowlands; guanaco were to be found only in the highs, well above the fields; and now, as they came to the fork in the way, they had to decide which it was that they were to hunt.

"We'd best go down," Lors said, trying to give his words the sound of judicious reflection. "We can get deer quicker and not delay our guests."

Duro at once countered, seemingly innocently, "And then you can get back and away quicker, and on top of Mia."

The younger boys laughed; the newcomer smiled. Lors wondered if he should hit his brother, decided against it for the moment. "I was thinking only of our guests," he said with dignity. And added, "How do they call you, guest?"

"Tom-small," said the guest, putting the boys to giggling again. He was about Lors' own age, and a rather large young man.

"I shouldn't like to have to share a sleeping-hammock with Tom-big, whoever he is," said Duro. This was an acceptable excuse: Lors hit him.

"No way to talk to guests," he said, righteously.

"He's my uncle," the guest said, unannoyed. "I *used* to be smaller than him, but the name sticks. . . ." He looked up the fork to the right, raising his head toward Mount Tihuaco, only partly obscured by drifting clouds. "I've never been up there. I've heard . . . it's said that on a clear day you can see the ocean on all sides, the whole coastline, from there. . . ." His voice ended on a vaguely questioning note. He was a diffident, amiable one.

Duro said, "Yes, maybe, but I've never seen the day that was that clear. There always seems to be at least some part of the coast you can't see."

Lors understood what Tom-small had in mind. "We really do not have time to go that far today," he pointed out, kindly enough. His eyes were blue-gray, his hair was long and black, his skin a light brown. "Maybe, if you stay over, we could make a special trip—" A half-smile of pleasurable, anticipating assent lit up Tom-small's broad and open face. Lors went on, "But right now we have to get meat. So: it's downward ho for us. Let me tell you the plan.

"There's a spring which the deer favor. And we usually set salt there for them, as a further attraction. The boys will go ahead and around to beat them back this way—if there are any there now. I'll show you, by and by, where we crouch for them along their trail. With three boys, we ought to have luck. Oh! Say—you're all right for hunting, aren't you? I mean, you haven't touched a corpse or a cat or a fluxy female today, have you?" Tom-small shook his head. "That's all right, then."

But Duro wasn't sure it was all right. "How about Mia?" he asked. *"You were touching her!"*

Lors had forgotten. His heart gave a thump, and the blood ran into, then away from his face. How could he have forgotten? But after a second he said, "No, I'm sure it's all right. She knows better; she wouldn't have let me, if— Besides, Popa saw me. He must think it's all right, too, or he wouldn't have sent me."

Satisfied, they started off down the down-slope branch of the fork. Far off below, through a break in the hills, they saw the blue sea. Lors pointed. "That's where the first Rowan landed," he said.

Tom-small looked impressed. "Before the Devils came," he said.

Duro looked at him. "How could that be?" he asked. "If the Devils hadn't come, Rowan would have stayed where he was and not come *here.*"

The young guest looked confused. Then, dismissing the need to figure the matter out, he said, "Well, anyway, it was a long time ago."

It had been, indeed.

And it had all begun much further ago than that.

Earth had become like a woman who has, after a long and painful labor, given multiple birth . . . flat, empty, weary and bare. For the Earth was long enough over the final wave of outward, star-bound emigrants for the last trace of concern and excitement in it to have ebbed utterly away. And there was, it seemed, nothing else.

It had begun calmly enough, this move to the known hospitable worlds swimming around the distant stars. Mankind had waited long enough to be patient at first. No one could say at just exactly what point it all became a frenzy. The Earth went mad; contentedly, controlledly mad . . . and stayed so for centuries. For on the one hand there was instant and continual concern to solve once and for all the old problem of over-population. Those nations which were actually overpeopled—which was most of them—wanted to make an end at last, forever, to crush and hunger. The few that weren't did not and could not remain aloof, for they wanted just as much an end to the fear that the overcrowded countries would spill out of their borders in war. So all worked intently. The first wave of migrants wanted just to get away. Their zeal was negative. But it was nonetheless *zeal*. Then came those who wanted to claim a share of what they heard was out there—land, room, opportunity, adventure. Then came those who wanted just to see for themselves what it was like . . . they said. The next wave went to join family and friends. Finally it became indiscriminately contagious, a roaring wind, sucking up that which lay behind as well as driving on that which lay before it. Those who toiled in sending people out were themselves caught up in it and strove to be themselves sent out. And so, finally, there were comparatively few left behind.

The long morning had been filled with noise. The long afternoon was strangely silent. The silence at first was filled with remembered echo.

Earth's remaining people had worked themselves into an unprecedented fatigue. They had also, it seemed, finally and forever plundered their planet dry. Scarcely a trace of crude metals remained, and not even a trace of mineral fuels. The very wastes of the ancient mines had been reclaimed, reprocessed, redigested and reconsumed. In the last stages, the technicians had cannibalized their own technology, gobbling up factories and smelting down fabric and machinery to consolidate and produce the ultimate

ships. The near-empty cities were at last dis-
mantled for their bones and scrap, ruins ravaged
like pigs nosing for truffles.

Finally, no more ships were built on earth and
no more migrant parties sent off. For a while yet,
though, the old world Earth stayed in touch with
her children via out-world-built ships touching
down with visitors. But there were never many of
them; and as the Earth-born in the outer worlds
grew old and died off, there were ever fewer. So,
finally, even they ceased. There was no announcement, only that the perhaps penultimate
one bore notice, in the form of so few passengers,
that the children-planets had become too caught
up in their own concerns to care much about the
withered mother-world.

Yet no doubt habit alone might have served to
keep up a communication with some semblance
of regularity. The migrants had been as careful
as they might to purge and to protect themselves
against bringing communicable disease with
them as they swarmed out to the series of worlds
which later became known as The Inner Circle.
But when they learned of the presence among
them of the deadliest such disease of all it was
too late: it had blazed up, and it was not to die
down for centuries.

Its name was War.

And it was then, when all the other worlds of
human tenancy were so pre-empted and preoc-
cupied that the very awareness of the Earth-
Motherworld became only faint memory—less,
perhaps, than the memory of Juteland was to
England during her Colonial wars—it was then
that the Kar-chee came. Earth-planet may have

seemed sucked dry, worthless, to those who now lived or whose fathers had once lived on it . . . just as the rind and the pulp of a squeezed orange might. But that same would not seem worthless at all to a pig or a swarm of flies. Nor did it seem so to the Kar-chee. They left their lairs around the Ring Stars and swarmed down onto weary, exhausted, riven old Earth, to pick the bones and crack the plundered planet for its marrow.

The spring and the man-made salt-lick were well set up for hunting, the arroyo and ravine being so as to provide an almost perfect situation for ambush. Only the one narrow way led up to the water welling up at the foot of an abrupt cliff: as the deer went up, so that same way they had to come down. "Beating" was here not the most exact word—the younger boys went up to the top of the cliff-face by another and roundabout way and pelted any deer they might find below with stones and sticks. It was doubtless not sporting, but this was a conception unknown to them. They killed what they needed, and no more, and it made sense to kill as quickly and easily as possible.

Lors and Duro levered down their goat-foot crossbows and loaded them with a bolt each. Tom-small nocked an arrow into his short straight bow, and the three of them picked their hiding places among the rocks and hunkered down. They could, if need be, maintain the position for hours. But, as it turned out, they had to maintain it for something much less.

From above and ahead, faint but clear, after

perhaps a quarter of an hour, the three heard a series of whistles. Duro got up, swearing. Lors shrugged. To Tom-small, who looked at them inquiringly, he said, "No game at the spring. Well, we'll have to go all the way up there to see if there's anything along the path . . . and then come all the way down again, if there is or there isn't."

"Oh, Devil!" said Duro, again.

And there was nothing along the path.

There was nothing along the usual beats, either—no actual game, that is. There was spoor and trace, to be sure, and these signs made them all look at each other with faces wrinkled in uncertainty.

"Upland," Tom-small said. "Everything seems to have gone upland. . . . Do you know why?"

The brothers didn't. "I don't know who'd be beating up from downland hereabouts," Lors said. "I don't smell any fire, either." Automatically, at this suggestion, they all sniffed the air. As though to accomodate them at just that moment the wind shifted.

"What is *that?*" Duro asked, scowling.

No one knew. It was musty and pungent and utterly strange. It might be connected with the curious absence of game; it might not. "Let's go see what it is," said Duro.

Lors shook his head. "Popa didn't send us out for anything but to get meat, and the meat's all gone upland, it seems, so we just have to go upland after it. When we get back we can tell him about it, and he'll know what to do."

"By the time we get back with anything—if

we find anything—they'll all be hungry, anyway," his brother pointed out. He looked windward, made as though to reload his crossbow.

"The longer we wait and gibble-gabble, the hungrier they'll be. Up," said the elder. And turned and started. Tom-small and the younger boys followed at once. So, after a moment, did Duro. They went upland, all of them, but they came within shot of no game. Once they stopped stock-still at the sight of three deer outlined upon the top of a ridge, heads all up. For a moment nothing moved, nothing was heard. Then, far off and below, it came . . . deep and distinctive and strange, and it sounded again—the deer darted off and were gone—and it seemed to have ended upon a higher, a questioning note.

"It's no horn," guest Tom-small said, low-voiced, evidently answering his own unspoken questioning.

But as to what it was, none had any suggestion. They nodded when Lors said, finally, "All game gone upland . . . nobody beating besides us, that we know of . . . a bad smell, a strange smell . . . and now a strange noise. . . .

"My guess is that whatever made the smell is making the noise. It's gotten late. We'd better go back and tell Popa, that's the best thing, and we can kill stock for the guests and then we'd all better find out what this thing is."

As they started back, Duro said, "Maybe it would be better to find out as soon as can be, even if it's got to be done on an empty belly." His brother grunted his agreement. The smaller boys were all silent, and kept close instead of spreading out. The sun declined away behind

the mountain and the air felt chilly on their skins
—and perhaps it was not just the air.

They followed Lors without questioning when
he picked a trail over fallen rock which would cut
time off their return. And it was while the loose
shale was still sliding a bit under their feet that
they all stopped short with no more sound at
first than the hissing intake of breath and looked
down where his hand pointed and where it trembled despite all his brave effort.

Along the distant shore below, at that same
shelving beach where the first Rowan had
brought his tiny boat ashore, there, outlined
against the wine-dark sea, they saw the forms of
two utterly strange and utterly dissimilar figures
stalking across the twilight landscape—one
erect, though slightly stooping; the other on all
four giant legs which held it high above the sand.

Slowly, fearfully, they sank down and spread
themselves flat upon the shale. After an infinity
of time the two strange beasts passed out of sight
around a bend in the shore line. Then,
crouching, sliding, trotting almost as they
squatted and slid, spraddle-legged, the young
hunters vanished into the safe-promising shadows. And only when the dearly familiar walls of
the homesite, outlined by the vigorous fires still
burning outdoors, came into view did any of
them speak. It was the youngest and smallest of
the boys.

"Devil," he said. "Devil." He was not swearing. "Devil—Devil—it was the Devil!" he chat-
tered.

And Lors said, "Maybe. . . . Maybe. . . . But
—*which one?*"

II

THE RAFT WAS low on one side. Whether the underbeams had been lashed wrong, or if something in the wood had caused more and sooner waterlogging, or— No one worried or cared about that any longer. It was accepted with a brute resignation, like the burning sun and the scant food and drink, the waves which lapped up and over all around and left salt encrustations which itched and stung the swollen flesh. Three people already had gone off that perilous slope— one had slipped and slid, shrieking, while the others had looked on and blinked their burning eyes and licked their cracking lips and otherwise done nothing; one had simply rolled off, a scatter of rags and flailing limbs, uttering no sound; and the third, with a pleased smile and a look of anticipation, had just walked off at a brisk pace, knee-deep before he'd plunged out of sight.

Now and then a shark circled, leisurely, and those who still had the energy to do so crawled as high as they could, as though fearing that the great cartilaginous fish might suddenly sprout legs and climb up after them. And now and then a huge sea-turtle flippered by, paying them no attention at all; some eyed it hungrily, but helplessly: the small boat in which they might have pursued it had gone in a storm uncounted time

ago, and even had it remained it was doubtful if
any of them now would have had the strength to
man it.

Some few fishing-lines still dangled, some
presently without even hooks, and none with
other bait than a bit of cloth of similar counterfeit. It had been days since any of these had
succeeded in catching anything—a bony, ugly
thing, but the man whose line it adhered to had
eaten it at once, fearful and famished and secretive and swift. Then he had vomited it all up.
Then he had eaten it a second time, shameful
and slow and sick.

It had been months. It seemed like months.
Perhaps it was only weeks. Perhaps, by now,
years. Liam would know, if anyone knew, Cerry
thought. Vaguely, she considered asking Liam if
he still kept up his records. But the notion soon
ceased to interest her. She had too little voice
left, her mouth and throat were too dry, for her
to call over to him where he sat, crouching, motionless. He might be dead. But she didn't want
to face this possibility. If Liam were dead then
the rest of them were as good as dead. So she
made her mind consider other things.

Suppose the raft were to encounter flying fish.
A whole entire school of them. Then the sail and
the awning could be used as nets. Everyone
would have something to eat. And then—since
flying fish lived in the tropics and in the tropics
it was very rainy—then it would rain, and the
rain water would be caught in those same sails
and awnings. All at once everyone would be better, healthy, alert, in good spirits and humor.
Their luck thus once turned, obviously land

would be the next thing to appear. *Land!*

It would be a good land, with friendly people, not savage, neither terrible nor terrified. The land and people didn't know of hunger, and there were no dragons in that land and neither were there Kar-chee. And . . . and then . . .

Cerry wondered what was next, smiling and giving little nods. The bubble did not so much burst as simply vanish; and, the vision forgotten as though it had never begun, she wondered and fretted mildly how long they had all been on the raft. At least a month. She had had her courses just before they'd embarked—a minor discomfort and a common and regular one: odd that she should remember it against the background of that hideous time and trouble—and then, surely, she had had them again at least once since then, aboard the raft. She could not remember it having happened another time. Which meant that it had not been two months yet. Or, possibly, that her body no longer functioned as it once had. Small wonder, if this were so. But what if Liam were dead?

The fear was worse than the pain of finding out. So, slowly and so slowly, Cerry raised herself onto her painful hands and knees and began to crawl and to creep and to climb across the cant of the raft toward the figure which half-sat, half-crouched, in the splotchy shade of the tattered awning. And the gorgeous golden sun beat down unceasingly from the blazing blue of the silent sky. There was a child stretched out, face down, back moving in slight rise and fall of feeble breath. Cerry did not dare stop or try to move other than as she was moving. Neither did the woman move who croaked, "Murderers! Murderers!" as Cerry dragged herself over the child.

"Are you human beings?" the woman demanded. "Or are you dragons? Kill me, kill me, only leave my child alone. . . ." Her head, at least, at last, commenced to weave from side to side, but by then Cerry was past. "Help, help," the woman croaked, striking her head with her skeletal paw of a hand. "Human beings: help, help. There are dragons on the raft. . . ." The child gave a ghost of a whimper. "Yes, my precious. Don't cry, my dearest love. Mother's coming. . . ." She moved toward the child like a crippled snake.

A hot gust smote the sea. The torn cloth slapped and snapped. The raft shook. A wave hit it; it shook again. Something dead went floating by and someone not quite dead pointed and wept, but it was too far away. Liam had one brown eye and one blue eye and otherwise his eyes were red as blood. His sun-bleached, salt-encrusted hair moved in the light wind like clumps of dirty marsh grass. He didn't blink or breathe as Cerry came lurching and creeping. "Liam, don't be dead. Tell me how long it's been," Cerry asked. He didn't blink or breathe. She could see the wind moving the little hairs on his chest, but she couldn't see the chest move.

She butted his knee with her head, like a lamb forcing its dam to give down milk. He fell over on his side. "Don't be dead, Liam," she begged.

After minutes, hours, years, he said something. He made a sort of snoring noise. He said something. "What, Liam? What?"

She crept close. "Maybe a dream," he said.

She listened. She strained to hear. The man who had pointed to the dead thing watched them. He sat up a bit. He watched them. The mother stroked her child's face. But her eyes did not really watch the child. Her eyes watched them. "May be a dream, Cerry," Liam said. "But I think I did. One night . . . I think . . ."

It had not been a dream. He had. He really had. In the box with the rotting ropes and other gear and tackle, he had really, on that night he half-remembered, secretly and cautiously placed some food—then, when food had still been plentiful and all had been optimistic, for they would soon reach Gal; none had ever been to Gal but all had been sure it was only a week's voyage away—against the possible time when, if Gal had not been reached, they might well be thankful for the food. And of course they had not in any week's voyage reached Gal, they did not know now if it were one week or a year of weeks, if winds and currents had carried them forever past it or if Gal itself had been sunk by the Karchee. But the food was still there.

It lay in her hands as she brought it up to the surface for long enough for her to see that it was in a bag sewn of soft cloth, part of a dress, and by the feel of it potatoes. Small, gone soft, gone sprouty, but food. "It's to be divided," she warned herself softly. "It's to be divided!" she shrieked as it was torn from her hands. The man who had pointed to the dead thing in the sea and wept because it was too far to secure it for the raft did not weep now, but gibbered and spat and clawed Cerry's face with his left hand. The bag was torn from his right hand by the woman of the child. *It's to be divided!* screamed Cerry.

And it was divided, though not according to the calm and rational scheme intended. Who would have thought there was still so much life left in them all? So much evil, so much greed? The dead rose up from the deck which was their grave and screamed and growled and fought. They bit the hands which held the shrunken, blackened potatoes, and clawed them up into their own hands. But the woman of the child, when the cloth of the bag ripped and the black manna fell and scattered, did not use her hands to seize. She crawled upon her hands away from the scene, her sunken cheeks full and smiling. She crawled to her child and kissed the child mouth to mouth and chewed for the child and fed it as a bird is fed. The thin, scrannel throat moved, slowly, slowly. When the child smiled at last, the woman, her own mouth now empty of all but love, said, in loving and rapturous tones, *"There,* my darling. . . . *There,* my precious. Did you like that? Was it good?" She composed herself beside the child, carefully arranged some tatters of her dress so as to cover the small face from the shade, and then, still smiling, died.

The man who had pointed to the dead thing in the sea and had wept and then later had snatched the sacket of food wept again. Or so it seemed. Drops flowed down his face, but they were red and he lay still. And more than one looked at him and looked at each other and looked away from each other and then looked back at him. For the few and small bits of provision in the sacket were gone now, but the hunger which had been lying somewhat dulled and anesthetized was wide awake now and gnawing.

And the man himself was dead now and he was not at all too far away to be reached.

"Are you human beings? Or are you dragons?" one of them had lately asked. And now it might be that none of them was at all sure.

In ravaging and in ravishing their own world for its minerals in order to make the means to abandon that world forever for newer and fresher, richer ones, the men of Earth had carried on—more or less—as they had done for the mere thousands of years in which mining had engaged the attention of their species. The holes they dug were deeper and the pits they scooped were wider and both of course were more numerous. They had left the landscape scarred and fractured, but it was, when they had done with what they were doing, still recognizably the same landscape.

But long before the Kar-chee were done with it, it was no longer so.

The Kar-chee were ten feet tall and a dull, dull black, with heads which seemed tiny in comparison to their height and perhaps particularly in comparison to the huge anterior forelimbs. In this they resembled the mantis, but in nothing else did they resemble anything else with which the scattered handfuls of infinitely wearied peoples on Earth were familiar. *Kar-chee* they were called, from a real or a fancied similarity to sounds which they were heard to make by those few who had come close to them, close enough to hear them, and departed whole; but what they called themselves, no man knew.

There had been no dialogue between the two
species. Had there ever been between men and
ants?

So, the old dwellers called the incomers *Kar-
chee* in much the manner that a child calls a dog
Bow-wow—though the Kar-chee, of course, were
nothing at all like dogs. The Kar-chee, in a way,
were audible ants. Conquering ants. Ants which
brought with them their fulcrum, and, finding a
place on which to rest it, did what Archimedes
never could do, and moved the Earth.

Piece by piece.

Of old, in the lost land of California, came the
Americans and dug and washed the dirt for gold,
and left behind great heaps of soil from which all
profit was extracted. After them came the Chi-
nese, and washed the once-washed dirt again
and, counting labor and toil as nothing, extracted profit from the unprofitable, content
with tiny flecks of dust where only nuggets had
satisfied their predecessors. Neither of them, of
course, in the least understanding the other. But
understanding, at least, that there was something to understand.

This much seemed at least clear—the Kar-
chee had done this before. Their movements
were too practiced, their equipment too suitable,
their techniques too efficient, to allow for any of
it to be new to them. Scavengers of worlds
beyond number they must have been, for ages
beyond counting; and in those worlds
throughout those ages they had developed sys-
tems of working titanic changes in oceans and in
continents in order to get at and get out the veins
and pockets and the merest morsels of minerals
and such as were left behind by human ex-

ploiters. First they reprocessed the slag and the
tailings and the cinders and the ashes and all the
mountainous heaps of (to man) worthless by-
products. Then they scored great trenches on
land and sea and turned their contents over and
over again like earthworms, digesting and re-
digesting. They peeled the earth like an onion.
But all of this was the merest beginning. . . .

When they had done what they wanted with a
given section of land, for the present time, at
least (and who knew what "time" meant for
them? how long they lived? or how they died, or
where, or at all?), then with inhuman efficiency
and ineffable insouciance they disposed of it.
They triggered the long-set charge provided by
the pre-existent San Andreas Fault, and California in convulsions and hideous agonies sank
shrieking into the sea. And before the waters had
in the least begun to settle, they were convulsed
again as the floor of the Gulf of California arose
trembling and quaking and flinching from the
air it had not encountered in countless ages. The
Kar-chee barely waited for it to dry before they
settled onto it like flies upon a carcass and commenced to suck the hidden treasures of its sands.

There must have been some plan determining
which lands should live and which should die,
which perish by volcanic fire and which by the
overwhelming of water. But no man knew in the
least what plan there was. Sometimes, though, it
did seem that here a land was sunken and here
a land raised up, not because of immediate particular concern for either but instead because of
problems concerning the adjustment and read-
justment of the weight upon the Earth's surface.
Thus Gondwanaland arose again, and lost At-

lantis, and land-masses—subcontinents or great islands—were newly designed and surfaced, while the familiar terrains were often fragmented or destroyed. And all the while the vast equipages of the Kar-chee, like huge and mobile cities, alien beyond the phantasizing ability of the human mind, slowly and relentlessly roamed surfaces and sea-depths, turning and churning and extracting and processing. And the great black hulks of the Kar-chee ships came and went . . . endlessly . . . endlessly. . . .

And—meanwhile—what of man?

At first, then, of man: nothing. What of the ants, when man had first come to occupy and to use new territory? One might step on an ant, idly encountered. If they become too intrusive, too troublesome, then one might take means to prevent their incursions. One would not, ordinarily, think too much about them; they were too small, alien, insignificant. Who considered a possible "history" of ants? Or who reflected that ants might have a "prior claim," as it were, to any place? But if in time ants became more troublesome, then, and only then, would attention take the form of destroying ant-hills—or, ecologically, introducing natural enemies which might do the work of destroying them and allow mankind to go about its own and proper business of plundering and polluting the world man lived in.

Thus, meanwhile, *that* of man.

Some handfuls of them dwelt, drowsy and fatigued, in what had been called the British Isles, when the Kar-chee came. Some, out of curiosity, had investigated . . . intruded . . . had been destroyed. Others had moved away. And continued to move, as the Kar-chee and their gargantuan machinery advanced. There was no thought of fighting, of resisting. Man was too few, Kar-chee too many; the invaders too strong, the autochthones too weak, too disorganized and inexperienced. One might hypothesize a situation wherein the children-worlds became aware of Earth's plight, and had sent help. But the children-worlds were not aware, and after the few first generations had died away, the very memory of such worlds had died away with them.

Man, in short, adjusted.

Where there were no Kar-chee, the people slowly increased in number, slowly developed new skills, new forms, new views. Where there were Kar-chee, the people either perished or retreated before them. The remnants of Earth's wild life, where the Kar-chee did not yet venture or remain, and while man was still so few, increased as well. Once again the trees grew tall, the herbivores replenished their flocks and herds, the wild swine flourished in the marshes and masted on the nuts and acorns, the fish returned to the cleansed-again waters.

It was fortunate, providential, that the last centuries of the movement of man away from Earth had coincided with the last centuries of a cold cycle. It may well have made no difference to the Kar-chee what the climate of the northerly part of the Northern Hemisphere was, tapping as they did the molten heart of the planet for energy. But the return of a warm cycle may have made all the difference to the bands of men living there. And when Britannia proper sank beneath the waves it once had ruled, and most of Ireland

with it, when a new great island was created by
joining the Outer Hebrides and the Isle of Man
with much of Northern Ireland—then, great
though the shock was, it was the milder climate
which enabled the survivors to . . . survive. New
rivers flowed into the sea through new beds; for
a while they ran brackish as the rains washed the
salt from the new-formed land. Eventually the
whole new land was cleansed, and, richer than
the older lands now joined with it by reason of its
accumulations of eons of organic matter, it benefited by the milder climate and the longer growing season, and its people benefited even more.
For the Kar-chee did not come. Perhaps they
had intended the changes wrought in the south.
No one ever knew. What they did know was that
the Kar-chee did not come, and this was of the
most infinite importance.

Indeed, it might have been that what had occurred there had been done to balance what had
occurred in California, when Rowan the first
had fled, a sea-borne single Noah, an Aeneas
fleeing fatherless across the sullen seas. None
could say.

So the centuries continued to pass; there, in
the Kar-chee-created (yet Kar-chee-ignored)
northern land, as in the fragment of former
South America which Rowan found, man re-
discovered old skills and learned and developed
new ones. New societies began to form, were
formed, and new forms of civilization arose. A
distorted memory of what had happened remained with them in both places, as in others.
But for the most part a life was lived which concerned itself more with the present than with the
past. And then, in a village located on the high

hill which was once the Hebridean island of Ben-becula, men looked out and saw, with astonished anger, the Kar-chee coming at long last.

It was different this time than the first time. The human race had recovered from its fatigue, for one thing. For another, distance and the long, blind oblivion of time had hidden from Liam and Cerry and their fellows experience of how dangerous the Kar-chee really were.

The great war-horns sounded, the alarm-drums were beaten, the farmers came running from the fields and the herds-men from their kine, the fishing-coracles put in from sea. And while Liam and the other fighting men mustered on the palisades which topped the earthen em-bankments around the townlet, Cerry and the other women boiled huge earthen pots of water by dropping red-hot stones in them. Thus they had prepared themselves against attack by either local factions or pirate-raiders from across the seas; and thus, straining and pulling and pushing, they set the lumbering catapults in place and loaded them with cold charges and set the stone shot to heating in the fires. On the part of the men, then, all proceeded according to plan.

But the Kar-chee, seemingly, had other plans.

A miner takes small heed of the swarming of an ant-hill.

The men of Benbecula had no such things as surveying-instruments; they would not have rec-ognized them even had the devices been of hu-man manufacture. The local chief, peering through the single and ancient telescope the place afforded, saw only that enemies had engines and that these moved in direction to and fro, and when they paused a moment and seemed pointed and poised at his defenses, he waited not, but gave the signal to fire.

Probably not a single shot struck the cluster of tall and slightly stooping black figures, but the thumping and crashing of their various impacts nearby drew the attention of the Kar-chee. The tiny triangular heads whipped up from their instruments and peered around; the stout anterior arms unfolded and waved about. The Kar-chee commenced to move on. Perhaps they did so merely because it was time to move. But the men of Benbecula did not consider this. They had fired on their enemies and their enemies were beginning to retreat. *When the enemy retreats, advance.* Thus, the old maxim. And, thus, shouting fierce cries of triumph and menace, waving war-clubs and making feints with their bone-tipped lances, arrows ready to be nocked on bowstrings, the levy en masse poured out of the fortified hamlet and down upon the aliens. The wind shifted and suddenly smelled no more of wood-smoke and heather and human sweat, but of something murky and pungent and strange. The shaggy ponies on which the lancers were mounted, toes gripping leather stirrups, neighed, fought, bolted for a less hateful air.

The charge, to give credit, did not stop for more than a moment. Liam, frank, said later to Cerry, "We didn't dare retreat, for then they should have attacked *us*—and they had the longer legs!" Now the Kar-chee did retreat, it seemed, or most of them did. Others stayed and whipped about them with the tripods of their instruments (clumsy weapons, the men considered!), but, being to being and implement to implement, not even the superior height of the Kar-chee availed them victory. Their longer legs did not prevent their being clubbed to the ground, and if their chitinous exoskeletons protected them for a while against thrusting points, it was only a short matter to discover that this armor had unprotected under-folds. The lances entered, were pressed home, the clubs beat and threshed, soon the clickings and churfings of the aliens ceased; the alien limbs twitched but a moment more.

So, dragging bodies and booties behind them, and singing impromptu songs of victory—including several verses directed at the unhappy cavalry—the triumphant defenders returned. The postures of defense were abandoned as quickly as they had been assumed, and Benbecula plunged into a frenzy of drunken feasting and rejoicing.

But Liam did not entirely join in it.

"What's wrong?" Cerry asked him. She had never at all made the error of thinking that because his eyes were different colors and his appearance therefore odd that there was anything at all wrong with the rest of him.

His face twisted, and he shook his head. All around him drunken shouts resounded. She put her ears to his lips. "Don't like it," he said. "Acting as though they'd driven off a raider-bunch from Orkland or Norland. . . . This is more, Cerry—much, much more. . . ."

He mumbled, shook his head, frowning, like a bothered child: another of the things which made some people think him a mere daftie. She knew better. She listened. She heard him, reconstructing from his mutterings, explain what was vexing him. That not everything the old-mothers nattered about the Kar-chee as they sat warming their dried-up feet by the fire, not all of it was or could be true: of course not, else the Kar-chee would have arrived riding upon their dragons as in the old tales, flying through the air and throwing bolts of fire. Would have picked up the land bodily and flown it away to the Northern Hell, whence the sight of the flames could be seen of nights now and then. Would have dipped it in the burning waters and burnt them off like beetles off a burning log.

Well, then? she asked. If not true—and he reasoned well that it was not—why worry, then? A merrymaker came garbling up to him, waving what seemed to be a Kar-chee's foot, and Liam pushed him away with such force that he never came back for explanation or fight, but hunted a horn of honey-strong to soothe his bewilderment. Why worry, then? Because, clearly, not all the oldmother's tales had been false, either. For the existence of the Kar-chee, whom none of them had ever seen or smelled until today, was the very warp and woof and thrums of the old-mothers' tales. . . .

Now Cerry had the turn to frown and squint. Although sharing in the rejoicing, initially, and feeling no more misgivings than resentment at not having gotten to scald the attackers with boiling well-water, her long-felt and distinctive respect for Liam convinced her that if he thought something was wrong, then something was *wrong*. She tried to follow his line of thought, but it was too strange for her. So, instead, she tried to tell him what she felt for him and about him;

but all that came out was the old, conventional question: "Shall I take my sheepskin and come and be a while in your cabin?"

If he had given one of the old, conventional answers—say, if only, "Take and be"—why, that would have been good and she would have been happy; if, "You may take your featherbed and come and be in my cabin forever,"—why that would have been very, very good and she would have been very, very happy.

But now instead he looked at her straightly, one odd eye as brown as loch-water and the other as blue-green as the open sea itself; and what he said now was stranger yet: "You may take your sheepskin and follow after me, if you will, but not to lie by me as a woman lies by a man. For I fear there will be many nights upon the cold ground and many upon the cold, cold sea before ever we may think of love or bairns or houses once again."

The words sounded as through from an old tale, sung and chanted to the background of pipe or harp or drum; yet she knew that she had never heard them before. And fast and hard upon this she knew, quite suddenly, in her heart, that the times were now come about which songs were sung and tales composed; and that Liam was and had always been destined to be one of those men, seers and doers and heroes, who figured in those tales. And, like a hand taking hold of her heart and tightening on it, she knew she would and must go with him and endure with him as long as his tale was run, come what might.

Liam got up and left the sound and sight of the feasting and the fires and went out into the chill night. And Cerry followed after him and they took their sheepskins and their sticks and their little pots of fire and their sackets of food and they walked toward the north. Thus it was that when the dragons came to Benbecula Liam and Cerry were in North Uist and when the dragons came to North Uist he and she were part-way to Ulsland. The dragons were not then in quick haste to make an end of men, and indeed it did seem that they drew out their destruction to suit their pleasure and that of the Kar-chee, to avenge whom they had come. And by the time that the dragons began to stir toward the marches of Uls, Liam and Cerry were building in haste their great raft to carry them and those who believed in Liam and his warning over the seas to Gal.

Gal, however, they never found. Nor any other place which it seemed might do for refuge. They found bleak lands, all salt and sterile, all stone or sands, or crushed stones; they found lands all smoking and burning and slag; they found lands where naked men hid behind the rocks and then rushed howling out upon them. And once they found a land of grass and trees and they gave thanks before they prepared to go ashore . . . but then the watcher on the masthead cried out that he saw that there were Kar-chee and dragons already in that land; and they rushed to hoist the ragged sail again and gave greater thanks than before when wind and currents carried them safely past and out, even though it were to starve and parch, to sea.

And so, finally, there was no more food and no more water and the sky and sun grew hot upon them and they looked with greedy and sickened eyes upon the body and the blood of the one who had made to steal the last of the food; and they wondered if they dared not use it as food. Cerry wept for sorrow that her hunger had been aroused once again and for joy that Liam was not dead. Liam muttered, but not to and not about Cerry; he muttered words as confused as his own mind; he muttered about maps.

Maps! The very concept drew a blank look from all but a few of his countrymen. But Liam knew what a map was, knew what a book was; had seen both. Both were, presently, pragmatically, useless, referring to and depicting things which no longer existed. But the conceptions were infinitely important, and they stirred his mind with excitement and frustration. Inside his tattered trews was a rough, ungainly copy of a map which he had once made. It was, of course, useless as a guide, showing as it did lands which no longer existed and failing to show lands which now did. He wondered, fevered, sunstricken, famished and parched, if accurate maps of any sort existed anywhere at all. Not likely. He avoided the obvious admission: not possible. So, as Cerry had dreamed of flying fish and rain, so Liam lay dreaming of an accurate map, a true chart, showing lands and currents and winds. . . .

He saw the island as it came slowly into view and he did nothing. He watched the island change into a ship and he did nothing. He watched the one or two or three of the others on the raft who still had the semblance of strength, watched them creep and heard them croak and saw them gesture; he did nothing. The ship was

not that at all, it was a whale; the whale calfed,
the calf came toward the raft, men riding on it
. . . in it. . . . He watched his craft become the
captive of the whale and he suffered himself to be
carried into the belly of the whale. He did nothing. But after an age of darkness he felt wet upon
his tongue. And he swallowed.

Still later, he thanked his graybeard succorer,
whispering, "We would have died. We have no
maps."

"I know," said graybeard.

"Fled . . . dragons . . . killing, tearing . . . Kar-
chee . . ."

"I know. I know."

"No land . . . no refuge . . . no rain. . . ."

Said graybeard, "I know."

After a long pause, he asked, "Who are you?
And what is this place?"

Said graybeard: "I am the Knower. This is
the Ark."

III

A STOCK ANIMAL had already been killed and was in process of being eaten when Lors, Duro, the young guest Tom-small and the younger boys arrived back at the Rowan homesite. But there did not seem to be much pleasure taken in the eating by anyone. Lors wondered, shortly, why guards had not already been posted and the gates secured—or why everyone had not fled inland and upland—but before long this became clear enough, though it never became acceptable, to him.

They found guest Jow, a very dark-brown man with a fleece of curly hair, off in a corner with old Ren Rowan: now Jow talked, intently, and Ren gnawed on a piece of meat; now Ren expostulated as Jow bit into his own victual. They shook their heads, they waved their hands, they took each other by the arms and elbows and shoulders. But they spoke so low that no one else could hear a word of what they were saying.

But moods, of course, are as contagious as maladies. Jow may have bottled up whatever was on his mind en route to Rowen homesite, but he had not bottled it up any longer than it took to bring his mouth next to Ren's ear. Ren, clearly, was not disposed to take the matter as something light or easy. The arrival of the young men and boys caught at once the attention of the two older men, and a curious mixture of relief

and apprehension came over their seamed faces
as they spoke almost at once.

"Did you see anything?"—from Ren.

"What did you see?"—from Jow.

But before Ren's sons or Jow's son could answer, one of the little boys burst out with, "We
saw the Devils—we saw two Devils!" and broke
into tears and sobs of pent-up fright. A
moment's stunned silence. Women and girls
ready to laugh and dispell the tension, thinking
that the two elders were talking of some matter,
perhaps, of a threatened and serious feud: a love
affair discountenanced for weighty reasons, a
disputed inheritance, a man-slaughter or serious
injury done in anger, a land-quarrel—all sufficient to justify the mood of secretive agitation. It
was a mood they would be glad enough to light-
en; the women and girls ready to laugh looked
up and over at the older men's faces—

And saw no amusement in them, not even justified annoyance at boyish babbling; but saw the
muscles of Jow's mouth and throat writhing as if
he had been struck by an arrow, saw a look of
sick dismay upon the face of Ren Rowan. And as
though it was death's approach made visible,
the women and the girls began to wail and weep.
A log of wood collapsed into its own embers in
the fire and the sudden shower of sparks flaring
outward and upward illuminated the scene of ignorant alarm and confusion and fright—children screaming, dogs jumping up and barking,
babies awaking to add their contribution to the
clamor—

"Enough of this!" shouted Jow, his huge voice
felling the turmoil like an axe a tree.

And, "Women, be quiet," Ren growled, standing up and showing the flat of his hand. Noise did not altogether cease but it went from a scream to a murmur. "Better," he rumbled. "I'll give you more Devil, otherwise, than you can use.—You: little Tino, put some meat in your mouth. The rest of you, too. Now—my sons and Jow's son—and you, Carlo"—he beckoned over his eldest, a married man whose skilled hands made up for his bad leg—"come over here." Rapidly he made a decision. This was no mere inter-family matter. "And all the men and older boys, too. All of you. Over here."

Lamps were brought, shallow shells of oil or animal grease, and sticks were thrust hastily into the fire and then pulled out again to make torches. Flames flickered and flared, breaths were drawn noisily, and finally all were settled around the two elders.

"Now," said old Ren once more. "You, Tom-small; what did you see?" He didn't ask him to mind his voice didn't carry past the male circle, but pitched his own low enough to get his point across.

Tom-small gave a feeble, bashful smile, but went on with what he had to say firmly enough. "We saw all the game had gone upland and we smelled a bad smell none of us knew and we saw two creatures that none of us knew. They were big. We came back, host Rowan."

"Well told. Short. Anything to add, any of you?"

None had, until Jow, his face now expressionless, asked, "These two strange creatures—what did they look like?"

Attempts to describe them were made, but
were not successful. Then Carlo, Ren's oldest
son, said, "May I, then? So . . . so look
here. . . ." He took up a stick, broke it with a
snap, scratched in the dirt with the now-sharp
point of it. "Did what you see . . . did it look like
this? Or like this? Think before you answer, and
don't say it did unless you are quite sure that it
did. . . . Eh?"

His brothers and the young guest drew in
their breaths, hissing. They nodded, lips drawn
back from their teeth. And Lors said, pointing,
"One of them did look like that—just like that."
He pointed to Carlo's first sketch-figure, of
something thin and somewhat stooping, standing on four thin limbs, with two stout limbs
folded aloft. "And the other was like this other,
yes, except that in this picture it's upright, running on two legs . . . and when we saw it, it was
walking, walking on all fours. . . .

"But it's them, all right, Carl. . . . It's them.
It's them."

And he asked the same question his father
now asked, voice upon voice. "How did you
know?"

The oldest brother said, "In one of the caves,
far, far to the back, up through a crack in the
upper part, is a chamber . . . I think there's
more, even beyond there, but I never dared to
look past there . . . and only once, when I was a
boy and playing a game and hiding, I found my
way there. But no one else came after me and I
grew frightened. I had my fire things with me
and I made fire. What I drew here—that's what
I saw on the wall in that chamber. Someone had

drawn them there, with lamp-black and green clay mixed with lamp-black. Of course, when I saw them, I was even more afraid than ever, and I got out as fast as I was able. I even left my fire things there. They may still be in there, for all I know. . . . Anyway, the second I saw those drawings, I felt in my heart that they had to be Devils. It was a long time ago and I never told anyone, but I've dreamed of them so often I never forgot them."

All was so quiet upon the finish of his words that they could hear one of the llamas protesting in the stock pens. And old Ren said, "Well, now. . . . You saw paintings when you were a boy, in a sort of secret side-room in one of the caves; and you felt in your heart they must be Devils. Now, today, your younger brothers and some more young ones, they saw—seems clear enough, seems to be true enough—they saw, alive, what you saw drawn. And Tino, he said that what you saw was Devils. So. It seems to me that it's natural enough, whenever a boy sees something strange and new and frightening, for him to call it Devil. But, after all, we don't *know* what these creatures really are. Fear is easily come by.

"None of you, not even guest Jow, are old enough to remember my rogue uncle, Arno. Everyone was in fear of him, and largely it was because of a tale that nights, when it pleased him, he'd go and change his body into the shape of what they called a half-Devil, a sort of giant cat, all spotted, do you see. I never believed it, never believed any of it. Whichever body he was to die in, they said, he'd turn into the other. So. When news was brought me that he'd died at last, in

the caves there, down I went; found him dead
enough, and one of his women with him—a mis-
erable thing, she was, fit for him, but she was
loyal at least.

" 'Did he die as a man?' I asked.

" 'As a man,' she said.

" 'And has he changed his shape yet?' I asked
her.

" 'Not yet,' she said.

"So I had him brought out and we watched
him, someone always watching him, by day and
by night, till be began to moulder. Then I told
them and showed them how the tale was nothing
but a tale, and we buried him. So. Time passed.
Years. And once, looking in some old bales and
boxes from his time, Rogue Arno's, I'll tell you
what it was I came across—it was a pelt, you see,
the skin of a sort of giant cat, all spotted. Never
I saw such a thing alive, nor don't know where or
when it lived or died. But it was not a Devil, any
more than Arno was. It was a strange thing, and
easy to fear. He knew it, he dressed himself with
it by nights, played upon that fear . . ."

The words of old Ren, slowly, softly, calmly
spoken, had gradually softened and calmed the
mood of most of his listeners. But they had not
calmed Jow, who said, shaking fleecy head,
"You don't mean us to think, host Ren, that
whoever drew those pictures in the cave, and our
boys, today—you don't mean to have us think
that what they saw were *men?* Men who put on
strange hides to frighten us?"

Ren said, "I don't know. I didn't see them.
The boys today didn't see them close, either. I
know this: for one thing, if a picture of them was

made at the time or before the time that Carl was a boy, then the things the pictures were drawn of were either here then or had been here before then. Nothing happened then to make us fear them, so why should we fear them now? There are, of course there are, strange creatures on land and sea. What of it?"

Jow had vigorous ideas as to what of it. The land they lived in, he pointed out, was an island, and they knew of—though they had not themselves visited them—other islands to the south and east. But they all knew well enough that this land and those other lands had once formed one great land, long ago, before (he used the common speech-figure which meant long, *long* ago) —"before the Devils came."

"What did they do when they came?" Jow asked. "Didn't they split the great land apart? Didn't they sink most of it? Didn't they hold it under the water to kill the folk, the way you'd hold a kitten under to kill it? No, Ren. *No!* You say that fear comes easy. True. But so does the fear of fear, I tell you. I'd rather be afraid for nothing, for then, by and by, we'll find out it's nothing—if it *is* nothing—than let danger slip up and find us unaware and unprepared. Wasn't California sunk, too? Wasn't the first Rowan my oldfather, too, as well as yours? Ren! Have you forgotten what it was that he said—the same thing as was said by the other oldparents already here:

" *There is a thin Devil that has four limbs to walk with and two limbs to work with. And there is a thick Devil that walks on four limbs and runs on two: this is the thin Devil's scout, spy, and dog. And the smell of each is strong, but the thin one's strench is stronger. The thin Dev-*

il is all wicked mind and evil brain; the thick one is that, and teeth and claws as well. Flee before their coming; for the name of the one Devil is Kar-chee and the name of the other Devil is Dragon . . .' "

It was an old man, a net-maker in the days of his strength, and Jow's near neighbor, who—restless from the thin sleep of old age—had gotten up groaning from his bed before dawn was more than a thin promise on the horizon. First he walked because he could not sleep, next he walked because he had in his mind a certain warm spring which he thought might relieve somewhat his aching bones. Then he walked because he decided he was hungier than he was rheumatic and his intention was to return. And finally he walked and walked because he had gotten well lost. Then he saw what he had seen and hid half a day in terror and risked moving about only because it came to him at last that the terror of night is greater than the terror of day; and so he came upon Jow, off by himself inspecting his bee-hives.

Jow at first had inclined to disbelieve his frightened babblings, then sent him off home with strong advice to say nothing to anyone else. "I wasn't convinced he was right," Jow said later to old Ren; "but I wasn't convinced he was wrong, either. So I thought I'd take advantage of your thatch-raising, late for that though it was, and come and talk to you about it."

Now, his face taut and haggard in the fire- and torch-light, he said, *"Flee.* . . . There is nothing else for us to do! Who can fight Devils? We must leave everything behind and sail to the other island, Zonia or Aper or the others. If there is no wind, we must paddle. And if the people there will receive us as we received Rowan, then good —if not, we must fight them and take their land. We must—"

Ren sighed and gripped his friend's knees. "*Must.* Jow . . . listen. 'Who can fight Devils?' No one. True enough. But how do you know for sure that we must fight? That we must flee? That the Devils are here to destroy either us or our land? Obviously they are here. Obviously they have been here before—but our land is still here. Isn't it?"

Jow nodded, half-reluctant, half-reassured. "But . . . Ren . . . you know . . . lots of times I warn people against danger and they laugh and say, 'Nothing has ever happened before.' And I tell them . . . listen, Ren . . . I tell them: *'Nothing ever happens until the first time it happens . . . !'*"

This was so true as to require no comment. Ren therefore made none and went on, grave and calm as before, "It is dark now and we can do nothing. Stay with us, be our guests. And tomorrow you and I, Jow, you and I will see for ourselves whatever is to be seen. Our boys are good fellows, but they are only boys. *Woman!*" He got to his feet.

From beyond the fires came his wife's voice. "Ren?"

"Our guests will stay the night. Get things ready for them." The women visitors broke into louder talk, deploring face-saving . . . as the relieved note in their voices showed. They did not know what was wrong, but they accepted that they need not know until the men thought fit to tell them. Yet it was a long way back, they were tired, their younger children were sleeping, and they welcomed the invitation to stay.

In the night Lors awoke to find his father's right hand on his shoulder, his father's left hand over his mouth. No word was spoken as they slipped out into the chill night air, the drops of the first dew dripping like the lightest of rains from the trees; the very stars, huge and swollen with lights, seeming themselves to be swimming down upon the earth through a black and liquid sea of night. He followed Ren across the compound to the most distant fire-pit, and there sat down beside him. Warmth still arose in a faint mist. The father took a stick and brushed off the embankment of ashes and blew upon the coals; as they went from gray to red he placed a small twig on them. In the brief half-light, his face shown ruddy and haggard.

"Lors," he said—and stopped. He swallowed.

"Popa?"

"Lors. Could . . . It is no disgrace to be mistaken. . . ." His voice was a bare whisper. Lors leaned close to listen. "It would be about the wrongest thing possible to allow so many people to be frightened for an error. . . . Or for a game. . . . You would not—Lors?—is it not possible that you are not really sure that you did see what you say? Perhaps you jumped too quickly to conclusions. Perhaps—"

Lors put his hand on his father's knee. "No, Popa. Don't think that. It's no game. It's no error. We did see them. We saw the thing that Carlo drew. We did. We saw them." His voice, despite his resolution that it would not, trembled. Not so much from fear of what he had seen as from his shock and grief at seeing and hearing his father so shaken. He gave a little sound of anguish as he heard his father moan at his reply, saw him rock back and forth.

"Popa—there were only two of them! Only two!"

Barely audibly, old Ren said, through the hand which covered his face, "There will be more. There will be more. There will be—"

Lors seized the hand and shook it. "Then we'll do what Jow said—we'll leave this land and go where they can't find us!"

The hand came away from Ren's face. His son felt the track of the tears upon it and, try as he would not to, began to weep, himself.

"Where is there a place where they can't find us? And if we knew of such a place, how would we get there? In our fishing-canoes? They wouldn't hold a hundredth-part of the people, boy. Are we to build more? Bark trees and wait for them to dry and cut them and hollow them and season them and prepare provisions— enough for who knows how long a voyage? Will they give us time? Or are we to try and make our escapes in boats of green wood and watch them founder under us? Jow didn't think of this. He didn't think!"

Ren wiped his face. "You see why, Lors? You see why you have to be wrong? Because even if there were the possibility of us all getting away, why?—what for?—to wait in some other island for the Devils to get around to coming for us? To spend the rest of our lives in that fear and then,' if we die in our beds, to hand that fear down to our children like an inheritance?"

His son said, unsteadily, but not without courage, "But what's the choice? Either we stay and fight, or we turn and we flee. What other choices are there?"

His father raked the ashes back upon the embers. His voice came from the darkness, thick and dull. "No choice. We can't stay. We can't escape. We can't fight. We have no choices. None. None. . . ." His voice died away. He did not move. Then, slowly, his head sank down upon his knees. But he moved no more than this. And he moved no more.

Lors stared. He swallowed. He wiped his nose with his hand. He could have sat, himself, or crouched, motionless for hours beside a game trail. But he could not sit still for this. It was horrible. Death was only a theory to him, and the deeds of Devils something he had merely heard of it. His mind could not encompass either his own destruction or the destruction of his land and family and friends. What tore at him now was the incredible and shocking spectacle of his father, that roof-pillar of strength, reduced to tears and to utter despair. This was intolerable. He jumped to his feet, filled with a childish urge to run away and run and run and stay away until he could come back to find everything in order once again, trouble forgotten. Even as he turned to set his feet, and even as he realized how useless and impossible this impulse was, the night vanished in a burst of rose-colored noise which ceased on the instant, leaving him blinded and deafened—

Again the blaze of ruddy light—his father's face open and aghast and all the homesite—again the ear-shattering, mind-benumbing noise—

Again the darkness and the thick, echoing silence.

From the house came the sound of a woman's voice, a hooting, ululating, uncontrolled, almost sexual sound. And upon this breakthrough every conceivable human and animal noise followed. The people poured out of the house, stumbling, trampling, crying, calling, shouting, shrieking; children wailing, women wailing, boys trying to assert manhood and courage but betrayed by breaking voices, men demanding to see the faces of their enemies—

"Earthquake!"

"Devils!"

"Attack!"

"Devils!"

"Raid!"

"Devils! Devils!"

"A volcano in the sea!"

"Wild men!"

But, louder, shriller, deeper, more often, more deeply felt because more deeply feared than any of these—again and again and again: *"Devils! Devils! Devils!"*

They fell upon their knees, fell and sprawled full-length, stumbled, were knocked down, and they bellowed like the beasts in the pens. And, looking up, they saw two trails of fire across the sky, greater than the greatest meteor, and again came the blast of light and the rose-flambeau of sound, and now, looking upward, in the instant brief as lightning-flash, they saw the huge black hulls of the Devil-ships as they wheeled—*blaze! blast!*—and circled—*blast! blaze!*—and wheeled —blazing! blasting!—inward, downward, turning, turning—

And vanished toward the south in one final smash of sight and sound and staying forever upon the seared eyes, only turning colors, on! off! as the astonished lids sprang down and up and down: blink, blank, red, black, hull, horror, chaos, Kar-chee, dragon, dark, fire, flame, burning light, Devils, Devils, death.

Daylight came at last, and when the morning mists had cleared away some strange disturbance in the air was seen toward the south, where the black sky-ships had gone.

This was the morning when Ren and Jow and the other men were to have gone to see for themselves the truth, if any, of the reports of the boys and the doddering oldfather.

They did not go.

Nobody went.

Nobody did anything.

Now and then a woman, movement automatic, perhaps more in response to habit or an aching breast, thrust her nipple into a tiny screaming mouth. Older children, not old enough to have quite succumbed as yet to the general paralysis of mind and body, either found food left over or went without. Now and then a groan or a sigh or whimper was heard, a rattling cough, a wordless and toneless murmur; nothing more. The wind spoke and the cattle complained, but nothing else. The very dogs were silent, scarcely bothering to crawl out of the sun. The very songbirds in their twig cages seemed to have caught the contagion and were silent.

It was close to noon when old Ren's wife appeared in her doorway. She looked around, made a gesture of dreadful despair. Her hair hung in witchlocks, sluttishly about her pendulous cheeks. She walked with melting strides toward the tiny cages hanging under the eaves of thatch, one by one flung open the tiny doors. The little birds fluttered, but none fluttered out. She opened her mouth and breathed painfully. Then, as though each gesture cost her infinite effort and infinite agony, she reached her hand into every little pen and closed it around each bewildered creature and drew it out and flung it away from her. "Go," she muttered. "Go . . . go. . . ."

When the last of them had been released she looked around her once more, repeated her gesture of horror and hopelessness. For a moment only her expression changed to something approaching bewilderment and she shaded her eyes and peered as though looking for, as though missing something . . . someone. . . . The moment did not long last. She melted back into her house. And all therein was silent.

Duro held his crossbow by the butt. He gazed, slack-mouthed, into space. Then his mouth closed, tightened. He swung forward on his knees and lifted the bow as though he were going to smash it into the ground.

Lors put his hand out. "Don't."

"Why not?"

The older brother's face and hand and head
did not move much, nor did his eyes. But Duro
knew him well enough to understand that an answer existed and would be presently forthcoming. He sank back and waited.

"Listen," Lors began after a long while.
"When I was on my first overnight hunt, way
out in the uplands," he began, looking straight
at his brother, no trace of condescention or rival-
ry in his voice: equal to equal now; and Duro, for
the first time since the trouble began, felt pleasure grow in his heart; "—you've heard me tell of
that?"

Duro said he had. "But tell it again," he said.
The story was obviously intended to make a
present point; besides, the hearkening to a story
makes a pain to be forgotten (so the old proverb
went).

A squall of snow, unseasonal and—peculiarity
—driving downward from the middle upper
ranges, had driven the hunting party even
further up and out of their intended path. And
up there in the clefts and rifts of the slope of
Tihuaco they had come upon a hamlet of the
dying and the dead and of the living-dead as
well.

"The sickness had come on them," Lors said,
recollection making his mouth twist, "and it was
still on them, so—you can imagine—we didn't
stay. But we stayed long enough for me to get the
picture of it in my mind. Later on, hearing the
older ones talk about it, I got it all clear and
fixed. There's no cure for the sickness—either
you recover or you don't. But those who were
already sick just lay there as though they were

already dead, and those who weren't sick just lay there as though they already were. They could have left, but they didn't. And not because they didn't want to risk infecting others, either, because they never opened a mouth to warn us off when they heard and saw us coming. It wasn't, either, that they stayed there to tend to the others, because we saw them begging for help and no one fetched them water.

"They just stayed and waited to die the way a rabbit does when it's face to face with a big snake. It trembles but it doesn't run. Even a rat will run or fight if it's cornered."

He paused and took a deep, shuddering breath.

"I saw Mia on my way out before," he said. "She just lay against the wall and breathed. . . . Yesterday you said I was in a hurry to get back and get on top of her. Well, I could have gotten on top of her right then and there and she wouldn't have said *No, Yes,* or *Oh, more.* But it would've been like mounting a corpse.

"Is it like this everywhere, Duro? It must be. If even Popa and Moma have given up, then who hasn't? They're all just waiting to die. They seem to think they're already dead."

Duro's head bent lower and lower. Then he lifted his hair out of his eyes as though it were very heavy, and said, "Who hasn't? You haven't. And I haven't. Thanks for not letting me smash the bow. If there's only one bolt left in all the world, then, brother, there'll be one dead Devil." And, just as Lors had made no stand of being older and in command, so Duro now made no stand of being younger and defiant. "Tell me what to do and I'll do it." Their eyes met in perfect understanding. They had never been so close before. They would never again be as far apart as they had been.

"I don't know what to tell you to do," Lors said, softly. "I don't know what you should do or what I should do. Something happened yesterday and something happened last night and something is happening today and probably they're all connected.

"But I don't know. . . .

"And even if they are connected, I still don't know. . . . We heard our fill of oldfathers' tales about Devils' and big Devils and little Devils. What does it mean? Maybe no more than the ones about Arno Half-Devil—and there are *still* people who'd stake their privates on his changing into a giant cat in the night! What can I tell you to do? I don't know what's right or what's wrong. I only know what *I'm* going to do."

He got to his feet. Duro did the same. They both knew.

They hadn't gone far when someone swung onto the trail beside them. It was Tom-small, but not the placid Tom-small of the day before. They exchanged looks. "You're going south to see what's there," he said. It was a statement.

"Yes."

"So am I." That was a statement, too.

It did not fail to occur to them that if they were capable of smelling the dragon-Devils, the dragon-Devils might be equally capable of smelling them. The thing, then, was to keep the wind in their favor . . . but this was a figure of speech:

they could not of course keep the wind, they had to keep with the wind. At the moment there was none discernable, and this gave them time to reflect on the other part of the equation, which was the matter of where the Devils, thick or thin, might now be.

"Maybe along the beach-coast," Duro suggested. There they had seen them yesterday, after all. Lors pointed out that it was no mere disinterested desire to find the creatures which alone had brought them, all there, upon the trail.

"There's a way down to the beach not far from here, at Goat Rock," he said. "And that's all the way, either up or down, from here on south, until you get to the caves . . . which is quite a ways."

Duro didn't see what he meant. "It's no ways at all; we can walk it in an hour . . ."

"And suppose we get caught half-way? How long would it take us to *run?* We can't sprout wings and fly, you know. And I wouldn't want to have to try swimming, either."

The point was conceded. Here and there, almost automatically, one or the other of them pointed out clumps of hair frayed against a tree; but no move was made or intended to pursue these signs of game. It was not venison that they were after now, descending the forest trails—indeed, none of them was quite sure what they *were* after. A sight of the strange creatures, to be sure . . . a safe sight, certainly. But then what? And after then, what? Such questions were equally unspoken and unanswered. Now and then, warily crossing open terrain, they felt the sun hot upon their heads and shoulders; but in short moments they were back in the shade once more. It soon became obvious that Lors was not intending to make for the beach by the nearest way, if at all. Duro and Tom-small said nothing; they followed. Few signs of life were observed, but now, so close to noon, when most live things favored rest and shade, was never a propitious time of day for such observations. Now and then a faint taste of the sea came on the light and intermittent breeze, or the familiar smell of sap and grass and rotting leaves; once, a stronger scent, a musky one, of some male creature's harboring or staling. But these were of only negative significance. The wind—such wind as there was —was still toward them, and it carried no warning on it.

There was no river in the land worthy of the name, but there was a point within sighting from their route where within a short distance a number of streams joined to make what was called, as it ran coursing through the savannah, the Spate. Such was its noise that they were long in hearing the other one, and did not recognize it when they did. They slowed their gait, they moved more cautiously, they frowned in concentration. . . . Logs, perhaps, thudding against each other or against rocks . . . logs perhaps escaped from woodcutters in the farther uplands, or perhaps intended by them to be thus moved downward . . . or trees, it might be, dislodged by the undercutting of some distant embankment by the eternal action of the streams. . . .

Such notions did not long bemuse them, for, the Spate and the savannah coming suddenly and alike into sight, they saw far off and below down the gentle incline three huge black hulks pointing blunt snouts at the silent skies.

They rested there as the three points of a wide-based triangle and it seemed in that second that each one was an eyeless face from which protruded a long and rippling tongue. One rooted up rocks and earth and licked them along, one sucked up water, and one conveyed the mixture into a single black cube from which, it seemed, the rhythmic thudding came. It seemed to them that things moved in the open side of this cube, tall things, thin things, things with other things in their great claw-hands . . . it seemed . . . shock and the distance made semblance uncertain. The wind shifted.

The rank and alien odor struck them like a blow, so benumbing them that they looked all around ahead for the source before it occurred to them that it was against the crawling hairs of their napes and the backs of their heads that the breeze now blew. And therefore the dragon was behind them—

To cock and load and aim and fire a crossbow while lying on one's back is probably not the most difficult thing in the world, but neither does it rank among the easiest. The dead and heavy tree limb still dangling from the breach in the branch was just within bow-shot. Lors's bolt split the flap of bark; almost the instant the small sound of this reached them they saw the bulk of withered wood fall and saw the dust spiralling in the beam of sunlight, and then they heard the sound of the crash. Hard upon this, forgetful of harsh spikes of grass or roots or

stones against their flesh as they embraced the
ground, they heard another sound: a hiss, louder
than the hiss of the largest serpent they could
conjure fantasy of. They heard it so short a time
that they might almost have imagined that they
had imagined it, but even as the sound vanished
in their ears they felt along the whole supine
lengths of them the ground shudder (they felt it,
did not hear it), saw the great green-black form
move so delicately diagonally toward the place
where the limb had fallen from the tree that although they could not see they could imagine
with dreadful detail and probable truth how the
grained webbing between each great toe would
fold in as the foot was silently lifted and then
expand as each great foot was silently, swiftly set
down again.

Oblivious of pain or anything else but flight—
instant flight!—they crawled upon their bellies
backwards and sideways and vanished into the
concealing covert of the thickets. Thorns tore at
them and took toll, bushes resisted parting, but
they pressed onward and away.

The Devil-dragon must have found the
crossbow bolt—they afterward agreed on this—
must, in that moment of sight, have understood
everything: that there was nothing there of itself
to draw a shot and even if there had been they
would not have ventured to shoot at it so close to
the alien encampment and that therefore the
bolt had been loosed for no other reason than to
part the heavy branch and use the noise of its fall
to draw away pursuit. Upon understanding
came rage—at least rage; perhaps more—a sig-

nal, an alarm, an appeal—

—From behind came the hiss again, this time not cut short, and, after the air had ceased to quiver from the hiss, came a great burst of gutteral sound, the coughing of a giant; and then noise for which no words existed for them. Roaring? Bellowing? Thundering? They had no need for names or words. They responded by the shrinking of their cullions and the swelling of their hearts and the cold sweat upon their skins. And by pressing on, writhing, sliding, ever away. Long after the noise behind them ceased they still had not dared rise up to run like men: and perhaps they owed to this that they were still live men.

And they did not rise to their feet until Duro saw before him the tumbled, fissured mass of rock like half-melted honeycomb, which he knew ran on and on and on, if not forever, at least for long enough for him to breathe deep and know he would draw at least a several few breaths safely thereafter:

The caves!

IV

THE RAFT as such had ceased to exist by the time Liam was well enough to come on deck, half-expecting to see it bobbing behind. A pile of its timbers were stacked neatly about; a few more were in the process of being split into planks; a few piles of such planks were pointed out to him, as well as a bin of fragments from which an old woman was feeding a fire-box well bedded in sand.

"You seem to have made good use of it," Liam said.

"'Waste not, want not,'" graybeard Gaspar intoned. "A saying of our wise ancients, as true today as the first day it was uttered. I am sure it relieves you to know that you have already payed your own way."

Liam looked at him just a trifle askance. On the once hand, he was of course grateful and glad for his life; glad for the food and the drink and the care: hence, yes, pleased that Gaspar and his people considered that the raft had paid for all this. On the other hand, he entertained a view of the whole matter which could not be fitted into a frame-work which contained the conception of payment in goods for saving lives. And he wondered what Gaspar the Knower and the others in the Ark might have done if the raft had not been there to serve for payment. But this was like wondering about a two-sided triangle. . . .

And not every life had been saved; small wonder if fresh-baked bread and dried fruit and smoked meat and broth of parched vegetables and cool water and shelter from the burning sun, wonders though they were, did not come in time to make up for the so-long lack of them.

There had been those who had clung to life with tenacious avidity even in the face of famine and drought, only to let go their hold on life with food and water still on their lips. And others to whom strange fantasies had become, if not facts, at least attitudes: that the arkfolk had not merely —fortuitously or providentially—in saving their lives done a deed of mercy, but that in some unknown, but not unsuspicionable, way the arkfolk were part of an overall scheme . . . details infinitely vague . . . a scheme in which Liam (to the minds of some of them) might be also involved, wittingly or otherwise. . . . "Weary, wary, cynical, grim, bitter," they declared by their manner if not by their words that they were not to be cozened or deceived any further; that they had suffered enough so far; that henceforth they were to be exceedingly canny and cautious and that the burden of proof lay upon everyone else.

And the fact that they had never heard of an "ark" merely added to the bitter mystery of things.

Liam, moving slowly, slowly around the deck of this curious vessel, sometimes holding to the side and sometimes to Gaspar, as yet did not fully grasp the meaning of the odd looks cast him by a few of his followers, themselves crawling cautiously about or merely reposing on the deck of the ark in the positions which had become habitual to them through reposing on the deck of the raft. His eyes and mind were both at work, but for the moment, satisfied that his people were not in want, he preferred to concentrate on other matters.

"Another thing our wise ancients used to say," Gaspar went on; "our wise ancients used to say, 'Knowledge is power.' Do you understand that? No, you don't, you only think you do. If you had understood it you wouldn't have been dying of hunger and thirst. You *were* dying of hunger and thirst, so that proves you didn't understand it. But the fact that you had made an attempt indicates that you are capable of understanding it. Listen to what I tell you, young man, and then you will understand, you will become knowledgeable, and hence powerful.

"Do you see how well prepared this Ark is? How cleverly and how sturdily it is made? How it is provisioned with food and fuel and water? Look at the drain-gutters and pipes and barrels —if a sudden shower occurred at this minute not a drop of water would be lost. Observe how all of our people are engaged in assigned and useful tasks, not sunken in corrosive sloth or corrupting idleness. See how well-cared for our beasts and poultry are. Do you notice the young people at their lessons? You do. May I ask you the rhetorical question, 'Did you make any of these beneficial arrangements for your own vessel and people?'"

Liam put one peeling foot down carefully in front of another. "There wasn't time," he said.

"You did not. Exactly. Time? Wasn't time?

There is always time. It depends what one does with time. You are the product of a society given over to violence and self-indulgence, confusing knowledge with knowing. By suffering the hypocrisy of a regime which ignored the laws of Nature, you saw that society met its inevitable destruction. Can Nature be successfully resisted? Of course not."

Liam resisted the temptation to say, "Old graybeard Gaspar, you are babbling." For one thing, it was not courtly; for another, it was not ... hardly ... safe. And besides, there was just a germ, a grain of conviction in the fact that the ark *was* exceedingly well made, arranged, provisioned, and ordered. Gaspar's words were persuasive of foolishness, but the existence and circumstancing of the ark seemed anything but folly. Liam resolved to listen well and long before voicing curt conclusions.

Gaspar passed his hand over his beard in a smooth motion, said, equally smoothly, "You perceive how unanswerable my argument is. Very well. To continue. The man of the multitude, contented with little, observes that a thing happens, and to him it is as though the happening has neither past nor future: as though something materializes from nothing and will subsequently dematerialize into nothing. But this is not so. Am I correct? Of course I am correct. Follow me closely, now. *Nothing happens without a cause.* The acceptance of this maxim is the solid foundation of all human knowledge, progress and hope."

He paused to watch and nod approval as the hide of a just-slaughtered bull-calf was carefully scraped with a sharp stone to remove the hair from one side and the fat from the other. Even these were not wasted and went carefully into containers provided for them. The fat was edible and the hair could be used to make brushes. "And therefore—" Liam gave the conversation a polite nudge. He scanned the horizon. Nothing in sight but water. Nothing. Surely Gaspar and his people did not intend to remain afloat forever?

"And therefore," Gaspar took up the thread once more, "it is necessary to inquire as to the cause of a thing, and this is to say that it is necessary to inquire into the causes of all things. Does this not follow?"

"Granted."

"So. Suppose a man neglect or abuse his body. What is the inevitable result? The inevitable result is disease, blemishes, decay, breakdown, the appearance of evil sores and destructive parasites; all of which attack the body further. The foolish man bewails what has happened to him, not realizing that it has not merely or actually *happened* at all—but that he, through his folly, has *caused* it to happen! Now, fellow from a far country, let us apply this knowledge to the social body as well as to the individual body. Follow me closely. Suppose the social body, or, if you prefer, the body social, is neglected or abused. What is the inevitable result? The same . . . only, of course, on a much wider scale. *Disease*—a plague spreads. *Blemishes*—accident and misfortune vex the land. *Decay*—more people die than are born. *Breakdown*—bridges and boats and buildings are destroyed. *Evil sores and destructive parasites*—this means dragons and Kar-chee. Now—"

Liam blinked and gaped. He put out his hand and Gaspar politely raised his eyebrows. "Yes?"

"'Evil and destructive' means *what?*"

"You have not listened carefully. However, I make allowances for the several circumstances of, firstly, you grew up in a benighted outland and not in a community of Knowers; secondly, you have suffered physically and mentally from your ill-managed venture upon the raft; thirdly, I do not wish to dwell upon it and perhaps hurt your feelings, but I must testify to what I see and in this case I see that you suffer from a physical malady: to wit, your eyes do not match, and from this it follows that—"

Liam, trying intensely hard to recall the Father Knower's exact words and stem the flood of rhetoric, said, rather loudly, "'*Destructive parasites.*'"

And Gaspar immediately said, "Kar-chee."

He was about to say more but a young woman of the stranger people, lighthaired and not ill-favored, rose from where she was sitting and stroking a small gray lamb, and said, "Liam!"

Her friend began to smile, then made an abrupt, impatient gesture, and she started to back away. He grasped her hand and drew her along, saying, "Father, your pardon, but—"

"Granted. Young person, your name has not been made known to me."

"Cerry . . . Cerry, I'm called."

"Have all your wants been made known to the Mother?"

"Yes. . . . She's been very kind."

"'Kind,' a word of insufficient exactitude. The Mother knows her work; if you have made known your wants to her they will by now have been supplied if it is proper and convenient for them to be so. Has she informed you on the subject of cohabitation? You flush. How becoming and proper. So be it. Accompany us on our conversational circuit of the ark if you wish, but feel no compulsion, and on no account interrupt us further or again."

So on they went, past the sheep-pens freshly littered with sawdust, past the woman plying distaff and spindle, past the sick-bay where some of the raft-people still lay, down to the close-packed but neatly arranged living-quarters— hammocks lashed and stowed; bachelors' section here, single women there, nursery, married couples' quarters; supplies: food, seed, tools, cloth, yarn, hides, salt, spices, water. Father Gaspar checked everything, inspected the rude but serviceable pumps, peered into each of the tripart hulls—and talked . . . talked . . . talked. . . .

After a long, long time he informed them that it was his period for rest, and politely dismissed them.

Back up on deck, in a niche which, as no one else seemed to have claimed it, they made their own, Liam looked at Cerry. And she at him. After a moment, he asked, "And what, exactly, did the Mother inform you about cohabitation?"

She half-smiled, half-scowled. "Oh . . . since no one knows for sure how long we'll be at sea, and since pregnancy and childbirth would be inconvenient for the duration of the voyage, all cohabitation has to be, well, 'qualified' was her word for it. I can go into details if you'd really like."

"Not necessary."

"That's what I thought," she said, moodily.

"I haven't forced you or distrained you. I don't now."

She blew out her lips. "Thank you, brave one. I understand that I am free to take my sheepskin elsewhere for qualified cohabitation. . . ." With a quick expression of her face she showed what she thought of that, and with a quick glance of her eye and pressure of her hand on his she showed what she still thought of Liam. Then, "Well, the Mother is not a bad old one, considering that she's been the sole wife of old Father Know-it-all for thirty years. Tell me, Liam: are they all quite mad? Or just him?"

He said, "I suppose it's a sort of qualified madness, one may say. Don't laugh, lewd woman. . . . I don't know for sure what to think of it all. Except that I think for sure that I am glad this vessel, *ark,* as they call it, was there when we were there . . . wherever we were. . . . If we just had a map . . . Well. *Every man hath his own madness.* A saying from our own wise ancients. . . ."

He ruffled her light hair. The ark women had been obliged to cut it short, so tangled had it been. "This is no single, simple thread we have to follow; this you know, Cerry, don't you? It goes weaving in and weaving out, it leads through the fire and the sea and storm, it's full of knots, but the knots are proper parts of it. The Knowers are one knot. We'll unravel it yet. And we will be sure of finding use for the slack as well. I'm sure of that."

He was sure of little else but that. The ark folk were kind enough—"imprecise" though their captain-priest-father might find the term; they went about their duties with efficiency. If Liam were pressed to name a particular impression received from them, he might have inverted the reply by saying that he was most impressed by a lack of any strong impression. Listless was by far too strong a term. Browbeaten was equally untrue—Gaspar, the Father Knower, might perhaps have simply overwhelmed them all by his ceaseless flow of wordage. Chiefly he felt the lack of any stronger personality, single or collective. And if there were more to it than that, then he did not know.

The vessel was both the largest and the oddest he had ever seen. It had stepping for a mast— and, indeed, several mast sections as well as huge rolls of matting doubtless intended for sail were all clearly visible on deck—yet the mast was not stepped and the breeze did no more than cool the air . . . cunningly diverted belowdecks by screens set for the purpose at the ladderheads. Also, thole-pins were in place and sweeps of a size for them all neatly arranged; yet no oar was set up; only the tiller oar, and that was lashed fixed. Still, the ark did move; it moved—as Liam observed, having for that purpose tossed a chip overboard—at a good pace. It seemed, then, that the ark had gotten into an ocean current, a mer-stream, and that old Gaspar knew enough about it to be quite confident as to where it was taking him, and at what speed, and for how long. Whence it was a reasonable assumption that eventually the mast would go up and the sails; too; and then, though not necessarily at once, the oars.

Liam had a strong sentiment that, in some

things at least, Father Gaspar was, indeed, and literally, a Knower.

The sea had long since come to seem to him the natural element; memories of the land behind receded; the land (or lands) before remained as yet but unformed hopes. He watched the sun plunge into the sea, a descent so much more swift than the long, slow sunsets of his lost northern homeland. The luminous washings of the night waves seemed now merely proper and familiar and no more, no longer sinister. Something was happening to the forms of the star-clusters; he wished now with all his heart that he had taken thought to make a map of the constellations long before now; but it was not too late . . . he could ask the Father Knower for sketching materials tomorrow; if they were refused (or, a likelier negative, smoothly and reasonably declined), he would manage to improvise them somehow.

His mind was filled with this as he sat on deck with Cerry, beneath a sort of high chair in which sat a young man who had the lookout watch. And presently they became aware that someone else had joined them. He thought at first it was probably one of his own, the raft people—although with that thought came another; were they still "his own people"? and how many, if any? and which ones?—but before the faint star-gleam and almost equally faint sea-gleam could reveal the lineaments of the face, the accents of the low, soft voice told him it was one of the ark's people.

"You don't know . . . you didn't, ever, know Serra?"

"I'm sure I never heard of her. Or—him?"

The young man laughed, softly, shyly. The laugh ended abruptly. Someone else had joined them. After a moment: "No . . . oh . . . Serra is the place where we used to live." The name still meant nothing to Liam. But he now knew that the conversation was a clandestine one, that the speaker had for a moment been concerned about the identity of the last arrival, but was now content about it.

"In which direction did Serra lie? And what sort of a place was it?"

A hand was waved vaguely. "Back that way. . . . It used to be a part of—do you know the old names?—of Africa. But we aren't of the old Serran stock. Before, although I don't remember it, we lived in Sori. And before that, we used to live in Jari. Adn before that— But it doesn't matter. My name is Rickar."

Even softer, from the other: "And mine is Fateem." It was a girl's voice.

There was a curious silence.

Rickar, launching his speech upon a sigh, began to tell them of life in Serra; the rich, intensely-cultivated soil, the games played, the songs sung, the names of the towns and what each was specially noted for—this one for the friendliness of its women, that one for the strength of its men, another for commercial cunning, a fourth for cloth of good weave, a fifth for its famous view. . . . His voice died away upon another sigh.

"And which one," asked Cerry, "were you from?"

Rickar made an abrupt sound in his throat. "We weren't from any of them, really. We kept apart. We were the Knowers. We worked, traded, studied . . . but all the while, you know, all the while, we waited."

"Waited for what, Rickar?"

"For the sinning to start. For the punishment to follow. For the time to come for us to leave and move on again. You must know about all that. You were with my father so long this afternoon. I know he was the same man this afternoon as he was this morning, so I am sure that he must have explained it all to you."

Neither Liam nor Cerry denied it. They said nothing. Rickar nevertheless began to repeat what he knew that they knew, and they suffered him to do so. It was like looking through another window; the sight was the same, but the angle was different—if some details were lost to sight, others were thus revealed.

And another crept up through the gentle darkness, and another, and another.

". . . then the village headman stole some of the tax-goods, and my father and the elders and elderesses shook their heads . . .

" . . . but her second husband sold her property and spent it on other women, and when my mother heard of this she said . . .

" . . . it was said that the bridge was almost a hundred years old and a wonder it had stood up so long, but when it collapsed . . .

" . . . so we began to assemble the ark again and get things to be ready, and, really, that was many years ago, and all those many years the people—the other people—laughed at us. But my father said it was useless to warn them. Well . . . it's true. The Kar-chee Devils and their dragons did come, they were sighted at the

western end of Serra, and the whole place began
to boil like an ant-hill. You never saw such prep-
arations for war!"

Liam said, even more softly than Rickar,
"Perhaps I have. . . ."

Abruptly, Fateem spoke, her voice quite
young and very sweet in tone. "You attacked
and defeated them, didn't you? You really did!
You really did!"

"Ah, well, no as well as yes," Liam began. But
there was a stir in the darkness, and those there
had no mind for equivocations or even for explanations.

Yes, he had attacked the Kar-chee Devils!
Some of the other raftsmen had told about it.
(The tale, quite clearly, had grown great in the
telling.) He had defeated the Kar-chee Devils!
And the stinking dragon Devils! Shot monstrous
stones and monstrous arrows at them with tremendous engines! Left their encampments burning and smoking! And then—

(And here he thought they were all about to
overwhelm him and smother him with their
youthful eagerness and touch him for a touch of
potent luck as though he were a mage-tree or a
sage-stone.)

—And then he and his men and his women
had, in more zeal than cunning, set off in the raft
to bring the news to other peoples that the Devils
could be defeated!

"That they are only beasts of flesh and
blood," Fateem declared, her slight voice trembling. "You *did!* You *did!*"

It seemed almost as though she defied him to
deny it. And he did not quite accept the
challenge. "There is a time for telling and a time

for dwelling," he said, evasively. "Not every new thing heard is true and not every old thing heard is false. I think it would be best for you to please me by speaking no more of this matter for now. We are guests and strangers aboard your craft. Do you understand? Then go, as you favor me, go one by one and quietly to your places and to sleep. . . ."

Long, long they sat there, after the young ark-folk had gone. They watched the sea and they watched the sky and after a while they saw a piece of a star come melting down and by this sign they knew that great matters were a-wing; but they did not yet know what.

Liam said, "I think we'll sleep ourselves now. First I'll go slumber with my gray eye open and my brown one shut, and then I'll change about. I don't think that anyone aboard will try to slip up and wrong me, but I am not utterly convinced of it."

Later, as they lay between the sheepskins, Cerry heard him murmur, "There never was a religion lasted even two days yet without a day-old heresy. . . ."

The Mother Knower—Gaspar's wife and Rickar's mother—was a tall, stooped, flat-chested woman, with large sunken eyes. Some whisper, some rumor, of the prior night's clandestine gathering must have reached her ears, for late the following morning she betook herself from her duties and came to ask Liam if he could be of help in sorting wool. Certainly there must have been among the arkfolk others whom she knew to be of use in this; equally certainly he would not refuse . . . so his thoughts ran. He was feeling, it seemed to him, stronger by every hour.

"This is not our kind of wool," he commented, fingering the pile, dirty-gray-black on the surface of each fleece, and underneath ranging from pure black to creamy-fawn to pure white. "But it smells much the same."

Mother Nor smiled faintly. "I never minded that," she said. "It is a healthy smell. Of course, wool was not much suited to the climate of Serra —or, for that matter, Sori or Jari. The sheep came with us from Amhar, our first home. Perhaps someday we will live in a cooler place; then we will see fulfilled the counsel of our wise ancients, always to bring the sheep with us."

His hands picked and pulled and placed, the familiar feel and scent of lanolin bringing memories before his inner eyes.

"Had they good sheep, in your own home land?" she asked, softly.

"Yes. . . good sheep. . . . Good men, too."

She sighed, shook her head. "But not good enough. They sinned greatly, or else the punishment of the Double Devils would not have been visited upon them . . . don't you see?"

Liam thought he would change the subject. "Do you think eventually to find your way north once more, to a cooler climate?"

The sunken, gentle eyes looked at him with mild surprise. "It may be so. We do not know. But it would not be necessary to go north in order to find the climate cooler, for it will become so eventually if one ventures far enough south. Didn't you know that?"

He shook his head, perplexed. "I had always

been told that it grew always hotter as one procedes south, until eventually no one can live because of the intense heat of the Southern Hell. I wasn't sure that I believed in the Southern Hell —or, for that matter, in the Northern one. Still . . . there must be something up in that frozen place, because we did see the lights. Have you ever seen them? They shone not long before I left . . . as though a great bowl of shimmering green had descended upon the night sky. So . . . it seemed reasonable that if there was a Northern Hell that there should be a Southern one, too. But I was never sure."

Now it was her turn for head-shaking. "No," she said. "Oh, no . . . there is no such thing as a Southern Hell. It grows hotter only up to a point, and afterward it commences to grow cool. As for these so-called lights, they are probably a delusion. A delusion," she said, firmly, "like the delusion that the visitations of outraged nature can or should be resisted."

He gave up trying to change the subject. Let her have her say and say it out; everyone else was doing so. "The Kar-chee, you mean. And the dragons."

She meant. Yes. The Double Devils. Could it really be that his own landsmen, not content with bringing this punishment upon themselves by sins and breaches of judgment and neglect of proper ways, had actually been so blasphemous as to *resist?* To *attack?* He assured her that they had, indeed. She was truly, genuinely shocked. "And what happened afterward, Liam? Wasn't there greater destruction than before? Surely there was! And did that not prove it? Was this not evident, obvious proof of the—not merely futility, but the absolute *wrongness* of resisting the Double Devils?"

"But . . . Mother Nor . . . what would you have people do? Submit, supinely, and see their land destroyed?"

She took his hands in hers. "Young Liam, can they, by resisting, prevent their lands from being destroyed? The destruction of the land, like the appearance of the Kar-chee and the dragon, is an act of Manifest Nature. Man can no more hope to resist it successfully than he can hope to subdue the waves with a broom, or bring down the stars with a noose. Salvation does not lie in resistance. Salvation lies in *compliance!* Man is but clay in Nature's hands. A course of action has been outlined for him and it is for him to follow that course. Proper action, correct deeds, the application of justice and equity: *these* will bring safety; these alone.

"What should the people of your home land have done when the Double Devils appeared? They should have built an ark and departed in search of a place to settle in—"

He broke in, "And waited there, passively, until the next visitation?"

But (she protested) if they would only be virtuous, obedient, diligent in the pursuit of proper conduct, then there would *be* no "next visitation"!

"Not 'passively,' no. Activity—but active in the correct way. Have you never thought to wonder *why* the Double Devils exist at all? Surely you know that nothing happens without a cause, and that no cause exists without a purpose? I'm told that your people believe that the Kar-chee come from the stars. This is mere superstition. No— this is *rank* superstition! The stars are made of purest fire and nothing comes from them but burning embers . . . sometimes we see them streak, flaming across the sky at night; sometimes we find the burnt-out coals upon the ground. But no living thing comes from the stars because no living thing can live in the stars. Why? Because the stars are fire and living things cannot live in fire." Her voice was earnest and sincere and she looked at him to see if he understood.

Liam, suppressing a sigh, said, "Well, Mother, your arguments are persuasive, and it is perhaps not for me, being rude and unsure, to say that they are not correct. You speak of it being possible to prevent the visitation of the Kar-chee. To me, their non-appearance would be a miracle. But you say that in order for this to happen, all mankind must become virtuous. And, to me, Mother, this would be an even greater miracle."

She swept up a pile of tufts of wool with her hand. "My son, it is necessary, then, for you to learn that man can compel the performance of miracles, that it lies within his power to do so; and that, indeed, he *must* do so, for man is a miraculous creature."

"Land is near," Gaspar declared, approaching Liam in his usual majestic fashion, and leaving moderate excitement in his wake. "All things, of course, are comparative: in terms of walking, or, to be more accurate, swimming, land is still very far. But in terms of the distance we have voyaged, land is rather near. Yes, yes," he said, contentedly, stroking his vast gray beard.

Liam asked the obvious question.

"How do we know? We are Knowers. It is our duty to know. But to reply more specifically: buy the observation of the clouds, by the flight of birds, by the scent and direction of the winds, by the nature of drifting wood and weeds, by the color of the sea; and by many other numerous and significant things. We *know*—as you could, too, if you were one of us. But we will leave that matter for the immediate present. Only for the immediate present, though. By and by we must take it up. We are determined that our stay in this newest land, if it is suitable for habitation, must be of long duration. From which it must follow that we can harbor none among us who are not of our knowledge and our ways. Otherwise the same sorry story of sin, injustice, and iniquity, followed by punishment and Devilish visitation and destruction will repeat itself. We are wearied of it. Yes, Liam, we are wearied of it."

With a firm nod of his head he passed on, leaving Liam with much to think about.

But within a few moments his meditations were interrupted. Gaspar was giving orders. The helm was unlashed and a man stationed on it. The mast was stepped into its socket, and the sails of sewn-matting bent in place to the yards. Oars were gotten ready. So far, evidently, they had ridden with the current (though presumably sail or oars had been needed to get them into it, in the first place)—but they were going to take no chances now, either of the current's taking them past the land or perhaps wrecking them upon reefs or shoals or shores or shallows.

All day long they watched, the arkmen abating somewhat their attitude of abstraction, and the raftmen theirs of suspicion . . . but no land came into sight.

And that night Rickar and his friends returned again for whispering heresy. Liam hardly felt that he could either encourage or discourage them. He agreed that something better than the present group of choices should exist, but he did not know what that something might be. Pressed, urged that his "experience" demanded him to know more than the Knowers, old or young, at least upon this particular subject, he scowled . . . paused . . . said, at last, "We could hardly know less about Kar-chee and dragon than we do. Perhaps if we knew more we could do more . . . perhaps not. . . .

"But if we should find them here, or anywhere —or if they should find us—I wonder if we wouldn't do better—rather than at once fleeing, or at once fighting—oh, I'm *sure* we would do better—to lie low. Not let ourselves be seen a while, or seen again. And concentrate everything on finding out as much as we can about them . . . without their finding out anything about us."

Rickar said: "Hiding and skulking?"

"Put a stinking name to it and say it smells bad, if you like. You're vexed because I won't offer to lead you in a charge, aren't you? If I thought it would do more than momentary good, I would. If I ever do, I will. But meanwhile . . . Knowers? On this subject, let us all become knowers. Father Gaspar's proverb: 'Knowledge is power.'"

A sudden, dull glow of light suffused the horizon.

"Heat lightning," someone murmured, even as it vanished. It appeared again, twice more. The air seemed to quiver. Then, darkness, and the silent stars.

Late the next afternoon land appeared—lying upon the rim of the sea like some crouching beast, and, presumably far inland, surmounting the high-massed land, a mountain peak with a long wisp of cloud pendant to it.

Gaspar had appeared to welcome the suggestion of Liam that he and other raftmen accompany the arkfold chosen to make an exploratory landing. Perhaps because this way, should anything untoward happen to the makers of the first landfall, the losses to and of his own people would be thereby diminished . . . or so thought Liam.

But Gaspar would not allow the ark to put in close until the next day. For the remainder of light time they stood down the coast, making soundings, but finding no bottom anywhere. And toward the last he gave a little sound of satisfaction and pointed toward a line of white or yellow in between the dark water and the darker land.

"Beach-coast, you see. Just the place for a small boat to put ashore—" He was interrupted by a shout. Bottom had been found at last. "Good, then. We'll anchor and ride here tonight."

It was cold and the stars were just beginning to pale when Liam, Rickar, an older Knower named Lej who was the uncle of Fateem, and the raftsman Skai descended into the small craft, hoisted a small triangular sail, and let the wind take them in. Day crept out, the sun leaped up, something moved upon the beach, and presently they saw it dissolve into three things . . . three men. Warily they checked their weapons. The three men were soon seen to be three very young men, two of them evidently brothers. Surprise and suspicion jousted for place on their faces; Liam felt he knew exactly how they must feel.

Lej was the first to speak. "War is not our wish," he said. He took a tiny pouch of flour, emptied it into his hand, tossed it north . . . south . . . east . . . west. "Peace and plenty to the four quarters of your land. May the blessings of Nature be made manifest upon them and upon you and upon yours."

The three young men looked uncertain, perhaps regretting a ritual of welcome which they didn't have. Then, after exchanging glances, they stowed their bows and stepped into the water and helped beach the canoe. The older brother said, "All men are welcome here now, I think. . . ."

They looked around them with something close to fright, and they lifted their heads and sniffed the air. Some of the near-fear seemed to ebb. And the younger brother said, "There are dragons hereabouts. . . ."

V

REN ROWAN now seemed old enough to be the
father of the man he had been but a few days
before. The homesite already had a slovenly and
half-abandoned air to it. He gazed at the new-
comers blankly at first, squinted and gaped at
his sons, frowned as he observed the signs of decay quickening about his yard and house. Then
he said, after several starts and stops and with
idiot soundings and smackings of tongue and
palate and throat, "So. . . . Came here to die. . . .
Could have died at home. . . ." Then he looked
at them with the dull, sick look with which a
man painfully and irrevocably ill may reproach
those who do not share his pain.

Lej's answer was brisk. "Everyone has to die,
but no one has to die just yet. This man here, he
with the strange eyes, he and men and women
from his country, were found by us at sea on a
raft. They had despaired to do other than die,
but they are, as you may see, alive and well
nonetheless."

Liam listened with wry appreciation, noting
how Lej said nothing of the raft people who were
not now "alive and well nonetheless." He noted
with some surprise that this seemed to be a different Lej. Aboard the ark he had apparently

been in some sort of suspended animation, with
nothing to do except perform his duties and listen to old Father Gaspar. Now the mantle of
Gaspar, the principal knower, seemed to have
devolved upon him by proxy and by right of sen-
ior age. This was not now the obedient sub-
ordinate speaking; it was the true believer,
preaching to the ignorant.

"Needn't die just yet. . . ." Old Ren repeated
the words. A very faint flicker passed over his
face. It was not hope—not yet—it may have
been only disagreement. But it indicated the return of some emotion other than lethargy and
absolute resignation. Lors looked from Lej,
smooth, utterly confident, to his father, so suddenly and prematurely bereft of hope and
strength and even manhood. He did not know
what Lej was about to say, but he felt at that
moment that if it would restore his father to the
man he had been, then, whatever it was, he,
Lors, would follow and obey.

"There can be no right action without right
knowledge," Lej went on. "I see this house
building, these outbuildings, these fields and
groves and cattle and stock; and I observe that
they do not pertain to savages nor to barbarians,
nor to men who live like brutals with no inkling
of the social complex. I see here a settlement of
civilized people, of people who possess knowledge and the ability to know more."

He paused to let this sink in, and turned his
head to look at the others, some of whom had
already begun to look up from every conceivable
moribund posture. His eye seemed to draw them
up, draw them out and away from the all-con-

suming terror which had blunted the senses. The wind blew sweet from the grasslands and woods and a bird sounded its territorial note, liquid and prideful. The trees rustled and shook a powdery shower of tiny blossoms down upon them where they lay or crouched and slumped. Already, merely by the intrusion of the stranger with his strange words, they had suddenly become aware of many things which had been forgotten.

"But I see here, too," Lej went on, "a community which does not yet know enough . . . one whose knowledge has not been sufficient to save it from nearly dying of fright. Friends! Listen to me! I have very important things to say to you! Only men themselves, and women, are capable of totally arbitrary and capricious actions. But Manifest Nature is not. Manifest Nature does nothing without a cause, nothing without a purpose. The fearsome demons who have, I am told, now appeared among you, have been sent here by Nature for a purpose, and that purpose is not to destroy you, utterly. *Is not!*

"Only if you are foolish and sinful enough to resist is destruction certain. But if you will examine your inner selves, admit that you have done wrongfully, if you resolve to learn from the Knowers how to avoid future transgression, and if you are determined, friends, not only to learn what to do *but to do it!*—then salvation is possible. If you wish to learn, we will teach you. If you, having learned, having come to know and having joined the community of the Knowers, then take the next inevitable and logical step—that of leaving the land tainted by former transgressions—"

Old Ren groaned. He struck his head with his hands.

"Leave? What for? So that the Devil can follow us? If we're to be killed, then let's be killed here. . . . Here! Where we were all born and where we've all lived. . . ."

Lej almost smiled at him. "But, old sir and friend, that's what we've come to show you: that you need not any of you be killed. Not here and not anywhere. Animals kill because they are hungry. So do sharks. But Devils are not animals, they are Devils! In their actions toward mankind the creatures of Devilkind aren't moved by necessity of hunger. If your children do wrong, you cut a switch and you punish them. The switch is not moved by any intelligence or force of its own. The switch is moved by you! *You* are the one perceiving the necessity of punishment, but the switch itself perceives nothing. The child fears the switch itself only if he lacks the wit to understand that he should rather fear his father's arm . . . but it takes only a little while for him to realize that *if he will not misbehave he will not be punished!*

"Are you beginning to see? The Double Devils are merely the implements by which we, children of Manifest Nature, are being punished. They have no mind of their own, you know. All we need do to avoid them is to cease deserving them. And if you should ask, in that case why need we build the vessels which the Knowers call *arks* and why should we prepare food and drink and timber and seeds and stocks of goods and select the best of our beasts and why need we venture into exile upon these arks?—why will it not suffice if we repent and begin to follow a proper course of actions right here where we already are?—"

He had either made this same address often before, Liam considered, watching Lej's very ordinary face suffused with a confidence which seemed to lift him above self, or else he had heard it so often before that he had soaked it up and was now disgorging it word for word and point by point.

"If this is what you're about to ask, friends, then you needn't wait long for the answer. The exile is itself a necessary form of the punishment. Do you see it now? Of course you do. It's so very simple isn't it? This land has been tainted. The appearance of the Devils proves that—if it weren't tainted they wouldn't be here. The land is seeped and soaked in sin; it's running over with it. You *can't* stay here; you *couldn't* follow a course of genuine knowledge and proper conduct here; you *must* leave it and venture out upon the cleansing sea and reflect and ponder and—"

His words went on and on and on. He had an answer for everything. The Kar-chee weren't everywhere at once; neither were the dragons. They did not move with the speed of the wind, they moved, indeed, rather slowly in their work of purifying the land from sin. It was only necessary to keep out of their way as they went about their pre-ordained and essential tasks. If they came near, then move far. And, meanwhile, let trees be selected for felling if seasoned timber enough was not available: there would be time. Oh, yes, there would be time. Haste makes waste. Knowledge is power. Meanwhile, the very palisade of the homesite itself was useful timber, and there were the beams of the houses, too. The Knowers knew how. The Knowers knew why. And when. The Knowers, in short, *knew*.

Skai, a pale-faced and scant-bearded man, standing next to Liam, said, "Makes sense. Makes sense. Wouldn't you say, Liam?"

Liam said, "It makes sense of a sort. But there's more than one sort of sense . . . wouldn't you say, Skai?"

The man blinked, mumbled wordlessly. After a while, Liam noticed, he wasn't standing next to him any longer. He was up front, crowding close, listening to Lej. And nodding . . . nodding . . . nodding.

A sheltered and concealed cove was found for the ark, and Gaspar directed her putting in to there. The vessel was warped in quite close to shore, the depth of the water there permitting it; and then Gaspar, in whom common sense was never totally obscured by either verbiage or dogma, directed that leafy branches be cut and placed over the topside of the vessel. More: he had them changed daily, as soon as they began to wilt. Perhaps he might have preferred not to tarry at all, but there were many things inducing him to stay a while. So he carefully camouflaged his vessel and began to see to those things.

Shelters were set up ashore for the ill, both of the ark-and the raft-group. (Work of prose-lytizing among the latter proceeded apace, a captive audience being in Gaspar's view the best audience of all.) The ark itself was overhauled, repaired, refurbished. A part of the livestock was taken ashore, turn and turn about, to be grazed.

Meat was killed and fish caught and both salted, dried, smoked—but a portion of kill and catch consumed as part of the daily rations. Ebbing supplies were renewed. The disrupted state of local society had almost destroyed the opportunity for regular trade, but the Knowers managed to procure what they wanted nevertheless.

And all the while they preached their message —vigorously, urgently, persuasively, incessantly.

And not without success.

Yet, curiously—and whether old Knower Gaspar noticed or not, it seemed to make no difference to him—his campaign seemed to be a two-edged blade. On the one hand, he drew many to him. On the other hand, he pushed many away. Some there were who had been willing to lie down and die who now arose and with all vigor engaged in scrutinizing their past deeds and prepared to repent and to migrate. Others there were who had been in the same comatose condition who now recovered and rejected not only their previous condition but the doctrinal preaching which had aroused them from it.

"What does he mean, Devils are only a switch to beat us?" demanded Jow. "Did anyone ever see a switch move around by itself? These Knowers—how many places have they moved to? So many, most of them don't know, themselves. They ever convert any place—*really* convert it—so good that it *stayed* converted, so that no Devils ever came there? It's plain that they didn't."

Jow, apparently, was going to be a hard nut to crack. If, indeed, he cracked at all.

Some of the raft-people, minds still afire with reflected memory of the destruction wrought in New North Britland, wanted nothing but to keep as far away from Kar-chee and dragon as they could. They took it for granted that Liam, having led them in on migration to safety, would certainly not stay behind after the next one. Others had second thoughts. Devils *had* been defeated once back in the old home land in the northern seas. Chop it and change it as one would, that fact remained. Which was reducible to a very simple formula: *The Devils could be defeated*. Liam, to these, was not a man who had fled from the folly of further resistance; he was the very leader of resistance, his wisdom being only further enhanced by having realized—concerning a second stand to fight back there and then—that *the time had not yet been right*. Liam, to these, was only waiting for the time to become ripe and right. This might be after the next migration; on the other hand, it might come right here—in which case, of course, there would be no migration . . . at least not for them. Let the proud-nosed old Knowers move where they pleased.

And all the while the proud-nosed old Knowers bent to their tasks, from preaching their word to pouring melted deer fat into dried deer bladders—dutiful, efficient, coordinate; and all the very while rebellion simmered below the surface. It took the form of advocating the blasphemy of resistance to Devils, but it might have taken another or other forms. Once, in ultra-ancient Byzantium, at a time when religion and chariot-racing were the national preoccupations, each faction in the church had had a corresponding faction in the hippodrome; historians had tended to believe that those who supported the chariots of the greens did so because they were Monophysites: but it might well have been that those who supported the doctrines of the Monophysites did so because they were Greens. So perhaps it was here. The younger and rebellious among the Knowers may perhaps have most resented, say, the ban on "unqualified" cohabitation—or the earnestly endless solemnities of their elders—or the fact that they themselves were tired of being reproved for levity—or excluded from making any but the most minor decisions.

But it was not such terms that Rickar used when he and Fateem and Cerry, Lors, Liam and a few others found themselves together and unobserved one middle morning. Their official mission there was the bringing down of a supply of choice seed-corn from a granary high up above the uncultivated thickets. When people are determined to be together for any reason the events of life lose much of their casual nature and occur only either to gather or to separate them. So it was now. The mission was a chance to be free of being overlooked and overheard. It was seized upon.

The llamas would much rather have been allowed to remain loose to gambol and nuzzle and dance about, and did not submit without protest to having the paniers laden onto them. Up the trail they all went, lighter of heart than any of them might have been willing to admit.

Lors said, almost as though the words were

unsafe, "We haven't seen anything more of the Devils since you came. I think it was a lucky thing for us that you did." Rickar, determinedly grim, said, "It may be luckier for us . . . for some of us, anyway."

"I think that Father Gaspar is right in one thing, anyway," Liam considered. "It's better to keep away from them, generally speaking, than not to keep away from them."

Rickar grunted, probably annoyed to think that his father could be right in anything. Cerry was thinking that it was a relief to be away from the eternal self-righteousness of the arkfolk. She looked down to where the vessel lay harbored, but only undisturbed greenery met her eye. Gaspar had seen to the work of concealment well. She said so.

Fateem shook her head of soft, brown curls. Everything about her was small and clear and, somehow, managing to seem at the same time delicate and sturdy. "Conceal," she said, bitterly. "Hide. Run. Preach."

She flung up her head and looked at Rickar. "Why do we stay?" she asked. "We don't have to. When the ark, when all the arks, are ready to leave, why don't we just stay behind?"

He was more than startled, he was shocked. In a moment he seemed to have withdrawn, not only from what she had just said, but also from everything which he himself had said. He half-turned to look back down at where the ark was concealed, then quickly looked back, embarrassed. His eyes met no one's. "That's a rather big decision to make," he said, in an uncertain, unhappy voice. Then, a satisfactory answer to her question occurring to him, he looked up and said with more assurance, "It will be a while before anything can be ready to go. That gives us a lot of time to think about it. . . . Anyway, we've got this seed corn to load. It's very different from our Serran-type of corn, isn't it, Fateem?"

She blew out an angry breath, but made no other answer. Nor did she answer him afterward, either, until, annoyed, he switched his conversation to Cerry. "We saw no such light-haired women as you before we saw you," he told her; "although we had heard about them. And how red your skin was from the sun! But now you look exceedingly well."

Lors, from time to time, seemed on the point of saying something, but never did. They filled basket after basket of the thick and twisted ears of corn, so different from the thin and slender ones of the type of Serra, and dumped them into the painers. Presently they paused to eat and drink, and Liam found himself sitting apart with Fateem under a tree. From time to time Rickar would look up at them, his face an unsuccessful mixture of anger and unconcern; then he would turn to say something to Cerry and laugh.

"These cakes are good," Liam said. "We didn't have this corn at all in Britland—just rye and barley and wheat. . . . Come," he said, "don't stay angry at your young friend. Give him a chance to adjust to your ideas. Think what it means for him to leave all his family and friends and—"

She burst out, "It should mean no more to him than it means to me!"

"Well . . . there's that."

"He was the first to talk of this among us, and he talked the longest and the most. I was contented, before. I would probably be still contented—believing what I was taught, doing as I was told. Receiving the wise words of the ancient elders, humbly accepting everything. But I can't, anymore—and it's all Rickar's doing! If he wasn't willing to face leaving the Knowers, why —well, what did he *think?*" She sat up, facing Liam indignantly. "Did he think that a miracle would occur? And his father and his mother and all the others would suddenly come around to his way of thinking?—when they haven't any of them the slightest notion in the world of the things he's been thinking of! And now for me to find out that it was all just thinking—and all just talk!"

Again, Liam was pacific. "Be patient—" he began.

But this was what she could not be. "No. No. But it's just as well that it's happened. I should have known better—I *will* know better—than to trust a boy!" She threw a fleeting, disgusted glance at the unfortunate lad, then turned her face, alive with indignation and disdain, to Liam again. "But *you,*" she burst out—"you are a man!"

"True . . ."

But he said nothing more; after a moment, she demanded, "Then don't tell me that you are really going to become a Knower and run meekly off with the rest of them? You'd better not tell me that! I wouldn't believe it, but I'd hate you for lying to me!"

He took the small hand she had held out to

him. "No, don't hate me," he said. "I can't tell
you for certain sure, Fateem, what I will do. I
rather incline to doubt that good Father Gaspar
will be wanting me on his next voyage. And I
wouldn't want you to make up your mind, and
make it up not to change it . . . now . . . that
you'll be leaving your people so certainly—not
on the chance of anything I might be going to
do."

Something like despair came into her golden
brown eyes. "Oh, but I thought I might depend
on you," she said, low-voiced. She frowned,
slightly. "Is it because of her? Cerry? Because . . ." She stopped, confused.

He rose, still holding her hand, and pulled her
to her feet. "It's not. You can talk to her as you
talk to me. If you want . . . from me . . . any
more than that, I'm sorry. I don't speak of forever or for never, but for now. But this I can tell
you, Fateem: as I will tell her of what my plans
may be, when I have a better way of knowing
what my plans may be, so I will tell you. And
just as she will be, as she is now, free to decide if
she will go or stay, or whatever, so, Fateem, will
you.

"And now, let's go back to our corn. Whatever
happens, and wherever it happens, there must
be seed to sow."

It was on the way back that Rickar, carefully
not looking toward Fateem, said, in a determined voice, "Liam, what you said about
learning more of the Devils—"

And Lors, in a relieved tone: "Ah—!"

None of the party was willing to stay behind

with the laden beasts; none wanted even to risk it by drawing straws. So the llamas were "deposited" in a small blind-end barranco and the narrow mouth of it plugged with stones and branches. Then, free, they followed Lors at a rapid pace which soon took them far from the main trail, and after that the pace was no longer quite so rapid. They clambered over fallen trees, scaled boulders hot from the sun, plunged through obstructive thickets; came at last to a sort of slot in the rocky face of the hill through which not more than two of them at a time could look down a long stretch of deep and narrow gorge.

A hawk rode upon the air, floating, rising, falling softly, rising again. "It would be nice if we could do the same," Liam murmured. Then: "What's beyond the end, there?"

Lors said, "Wait." They waited quite a long time, looking at the stretch of empty ground beyond the farther end of the gorge. At length he clutched Liam's arm. Something which perhaps both of them had assumed to be a tree now detached itself from a shady mass of obscurity and moved across the landscape. They could not see it at all clearly, nor could they see clearly the shapes which followed it. But they could see them move and pass and vanish. It was certain that they were large, certain that they were strange, certain that they could not be trees. Nothing more moved, down and afar off, though they waited a long time further. But at last they felt the breeze in their faces, and the breeze told them that what had been known without proof was indeed true.

Devils!

But they saw nothing more.

Cerry said, "We can't learn very much about them at that distance, can we?"

"We can't learn anything at all about them at that distance," Liam said. "Except that they're there. Or at least that some of them are there. No—

"Lors, is there a way through? A safe way? Or at least safer?"

"A safer way to what?"

It was not the words of the question which brought them up short, dismayed, nor the tone of voice in which it was asked, for the tone was mild enough. But they were so thunderstruck at seeing Gaspar, the Father Noah, up here that astonishment made them all for a moment mute.

Rickar it was who broke the short silence. "A safer way, in case one should ever be necessary, through to the coast, father. . . . But what brings you here? Is anything—"

"Wrong? No. But it is well to look about on all sides and to know what lies behind as well as before. Indeed, is this not the very motive which inspired the question of Liam? And a good question, too. Is there an answer, Lors Rowan?"

"Not the way we have just been," Lors said. "But it's possible that there may be one by other ways. If we might take time out to look . . . ?"

Gaspar stroked his beard and pursed his lips reflectively. He nodded. "Speak to Lej," he said, after a moment. "He is this week's Orderer of Schedules. . . . But I see that you are all here. Where, in that case, are the animals? Not unguarded, I hope? And the seed corn? What of

that? Lors Rowan's father's generosity should
not be repaid with carelessness."

He was somewhat appeased on being shown
the effectively-blockaded animals, all comfortably sitting down and ruminating their cuds.
Lors took the occasion to deliver a running lec-
ture on the intelligence and habits of llamas,
which occupied the rest of the return trip and
which (they hoped) effectively prevented the old
Knower from entertaining suspicions.

"Clearly," he said, when Lors at last paused,
dry-mouthed, and at a loss for further comment,
having already repeated himself at least twice;
"clearly, we must take a breeding stock of these
intelligent and useful creatures with us."

"There is another breed related to them that
runs wild in the Uplands—guanacos. They're
smaller, but the fleece is softer."

"We must have those, too. I will make a note
of it."

They watched him leave as they started un-
loading the seed-corn. They indicated neither by
word nor conscious expression any fears not yet
laid quite to rest. But evidently nothing more
than a routine inspection of yet another aspect of
the work of preparation had brought Gaspar up
to look at them. It was probably fortunate that
the inspection had not been made by someone
with younger legs and keener eyes who might
have traced them up the vantage-point and overheard what they were saying there.

Thus, as on the raft, consultation awaited the
fall of night. When they were together again
Lors said, "My brother—Duro, my younger
brother—has an idea which might bring us to a

safer way through the hills."

But Rickar was feeling somewhat dis-
couraged. "I did speak to Lej, but he said that
three people were enough for a scouting trip. Not
that the others are especially needed for anything else; it's just the Knowers' frugal way: if
three are enough, then only three will go."

Liam, in the darkness, felt someone settle next
to him, felt an arm touch his—a smooth and not
a hairy one. A woman. He reached, gently, and
his hand encountered a soft mass of curls.
Fateem. He patted them, and heard Rickar ask,
"What now?"

Liam said, "Now we ask Lors to think of
where we'll all rendezvous . . . after he arranges
for the rest of us to start out for the Uplands to
see about those—what did you call them? Ah,
yes. Guanacos. Can't a rendezvous be set for—
where is this place your brother has in mind,
Lors?"

Out of the darkness Lors said, "We call it the
caves. . . ."

VI

THE SCHEME had worked . . . so far. Rickar, Duro, and Cerry had gone off to the caves. Lors, Liam, Fateem, a raftsman named Dunal, and Seqah, one of the young and crypto-heretical Knowers, were the Uplands party. Lej had felt himself obviously less certain as to the number required for the unprecedented task of seeing to the acquisition of guanaco breeding-stock, and Lors had been insistent. Lej's final statement— "Since they are smaller animals, then, five people should be enough"—seemed to indicate that he perhaps thought they would each carry one of them slung across their backs!

What they did carry, slung across their backs, were several days' rations apiece. And so, when they came across him, was Tom-small.

Tom-small shrugged. "My popa has been building canoes in a fury. He claims that even though the strangers seem to have taken over the country, at least they've attracted enough fools —your pardon, friends—so that he can handle the rest of ours who've stayed faithful. *Then* (he says) if it's really necessary to flee, he'll find out where the arks intend to go, and he (that means us) will make damned sure to go somewhere else. . . . He won't admit, but he's following Knowers' advice in at least one way. We're living

97

in brushwood shacks now, for the most part, because he's having the houses pulled down for boat-timbers.

"He says that if we've got to leave, then the houses won't be of any use to us. And if we haven't got to leave, we can always build new ones. Any news of the thick-and-thins?"

Lors exchanged quick looks with the others. They raised their eyebrows, shrugged, leaving the decision to him. He said, "The two kinds of Devils, you mean. . . . Well, Jow's son, we have some hopes of our finding out some news before very long. But it's got to be private news . . . if we get any . . . for the time being, at any rate. Understood?"

Tom-small straightened the skin bag of supplies slung across his broad shoulders. "Understood. Where's Duro, then?"

"We'll meet up with him at the caves, later on."

"But this isn't the way to the—"

"The longest way around is sometimes the straightest way there. A saying from the wise wisdom of the knowledgable ancient old Knowers, which I just made up. . . . What do you know about chasing down the wild guanaco, shorty?"

Jow's son grinned. "Not a thing. Why?"

"You'll soon know something. Knowledge is contagious. And now, talk more if you like, but I'm going to save my breath for climbing."

The thickets thinned out, were succeeded by farmlands, which in turn gave way to moor. The winds began to nip at them, and they were glad for the extra clothes Lors had had them bring; and, when night began to settle, glad for the

warmth of the fire in the grove they picked for
their camp: not only did it serve as a windbreak,
but it was naturally supplied with wood. They
ate, drank hot infusions of herb, and, well-tired,
turned to sleep.

After a while someone came and lay down
next to Liam and he felt arms close softly around
him. There was a whisper: "It is me—Fateem."

He grunted. "I'm relieved it's not one of the
boys, behaving so."

She breathed angrily. "'Behaving so—' Silent
hero, cautions, careful, stiff and aloof! Should
we all behave the same? I won't. I can't!"

He sighed. "What do you want, then?"

Her whisper trembled, broke—perhaps still
with anger, perhaps with cold—but went on
again. "I don't know what you—I can't go
along, waiting forever. I can't be alone like this
any more. Before, there was the safety of the
family and the folk. Then there was the ark . . .
and Rickar. What's Rickar? Very little. I—
Tomorrow the entire ground may give way beneath our feet. And you go on, as if—What do I
want? I want to know that I'm not alone, not just
one of a band of brothers or something like that.
I want to know that I'm something special to
some special person. Not forever. I don't know
about forever. I know about tonight—

"Tom has his father, Lors has his brother, you
have your secret dreams, I—what do I have?
You know what I have. Tonight is not for dreaming! Aren't you a man, made like other men? Ah
. . . yes . . . there . . . so . . . I knew that
you were—" Her voice broke off, then began
again, even lower, without words.

                        *   *   *

Morning was cold and wet and there was very
little in the way of talk until more hot herb tea
was made and drunk; then they went on, following the path with lowered eyes, the dim light of
sunrise made further dim by the thick mists.

And then, as a portion of the mists blew away,
they saw three figures: as strange to all but Lors
as they were suddenly come upon . . . and even
somewhat strange to him.

Three men stood athwart the trail, tall, each
one with a tall staff in the crook of one arm and
a bow as tall as himself resting, unstrung, in the
crook of the other. The pelt of the wild, fleet
guanaco was their clothing, and the mists and
dews distilled in droplets in their thin, dark
beards.

One said, "Hey, people!"

One said, "Where do you go, people?"

One said, "Only maybe not, eh, people?"

They straggled to a halt, irresolute. Tom and
Lors, in turn, identified themselves, and began
an explanation of their purpose. But presently
they stopped. The three men were not listening
to them, were not looking at them. They were
looking at Liam. Intently.

One said, "Hey, person, your eyes don't
match!"

One said, "You've got power of a sort, person?"

One said, "Only maybe not, eh, person?"

Liam said nothing. He returned their looks.
By and by the long silence was broken again as
the men touched their breasts in the identification which was, evidently, among them a
form of greeting.

"This is Lehi."

"This is Nephi."

"This is Moroni."

And again there was a silence. Then Liam said, "It's been told you what is wanted of you. You are not obliged to agree. You may answer *Yes*, you may answer *No*, you may answer *Maybe*. But, persons, before the sun is warm enough and the air is dry enough for you to have safely restrung your bows, persons, you will have answered." And he touched his breast and said, "This is Liam."

And he was correct. They thought him perhaps the only sane man among madmen—but only perhaps—but they were willing to provide the live guanacos . . . for a consideration. For what consideration? That, it was stated clearly, would have to await further thought.

"Three men alone cannot catch the wild ones alive, person. Many men will be needed to catch the wild ones alive. Some to creep up on them . . . slowly . . . slowly . . . so . . . dressed in the skins of the wild ones. They will be suspicious at first"—Lehi mimed how the wild guanaco would lift up his head and look dubiously at the odd "guanacos" so slowly "grazing" and advancing—"but by and by and little by little, they get used to it. They forget."

"Only maybe not," said Moroni.

"They never get completely used to us, they never completely forget their suspicions of us," Nephi conceded. "To hunt them to the death is difficult, yet we must do it, for such is their fate and such, for that matter, is ours."

And then the three of them, with words, with gestures, mime, and dance, enacted for them the

rest of the hunt of the wild guanaco: concealment and disguise, gradual approach from all
sides, the off-throwing of disguise by one group,
the blowing of the horns, the swift flight of the
alarmed animals, the rising up of another group
waving flags, the wheeling and turning and the
fleetly flying yet again of the wild ones until,
their sides turned most advantageously to the
hidden archers lying low, they were at length
shot to death.

"We do not slay them all, hey, person," said
Lehi.

"We spare the colts and the mares, eh, person," said Nephi.

And Moroni said, "Only maybe not."

The other two conceded that such conserva-
tion represented the ideal, but not, invariably,
the actual practice. "But capturing the wild ones
alive, hey, this is something else. We must build
corrals, eh, and station many men with horns
and banners. But we will do it, persons; tell us
how many you want, and we will supply them,
every one of them."

"Send us someone in a week's time to tell us
the news you have to tell," Liam said. "Meanwhile, what do you intend to do about the Kar-
chee and about the dragons?"

They shrugged. They mimed the stooping gait
of the Kar-chee, the dragon on four feet and the
dragon on two. They would deal with them as
they dealt with the wild guanaco: hunt them—
confuse them—destroy them. So. That was what
they would do. Moroni as usual had the last
word. "Only maybe not," he said.

One last question they had for Liam as he and
his friends prepared to go. "You are not of this

island-place, person. How did you get here?"

"I came on a raft with others," he said.

The sun's rays came slanting through the clouds, and the hunters looked slantingly at each other. "Persons have ventured far on rafts before," one said. "And perhaps will venture far again," said another. And the third said, "There is no end; there are only beginnings."

They strung their bows and hefted their spears and strode away across the moor and rolling hills, upward, upward, and up. Mists closed in, parted, rallied a last time, were burned off by the sun. And when Liam last looked back there was no one in sight.

Long, long, on the long downward way, with Fateem silent but serene by his side, he considered. What was his duty toward these hunters, for example? For even if their wild, free life on the open heights were doomed, surely they themselves need not be? That is, unless the whole house of mankind need be. . . . That is, unless their own stubborn intransigence might turn their fate to *need be*. What was his, Liam's, own duty toward them?

Toward those who had followed him from Britland on the terrible raft?

Toward those who followed the Knowers?

Toward Lors and Tom and their fellow-islanders?

Toward Cerry, who followed him and asked for nothing and had received little more? Toward Fateem, who had asked for that which he had determined not to give . . . and yet had, like any other man, gladly in the moment given?

And—for that matter—toward himself?

The moors gave way to farmlands, fields, for-

ests, thickets, rocks and sand; and all the time
his thoughts roamed and prowled and always
they came out the same door they had come in.

His duty was to learn all that he could learn
and by whatever means and at whatever risks
about the Kar-chee and about the dragons.

Duro felt his responsibilities so keenly and
weightily that it abated his pleasure in being
more-or-less in charge of two older people. He
was also unable to forget what had happened the
last time he had come down to the caves. The
recollection was like a heavy hand upon his
stones. He and Lors had agreed to rendezvous as
far away from that particular part of the region
as possible, but . . . still . . .

"We have some caves in our part of Britland,"
Cerry said, as she looked about, awed, "but they
are not so regular as these. It looks—of course,
that would be impossible—but it does look as
though they had been *dug* here! Right through
the solid rock. . . ."

Rickar smiled at the absurdity of the suggestion, but Duro nodded his head. "They say that
it was so. They say that in the oldest days there
were, the days before the old days, that these
hills were full of *metal*"—he spoke the word with
awe—"and that the men who were alive then
dug these caves with tools of metal to get out the
metal that was here.

"And I've heard Popa say that when the great
land that was before the Devils came split up
and parts of it sank, you know—that the whole
fore-part of this region was split away and sank,
too, and this is what was left after that."

They lifted torches and peered about them, s

lent and reverent and almost overwhelmed. Here the walls were far apart and the ceilings high; there, everything narrowed and closed in upon itself. For a long while the passage ran straight as the path of a well-made arrow, then it curved with measured symmetry; now it was level, now it rose up, now it sank. Strange markings were found in the rock from time to time. And once they came upon a place where water dripped from a cleft in the wall and formed a stream which found its way into a deep pool which reflected the light of their torches.

Cerry shivered. In the low voice which had become natural to the three of them, awed by the initial echoes, she said, "I'd be afraid to be here without light. . . . The truth is, I'm afriad to be here, even now—"

"We'll go back," Duro said.

They set up their meager camp in a chamber he showed them, off a short side passage; it was entered from below, and they closed the way up, once they had ascended, by pushing over a shard of broken rock; but not so completely that air couldn't enter. Then he set up his lamp, a clever and curious thing whereby oil trickled slowly through a series of pierced egg-shells, replenishing the bowl as the small wick consumed the fuel. The light flickered for a few moments, dancing wildly, then it settled down and commenced to burn steadily, if a trifle smokily. They ate lightly, conversed a while in the tones now dared to be raised a trifle louder. Presently the older two became aware that Duro had dropped off to sleep. They laughed, then yawned, then did the same.

And in the night-time, Cerry wept.

Rickar awoke to hear her sobbing. "Are you ill?" he asked, raising himself on an elbow. "Have you a pain?" She shook her head, her face concealed in her hands. "Then what's wrong?"

But all she would say was, "Liam! Liam!"

And after a while she fell silent and turned her back. So Rickar sighed and blinked his eyes and then Duro was jogging him and beckoning him to follow. Daylight filtered in, dimly, below. He followed him, wondering, waiting for the boy to speak, but all he did was stop and face against a wall. "Well?" Rickar asked, after a moment. "What's the matter?"

"Matter?" Duro asked, over his shoulder. "Don't you Knowers have bladders, too?"

"Oh," Rickar said, blankly. A mildly insistent internal pressure supplied the answer. "Yes," he said, "we do. Uh . . . yes . . . thanks."

"No fee to guests. Sleep well?"

"*I* did, yes. Except when Cerry woke me up. She was crying. You didn't hear her? I thought not. Wouldn't say what was wrong."

Duro adjusted his breech-clout. "Well," he said, cheerfully, "that was your opportunity. You should have blown out the lamp and taken her into your arms and kissed away her fears. Oh well. Crying, hmm. Too bad. Probably had a bad dream. You all finished? Then let's get back before she wakes up and gets scared all over again." He started back, nodding his head sagely. "No accounting for dreams, you know. No accounting for them."

In after ages there came to be much marvel at the technology of the Kar-chee. But there could never have been much marvel at their technology of what an earlier age would have called "security"—except, perhaps, to marvel at the almost complete absence of it. Yet this was not without reasonable cause. Just as there are organisms who cannot digest anything which has not been already partly pre-digested by decay, so the Kar-chee's social-scientific organism could digest no planet which had not been already partly pre-digested by decay. Hence they picked none for their attention which had not already been either abandoned or as close to it as made no matter of difference. In such cases there was little or no capacity for resistance by the few remaining inhabitants. A man, in the days when men had still been scanty upon the surface of their own mother-world and still exploring newly-found portions of it, might have been clawed by a bear or nipped by an owl, but he did not think that the owls or the bears were *resisting*. And no matter how many such accidents or incidents occurred, it still never came into the mind of man to establish a system of "security" against owls or bears.

It was the notion of Lors and of Liam to pick their way cautiously through the honeycomb of caves and come out high up on the other side, where they might be able to peer down, seeing without being seen; and even, perhaps, at night, creep down with infinite caution and spy about the outskirts of the enemy camp. What happened was rather different, of course.

None of them had ever had personal experience of any engine or device more complex than a loom or a wine- or oil-press. The meaning of what lay far below them there on the floor of the vast cavern was thus largely hidden from them. An infinity of lights, a multitude of great black cabinets (so they thought of them), a profusion of moving parts, odd noises, hummings, buzzings, shrill-high batlike squeakings, rumblings . . . sounds for which they had no names. Kar-chee came and went, bound on tasks which —concerned as they must have been with the machinery—were meaningless to the unobserved observers. There were no dragons immediately below, but at the opposite end of the cavern, a good distance off, there were a number of them, milling slowly about.

To Cerry, what was going on below made no more sense when she last looked at it than when she first looked at it. Except for the presence of the Devils, it simply was not something to be comprehended. But with Liam it was otherwise. His eyes roamed slowly and systematically over the entire area, back and forth, back and forth, up and down, up and down. Again and again. Again and again. And so, gradually, line upon line, principle upon principle, here a little and there a little, something of what was going on below began to fall into a sort of a sequence and to make a sort of a sense to him.

There was a continual flashing of blue points, a rushing of waters, crashing percussions, dust, a flow of crushed rocks in moving paths, Kar-chee bending and stooping and rising, the air shuddering, the solid stone shuddering.

But, now, as he looked and looked, he began to believe that although all this was going on simultaneously, all the *these* which made up the *this* were going on separately. He perceived repetitions, from the repetitions he perceived sequences, and from the sequences he derived causes and effects. As yet he could not in any manner understand purpose. But that might yet come. It might yet. He inched forward yet another little bit, and stared intently, trying to isolate a sequence and follow it through from start to stop.

A great serpent of metal mesh and joints reared itself up, extending and extending, stretching and stretching, rigid where it had been flaccid, its head all monstrous gears and metal beak. At a height higher than that of ten men standing on each other's shoulders, the head struck. Plates fell into place, protecting the gears as the beak imbedded itself in the rock. And bit. And burrowed. The head vanished; the "neck" stretched and extended. Dust and new-made sand, like dry dribble, came from the orifice. The head withdrew. The plates opened. The monstrous beak sank down . . . down. . . . The body withdrew into itself, turning, serpentine, retreating across the floor of the cavern. And at length it paused by a Kar-chee and, in a movement which made Liam, watching, shudder, so closely did it counterfeit life and affection, it raised its head to the Kar-chee and the Kar-chee lowered a monstrous arm and laid its hand upon the monstrous head.

But this curious simulation lasted but a second. The Kar-chee hands contained implements, which removed the beak-drill and placed it in a container; then the Kar-chee hands dipped into another place, came out with one of the curious objects Liam had come to think of as *points*, and—

But then, far down the immense cavern, a section of wall slid away, revealing an immense corridor leading off into obscurity and fitfully illuminated with reddish light like the reflection of enormous fires, and from this emerged a blast of heat which made the humans fight for breath. Out and up from this inferno crawled a long and armored Something on many clanking feet; mud and water dripped from it. Behind it, very far behind it, a door slid shut. And before that, another. And another. Another. . . .

It was as though there lay something very strong and dangerous far below there, which had to be caged and fenced and walled away. . . .

The Kar-chee, all of them, looked up and paused in their doings and walkings and watchings. Farther away, the dragons did the same, lifting their heads up and some even rearing on their hind legs. All turned, all regarded. Something of greatmost importance seemed imminent.

But what this might be, Liam could not know. He could suspect, however, and his suspicion turned his courage into terror. But not for long. The greater and nearer the danger, the sooner and more effectively the quest for knowledge must be accomplished. He returned his intent gaze to the glittering and flashing blues . . . his eye and his attention had been caught by them at the first. In terms of language with which he was not familiar it could perhaps have been said that his subconscious mind had made an important discovery which his conscious mind had yet to make. Liam did not think in such terms. He knew only that he must now start over again in trying to discover a sequence and trace its progress along its circuit.

The metallic serpent, thick and gross as any

python, but, even at its shortest length, longer
imcomparably than any serpent or python of
flesh and blood—

—raised its head—

—the Kar-chee—

—placed the point, rather like a longer, larger,
cross-bow bolt, flashing in every shade of blue, in
the "head" of the serpentine machine, as though
it were feeding it—

The thing retracted, retreated, undulating
across the floor of the teeming cavern until it
came to the rocky wall-face, reared up, entered
one of the drill-holes once more, retreated from
it, more slowly this time, emerged entirely and
withdrew . . . withdrew . . . withdrew . . . the
head moving backward and ever backward but
always keeping in direct line with the opening. . . .

An object whose precise shape Liam could not
make out appeared briefly in the front of the
monstrous "head" where its mouth would have
been had it been a living thing.

This it spat and, having projected it, at once
the whole equipage subsided and Liam did not
watch it. He observed the object shoot forward
and enter the drill hole. And the drill hole vanished and all the wall of the rock about it vanished too as it came bursting . . . shattering . . .
flying forward. . . .

Noise upon noise, crash upon crash, sound
upon sound, rolling and thundering.

Below, vast engines which had come into
place received the expelled rubble. Moved it. Deposited it. Transported it. Washed it. Sorted it.
Carried it away.

And the sequence began all over again.

The thing had been going on when they had
first emerged at the abruptly shorn-off end of the
old mine-tunnel, to discover this vast and (so
Duro and Lors said) new-made cavern. But until
Liam had set himself to analyzing and tracing
the sequence, all had seemed chaos and Devilish
confusion. He now had at least a part of it all
clear in his mind. As he cast his eyes around
again to see what he should next concentrate on,
Cerry made a shuddering noise and Rickar
made a sick one. The Rowan brothers hissed
and half-started to their feet—but abruptly they
lay down once more.

And Liam, his eyes now following theirs, saw
a dragon walking down the floor of the cavern
and pausing slightly from time to time to move
its head as though to fix a better hold on what it
carried in its mouth—arms flailing, legs
thrashing, mouth opened to utter unheard and
unavailing screams and cries—

—a man.

The brothers looked at Liam, scowling—
masking shock and outrage and bafflement.
"Get down?" Lors repeated. "To rescue that
one? It's madness—"

"How could we do it?" Duro demanded. "We
couldn't do it! We would be killed, simply . . .
or"—he winced and shuddered—"not so simply."

They could hear him now, for the machines
had fallen silent and the blasting and the fall of
broken rock had ceased. They could hear the
hissing of the dragons and the clicking and shuffling sounds produced by the Kar-chee. They
could hear the pad-pad-pad of dragon feet and

even, if a second's silence fell, the running of the feet of the man down there below. But over all of this, almost incessantly, they could hear the man's voice—the voice of terror and of the fear of death—human, because it was neither dragon nor Kar-chee, but otherwise scarcely human in its absolute loss of control.

Man's voice screaming as the dragon lifted and tossed him and caught him in its mouth. Man's voice shrieking as the dragon shook him as a dog shakes a rat. Man's voice babbling witlessly as the dragon released him. Man's voice gibbering as man's feet tottered and ran. Man's voice screaming as the dragon came after him again.

There seemed no end to it.

They had formed a circle, the Devils had— Kar-chee on the inside, dragons on the outside. The man ran blindly, stumbling, drooling and piddling in terror. The Kar-chee cuffed him back. He fell, he crawled, he got up, he ran. The Kar-chee cuffed him back. The dragon caught him up again. Blood streamed down his naked sides. And suddenly the dragon, as though tired of the sport, closed his jaws with a crunching, mashing sound. The man's voice continued for another second, still, high and thin, like an insect's screech; then it stopped. The dragon tossed the mangled body aside.

Rickar was sick. Cerry moaned, eyes closed, hands to mouth. Duro said, through clenched teeth, "So he's dead. No reason to go down now. We'd be dead, too. He's dead. No reason—"

And Lors, his voice high-pitched and trembling, incredulous, on the point of breaking: "Oh—Oh—Another. Another—"

They had not known the first man, and they did not know this man. They felt his pain, his anguish, fright, terror, the body that hopped and ran and bled and screamed . . . and screamed. . . . And it all began all over again, everything as before.

"We—must—go—*down!*" Liam said, hoarsely. "To save him? I don't know. But—look you, all of you: *They* are down *there*. Down *there*. All of them. So—"

He forced them to listen; he seized them by the hair, struck them in the face. He dared not raise his voice, but they listened to the voice— the voice of Liam—and slowly, unwillingly, in fear and in trembling, they listened. But now and then despite themselves their eyes would move, only to jerk back to his eyes, away from the hideous gathering below. Their eyes were fixed by Liam's eyes and they listened and they nodded. And, slowly, slowly, scuttling sideways like crabs, they retreated.

The screams were still going on when they emerged through the half-buried fissure three-quarters of the way down the side of the cavern wall. The cavern itself was more or less horizontally cylindrical and so they had reasonable purchase for hands and feet as they descended. From far away the screams still sounded, but they could not tell if they were still coming from the same man or from another. They did not stop to try and decide. Uppermost in their minds was that they not be caught. And next in claim upon them was to follow Liam, which they did, instinctively crouching as they moved. A thick and bitter odor overlay the air, mingled as it was with several other ones—the dust of the shattered rock, the smell of sea mud which had come up from the now-closed cavern, various unfamiliar reeks probably pertaining to the machinery—but over all was the bitter odor of the Kar-chee and the thick stench of the dragons.

Liam had no easy task orienting his passage here below in terms of what he had seen from high above. But he managed it, somehow. The mesh reticulations of the serpentine bores lay motionless, but they stepped over them fearfully as though not certain that they would not, if touched, spring to dreadful life. On and on in the curious lighting and the rubble and clutter they moved, bent over. Trying not to listen to the sounds of agony from far ahead. And at length Liam found what he was looking for.

The Kar-chee had reached down into the container. Liam had to climb up—but not very far up. He reached out his hand and he noticed that it trembled. The blue points shimmered and flashed. He took one in his hand. It seemed to feel both hot and cold at the same time. He seized it firmly, thrust it into the sacket which had been emptied of food. Thrust in another. And another. And another. . . . He filled the bag, handed it down, received another one. He filled them all, filled the sheepskins, tied them up, and then descended, carrying the last of them.

"Don't stumble," he warned them. "Don't drop any of these. Don't run—but if you *do* run, lay them down—gently—first, and just leave them lie."

Off they started, back the way they had come, walking delicately, stooping beneath their burdens. The cavern echoed with the mind-shak-

ing sounds from behind, but they did not stop.
Liam had carefully observed his landmarks. *Here*
a spring of water gushed from the rock face into
a sluice; *there* two serpentine borers lay coiled together as though in some cold, loveless pythonic
embrace. He gave a short hiss, turned. Behind
them the screams suddenly ceased. There was
another hiss . . . not from Liam. And another.
The air was filled with them. And then came the
first bellow. And the pad-pad-pad of dragon feet.
This became a quick and thudding and ground-
shaking stamp. They climbed the slanting face of
the cavern wall. They did not look back. They
knew they were discovered.

"Duro and Lors, drop behind—you others, up
with you! Don't wait for us, don't drop anything
—*go!*" As he spoke, he drew open the mouth of
a sacket, took out two of the blue points and
stood there with one in each hand. "Cock your
bows," he directed. They did so; took the points,
once each, loaded, followed Liam's pointing finger; fired; turned and were scrambling up again
when the double blast behind caught them and
flung them. On hands and feet they crawled
back, crept upward, slowly, carefully, the lips of
their sacks between clenched teeth, echoes roaring and rolling, dust and gravel; on hands and
on knees they reached the safety of the cleft in
the rock and sidled through.

Through the obscurity a dragon came thundering, pounding upright on two feet, the claws
of its forefeet slashing at the air, the nodules on
its cheeks swelling and puffing, body a dark-
green-black along the back, a paler tint below. It
shattered their eardrums, so it seemed, with its
bellows. And then the finger on the trigger of the

crossbow tightened, the blue point flew flashing through the air—the flashing seemingly reflected in the flashing irridescence of the great faceted dragon-eyes—the point and the dragon alike vanished in a cloud of thick dust and darkness and the noise of it rolled and roared.

Lors' chin was bleeding where a sharp stone had cut it in ricochet. He grinned a twisted, terrified, yet quite triumphant grin, shot his hand inward, directing. "Go on, Liam! Go on! I'll cover you! Go —"

But Liam shook his head, pulled out two more of the strange but unquestionably potent points, handing as before one to each brother. "Shoot these—*there*," he said, pointing. "And try for as much distance as you can get."

The clouds rolled around, thinned, thickened again. Here and there something lay upon the ground, still; here and there something thrashed and bellowed and bled. Lors and Duro nodded. Their other shots had been of need hasty and impromptu. Now, for the moment at least, nothing seemed to be pursuing them. They hefted the points, spoke briefly to each other, made swift, skillful adjustments of their crossbows, downed them, foot against lever for the pressure that hand and arm couldn't give, cocked them, raised and loaded, aimed, holding them a bit higher than before.

They shot.

Through the haze they saw a group of Kar-chee, black chitinous exoskeletons covered and gray with dust, chirring and gesturing in front of that great closed gate which led—which led where?—which led below, wherever or why-ever—

Thud-thud—

As they dashed for their lives deeper into the fissure, and, suddenly remembering, slowed, clutching more tightly on the sacks and skins containing the explosive points, they retained one single swift-flashing recollection of the great blast of fire and steam and scalding air and boiling mud that came vomiting up and out from that hellish corridor where once the Kar-chee had chirred and gestured and where once that door had been.

And Liam, too, clutched at the sheepskin packed with the blue and flashing points, but even tighter was his grip on the curious object that had been standing so casually there among the engines where the Kar-chee had stood distributing the points; the object between his shirt and skin, warming his heart. He had had no chance to take more than the most rapid and inconclusive glance at it; it was perhaps even likelier that he was wrong than that he was right. . . .

But he might be right!

And in that case what he held would be a map.

VII

AFTERWARD HE was to compare their retreat through the mine-caves to the passage of a troop of ants crawling through a sponge caught in a high wind. Over quivering ground, pelted by falling debris, half-stifled with dust, singed by burning air, more than once finding that either the roof or the floor or sometimes both the roof and the floor of a corridor they had planned to take had given way—such was their trip from the Kar-chee cavern to the world outside.

But the world outside seemed little if any more stable. No sky appeared likely to fall down in upon them, true, but the land quivered. Off-shore, far off-shore, a great bubble broke the surface of the water, and a great puff of steam rose and vanished into the air; presently the hot and muddy breath of the vexed sea-bottom reached them. Again and again and again. . . .

While they watched, fascinated, alternately sweating and chilled, an entire headland slid, sighing and rumbling, into the ocean. Their ears were next buffeted by soundless concussions. As they stood, straining to hear, the earth rose and fell and rose again. Carefully they lay down their sacks and skins of warheads and subsided into sitting positions. Cracks and chasms opened, closed again with the sound of thunder-claps, only to reappear—so it seemed to their bemused and confused sight: as though a chasm was a living creature, now hiding and now disclosing himself—elsewhere.

And after these great shocks came stillness and silence.

Several of them made as though to get up, but Liam gestured them to remain where and as they were. His eyes were rapt and intent; the eyes of the others followed his without being able to see what he could see—but never doubting that he did see. "Wait. . . ." he murmured through slightly parted lips. They waited, uneasy but content. Cerry felt as she had upon that night when she had known that it was for him to lead and for her to follow and that he was one of those about whom tales were composed and songs sung: seers and doers and heroes. . . .

And after the silence and the stillness came another quake, and this second one was greater than the first. And after that one they looked at him again and still his eyes (the one brown as loch-water and the other as blue-green as the sea itself) were focused afar off and again he said, this time in a whisper, "Wait. . . ."

The third shock was mild and brief, and after it subsided Liam rose to his feet in one swift motion and stooped and carefully picked up his burden and walked off, silent and absorbed. And they silently followed them, all of them.

The face of the land was much changed in places. Here had been a stream and now already the gravel of its bed was drying in the sun; there had been an old water-course dry except in the

rainy season: now it rolled to the roiled sea in a
torrent of liquid mud and it stank of the bowels
of the earth. Once they had to detour inland because where the path had led now lay a new
lagoon of water still faintly streaming and full of
dead fish; but once they were able to proceed
straight on through because what had been a
high ridge of rock was now a flatland. Such
marvels were many, but most marvelous of all
was a hushing pillar of flame where natural gas,
long imprisoned beneath the earth, had been
freed and, rushing to the surface, had been met
by a transforming touch of fire.

It was having gone but a short way beyond
that they saw the Kar-chee.

There were a number of them—six, perhaps,
or seven—and they stood upon their four lower
limbs with their huge two upper limbs in the
folded manner common to them, as though engaged in silent meditation and prayer. Only one
of them looked up as the people came suddenly
out of the woods, and this one made no motion
other than the lifting of its head. Liam turned
back on a diagonal course; Lors did the same; so
did Duro, Fateem, and the others . . . except
Rickar. He, as though unseeing, continued walking as he had been. Liam snapped his fingers.
Clicked his tongue. Said, finally, low-voiced,
"Rickar—"

A second Kar-chee lifted its wedge-shaped
head. And a third. And Rickar gasped and
halted. He looked wildly around him. What happened next was probably attributable to the fact
that his whole mind and body told him to run
but that he remembered—now!—Liam's words

of warning in the cavern: *"Don't stumble. Don't drop any of these"*—the blue detonation points.— *"Don't run—but if you do run, lay them down—gently —first, and just leave them lie. . . ."* So he bent forward and deposited the sack he was carrying, and turned to run away after his friends.

And a fourth Kar-chee lifted his head, and a fifth.

And Rickar took two long steps. And saw that his friends were not running at all, but walking at a steady pace. He walked after them, perhaps half-a-dozen paces more. Then he realized what he had done. And he tried to undo it. He turned around and went back.

The act was confused, but it was not cowardly, and he might in the end have gotten away with it—if he had walked. But he did not. He ran. He ran back and he stooped. And the Kar-chee broke out of their own introspective detachment, or whatever mood it was which had been holding them fast; the Kar-chee were all around him and the Kar-chee were upon him and held him fast. One low and mournful cry he uttered; then he was still.

It was but a moment before they had the sack and knew what was in it. Perhaps they might have killed him then and there . . . but, although the people had seen, all of them, the Kar-chee cuffing the man in the cavern back to be baited by dragons, neither then nor anywhere else had they seen, nor heard—save in legend—of Kar-chee actually killing any human being themselves. This they seemed to leave to the dragons. And there seemed to be no dragons about.

Rickar's friends looked on to see him dragged

away—but for a moment only. They dared not use the blue warheads, of course—but the brothers Rowen still had in their pouches conventional crossbow bolts. At Liam's nod they shot once . . . twice . . . so that the bolts landed in front of the retreating Kar-chee. The Kar-chee hesitated—but they did not stop. So Lors and Duro loaded again. And this time they loosed their bolts into the bodies of the two Kar-chee carrying Rickar between them, dangling. He fell. The Kar-chee stumbled. And then—and this was curious—it was as though the same train of thought now passed through the minds of the Kar-chee, for the one carrying the sack of blue detonators stooped and laid it on the ground; as he was doing so, two others seized Rickar, who had been too dazed to escape. And the others surrounded the injured Kar-chee; and all of them began to run.

They were heavy-laden, but they had four legs to run with, and the recocking of the heavy crossbows could not be done in a second. Then, from far off, but again and again, and each time nearer, came the call—the questing call—of a distant dragon. The people saw the wounded Kar-chee fall, saw the others—Rickar now swinging limply back and forth—race away. And then, at another command from Liam, they turned and walked rapidly off.

Old Gaspar trembled and shook. The quake had not unmanned him as this had. Liam felt for him; he had not realized that the Chief Knower had so much softness in him.

"My son, my only son . . . what a blow . . .

what a blow," he repeated. And then, shaking his head, lips trembling and eyes brimming, he asked, "How could he have done it? *You*—you have lived in ignorance; but *he* was a Knower. I knew that all was not well with him in his heart and that he lacked proper zeal to fulfill the obvious intentions of Manifest Nature . . . but still —but still! To engage in the blasphemous futility of resistance—!"

And his wife, old Mother Nor, covered her face with her hand and withdrew, silently, silently shaking her head.

The ark—and the other arks in process of building—had inevitably sustained some damage in the upheavals. Gaspar and his council of elders now set to work at quickened speed to repair, finish stocking up, and be gone. "For already the work of punishment and destruction has begun!"—thus, their cry.

But Liam had not quite the same notion.

"There's no doubt that the Kar-chee had begun to put this place through the usual process. But I doubt that they're ready for it yet. In fact, I'm confident that they're not," he told his small band of followers.

"Do you think that what's happened has been just natural phenomena?" one of them asked, somewhat doubtfully.

Liam shook his head. "No. I'm sure that we set it off ourselves by firing the blue thunderheads down below, there! That cavern?—and the corridor we saw leading down from it? From the looks and the smell of it it seems to me that the Kar-chee were mining or sapping or perhaps just sampling and exploring down there. But

likely not *just*—did you see how wary they and
their Devil-dragons all were when the door on it
opened? How they looked up and how they all
kept on looking till the door closed?"

Lors said, softly, "And we blew it open again!
We dropped the fire into the tub of oil. . . ."

"Something like that. But I've been wondering and wondering, now. . . . It does seem to me
that two fire-charges shouldn't have done all of
this. And the Devils weren't ready to have it
done, either—else they wouldn't have been
down below in danger of being crushed to death
like grubs or beetles. No. . . .

"I think there must be another explanation,
and I think that this is it: the Kar-chee had made
that corridor, that shaft, to tap the hidden fires
beneath the earth. And they planned to drive it
even deeper and they must, I think, have had a
great store of the blue fire-heads in that shaft.
What drew their attention and kept it there? Eh?
Danger!"

Lors repeated, "We dropped the fire into the
tub of oil. . . ."

The conversation was not slow, leisurely,
philosophical. It was quick, excited, grim. And it
turned, abruptly, onto another tack, as Liam
opened his shirt. "Look at this," he said, drawing something out.

This was a something for which they had no
name or word, having never before seen it nor
anything like it. They looked at it as he had
directed and made sounds of awe or bewilderment as it changed shape in his hands: he drew
it out . . . he pushed it back into a smaller com-
pass than before . . . he showed them to what

extent it was pliable in his hands . . . how now it
became globular and now cubical and now it
was flat. . . . And with each change, and, it
seemed—if one looked quickly and closely—even
without each change of shape, the designs upon
it changed . . . changed . . . subtly changed. . . .

"What is this?" Fateem asked, whispering.

"I am not totally sure," His voice had
dropped, too. "But I am almost so—I believe
this is what was called by men, *a map!* But it is
not a man-made map, it is a Devil-made map—
a Kar-chee map! I've always, as long as I've
known that such things had ever been, wanted
one. But not one like those very few I'd seen,
ancient and worn and crumbling and of no practical use because they showed things as they had
been, hundreds of years ago—"

"Before the Devils came . . . !"

"Yes . . . 'before the Devils came.' And, since
then, do we not know?—what changes occurred?
No! We do *not* know! Only that changes *have*
occurred. Look! Look here—Do you see this?"
His finger traced the curious outline upon the
curious surface. "Do you know what it is? It's a
map of this land, this island! I'm sure of it. Or
rather I should say, 'This is how this island appears upon this map.'—Now: Thus it appears as
though we were birds, looking down on it from
the air as though floating fixed in one place.
Now—" His hands moved, the "map" moved, the
design changed, flowed, changed, stopped . . .
more or less. "And this is how it looks as though
from the side, but at what angle I am not sure,
and . . . follow my finger . . . it goes right down
from the top to the sea and beneath the sea . . .

down . . . down . . . so . . . down, to where the island grows from the bottom of the sea the way a tree grows from, well, the bottom of the air—"

He groped for unfamiliar phrases to express unfamiliar conceptions. His eyes glowed and glittered and there was life and light upon his face such as none of them had ever seen before. But even as he spoke and they listened there was a distant rumble, the ground shook again, the sound of the surf was disturbed, and Cerry pointed a shaking finger at the outline of the map. And now it was she who whispered, "Look . . . look. . . ."

At one point upon the surface of the chart the outline altered as they watched. Shifted . . . flowed . . . was still.

"What? Liam? What . . .?"

He said, with a kind of fierce joy in knowledge, "The ancients spoke of things, of measures, which they called *dimensions*. Length. Width. Depth. Time. Most of their maps showed only two of them: length and width. Some, as they called them, *relief maps*, these showed *depth* as well." His fingers, scrabbing hastily in the dirt, tried to give evidence of what he was trying to explain and convey. "But none of these ancient maps ever showed or could ever show *time!* If an area changed, the map became obsolete . . . out-dated . . . useless. It was necessary to make a new one. But—somehow—I don't know how and it doesn't matter now—somehow this Devil-map does show time!"

And his finger stabbed the surface of the chart. "And here we have the proof! Just now, this moment before, we heard and we felt another portion of the land go sliding into the sea—no doubt another link in the chain of reactions from the first shock—and when we heard this and felt this, *we saw it, too!* This map never becomes obsolete or ancient, for it is somehow a mirror reflecting every aspect of the earth-sea surface— *and responding to every change in the earth-sea surface!*"

There was brief silence. Some implication of what he was trying to imply came through; more confusion than enlightment remained. But the conversation now shifted, and abruptly, for the third time, as Fateem said, in a dreamy, stifled voice, "But the Devils have Rickar, and we know what they will do with him. . . ."

Gaspar would not listen. That is, they spoke to him, and they refused to stop speaking until they had told him in complete detail just what they had seen the Kar-chee and the dragons doing to the captives there in the cavern; and in a physical sense he could not have helped but hear them. Once or twice his eyes blinked very rapidly, but there was not a tear in them, and he neither replied nor even stopped in his moving from one place to another nor in his giving ceaseless orders and directions. His ears must have heard. But his mind would not listen. It was entirely possible that after they had done with talking he could not have repeated a single thing they had told him, even if he had wished to.

In his own way, certainly, he had loved his son —and from any ordinary danger he would certainly have risked his own life and the resources of his community in order to try to save his son's

life. But his commitment to the axioms and principles of the Knowers was total: Manifest Nature
made certain demands of mankind, not
capriciously but of necessity; if these were
flouted the inevitable result was the punishment
consisting of the double-Devils; the double-Devils were produced by unjust and sinful conduct;
to resist them was to square the transgression,
and—certainly—an attempt to aid one caught in
doing so would be (at least) to cube it. Therefore
Gaspar did not, would not, dared not, could not,
allow his mind to consider what Liam and
Fateem or anyone else was trying to tell him—
that it was possible for Rickar still to be saved,
perhaps—that it might well be that, in the shock
of the quakes, no man-baiting had been held—
and that, if Rickar were still living, it might be
possible . . . somehow . . . somehow . . . to save
him.

In which case it was imperative to try.

But Gaspar, clearly, would not try.

He would not even try.

Nor would any Knower.

What then?

While all those who followed Gaspar, whether
of his original following, or the converts from the
raft people, or those of the island's people who
had been persuaded that there was no hope or
answer save in the arks—while all these toiled
and troubled and swarmed like ants to bring
their departure to as soon a moment as possible,
Liam spoke his mind aloud to those few who followed him and who looked to him for hope and
answer.

"He came with me because he trusted in me, and he trusted in me because I had once been in arms against the Kar-chee. He himself had never even seen them—to him they were just part of what the older people nagged on and on about. Probably he didn't fully realize how dangerous they really are. But I did. And I let him come with me. Why? I wasn't trying to defy people who had always been telling me what to do. . . . No, it wasn't mere rebellion with me. I wanted to know more about the two Devils, and I wanted to know more so that the next time I resisted them I would feel that something more than flight or slaughter would be the result.

"And he trusted and he followed. Now, the trip wasn't for nothing. We've learned a few things. We know what they use to make the thunder that splits the rocks apart—and we've got much of it with us, too. And we know that what we saw in the cavern isn't all that there is to see about the Kar-chee. There's something more, much more, and it lies below—deep below. Well—

"Easy to say he was taken because of his own act. His act was based on my words and my words were meant to save the blue thunder-heads. He did his best for them . . . for us . . . me. . . .

"Shouldn't we do our best for him? Should we? We saw something of the risk. Are we to take it? And if we aren't, then what are we to do in place of it which justifies anything we've already done?—and particularly Rickar's capture —"

His voice broke off. Not more than a few paces

away three men trotted by, driving a group of
llamas en route to the arks. The men's face were
grimed with the sweat of their haste and the dust
of the path which rose and swirled around them.
They did not notice the others; the others, intent
upon Liam and on Liam's questions, did not notice them. But Liam noticed them. And as he
did, there welled up in him the thought that here
was his answer—

But when he sought words to frame the answer he could not find them, and when he tried
to resolve his thoughts he realized that he had no
clear pictures of them. Yet the certainty persisted. The brown and white fleeces of the
llamas, then, aboard the older ark . . . the newer
ones, too, if they were readied in time, presumably. . . . And then the answer, like a bubble,
welled up and broke upon the surface of his
mind.

He saw the relief mingled with excitement on
the faces of his friends as they saw the change on
his face. They listened, intent, undoubting, willing, absorbed, as he told them what was to be
done. Their numbers were to be divided—thus
and thus and thus—and, with them, the quanti-
ty of thunderheads; immediately the blue points
were carefully separated. A few more directions
were given, places appointed, hands shaken and
withdrawn regretfully, caresses briefly exchanged.

On all sides sweating people streamed like
ants to and from carrying provisions and materi-
al to the arks. Liam, Lors, and Duro walked,
rapidly, apart, bound upon this mission of their
own. The others watched out of sight, then part-

ed upon their own assigned tasks. They had made their decisions. There was to be no room for them in the arks.

The two tall, gaunt dusty-black forms lay where they had fallen. Either the Kar-chee felt no impulse toward retrieving their dead for burial, or else the necessities of their present condition had allowed them no time to come back for this purpose. Still, the men had no way of knowing that the Devil-things might not come back at any moment. Prudently, Lors and Duro stood on different rises of ground, standing watch—but, equally prudently, they first pulled out the fatal bolts with their obsidian points and vanes and replaced them in their ammunition pouches.

Liam and Tom had in their time flayed and flensed many a carcass, but neither had ever dismembered a Kar-chee carcass. The task was inherently unpleasant, and was made more so by the bitter reek. Tom, his mouth twisted, said, "They have no bones, then . . . *okh!*"

Liam said, "They have, in a way, yes. This . . . this armor . . . on the outside—this is their bone. But as to the rest, I am in full agreement with you: *okh!*" He carefully pried and scraped. They had to use exceeding care, but they were infinitely hampered by their ignorance of the alien anatomy.

"If we had the time," he said, "and if we had a vessel big enough, we might boil them like lobsters." He grimaced and grunted, went on with his digging. They were not so much skinning these cadavers as excavating them. "This is one sort of armor which must have a chink in it. . . ."

He wished that the three vigorous guanaco-hunters from the Uplands were here with them now. It had been the sight of the drove of llamas which had started the quick train of thought which led to guanacos, "cousins" to llamas; and simultaneously to what Lehi, Nephi, and Moroni had said about their methods of hunting the wary and windswift cameloids. Experienced in this technique, the Uplanders would be very useful in this present and dangerous enterprise . . . were they but here. But they were not; and there was no time to fetch them here.

Wind sounded and sighed in the trees, the surf (now unvexed in its timeless, ceaseless motion once again) murmured, and Liam and Tom, with teeth clenched and jaws set, worked at their grisly task. And at last they had done the brute and greater part of it; now came the part of more cunning and craft. Cords of sinews were threaded through and inserted and fastened, sticks put into place, the crossbows themselves—vertical—acting as excellent frames and braces. And then—

"Who's to go inside?" Lors asked, eyeing the rude, quick jobs of taxidermy with a mixed air of admiration, doubt, caution, and impatience.

"I, not," Liam grunted. "For I must have fully free movement of head and eyes to look all about and see what's to be seen. Let the three of you choose amongst you."

He had stripped before beginning work and so had only his hair and beard and skin to wash, squatting in the small pool left to dry up gradu-

ally when the brook had been ripped untimely
from its accustomed bed. They had none of the
coarse soap along with them; he ripped up grass
and wadded it and scrubbed, then he scooped up
sand and scrubbed, wincing, but nonetheless
grateful that the abrasion removed the thickened, gummy ichorous exhudations from his
skin and hair. It should not have taken them
long to choose, and, since Tom did not come to
join him in the pool, he assumed that Tom had
lost the choice; he was right.

Prepared as he was for what he saw, still he
started at the sight: Two Kar-chee, erect and
towering (but stooping a bit as was their way)
over Lors, who—on seeing Liam stop and stare
and then come on—assumed the stunned and
hang-head look he evidently believed appropriate to a captive. And Liam, once into his
clothes again, and thinking the other's manner
was right enough, assumed it, too. The pair
started off, and, behind them, heads bobbing a
bit, extra legs dragging a bit, from time to time
uttering muffled exclamations, came Tom and
Duro, concealed inside the armored skins of the
dead Kar-chee.

VIII

TWICE THEY SAW Kar-chee off in the distance but could not tell if they themselves had been seen or not. And once a dragon lifted its head and flashed its faceted eyes at them; but then its head went down again and, with no more than a rather plaintive lowing, it ignored them as before. Once they heard the voices of men and themselves turned aside so as neither to encounter nor to be encountered. And once without warning a young girl and a much younger boy crossed their path. One of the men began to say something, but before his useless caution *Don't be afraid* could advance more than a syllable the girl had snatched up the child and fled, silently, the long vocable of the boy's wail floating behind them after they had gone from sight.

There was no need for them to go seeking for the right hole in the cliff-face which would lead to the right cave—for the cliff-face itself was rent apart as though it were a rotten piece of cloth; the immense rift running from top to bottom. And there, far within, beyond the fallen rubble and the shattered rock, like a cavity in a rotten tooth, they saw what they wanted.

The cavern they had formerly been in was recognizable by an occasional fragment of machin-

ery protruding from beneath the caved-in roof.
Very likely the store of thunderheads, detonated
by the collapse of the rock overhead, had done
more damage than the quakes themselves. Liam
feared that the way below might have been covered up altogether; and, indeed, he was never
sure that it was not, for the corridor-shaft they
found at last was located on altogether the other
side of what had once been the immense
chamber, its doors lying twisted and shattered
beside the gaping orifice.

The strange and curious lamps which had
once made the cavern a mixture of hissing, off-
color lights and heaped-up shadows were now
for the most part dim and silent where they were
not vanished altogether . . . but only for the most
part. Here and there a lamp lay on the uneven
ground or protruded askew from a twisted wall
or hung perilously from the rocky overhead, its
sound reduced to a faint sibilant and its light
reduced to a pale flicker . . . but it was enough
for them to pick their way along by.

The smell of dragon was missing here but the
smell of Kar-chee was musty and strong—not
that Duro and Tom, inside their Kar-chee husks,
would have noticed, half-stifled as they were by
the smell of their own concealing cortices! They
went, peering and pattering and picking and
stumbling their way through the dim and tor-
tured corridor. The ground trembled faintly.
The way led steadily down and around.

Presently Liam stopped and held out his
hands for the others to stop. After a moment,
"Listen. . . ." he said. He lifted his face and
stared at the rock above.

After a while the others heard it, too. A whisper at first. Then the sound increased . . . ceased . . . was repeated more faintly . . . and again and again. . . .

"What is it?" Lors asked.

"The surf. We are under the water now. Not very far under, but—"

Lors finished the phrase for him. "But the farther on we go, the farther under the water we'll be."

Liam nodded. He listened another moment to the long sound of the withdrawing/advancing/withdrawing waves up, up above and over them. Then he shrugged. Then they went on.

But, curiously, the trembling of the ground did not decrease as they went on. Liam at first thought that this might mean that the descent of the beach was matching the descent of the tunnel. It took not long for him to realize, however, that this implied by far too prolonged a beach, an interminable shallow which would have exhausted the drive of any surf. And, by and by, the trembling took on a rhythm which was different from that of the surf altogether.

And therefore the source of it, as it did not lie above, must lie below.

His preoccupation with this was such that he did not become fully aware of the other sounds until some time after—he realized—he had first become aware of them at all.

For a moment he thought he recognized those sounds: the dragging of the Kar-chee feet, the supernumary "extra" pair which were not animated by the human legs of Tom and Duro. *Scrape . . . scuffle . . . rustle . . . drag. . . .* Again he stopped and signaled the others to stop.

Scuffle . . . rustle. . . .

Scuffle . . . rustle. . . .

Tom and Duro had stopped, but the other sounds persisted—only to stop, themselves, abruptly. He moved on, signaled the three others to follow.

Scrape . . . drag.. . . .

Scrape . . . drag. . . .

And then—

Scrape . . . scuffle . . . rustle . . . drag. . . .

Now he knew the sounds that Tom and Duro made, by themselves. And now he knew, too, the sounds that whatever-it-was-behind-him made. And it was clear now, too, that whatever-it-was-behind-him knew that there was something ahead of itself: hence the stopping and the waiting when they stopped and waited. Did whatever-it-was-behind-him have a clear notion of what they were, there, ahead? Was whatever-it-was being merely cautious and avoiding catching up for no other reason than safety? Or was whatever-it-was fully aware of what Lors and Liam and Duro and Tom were?—and was it following them?

Such speculation might go on forever and leave him none the wiser; he might still be speculating when the boom dropped or the roof fell in, or—He looked ahead and around him for a favorable lay of land. *Scrape . . . scuffle . . . rustle . . . drag. . . .*

The pallid, shuddering light faded away behind them. Shadows crouched, simulating rocks, doors, monsters, beasts, pools. The air was tight and close and thick . . . thick as the shadows.

Scrape . . . scuffle . . . rustle . . . drag. . . . But only part of this series of sounds was significant, now. Tentatively, he thrust his foot into a heap of shadow; turned, gestured to the others to go on; withdrew into the shadows, into the cleft of the rock, as silent as the shadows and as the rock itself.

He watched Lors continue on his way, watched the two masquerade-figures go after him, each with head bowed, fore-limbs folded, lower-limbs two moving slowly and stiffly and two scraping and dragging.

Liam hid. Liam waited.

Before him in the half-light and the half-darkness, the sound of *scrape* and *drag* became fainter; the sound of *scuffle* and *rustle* became louder. Ever since the sound had first reached him, he had known what it must have been. A multitude of images had clustered and gestured: Old Gaspar muffled in a cloak and bound on the mission of exposing blasphemous resistors. A raftsman still resentful of Liam's leadership and now intent on vengeance. A friend or kinsman of young Rickar, brooding over Fateem's transfer of affection and awe . . . Others. Others. Many others. But he had all along known them for what they were: illusions. And now came truth.

And truth came, as he had known it must, in the form of a Kar-chee.

The strange procession continued on its way down and along the twilighted corridor, the twisting and tubular corridor which the invaders must have made and made quickly, as naturally and as easily an ant-hill or a wasps-nest is made.

First went Lors. Men: Captive. Then came Duro
and Tom. Men: Masked: Pretended Captors.
Then came the live, the real Kar-chee. Then
came Liam, not so much pursuing the pursuer as
tracking the tracker.

It was impossible to say with surety that the
creature was suspicious or alarmed or that the
creature knew exactly what had happened. How
could any man know these things? Yet everything seemed to point toward the Kar-chee's
being aware that all was neither right nor normal. It had been following them for some time,
now. It had not intentionally made its presence
known. When they had stopped, it had stopped,
too. Liam tried to imagine . . . suppose that two
smaller Kar-chee had slain and flayed two men
and concealed themselves in the skins—somehow—The image would not itself be imagined;
Kar-chee were even less fitted for that imposture
than the other way around. Still . . . still . . . was
it possible that he, Liam, could be deceived?

The dragon had clearly seen them in the daylight and had done nothing. Had seemed neither
alarmed nor in the least suspicious. So why—
now, in the darkness—should this Kar-chee be
stalking them? But even as he asked the question
he admitted to himself that the question was no
proper question: it was comparing apples with
onions, or seals with foxes. The dragons were the
creatures of the Kar-chee and no man knew just
how close the relations between them were . . .
but the dragons were, after all, *dragons*. And not
Kar-chee. What, therefore, the Kar-chee had in
mind was known and could be known only to the
Kar-chee itself.

Which the Kar-chee proceeded soon enough to reveal.

The shadows had begun, faintly but perceptively, to lengthen in Liam's direction. And shortly the light ahead of them came into sight. And the Kar-chee "spoke"! The three ahead, as they heard the loud challenge, the chirring and clicking that resounded and echoed; jerked and started and had begun to turn around—all quickly and in an instant—

But the Kar-chee moved more quickly and it hurled itself forward on its four hind limbs and raised its two huge upper limbs as though to strike.

Liam ran and leaped and hurtled upon it, hitting it low down but catching hold at once as it staggered. As it gibbered and threshed, he threw his whole weight forward. The Kar-chee staggered, struggled desperately to keep its balance, jerked and clashed its "arms," fell forward.

Lors slipped his knife into it just below and behind the head, twisted, slashed. The Kar-chee writhed, then lay very still.

"If I hadn't noticed that soft spot there, when you were skinning it—" Lors panted. "If I hadn't noticed it—!"

Liam hissed for quiet. Tom and Duro stood about, helpless as they had been during the brief struggle. Something sounded from ahead and below. Liam and Lors dragged the body back and into the shadows, and the younger concealed the knife once more in the scabbard hanging within his shirt; then he and Liam resumed their position in front as before and they all went on.

Light burst in upon them.

They came out upon an immense shaft which seemed to extend as far above them as it did below them. Their passage, and others which they could see, entered upon a spiral ramp which threaded its way from top to bottom, winding around and around and around. Above was an immense dome and around the rim of this water dripped and ran incessantly and fell in sheets and torrents. Strange engines crawled around and around the framework below the rim, clicking and clacking and moving slowly; where each one passed, the inflow of water ceased; then it began to drip once more. And below—

Even at the first glimpse of the gigantic vertical tube two—at least two—possibilities had come to Liam's mind. Either this enormous work had been done in the short time since the Kar-chee had entered the island . . . or it had been prepared by them at a previous visitation: perhaps at the time they had split the area off from the mainland and, having mulcted and milked and crushed and washed and wasted most of it, sunk the major part beneath the sea. Subsequently a third possibility occurred to him: that it was not a Kar-chee work at all, but was a remnant of the ancient works of man. But all this was theory and speculation and of no immediate importance or assistance.

For below was a scene which dwarfed even the one they had seen in the great cavern above. Catchment channels received and carried off the flow of water—this was essential, but this alone was, comparatively, nothing; for on the floor of

the immense pit below the Kar-chee swarmed
and toiled like ants. An enormous ramp led up
from the floor and was lost from sight to them
looking down from above as its length went out
of sight and out of the pit. But as to what its
purpose was and what had used it recently, they
were left in no doubt. The sky-ships were a dull
black which seemed the negation of all light.
Even at that height they were gigantic. One of
them seemed to rest a bit askew and its lines appeared vaguely assymetrical at that point where
Kar-chee and machines most closely swarmed
around and upon it; a second received at least as
much attention and had had a part of its hull
peeled back. It was like looking into the inside of
an insect-nest—cells and passages pullulating
with quick, inhuman life. And the center and
seeming source of all this fevered energy was the
third ship. Nothing at all untoward seemed to
have befallen it and evidently it was serving as
principal energy source for the repairs which its
two fellow-vessels were undergoing; they and the
clustering engines were attached to it by a multitude of throbbing and umbilical-like connec-
tions.

Deprived of one subterranean passage by the
quakes and crashes, the Kar-chee still had another one and still their engines toiled into and
within and out from it. Despite all of Liam's
scepticism, the sight of those flickering flame-
shadows and the recollection of those blasts of
heat and the hot-steamy ocean-muddy smell
brought to his mind an unwanted speculation:
that perhaps the several Hells of which the old-
mothers had prattled and nattered had a coun-

terpart somewhere here below. . . . And, as before and elsewhere, great armored engines crawled and humped themselves along this route until they, too, vanished from sight.

"There," said Lors, slightly inclining his head to indicate direction; "there are the things which we saw in the sky at night before the ark came. Those great black things—with thunder and lightning—What are they, Liam? Do you know? And how did they get here? And what is being done to them?"

Equally low-voiced, Liam said, "I think that they must be the things the Devils came in . . . a sort of, well, *ship* . . . that rides the air instead of the water. I don't know how. There must be a huge passage into this place from above to below. Here is the Kar-chee headquarters, no doubts of that. And here they are repairing the damage done by the quake. Here they are . . . and here *we* are. And now, what are we going to do?"

"Look for Rickar?"

"Yes . . . we came here for that. He's not down below on the bottom, as near as I can see. Where, then? It's possible, I suppose, though I hope not, that they might have killed him before bringing him here—didn't bring him here at all, I mean. But somehow I doubt that. No. . . . And clearly they're in no mood for games down there right now. But—when they're done—

"So. If not there, where?"

Suddenly he began to whistle, and he went on whistling. There was no reaction from any of the Kar-chee, either down below or anywhere on the winding ramp. Possibly the noise of the repair-work at the bottom masked the sound down there. But it must surely be audible for quite a distance and at levels far enough removed from the mechanical noises. Quite possibly the sound simply conveyed nothing to them. It was unlikely that any human had ever before deliberately undertaken to whistle in the presence of Karchee; it was, after all, an occupation inseparable from leisure and from peace of mind. Or it might be that the sound was not registerable on their auditory equipment . . . whatever that might be like, and if indeed they had any. Just as there were sounds which dogs and other beasts could hear but humans could not, so it might be that this particular sound made by and hearable by humans was simply not hearable by the Karchee.

Now and then some one or two of the Karchee bent on errands of their own looked up or down or across the great pit at them and fixed gaze upon them for a while; but it was never a long while. In a moment the gaze passed on, and so did the Kar-chee. For all that he could observe to the contrary, Liam's hope and scheme that other Kar-chee would merely assume that he and Lors were captives of the two supposed Kar-chee behind them was working out so far.

It had gotten them a good way into the enemy camp. But whether it would help fulfill their mission there and get them all out safely again remained to be seen.

Lors said, "Stop."

It seemed to Liam that he could hear a faint, shrill sound far away upon the close air. Whence had it come? From the corridor whose doorway

they had just passed? Or from elsewhere? Liam
started on again down the ramp.

Duro said, "Stop."

His voice was muffled by the concealing
carapace. He had moved so that he was facing
across the pit. A Kar-chee was there, facing
them. His chirring and clicking was only faintly
audible, but if that and the precise meaning of
his gesticulating was incomprehensible, the
direction in which he was gesturing was not.
Back, the gestures indicated. *Up—back—*

Liam said a word or two. The four of them
exchanged places, reversed directions, proceeded up and back the way they had come, entered the doorway they had passed before. The
other Kar-chee proceeded on his way with the
same deliberate pace as before.

There was only a doorway, there was no door.
Whether this was usual or not Liam could not
say. There had been doors and more than one
door, in fact, in that glimpse of the deep-driving
undersea caverns. But no door on any corridor
here. As for the gaunt, black Kar-chee castles
which legends place here and there in far lands,
legend did not report on any man who had returned to speak in detail on the subject of doors.

The hallway wound down and around as well,
through on a lesser incline than the main ramp,
and it smelled mustily of Kar-chee and it was lit
in the same odd fashion as all their other habita-
tions; Liam wondered if this might be due not
only to differences in mechanics but to difference
between Kar-chee and human eyesight . . . and
he wondered, rather more pressingly, if the Kar-
chee who had gestured them hither had done so

because he had seen through the disguise and was calmly sending them to somehow their death, or because—

Lors had said *Stop* and Duro had said *Stop* but Liam now merely held up his hand and held it out, holding the others back. Not far ahead, but hidden from sight by the curving corridor, a single Kar-chee "spoke." Another one, sound just perceptibly different, "answered." Then the first one replied . . . or at any rate "spoke" again. There was a groan, in the midst of which the second Kar-chee resumed his speaking. The strange dialogue continued, thus, intermitently. But there was not another groan. Liam's hands made swift motions. And things began to move.

He and Lors helped, as quickly as they could —unfamiliar task—Duro and Tom to wriggle and squirm out of the Kar-chee carapaces. They emerged, ichorous and odorous and with faces indicating pleasure at being out and loathing at having been in. The cross-bows, which had served as framework to hold the upper parts of the scarecrows in place, were next extracted, and Liam pulled off his shirt for a rag to clean them —quickly and hastily and not totally effectually, but well enough, so that the cord was not likely to slip or the bolt to stick.

Then the four of them went on . . . Tom and Liam first, propping one of the Kar-chee-things up and holding it up and holding it so that it projected ahead of them. It was not an easily performed task, and they went on slowly, slowly . . . slowly. . . .

It was not too hard to conjecture the feelings of two men, conversing together, if suddenly the

head and upper torso of another man came into
sight round the bend of a corridor—head drooping, torso at a probably impossible angle—and
then, equally suddenly, vanished from sight
again. The men who witnessed this might have
thought . . . anything. But it is reasonably sure
that, think what they might, part of their natural
reaction would be to go and see *what*—

And thus did the Kar-chee.

The first one came into full and almost immediate view, incautiously, and, as it turned out,
almost immediately fatally: Duro, to whom first
shot had been assigned, caught it with a bolt
which pierced an eye and emerged through the
top of the brain pan. The second showed himself
just as the first was falling, took in enough of the
scene to be warned, and withdrew—but not
quite soon enough. They were never sure just
where the second bolt had pierced this one, so
swiftly had it turned and tumbled, threshing
about; they did not pause to find out, but flung
themselves upon it, knives in hand, seeking for
the soft and unprotected hidden places in the
chitin, the chinks in the armor; trying all the
while to avoid the blows of the huge and
murderous-looking anterior fore-limbs.

They found what they had sought.

And found too, in a chamber opening onto the
corridor, naked and bleeding and bound . . . in-
coherent . . . Rickar.

They unfastened his curious bonds (there was
actually only one knot, and that behind, where
he could never have reached it: yet it gave upon
a single tug of the short, protruding claw, and

fell in loose folds away from him) and he moaned; they rubbed his limbs, and he groaned; they spoke to him . . . softly . . . sharply . . . he rolled his eyes . . . and, at last, they slapped his face.

He stopped rolling his eyes and whimpering. He saw the dead Kar-chee and he screamed—a cry which caught them so by surprise that he had time to catch his breath before they muffled his mouth with their hands.

What the Kar-chee had done to him, or what he had thought they might do to him, they did not know, and had no time to ask. "Listen, Rickar," Liam said, urgently, "we have risked our lives in coming here, and we have come here for *you*. So get hold of yourself, and now!—so that we can get away from here, all of us!"

Rickar's eyes had begun to focus and now seemed fully sensible; he nodded.

"Can you walk now?"

"Yes. . . ."

They helped him to his feet and he hissed in sudden pain and pulled away. They eyed the cruel marks on his lower fore-arms where his captors had gripped and carried him away. And then, though they had been in full haste, they now came to full stop. Something forgotten lay before them—the husks of the dead Kar-chee, which two of them had for a while inhabited. And both two now said, simultaneously, "Not me, this time!"

There was only a second's hesitation, then Liam said, "No time for anyone, this time!"

Out the winding corridor and up the winding ramp they went again, hugging the wall in hopes

they might not be seen from below, and in fear
that they might encounter any coming down
from above. From far down below the ceaseless
clangor of repairs testified to the continued presence of the many Kar-chee there. Above, visible
between the struts and bars of metal scaffolding,
the great and ponderous engine crept around
and around with infinite slowness along the inside of the dome, sealing and resealing it against
leaks from the sea above and outside which
pressed forever down upon and against it with its
terrible and eternal pressure.

But on the middle areas, where their route lay,
there appeared no one and nothing except themselves, as up they toiled, around and around the
inside of the pit, like insects on the screw-thread
of an enormous cylinder. And then from below,
though not very far from below, a new sound
suddenly burst upon their ears, like the noc-
turnal screech of insects, but magnified ten-
thousand-fold.

And from farthest below, a background of
equally sudden and ringing silence, came awareness that the mechanical noise of repair had
ceased.

Duro and Rickar, ignoring or perhaps not
even hearing Liam's hissed warning not to stop,
went almost instinctively to the edge of the ramp
and looked. Below and across stood a single Kar-
chee, head thrown far back and thorax visibly
vibrating, and from this one came the shrill high
chirr of alarm; in its foreclaws was the flayed
integument of one of the dead Kar-chee. Again
and again the earpiercing tocsin sounded, then it
faded . . . and then it suddenly rang out afresh

and with a different note as the Kar-chee
gestured for attention with one fore-limb and
with the other pointed up and over to the two
who stood, as though ossified, where they had
stepped—on the rim of the ramp and plain to all
view.

"Come back! Away! Come away!" Liam
cried, knowing it was too late anyway.

But still they didn't move and still they stood
there and still the dread shrill chittering and
chirring of accusation and alarm stirred the close
air of the great pit and beat upon the shuddering
ear-drums. Swiftly flashed through Liam's mind
the possibility that the sound was intended perhaps not only to alert the Kar-chee of danger but
also as a sort of auditory fascinating directed
against the creature posing the danger . . . something instinctive and reactive, likely—and what
inner Kar-chee realizations must have taken
place, now, here, suddenly, *now!* for them for the
first time thus to react to mankind or any of its
deeds. . . .

Liam and Lors rushed forward and seized the
recalcitrant pair and hustled them back and
away, breaking the spell; they ran, they ran,
they all ran, fleeing and sounding in swift and
troubled breath full awareness of danger: but
Liam and Lors, in doing what they had done,
had also exposed to the enemy their own pres-
ences—

From below arose great and shuddering, shattering sound which made the very air to tremble,
as all the Kar-chee below broke into the same
clamor of alarm—and, abandoning engines and
machines and tools, toil and repair alike, poured

up the winding ramp in pursuit.

The men caught one glimpse of this and then dared look no more either behind or below, but tore up the incline with flying limbs and quavering breaths, not attempting to think how many more turns or how turns were to be measured before they reached the corridor which would lead them eventually to the outside and (they hoped, perhaps without much reason) to safety. Hearts swelling, bodies sweating, feet pounding, knees bent—

"Blasphemers!" cried Gaspar.

"Recusants! Rebels!" shouted Lej.

And they barred the way.

"For the sake of our life—of all our lives!—yours, yours!—don't stop us now!" cried Liam, seizing the old Knower and trying either to thrust him aside or to pull him along. But he stood there, fixed and firm, like stone, immovable. And so did Lej and so was Lej.

"Father, father," wept Rickar. "What they did to me—! Let us go!" he implored.

But Gaspar's face showed no sign of joy on seeing his son among the living; it became clear to Liam, afterward, that most of the old man's sorrow—perhaps even all of it—had been for his son's defection and not for his actual loss. "Impious child," he declared, shaking his head so violently that his beard and his long hair whipped about, "do those who have entered the grave seek to crawl up from it to instruct the living?"

Shouting, "Look *down* there! Look! Look!" Lors threw himself upon Lej, who thrust him back so quickly and strongly that he almost lost his balance and fell into the pit.

"Down there is nothing but deserved judgment and punishment for you!" cried Lej.

"Deserved or not, it will be punishment for all of us," Liam shouted, frantic at the thought that, having thus far escaped all perils, they were now in danger of perishing from this pair's fanaticism. Previously, however absurd old Gaspar's arguments had been, they had still been presented calmly and with some show of logic. But now the old Knower acted like one unhinged.

"Rogues!" he shouted. "Scoundrels! Rebels! Is it not enough, the damage you have already done? As a result of your wicked resistance we suffered the crippling quakes and waves which have delayed our necessary departure. And now you wish to tempt and provoke Nature even more, and thus destroy us all!"

Little bubbles of spittle lined his lips, and his hands clawed the air; then, abruptly, he hastened to the rim of the ramp and in a voice between a scream and a howl he cried, "Devils, Devils! Just is your rage, but direct it towards these, to them who have defied you, and not against us! We have lived virtuously all of our lives, Lej and I and the rest of us, never resisting, never—"

Liam lifted his hand and rushed at Lej, who tensed and pushed to parry the blow; and Liam seized him and threw him heavily to the ground. *"Come on! Come on!"* He darted up and away, and Lors and Duro and Tom rushed after and along with him.

Behind they could hear Gaspar still shrieking

out his insane petition. Then, abruptly, his voice dropped, and he declared, quite calmly. "Let them run; from the Manifestations of Nature there can be no escape for long. . . . Devils, Lej and I will step aside so as not to impede you in your pursuit: but spare the others above—or at least spare those of them who . . ."

Distance, and the noise of their own running feet and the strident ululation, prevented the fugitives from hearing the rest of his comments. And then came a sound which broke their stride —and then another which brought them to a halt: Gaspar's voice, raised in one long and incredulous vocable of protest; and overwhelming that, Lej's voice, raised beyond a pitch they would have thought possible, in terror . . .

And in pain. . . .

Rickar's eyes bulged; his mouth swept back into a grim and almost skeletal grin; he half-turned. Tom and Liam grabbed him, Lors pulled, Duro pushed, and they all fled once more; and now their pace flagged never.

IX

WHEN THEY SAW the light of outside day, looking strange and pale, ahead through the rift in the curtain of rock, Tom-small it was who stopped to offer his first word of advice. His chest labored and shone with sweat, and his voice was faint; his gesturing hand trembled.

"If . . . if . . . if we have a firehead . . . should . . . shouldn't we . . ."

Block off the passage behind them?—so Liam understood him. He drew a shuddering breath and shook his head. They fled on, staggering, stumbling, not daring to stop: fleeing through the dying day like animals who dare not pause to look back for sight of the hounds they can no longer hear. . . .

Later, long later, when they had found refuge in a blind cave whose entrance they had closed by moving boulders across its narrow opening, then Liam, when he had caught his breath, explained his reasons.

"We don't know that they knew that was the way we came in," he said, throat still burning and lungs still aching. "For another thing, it wouldn't keep them from getting out. They know other ways out. But . . . us? do we know any other ways *in?*"

Rickar seemed not to have heard him. His head was cocked and he seemed straining to hear something else; his face still bore signs of the rictus which had seized it at the sound of what might have been his father's death-cry. Might: then again, might not: and perhaps they all had visions of Gaspar, stripped of clothes and faith and dignity and subjected to the cruel sport of the man-ring—baited and bloody. . . .

Lors parted his sodden hair with his hands, too tired even to toss his head to clear his eyes. " 'Any other ways *in?* ' " he repeated, aghast. "Are you as mad as those two were? By my mother's milk, what could ever bring us back in again?"

Duro said, "Don't say 'us.' "

And Tom added, "No, don't. Not me. Never."

But Lors, still facing Liam, and with a rising and incredulous inflection in his voice, asked, "What do you think of going back for?"

Liam said, his hands roaming aimlessly, nervously, among his sweaty body-hair, "I don't know. . . . I don't know that I think of—But I don't know that I don't." Then, less reflectively and more than a little more personally, eying each of them in turn, he declared, "And anyone who doesn't feel up to going wherever I go is free to go—well, somewhere else. . . . I haven't twisted any arms," he concluded, resentfully.

There was silence, broken only by their still laboring breaths. Lors broke it. "We've been going where you went," he pointed out, "not because we were bound to you by oaths or had lost to you in a game of forfeits or owed you a hereditary allegiance, or any of those things . . . anything like that . . . no. . . .

"We went with you because you had a sound purpose in mind, so we thought . . . so I, at least, still am thinking. To find out more about the Devils: wasn't that our purpose? All right, then. So suppose we just consider together and see what we've learned about them—before we either forswear ourselves never to go back or start getting ready to go back right now. Eh? Duro? Tom? Agreed? Well, then . . . Liam?"

Liam noticed the omission of Rickar, but a swift glance at that one confirmed that he might as well be omitted, at least for the moment. Certainly it looked not only as though Gaspar's son were not listening to what they were saying, but as though he were incapable of doing so.

"Agreed, then," he said. And he lifted his head, cleared his throat.

What had they learned about the Devils?

For one thing, they had learned that Kar-chee and dragon were not always found together; although they had seen both on the surface and in the cavern where the serpent-drills had been at work coring and sampling, they had seen only Kar-chee in the great cylindrical pit. What did this prove? Or, if it proved nothing, did it at least hint at something? That the dragons were not essential to the basic tasks of the Kar-chee and served only as, or chiefly as, a sort of army or watch-force?

Further—they had seen the great ships with which the Kar-chee (and, one must assume, the dragons, too) rode the air . . . and, according to some legends, the airless spaces in between the stars. They had seen these ships damaged, whence it followed that they were damageable. And they had seen the Kar-chee at work repairing them. And what this showed was certainly more than just a possible hint—

"You mean that they want to get away?" asked Lors.

"I mean that they want to be able to get away! I mean that they don't look as though they've come to stay," Liam replied.

But even as he stated this deduction so clearly and so definitely, a doubt nibbled at the edges and corners of it. The nibbling doubt went round and round, and round and round, and—curious!—try as he would, he could see no other motion to it, nor could he get it to stop so that he could look at it and see clearly what it was. . . .

"Anything wrong?" Lors asked, giving him an alert glance.

Liam roused himself. "No . . . no . . . not really. Well, to go on, then—"

To go on, they had had confirmed by their own eyes the information which Lors could have given them from his own experience in Britland: that men at arms were capable of physically destroying Kar-chee. It now remained to be seen whether or not this destruction would be followed by immediate attack—as it had been in New North Britland from Uist to Ulst.

"But I have the notion that it just might not be," he said.

Rickar muttered; they looked at him, quickly, then at each other. Duro shifted his weight from one haunch to another, asked, "Why not?"

"Because they would have acted after our first attack on them, they would have tried to avenge the death of the first two Kar-chee we killed . . . or . . . if they weren't sure that they were dead, wouldn't they have tried to rescue them? Still— We haven't learned *much* about them, whatever we have learned. Their notions of responsibility one to the other may not be the same as ours. On the other hand, remember how they reacted down there in the pit? Who could have predicted that? Was it only because there we were striking so close to home?"

The cave was dark and small and smelled of bat-mould and drying sweat. It seemed a strange place to be discussing, with almost academic detachment, the psychology of an alien race . . . and yet the fate of this whole island and all of mankind who dwelt upon it might very well have been hanging upon this discussion.

Liam said he wasn't sure what the reason was, but he thought it might well be that the Kar-chee were devoting all their energies to repairing their ships so that they could get soon away. And maybe they *had* been roused to frenzy out of fear that the invading humans were somehow capable of further injuring the Kar-chee ships.

"Then the ships," said Lors, thoughtfully, "are their weak spot. Maybe their weakest. . . ."

"Until they get them fixed. Then they might well be their strongest."

Tom seemed to struggle with an unfamiliar idea; he turned to Rickar, as though forgetting that Rickar had been tacitly deemed to be outside the discussion. "The ark people . . . the Knowers . . . you can manage big ships. Do you suppose that you could manage these big Devil-ships?"

Lors looked at him almost scornfully, Duro

gave a *Huh?* of surprise, but Liam—

Rickar, to everyone's surprise, answered, "I don't see how. Ours go by wind or oars and these have engines. Ours go on the water and these others go on the air. No . . . no. . . ."

Tom winced his disappointment. "Oh. Too bad . . . I was thinking that if you could, if any of us could, then we could go just anywhere at all and alert the men in every place, and then—"

"If we could manage their ships we might be able to wipe them out, Devils of both kinds, all by ourselves," Lors said, impatiently.

But Liam looked at Tom and his head slowly rose and slowly fell and, slowly, slowly, he nodded to himself.

As zealously as the Kar-chee had toiled to repair their own ships, so the Knowers, old and new, now toiled to repair theirs. Rickar's appearance at first produced no disturbance in the toil and labor; some did not look up to see him, others had never known who he was, some had forgotten that he had been missing, some now merely assumed that there was no truth to the report of his having been gone, others—

But one came forward now, with a cry of joy, her gaunt face transfigured, her worn hands raised and wavering: Mother Nor.

"My son, my son! I knew it, my son; I knew it! Your father could not look at you and not yearn to help and save you—ah, no. . . ." She caressed his face as he stood there before her; and now others began to gather around them— none actually leaving off the work of repair, but many pausing en route from having laid a burden down. "You were wrong, you and your friends were of course wrong: Gaspar knows that, who does not know that—but he was willing to harrow Hell for you!" Her eyes searched among the thronging people, brimming with tears and confidence. "Your father? Gaspar? Where has he gone to?" And her glance came back to her son and her face changed, suddenly, terribly.

"What has happened to him?"

Her voice was a scream. Rickar shuddered, his body jerked and trembled. His mouth opened but only uncouth clicks and barks came forth from it. His limbs twitched, his head sat stiffly to one side and the horrible and lipless grin returned to his face. A murmur of dismay and fright went through the crowd. And still Rickar remained incapable of coherent speech.

And so it was left to Liam to speak for all of them. He sighed very deeply. "Mother Nor," he said, after a moment, "things are not as you suppose. Gaspar didn't follow us to rescue Rickar from the Devils, but to drive him back to them! Oh, Mother—

"Is it possible for you to consider—not to accept, that may be asking too much—but just for a moment to *consider* the possibility that the Kar-chee have other functions besides that of being Devils in regard to sinful mankind? Just make-believe for a moment . . . can you do that? Make believe that the Kar-chee are living creatures like we are and that they have come here for a purpose of their own which hasn't got anything to do with us—neither with us here nor any other men or women anywhere else. Make believe, pretend that it isn't to punish that they've come here, but on a purpose which would be the same if we had all died long ago . . ."

He had to credit her, for she did make the effort to imagine it; he could see her doing so. That something extraordinary was going on, this she realized, and so for the moment she not so much abandoned her faith but stood, as it were, a bit outside and apart from it. Her thin lips moved, she still caressed her son's tormented face, and she asked, "And what would this pretended purpose be?"

Liam said, "We saw them down below in a great cavern drilling into the rock and taking out parts of the rock and washing these parts after they'd been crushed; and the way in which this was done, Mother, was the same way in which I've seen the men called *miners* working the rock and soil in my old home land on those parts of it which were raised up from the sea in the old, old days when the rest of it had been sunk beneath the sea. Washing it to see if it contained metallic traces enough to justify mining on a regular scale. All over the world, from all I've heard, are found evidences of mining which was done on a great scale; and it might seem, metal being now so scarce and rare with us, that this whole world has been mined out. But even after a carcass has been stripped of meat and the meat eaten and even after the bones have all been gnawed, still, you know, inside the bones is the marrow.

"And if hunger is deep enough and teeth and jaws are strong enough, the bones will be cracked and crushed and then the bones will be sucked for the marrow they contain. . . .

"I believe this to be true, but I ask you only to pretend that it *might* be true: that the Kar-chee have come here from someplace else, hungry and sharp of teeth and strong of jaw, to crack the bones of this earth of ours and to suck them dry of marrow. Only the marrow they seek is not really marrow, it is *metal!* Can you, if only for a moment, imagine this?"

The crowd muttered. Mother Nor compressed her forehead. A moment passed. She said, "And therefore—?"

"And therefore, Mother, therefore all of these great and monstrous engines which we have seen below—" He described them, turning to Lors and Duro and Tom for confirmation of what they had seen as well as he. "—These things are for mining, Mother. The Kar-chee have come here to mine. They dig deeply because only in the deeps and depths are rocks worth mining to be found. The sinking of lands, the raising up of other lands, all these are for no other purpose except as they connect with mining operations. The effect of all this on mankind is coincidental; as far as the Kar-chee are concerned, mankind is beside the point. They have not come with the intention of making us suffer, but if we suffer as a result of their coming, that is no concern of theirs. If we stay, they are indifferent; if we flee, they are indifferent. On only two levels, Mother, do they take cognisance of us at all—

"One, is if we menace or seem to menace them: they strike back. It is perhaps only natural. We have nothing in common except life and death and a desire to occupy the same space; we cannot communicate, our species with their

species. And so what else is there to do, if one
strikes out at or seems likely to strike out at the
other, except to strike back?

"I've said that this is natural. Not 'good'—
'natural.'

"But there's another level on which they interest themselves in us, Mother, and this seems
to me less natural, in the sense that it is less inevitable. *They sometimes use us for their sport.*"

The older woman's face changed; in a low
voice she said, "My child, you babble."

Lors took a deep breath and shook his head.
He seemed ten years older than the stripling
who, a short while ago, had had no greater concern than hunting a deer or lying with a girl. The
soft lines had gone from his face, his voice was
deeper and harsher, his movements at the same
time more cautious and more emphatic. "He
isn't babbling at all, Moma," he said, straight-
forwardly. "We've all seen it. We can't forget it.
That's what's bothering your son, I'm afraid.
Have you ever seen a cat playing with a mouse or
with a very young rat? Is that really *play?* Isn't it
a kind of punishment, too? The cat gives pain
and gets pleasure. And in the end, no matter
how long it takes, the smaller creature dies.

"Well, that's what we've seen the Devils
doing. We've seen the dragons bring in men, one
at a time, and the other dragons and the Kar-
chee form a circle, do you see? Then begins the
baiting, the sport, the play, the torture, call it
whatever you want. The dragon picks up the
man and tosses and worries him the way a dog
might do with a rat. But the dragon is careful at
first not to kill the man, as the cat is careful no⁴

to kill the mouse. It even drops the man and lets it try to escape. *But there is no escape!*

"The Kar-chee strike the man down when he tries to get away from the circle they've made around him. The Kar-chee drive the man back. And then the dragon begins to work on him again. Teeth and claw, claw and teeth. . . . We've seen it; we've all seen it."

Duro said, "We've seen it."

Tom said, "Yes. We all saw it."

And Rickar, in a low, low voice, grinding his teeth: "We saw it. We did see it. I saw it, too."

The crowd groaned. Mother Nor moistened her lips. "If you all did, then there is no need for imagining or making believe, is there? But this is only another form of punishment, of the punishment the Devils inflict upon men for violating the practice of justice and equity. My husband would never say differently, of that I am sure." She took her son by his arms. He looked at her now, his face still fixed in that dreadful grimace. "Rickar, tell me now—*where is your father?*"

"In Hell," he said.

There was a long silence. "He followed us down, he and Lej, not to help me get out, but to see that I never got out. It was better, he thought, for me to die so that he could still say that he was right all along than for me to get out and prove that he was wrong all along—"

"No, Rickar. My son, no—"

"And then they were all aroused, all the Kar-chee Devils, and they started after us all, and we fled—*we* fled—my friends who'd risked their lives to save me—but *they* didn't flee, Father and Lej didn't flee, no, not they. They stayed behind, you know that? They stayed behind to preach a sermon to the Devils to tell the Devils how right they were and how wrong we were and they urged the Devils on after us—

"But the Devils didn't take us! The Devils took *them!* And they screamed—and they *screamed*—and *we could hear them screaming!*"

And he threw back his head and he screamed himself, again and again and again, and then he pitched forward and fell upon his face with his eyes rolled up, and his mother knelt and gathered him in her arms and soothed him and cradled him and murmured, over and over again, "My son, my son. . . . My son, my son. . . ." She must have realized that she had lost her husband forever—and in his person not her husband alone but her leader, the guide of her life in its spiritual and communal aspects, the head of her people—and under circumstances the most cruel: cruel in the physical circumstances of her loss, and perhaps more cruel in that if his teachings were correct, as she had always implicitly believed, then he himself had been a sinner whom she had always deemed to be righteous, and if his teachings had not been correct then he had lived and died in folly—and in a void and a chaos all his followers were now to find themselves.

And in the night the alarm was sounded and the cry arose. *"Dragons! Dragons! Devils! Devils! Dragons! Dragons!"* The people rose up from their slumber and their beds and heaped wood upon the fire and then, confused, in terror and concern, milled around, uncertain of anything except their own fear and the very uncertainty which perhaps terrified them as much.

Liam had not lain down. He and his friends had eaten and had then talked themselves to sleep. He awoke to find his knees wet with the sweat of his face and had a confused recollection of having thus fitfully slumbered, half-sitting, half-crouching. He was afterward never altogether sure if he had *seen* the dragons, there, at the perimeter of the camp, upreared and immense in the firelight and the moonlight; or if the image had been nothing else than a vision of the night, a creation of the obscurity and uncertain illumination, the dream from which he had been ripped, the fears which pressed in and down upon him.

But the dragons had certainly been there. And they had flung their monstrous message into the enemy camp, the camp of men, and then retreated into the mists and darks from which they had come.

Message?

Messages!

Stones flung into an ant-heap were nothing in the creation of panic and swarming and fleeing compared to this. And no wonder. Liam saw the things as they came flying through the air and thudded upon the ground and bounced and flapped and then lay still; he saw this, but did not then in that split instant of fire-flickered and moon-silvered time see clearly enough to recognize it. It was not very long, though, before the ground was clear enough of people—screaming, maddened, gone off into the darkness—for him o venture out and over. And there he saw full

clearly what was there, and for the first time in
all this long sequence of events he felt something
as close to guilt as he ever came to it. He had not
felt it in Britland, leading his followers to (as he
had thought) safety and the sea; he had not felt
it in the raft, not even when famine and thirst
and death had laid heavy hands upon it; but he
felt something like it now—

"Gaspar. . . ." It was Tom who spoke, in a
stifled, sickened tone.

And Lors, his mouth stiff, made the second
identification. "Lej, too. .. ."

Duro said nothing. Rickar began to weep.
Liam looked. He knew what he was seeing, and
he knew immediately why he was seeing it. It
had been his idea to flay the two dead Kar-chee
and use their cortices for stalking-horses. The
other Kar-chee had been intent on carrying
away Rickar: true. But they had certainly been
aware that two of their number had been slain
by men. Yet neither then nor afterward had they
seemed particularly concerned. And when that
dreadful and strident Kar-chee alarm had been
raised by the discovering one in the great cylindrical pit, he holding the flayed integument of
one of the two over the rim of the ramp so that all
the others could see, and when the shrill sound
had come, repeating, echoing, prolonged, from
(seemingly) everyone of the other Kar-chee there
—when they had abandoned their works of repair and poured upward in pursuit—

Even then Liam had somehow assumed that it
was only the *death* of their fellows which had
aroused and concerned them, and nothing more.

But now, looking down, his heart pounding

violently, his mouth filled with a sick taste and the muscles of his jaw and stomach stiffened against nausea, the sounds of panic around the camp transmuted into a clamoring buzz; now, as he gazed upon the meticulously flayed skins of Gaspar and of Lej, skins which contained no bodies—now, at last, he knew better.

What synapses had been sparked or set in motion by the Kar-chee discovery of what men had done to those two Kar-chee, what reflexes or reactions set off, what deep instincts or emotions roused, Liam did not and probably forever could not know; but he could and did know that they had been exceedingly great. Some faint hypothesis occurred to him: perhaps only by this act of his and his friends had the Kar-chee suddenly or finally been convinced that the race of mankind was an intelligent race capable of intelligent i.e. malign i.e. *dangerous* action; not merely any longer stinging ants or biting dogs. . . .

But this was speculation and nothing more; it was not facts. The facts lay before them—the empty husks which had once covered Gaspar and Lej.

"This cannot go on," someone said. "This cannot be endured. It if can be done to Gaspar and to Lej, then no one is safe.

Liam turned to see who had spoken. He marveled at her control. "No one *is* safe, Mother Nor. And never will be until—"

Her face was like a mask in the lights of the spurting fire and the gibbous moon. Her voice sank. "If such things are done in the green wood, what shall be done in the dry . . .?" She threw up her hands. "What shall be done, what shall be done? What *can* be done? I would say, Flee, let us flee again, ready for flight or not. I would say, Let us leave this accursed land! But all the Earth is accursed, and there is no part of it to which we can go where these Devils cannot follow and torment us again.

"Always I believed that following the clear and just path of Manifest Nature, the path of charity and justice and diligent equity, would eventually see an end to suffering and punishment and flight—" Her face worked. Suddenly it became stiff and still and masklike again. Liam shifted; she put out her hand to stop him. Then, slowly, slowly, as he watched, wanting to move and be about doing things, unable to stop watching and wondering, her face changed and became certain and satisfied and vigorous once more; and yet changed greatly from her former face of days.

She said, "I see now quite clearly how it is. The Devils have over-reached themselves. They have ceased to be instruments and have begun to move of themselves instead of being moved by Nature. The results, of course, are evil, hideously evil"—her hand's sweeping gesture indicated the things on the ground she did not look at— "but at least now they have set us free. Resistance is no longer sinful, for it is now resistance against sin itself." She looked at Liam. "And we will have to consider, consider quickly, what form resistance can take. You will have thought of that, and as soon as the people are rallied and returned, you will tell us about that. Leadership must come from you, for I am too old."

He shook his head. Her face fell; her hands went out to him. "Rally the people, by all means, Mother Nor. And explain your new discovery to them. But I can't stop and wait. There is something I must do now . . . perhaps I should have done it before, but events . . .

"One thing only I must impress on you, and you must impress it on everyone else: *Get as far away from the water and stay as far away from the water as you can.* Do you understand?"

Faintly, she frowned. "I understand the words," she said, nodding. "But I don't understand the meaning which must be beneath them. Are you asking me to act on faith alone? All my life I have acted on faith, but it was never at any time only on faith, for always there was enough evidence that the ways of the faithful produced a better result than those of the unfaithful."

He told her that he had little evidence which was able to be looked at calmly and understood. But he had some such. And he would tell her what he proposed to do and what he expected would have happened by and by as the result, and what the results of the result would inevitably be. She listened further. She looked, and she nodded. "So may it be," she said. "I will tell them. And . . ." She ceased, suddenly, to be leader, became again mother. Liam understood her look, her gesture.

"No, Rickar I will not need. Let him stay here, and let him add his descriptions to your explanation." He didn't bother to add, *Besides, he is in no condition to go off and do anything else.* "Duro —get back to your father's place and spread the same word all around there, and do your best to

see that others spread it as far as can be. Tom—
that goes for *you, your* father's place, and you see
to it that the word gets as far around the coast
and all the lowlands. Have you got it? I'll give it
to you again. Listen."

*"Get as far away from the water and stay as far away
from the water as you can."*

The air was as close as ever before, and, as
before, it throbbed with the pulse of the engines
from far inside and below. "I hoped we'd never
have to come back," Lors muttered, as they
walked very quickly and very carefully down yet
another of the many corridors leading off from
the many caves . . . leading inward . . . leading
downward.

Liam said, "Well, it's for damned certain that
we'll never be coming back again." He grunted,
and his mouth moved wryly. "One way or another . . ." His voice died away. They moved
along, heads moving cautiously from side to side.

After a time they emerged once more onto the
ramp running threadwise down the inside of the
great cylindrical pit. They did not peer over and
down this time; it would have been a needless
and useless risk. And one other thing, too, was
different now from the last time—this time their
route was *up*.

The strange lamps cast their strange light.
They looked across and over: they saw no one.
They quickened their steps. Upward they
climbed. Upward and up. And finally they came
to the first strut. They did not know what kind of
metal it was or by what process it had been
worked or by what process cast. It was fixed into
the wall of the pit firmly and on all sides were

fixed into the wall of the pit firmly and on all sides were fixed the other struts, on this level and on levels above, supporting a framework or scaffolding which seemed to go up almost forever, up to the dome roofing over the pit itself.

Lors stroked it almost reverently. "So much metal," he said, awed.

"Up with you, or let me," Liam said, curtly. Lors sucked in his breath with a hiss; he reached out his arms, grasped, set his right foot down, then his left. Liam followed behind him. There were odd curves and indentations in the girder, their purpose unknown, but they provided excellent hand- and foot-holds. Upward and onward they climbed, and finally reached the first of the horizontal sparrings. Here they paused to rest a short moment, and in the comparative silence they heard the sound of water trickling, and beyond that they heard something else.

A voice. A human voice.

They climbed out and alone another distance to have a clearer view downward. The voice was muttering. Then it hummed something. Then it said, quite clearly, "I know you're there!"

Lors shot out his hand, grasped Liam's wrist. Liam pressed his lips together, shook his head.

"I know you are there. Don't hide. Why hide? No use hiding. I know you are there. I'll find you. I came here for that. Do you hear? Do you hear, Devils? Devils? Do you hear I'm here?" The man down below laughed, low at first; then, losing control, louder, loudly, a whooping sound which ended abruptly as though axed.

Only the thump of the engines, the dripping of the water. . . .

"Devils, Devils, I'm going to get you for what

you did to my father. He was the best father who ever lived. I didn't deserve him. It's my fault he's dead. I was bad. But it was you who killed him, Devils." The words sank lower, vanishing into gibberish which then became a low and agonizing moan which froze the hairs of Lors' neck.

Cautiously, he and Liam climbed farther out, cautiously peered down. It was, of course, Rickar. Sometimes he moved with exaggerated, almost ridiculous care, picking up each foot and lifting it high before setting it down again. Sometimes he walked sideways, like a crab, hugging the wall. Once he stumbled and Lor's hand dug into Liam's wrist—but Rickar did not go over the side. He landed on his knees, and, thus, still on his knees, continued on his way, crawling, creeping, crooning his insane warning. Downward. Downward. Down, down . . . down. . . .

Liam sighed. He shook his head again. There was nothing they could do for Rickar this time. Nothing.

Their route continued to be upward. They climbed the girders, struts and spars like clumsy monkeys; ground-apes, returning rather gingerly to the long-forsaken trees. The sound below had either ceased or had sunk below their capacity to hear. There was once again nothing but the slow drip-drip of water. And then, gradually, another sound began to make itself known to them. A slow, infinitely slow, but infinite and endless racheting. It seemed to repeat its dull, one-note message over and over again forever as they climbed and climbed . . .

. . . and climbed. . . .

The reticulations of the scaffolding finally

came to a visible end, and there, above them, a
railing surmounted the whole and circled about
beneath the dome. And there, riding the railing
and seeming to swallow it as it did so and then
to extrude it as it passed on, was an engine of
sorts . . . fastened right behind it, another engine
. . . fastened right behind the second, a third . . .
and then no more. The engines mounted up to
the rim of the dome. They grasped the rim, grap-
pled with it. The engines moved slowly, so very,
very slowly; they almost seemed not to move at
all. The struggle was a long and slow one. Water
oozed in along the rim, fell in minor torrents.
The engines approached . . . the engines worked
. . . at last, after longer time than Liam could
count in his head, the engines crept on along.

Before them, the rim was wet. Behind them,
the rim was dry.

The two men reached up their hands and
arms, took hold, and took the last few steps upward.

The rail itself was no simple single bar of
metal curved into a circle. It received part of the
engine carriage deep within itself and retained it
as the engine or engines crept around with de-
liberation and slow determination. Liam crept
up himself as close behind the retreating third as
he could. He peered within, and seemed to see
the glint of wheels. . . . He thrust his hand
within the bosom of his shirt, pulled it out.
Something flashed with a blue glint of fire.
Liam's hand, moving dreadfully carefully, vanished within the continuous cavity which was the
inside of the railing. It emerged. He repeated the
gesture. Again. Again. Again. At last his hand

groped within his shirt and found nothing. He grunted then descended. Lors took his place.

The engine had moved only a few inches in this time.

Blue fire flashed again, flashed many times. There remained nothing more inside of Lors' shirt, either. He got down from the rail. And now, alternately moving more quickly than they had in going up and, caution overcoming fear, more slowly, they made their way down and across. Once only, before taking earth, they allowed themselves one last glimpse into the abyss. But they could discern no new things: the three black-hulled spaceships, the tiny dots which were the swarming Kar-chee, the dull flaring-flickering glow as the mysterious gateways into the subcavernous cavern were briefly opened and quickly closed—all was as before.

And of Rickar himself they could see nothing.

"Here we go," Liam said, pointing to an opening in the rock wall.

"That's not the way we came in," Lors said.

"Well, that's the way we're going to go out," Liam answered, making his way toward it. "If we get to go out at all, that is. . . . You coming?"

"Don't move so slowly," said Lors.

X

JOW WIPED sweating forehead with his forearm and looked at his son. "We've been doing nothing but make boats," he said, partly annoyed, partly alarmed . . . and not a little confused. "And for what, if not to put them on the water and ourselves inside of them? Now you come along and tell us, Stay *away* from the water!"

"I've told you good reason for it, haven't I?—Popa, there isn't much time. *There isn't much time!*"

His father gave a deep sigh. Then he said, "I'd better believe you. Come on, then, boy!" He leaped to his feet, seized a length of wood which was only partly fashioned into a paddle, and rushed across to where the great wooden gong hung from the branch of a tree. He struck it once . . . twice . . . a third time. *Attention!* All around, all work ceased, all looked up, started rising to their feet. Fishermen heard it along the shore and commenced pulling in their nets. Women gathering shellfish in the shallow coves straightened up and began moving in toward shore. Boatmen about to launch another new canoe at the beach hesitated, slid it back a bit . . . listened. Everyone listened.

Jow struck the echoing wood once-twice, quite quickly. He sounded the double-note again. Again he brought down the improvised gong-

stick; and again. *Doom-doom . . . doom-doom . . .
doom-doom. . . .*
Danger!
The fishermen froze, a shell-gatherer stopped
with one foot in the air, the canoe-launchers
rolled their eyes at one another and did not otherwise move. They waited. Waited.
Doom-doom . . . doom-doom . . . doom-doom. . . .
Danger!
Then the great hollow sounding-board gave
forth three slow notes. And another three. And
another three. Then once again it sounded Danger; then once again three slow notes and for a
third time three slow notes. Then it fell silent.
Jow, Tom, the boatbuilders, the fishermen, the
shell-gatherers, the canoe-launchers, treecutters,
old men, children—everyone and everyone—understood the meaning of the last signal.
The hills. . . .
The hills. . . .
The hills. . . .
The net lay where it had been dropped. The
basket floated and bobbed about and the
shellfish began to be dimly aware that they were
in water once again, the canoe lay on its side and
was aware of nothing. A pot boiled over and
quenched the untended fire. A parrot called out
querulously, cocked its head at the silence, finally flew off, muttering.
The day was unusually clear. Away and away,
off in the Uplands, three men who had gone out
to scout for guanaco turned aside from their
quest a moment and glanced below. After a moment one of them spoke.
"I see many persons moving very fast," said
Nephi.

"Many, many persons, moving very, very fast," said Lehi. He paused, shaded his eyes, frowned. "And also," he said, "Many, many dragons also," he said. "many, many dragons also moving very, very fast. I fear that they will catch and destroy the persons."

"Only maybe not," said Moroni.

From the Rowan homesite the retreat to the hills had proceeded somewhat less precipitately, it being rather more removed from the water than Jow's place was. Not many people, in fact, were there—some had gone to join Jow's people and some had gone to join the Knowers. But old Ren and his wife were there, and their son Carlo and his family, and several others.

Ren seemed very old, very uncertain. Indeed, if his wife had not joined with her sons in pulling him onto this feet, he might not have moved at all.

"Up, up, Popa!" cried Duro. "Haven't you heard what I've been saying? Don't you believe me?"

His father did not resist, but neither did he much cooperate. "I don't know. . . ." he groaned, allowing himself to be pushed along. He reached out and grasped the pannier of a loaded llama, perhaps not so much for physical support as for the comfort of a familiar object. "I don't know . . . I suppose it will make no difference. . . . Here, there . . . today, tomorrow. . . . What does it matter? Mmm. . . . It doesn't matter."

The land had begun perceptibly to slant upward and they could see Mount Tihuaco for once all free of cloud, when they heard in the middle distance the cry of a questing dragon. Old Ren sucked his breath in between his teeth, fearfully, and trembled.

Duro took his arm, pressed him gently, firmly forward. "It's far away, Popa," he said, reassuringly. "And it's certainly not after us." The small caravan continued.

But when they heard the second dragon, and the third, and then the fourth, each nearer, and each from a different angle, Carlo voiced the inescapable conclusion: "Duro, they may or not be after us, but they seem bound to cut across our path. We'd better leave our path—"As if to confirm or to confound him then, it seemed as though every dragon in the world gave voice, from everywhere and all about, a pandemonium of hissing, roaring, bellowing. The old woman gave a little cry of fear and one of the babies started wailing.

Duro seized the lead llama and turned it at right angles to the path and pulled it along after him. The beast protested but it obeyed, and the other ones followed after. Duro, for the moment, was torn between the need to aid his trembling old father and his brother Carlo, whose lame leg was not well-suited for tripping through undergrowth and climbing steep inclines.

It was Ren who made the decision for them. "Help your brother, then," he said. His face was suddenly resolute.

"They may catch up with us, but we'll give them a chase before they do!"

Through bushes and thickets which tore at their legs and stones which tore at their feet, bent over and clutching at any support, between boulders which barely allowed the laden llamas to pass, the party went on, went up, and finally reached a bare place which allowed them to turn once again onto still upward-slanting but somewhat more level land; and here, as though ordered to, they all looked below. . . .

The dragons were moving in somewhat broken but clearly purposeful formation, in an irregular line at an angle of forty-five degrees. Now and then one of them reared up and stretched its neck and looked all about, its long and bifurcated tongue flashing as it flickered in and out to taste the air, and the unobscured sunlight glittered many colors from the faceted eyes. Fortunately, their change of route had taken them out of the direct line of the dragon advance; fortunately, too, the wind was in their favor.

And then the ground trembled and shook.

"Down!" cried Duro. "Down, down, everybody!"

The noise came rolling, thundering, roaring. The earth fell away beneath them, rose up and struck them, tossed them to and fro. Then, for a moment, all was still. Carlo gasped, pointed out to sea. . . .

In its place, for a long, long, very long way, was land which none had ever seen before. And beyond that was a great whirlpool. There were three sudden, sharp thunderclaps behind them. They turned just in time to see Mount Tihuaco blow off its top and vanish from their sight behind black clouds through which the lightnings which had slept in the earth now flickered and blazed like the tongues of giant dragons. They saw a vast plateau dissolve before their eyes and a valley vanish, shattered like a board whose back has been broken against a rock. Then on-rolling dust and darkness veiled all of this from them and, crawling toward each other for a comfort which was more than spacious safety, they looked out again toward where the sea had been, and there they saw that which made them—breathless as they were and dumbstruck as they had been—cry out, less at that moment in fright than in utter wonder: for the waters of the ocean, as though piled and heaped high upon themselves by a colossal hand, now came rolling and rushing and galloping in to reclaim their lost terrains once more.

In the momentary silence of the earth and the volcano they could hear very clearly the roaring of the on-rushing, in-striding, all-devouring sea.

Liam and those with him had taken refuge on a gaunt and treeless ridge. He recapitulated it all in his mind. The triple engine so slowly and deliberately inching its way ponderously around the inner rim of the dome. He and those at the Knowers' camp trying to reach refuge in the heights of land. Not all of those at the Knowers' camp, though, for—He urging that no one run and thus exhaust himself before reaching safety, but to proceed at a rapid walk. And the engines below racheting their slow, slow way around the inside of the dome. The first intimation that the Kar-chee, forgetting nothing, forgiving nothing, were intent both on their work of repairs below in the pit and on their work of punishment here on the surface via the dragons. The dragons relentlessly advancing. The engines relentlessly circumambulating. And then, before sight, before sound, the first forewarning quiver of the ground.

The engines, returning on their circuit around the track, had at last reached and touched and crushed the first of the blue fireheads.

Immediately, the earth shaking . . .

Sliding . . .

Trembling . . .

The first detonation setting off the second . . . the third . . . Explosion upon explosion there below—

Below, the Kar-chee trying to flee. . . .

Above, the dome, all repairs now annulled and more than merely that, the dome cracked and riven and shattered, and above the dome the tremendous pressure of the ocean no longer in the least restrained—the dome crushed forever, the ocean falling in—

The pressure of the air alone in that first second as it was compressed by the incoming water behind it must have killed them all and swept them and crushed them to the floor and wall and spread their ichorous blood and splashed and splattered it all about—

Only to be washed up and away in another second, and all their works, their engines, their great black-hulled ships crushed and twisted as the sea came thundering, rolling, twisting in, air as heavy as a wall of rock rushing into every tunnel and corridor and killing and expelling any Kar-chee found there.

And Rickar? Had he been still then alive? Poor Rickar—

The pit become one gigantic whirlpool and the waters of his maelstrom forcing their way down into the subcavernous cavern-way which, hot and steamy and lit with flaring light led— where?

When Mount Tihuaco erupted, Liam knew where.

The sea receded, made contact with that underground river of lava, that molten lake so deep beneath sea and earth alike, turned it into steam with a sound there was no one to hear, a sound which must have been at first like the hissing and then like the roaring and bellowing of a hundred million dragons—

Sea and Earth locked in violent embrace, spending their spasms, crying out, threshing and writhing and trembling. A moment quiescent. And then the sea cannonading in upon and against and over the land, climbing higher and higher and higher and higher—

The land shaking in every limb but holding, finally, firm, and so finally casting off the sea, casting it back . . .

The land lying spent and lacerated and bleeding and weary.

There were those who were never seen again, living or dead, and so had to be assumed to have perished in the destruction. Of those who rejected Mother Nor's counsels as a betrayal of the true and pure doctrines as preached by Gaspar and by Lej—rejecting, too, the very evidence of their dead elders' flayed hides as mere deceitful phantoms—and who in the face of all warning launched their arks and put out to sea, defiantly: of them no conclusive trace was ever found, either. Shattered timbers which washed eventually ashore, and shattered bodies as well, might as well have belonged to the arks unlaunched and to those who had sought refuge in the heights of land but had not found it before the sea had found them.

It was days before the last reaction and counter-reaction subsided; weeks before anything resembling coherence returned to human life. But eventually most of those who survived were found by Liam's messengers and most of these attended at the great council which he summoned. It followed the pattern of preceedings which he had laid down for it—a recapitulation of all which was known of the suffering of mankind at the hands of the Devils and the helplessness of mankind before the superior strength of the Devils began the talk; Liam delivered it. He spoke of how he had been among the first of men to resist the Devils in this age and of his first battle against them in Britland and of how he had led the bravest of the brave therefrom unto this land; and Cerry confirmed this, her eloquence undiminished by her recalling that this had not been precisely the way things had occurred in every particular. . . .

Cerry had known from almost the beginning that Liam was one of those about whom songs were to be sung and stories told, and this and her love was why she had followed him. She knew that song and story is never bound by the mere details of the events which give them birth, but that song and story are creators of values in themselves and of their own and are not to be hobbled or mutilated by mere alignments of mere facts.

Lors and Duro confirmed, and, after them, Tom (who was no longer known as Tom-small), how Liam had led them unfalteringly to spy out the Devils and learn the secrets of the caves and cavers, their Hells and hollows and their secret fires and weapons, how they had baited men and hunted men to bait them; their own narrow escapes time after time after time, their own unfaltering bravery and how it had derived its strength from Liam's.

Fateem testified how Liam had raised up among the Knowers a group which rejected the doctrine of non-resistance and she told of how Rickar, though grievously wounded by the Karchee, had been carried away to freedom by Liam and his men and how later Rickar had risen from his sickbed and followed after to assist them in their final work of destruction and salvation, only to die a martyr's death in doing so.

Mother Nor spoke briefly of Liam's having opened her own eyes to the duplicity of the Devils and how she was thereby enabled to persuade many of the Knowers to find refuge and salvation on the land instead of death and destruction on the sea; then she spoke of the need to follow the principles of justice and equity . . . but she did not speak of this for long, for she was old and tired and the death of her son had much diminished her.

And then again Liam spoke. He spoke sitting in a chair which had been specially made for him and carved out of scented woods and cushioned with soft, washed fleeces and precious guanaco skins, with a carefully fitted-up support for his injured leg, shattered in the earthquakes.

"No one has seen any living Kar-chee since then," he said, among other things, looking around in grim triumph. His wives, Cerry and Fateem (for in those early days he had only those

two and he accorded them equal status) sat
beside his chair. "It seems to be certain that
those who were not drowned were eaten by the
sharks and the other monsters of the sea; people
have testified to seeing this happen, and there is
also the dead shark found to have parts of Kar-
chee inside of him. I have shown how to destroy
the Kar-chee here and I will show how we destroy them everywhere else as well!"

All shouted at this and Liam's eyes glittered
and his fingers strayed up to the scar on his head
where he had received his second sacred injury
(nor did this one ever heal entirely, either: thus
did Liam suffer on behalf of all those whom he
had saved).

"It is true that the dragons still remain," he
admitted; "but you see how humble they have
become. They avoid us. But this will avail them
nothing, for I will show you by and by how we
may hunt them and bait them and kill them as
they once hunted and baited and killed *us!*" And
all shouted even louder at this and bared their
teeth.

It was at this great council, then, that the
basic great plans were laid down. With the aid of
the Kar-chee map of land and sea which Liam
alone knew how to read and to follow (and hence
had no need to show to others, he explained) and
with the aid of those who had been Knowers and
who knew the arts of navigation over long dis-
tances, Liam and those brave enough to fare at
sea with him were to make contact with every
other land inhabited by men. And so it was
done, land by land, year by year. In some places
Liam and his gentlemen (as they came to be
known) were properly welcomed and alliances

against the Kar-chee and the dragons were formed. There were not many Kar-chee found elsewhere, for most of them had been destroyed in the great destruction, and over those remaining victory was always obtained . . . sooner or later.

Sometimes, unfortunately, the men of other lands did not always properly welcome the gentlemen and it was essential to overcome their hostility, and to divide their lands and their women among those who had come only in friendship and unity against the natural (or unnatural) enemies of the whole race of mankind. But these battless and diversions did not long prevent mankind from wiping out its alien enemies, nest by nest and camp by camp; tracking them down and spying them out and destroying them with their own weapons. Eventually, of course, there were no more of the blue fireheads. But by that time the Kar-chee who lived afar off in the cold night in their lairs around the Ring Stars had coldly decided to cease sending replacements: there were other mineable planets with more tractable native life-forms, and thenceforce there and there only the Kar-chee concentrated their attentions. Only working Kar-chee had ever been sent to Earth, only neuters, incapable of reproducing themselves; and this decision of their own home worlds was thus the final death sentence.

The dragons, on the other hand, multiplied, and their eggs and chicks and cockerels were known in every woodland . . . but they seemed more and more subject to the control of man as their former masters died off. Liam delighted to watch the dragon hunts as he grew older and less

active, and many of them were held specially in
his honor.

Mother Nor still maintained her few followers
and continued to preach her moralistic ideals,
but without the rigidity and discipline it had
been subjected to under the regime of old Father
Gaspar the sect of the Knowers continued to
diminish. Further, it was unable to compete with
the attractions of the vigorous and continually
exciting adventure of life as led by Liam's gentlemen. But he himself would never allow the old
woman to be mocked or abused and it was by his
generous consent that she and her handful of im-
practical followers were allowed to settle in a
land all to themselves. There were those who
suspected that it was there that Fateem went secretly after her disappearance in later years, but
no one ever knew for sure; Liam neither spoke
nor allowed it to be spoken of.

Thus humanity renewed its strength and developed its newest ways of life upon its oldest
world, forgotten by its distant children for many
centuries yet to come. And as for what happened
after the other worlds remembered, this is not
the place to recount that; and as for the later and
the last years of Liam, how he bore all before
him, his slaying of the Great Kar-chee who held
the daughter of the Chief of Bran a captive in his
hidden cave and how Liam took her, too, to wife,
and of all his deeds and triumphs and those of
Lors and Duro and Tom, these are to be found
wherever songs are sung among men and wherever tales are told among women.

Rogue Dragon

I

THEY HAD FLUSHED the bull-dragon in Belrozc Woods and paced him for about a mile before he came up against the other line of beaters and turned to fight.

For a moment the whole hunt fell silent. Jon-Joras, feeling (so he thought) like a virgin at her first assignation, heard only the sound of his own troubled breath; felt sweat starting on face and body. The dragon seemed to crouch in his place on the far side of the clearing, his crest quivering. A moment passed. The great head moved a trifle, (uncertainly,) and the faceted, gem-like eyes rolled in their hooded sockets—blue, green, blue-green light flashing in the beam of moted sunlight which suddenly broke through the trees. Then, incredible how long it was, the red and bifurcated tongue leaped out from the mouth, quivered, tasted the air. It was blowing right towards him. Body rather than mind (if mind it had at all . . . and what thoughts must it think!) probably making the decision, the dragon darted off to the left.

Instantly the silence was shattered. The beaters were trotting left, clashing their cymbals and howling, the musics blared on their harsh-voiced shawms, the archers (all neat and trim in their green tunics and leggings) nocked their arrows and poised. The dragon halted. At a signal, so swiftly that Jon-Joras scarcely saw the motion, a flight of arrows was loosed; in another instant were visible only as feathery shafts ridged in the great beast's side.

To say that the dragon hissed was only to confess a limitation of language: ear-drums trembled painfully at a sound the auditory nerves could but faintly convey. The dragon *hissed*. A spasm passed along the great, pierced flank, and tiny runnels of dark blood began their paths. The dragon halted, turned its head from side to side in search of its tormentors, its cheek-nodules swelling with rage. The wind shifted, bringing a rank, bitter odor to Jon-Joras. He felt his skin grow cold and his heart expand.

Then the bannermen ran forward, teasing their flags on their long poles. The hiss broke off suddenly and the air vibrated with the roar which succeeded it. Here, at last, was an enemy which the dragon could see! Head down and neck out-thrust, it began to move towards it. At the first, slowly and ponderously, each immense leg placed with care. The bannermen seemed almost to dance, in their traditional movements . . . the figure-of-eight, the fish, the butterfly . . . faster now . . . the wasp . . . the flags, white and red and green and yellow, whipping through the roar-tormented air.

And faster and faster came the great bull-dragon, now at a lumbering trot, turfs flying as the great splayed feet came pounding down, shaking the ground. The cymbals ceased, the horns, too. The trot became a gallop, a charge,

and the men broke into a shout as, in one sudden
and tremendous movement, the dragon reared
up upon its hind legs and came bounding forward upon them, its forelimbs slashing at the
air. In one accord, the flags dropped to the
ground, the bannermen swiftly twirled their
poles, winding up the wefts at the ends of them.
The colored cloths had danced and teased—suddenly, suddenly, they were gone; furled,
grounded, hidden in the grass; and the bannermen crouched.

Bewildered, the great beast paused again.
Twenty feet above the ground the huge head
growled and rumbled and it turned from side to
side. From the left, a flight of arrows stitched the
now-exposed chest. The dragon screamed; the
dragon tore at the barbs; it plunged in the direction from which they came. And the cymbals
clashed three times and another flight of arrows,
now from the right, stitched the creature hip and
leg, and three more times the cymbals sounded
and as the dragon sounded its pain and fury and
swiveled its head, again the bannermen twirled
their palms and pinnacled their poles and once
again their bright flags played upon the air.

The dragon bellowed and the dragon charged.
Striped with the blood that coursed along its
paler underside, it thundered down upon the
bannermen. Once again flags and flagmen vanished. Once again the dragon paused. Again and
again it hurled its great voice upon the wind.
Jon-Joras saw, midway from throat to fork, like
a blazon on its fretted hide, the white X-mark.
He thought he could see the great pulse beating
in the mark's crux, and then—sight and sound

together—heard the crack of the huntgun behind him and the crux vanished in a gout of blood. The blood gushed forth in a great arched torrent. And the dragon stretched out its paws and talons, showed its huge and harrowing teeth in a scarlet rictus, sounded its hoarse, harsh death cry, and fell face forward onto the ground which trembled and shook to receive it.

"*Pierced!*" a voice cried the traditional acclamation, high and shrill and exultant and shaking. "Pierced! Pierced! *Dragon pierced . . . !*"

It broke off abruptly as Jon-Joras suddenly recognized it as his own. And all the music sounded.

The man who shot the dragon was a Chief Commissioner Narthy from somewhere in The Snake, that distant constellation whose planets all seemed to abound in precious metals and rare earths . . . and rich, hunt-buying Chief Commissioners like Narthy.

Actually, the C. C. wasn't a bad sort, though quite different from Jon-Joras's own superior. He joined the ring of men crowding around to congratulate him on his kill.

"A fine shot, Hunter!"

"Well-placed, Hunter!"

"—and well-timed—"

Narthy, sweating and grinning, mumbled his thanks, his shyness before other, vastly more experienced Hunters vanishing before his pleasure in the new—the so suddenly gained—title. Conscious of the cameras, he sucked in his pendulous belly and tried to look appropriately grim. Then the Master of the Hunt came over for the ritual, and the well-wishers fell to one side.

The Master was a stocky man with a sun-burned, windcracked face; his name was Roëdeskant, and, unlike most of the hunt masters, who were of the Gentlemen, he was not, although bred on their estates. He had been cool and sufficiently self-assured during the hunt, but now—aware of the cameras and of his low-caste accent—he fumbled a bit.

Partly because he was embarrassed by the embarrassment of Roëdeskant, and partly because the sight of pudgy, grinning Narthy being ritually bloodied did not much appeal to him, Jon-Joras turned and walked away. His own home world, the *beta* planet of Moussorgsky Minor, was nowhere near The Snake (where he had never been and never expected to or wanted to be). No one who knew him would see him in the 3Ds for which Narthy had paid a small fortune and which he would doubtless be showing to his friends, family, associates, subordinates and such superiors as he wanted to impress for the rest of his life.

The scent of the strong-smelling grass rose, pungent, as he stepped on it heavily in his hunt-shoon, but it was not quite strong enough to overcome the bitter reek of dragon musk. A voice beside him said, "What a rotten shot!"

Surprised, rather than startled, Jon-Joras turned, said, "What?"

It was someone he didn't know, dressed in the white garments of a Gentleman—a tall fellow with bloodshot eyes and grizzled hair. "Rotten shot," the man repeated. "Badly timed. Trembly trigger finger, is what it was. These novices are all the same. Why that bulldrag had at least another quarter-hour's good play in him! No . . . Don't tell me that Roë signalled him to shoot, I know better. Oh, well, *they* won't know better, back in The Lizard or The Frog or wherever 'Hunter' Barfy or what's-his-name comes from—"

He looked at Jon-Joras with shrewd, blue eyes. "Not a Company man, are you?"

"No. I'm one of King Por-Paulo's private men. Jetro Yi, he *is* a Company man, is going to arrange the hunt. I'm just here in advance to make his personal arrangements."

The man in white grunted. "Well, to each his own, I don't hold with monarchies myself, having to renew your damned crown every five years, make concessions to the plebs and scrubs: poxy business, elections. No. But of course, no reflections on your own local king, mind." Having probably a notion of quickly changing the subject of his probable tactlessness, the Gentleman added, "Kind of young aren't you, a king's private man?"

The subject of his youth being a somewhat touchy one with Jon-Joras, he brushed back his shock of black hair and said, a bit stiffly, "Por-Paulo is a good man." His youth—and how he came, despite it, to hold his position. Brains, ability, judgment, and a top rating at the Collegium, all good reasons, sufficient ones, no doubt. But when a young man *is* young, and the son of a young (and lovely) mother, when he cannot remember his father, and when rivals in his peer group are ready enough to hint that he need look no further for his real paternity than the Magnate with whom his mother is most often seen, why—

"No offense," repeated the older man. Then, "Your customs don't forbid self-introductions, do they? Good. Allow me, then." He stopped, put his hands out, palms up. "Aëlorix," he said.

Jon-Joras stated his name, placed his hands, palms down, on the other's. Aëlorix said, formally, "I am yours and mine are yours."

Thankful that he had taken the trouble to look into local ways, Jon-Joras said, "Unworthy." Behind them, the musics struck up a tune of sorts and Narthy was led around the dead dragon. Aëlorix raised his eyebrows and made a disrespectful noise.

"Base-born, I shouldn't wonder," he growled, indicating the triumphing chief commissioner with a jerk of his head. "Roëdeskant is a good Huntsman, none better. But *he* knows his place, more than I can say for a lot of basies, local and otherwise, I remember when he was one of my old father's chick-boys. Fact. Where are you at, in the State?"

An implausible vision of the hefty Chief Huntsman as a bare-legged boy chasing dragon-chicks through the woods and thickets made Jon-Joras think a moment before he was able to answer the question. The—the *State* . . . oh, yes . . . confusing local speech-way: if the City proper was termed "the State," what did they call the whole City-State? Answer: by its name, of course. In this case, Peramis.

He said that he was staying at the Lodge. "That's no good," Aëlorix shook his head. From somewhere deep in the woods a faint bellow sounded over the raucous music, and the higher note of another dragon almost at once seemed to respond to it. Instantly diverted and alert, the

Gentleman cocked his head, harkened a moment, pointed. "Off there. A big cow-drag, by the sound of her. Word of advice. When you hear those love-calls, don't go to evesdrop. . . . No, the Lodge is no good. Stay with me. At Aëlorix. What? Till your boss-chap arrives."

Jon-Joras, sensible of the compliment, flushed slightly. An invitation to stay at the Gentleman's seat, and the one from which he took his name and style—"Only proper, courteous, a king's private man," he heard his would-be host say— no common compliment, from all he'd heard and seen about the Gentlemen in the short time he'd been here on Prime World (*Earth,* the locals called it; name sounding so startlingly archaic on out-world ears). He could hardly refuse, of course. More—he wanted to accept.

He wanted to see for himself what the semi-feudal life was like at first hand. Then, it was his duty to his elected king, too: the more contacts he made, the more pleasant he could make Por-Paulo's stay. Only—

"Would it not be difficult," he said, slowly, "if I am there, where I wish to be, to coördinate my work with Jetro Yi?"

For answer, the Gentleman pulled out an instrument like a whistle, blew a couple of notes on it. Immediately a man detatched himself from the throng and came running towards them. "Company Yi," called Aëlorix, as soon as his servant was within hearing distance. The man nodded, made a sketchy, informal salute, and ran back. In a few moments he returned with Jetro, the latter not running, but coming at quite a brisk walk.

"Company, I want to host this young fellow at Aëlor'."

Yi made his eyes go round, as if astonished there could be any objection. "Of *course*," he said. "As the High Nascence *wishes*."

"You're to keep in touch with him," The Gentleman ordered, as casually authoritative as if he were a director of the Company, "twice a day. And have his things sent over as soon as you get back to the State."

"Of *course*—of *course*—"

"Get along, now."

As Yi, having bowed almost to his navel, departed, Aëlorix said, without malice, "Flunky . . ."

Narthy was now making the first cut in the green-black hide. The skinners would do the rest of the work later, and, before he left, the Chief Commissioner (now "Hunter," too) would be presented with his silver-mounted belt, his braided hatband, and enough dragon skin to upholster all the seats and sofas in his villa if he desired to. The cost of tanning, like everything else, was included in the immense fee—in this case, mined and mulcted from the rich flesh of The Snake Worlds—which he had paid in advance to the Hunt Company.

Somewhere downwind the cow-drag once again blared her presence and her need; again, replying and following, the bull bellowed. Aëlorix listened, his face puckered. He shook his head, seemed faintly puzzled, faintly disturbed. Jon-Joras asked if anything was wrong.

"No . . . Not really at all. I know the cow . . . don't mean we've met, socially, but one becomes familiar with the calls of all the drags around, sooner or later. . . . But I don't know the bull. Well, well." He took his guest by the arm. "Come along. Aëlorix, ho!"

Aëlorix-the-place seemed less an estate than a city-state of its own, repeating on a smaller scale the pattern into which all the civilized parts of ancient Earth had formed after the planet's emergence from the dark and painful chaos of the Kar-chee Reign. Its fields and groves were pleasant to see after the somber forests, and at first Jon-Joras could not tell which of the many wooden buildings clustering closely where brook and river met was supposed to be his host's seat.

A scene in the market-place or courtyard quickly diverted his thoughts from this. A group was gathered around two men dressed in dirty hides who were arguing with what, by his manner, appeared to be an upper servant. This one looked up at the entrance of the Gentleman and said, "Ah, here's His Nascence."

"Here's the Big," muttered one of the men in leather—expressing the same thought in cruder speech. They looked to be brothers. And they looked sullen. One of them now picked up a filthy fiber bag, tumbled its contents on the cobbled ground. Jon-Joras stepped back. They were the severed heads of animals, one huge one with mottled teeth and bloody muzzle, the others tiny.

"There, now, Big," the man rumbled. "Look a' them!"

"Mmm . . ." Aëlorix, noncommittal, gazed down. "What say, Puëdeskant? Eh?"

"They gets their yearly dole," his man growled, stubborn.

"But look a' the *size* a' she!" one of the brothers protested. "Now, Big, ain't such a karchen sizey bitch—and all o' them karchen pups, look how many!—ain't them worth a bonus, Big?"

Aëlorix grunted, prepared to move on, paused. To Puëdeskant he said, "Give them some fish, then." The brothers seemed a little appeased. Jon-Joras, looking back, saw the steward unclasp a knife and slash the ears of the strange animals. His host, following the look smiled. "So they don't take the heads elsewhere, try the same trick. Dirty chaps."

"But who are they?"

"Doghunters . . . Up here, guest—these steps." They began upon a long covered wooden walkway, curving gently upward and to the right, gardened courtyards on either side and potted plants and caged birds lining the rail below and above on the walk itself. The younger man admired the neatness and the taste of the scene, but tried to fit the spoken phrase into his recollection of his readings. *Doghunters* . . .

Suddenly the key fitted and the wards turned. "Free farmers!" he exclaimed.

He saw his host's mouth give a slight twist. "Fancy name," he said. "Doghunters. Useful in their way. But—dirty fellows." Somewhere ahead music sounded, as different from the elaborate orchestrations of his home world as it was from the crude—though, in its setting, appropriate—harshness of the hunt musics. The covered walk continued to curve on ahead, but the two took a broad branch to the left. The clean planking here was covered with soft reed mats on which designs had been traced in red.

The same motifs were extended and elaborated on the oiled-paper windows of the high screen door whose panels parted silently to admit them; and the melody grew louder. Jon-Joras found himself in a place so strange to him that he stopped short and drew in his breath. It was more a hall than a room, but it contained things in it never seen by him in any hall before. Built around part of a hillside, seemingly, it had a little waterfall plashing and purling in one corner of it; and the tiny stream moved in its channel across the floor to a pool in the center. Bright colored fish swam and darted there. In another section a garden of stepped-back semicircular shelves rose around and retreated from a tall, cylindrical aviary, a rainbow of birds which provided their own background to the music.

The source of this was in a floor of light from a windowed cupola: a dark-skinned woman in a full, embroidered robe. She sat, unseeing, at her instrument, from which came the flow of tinkling sounds, her ringed fingers moving across the keys with stiff but beautiful precision. Suddenly she saw or heard, perhaps felt, them. The music ceased. Jon-Joras might not have been there, for all the notice she took.

"Aë, what news?" she cried.

"The usual," he said shrugging. "A hunt—an outworlder. Usual kill. Too quick, though—"

Lustrous eyes, beautiful tan face expressed something between anger and distress. "I don't mean that! Don't dissemble—what *news?*"

He hesitated; she saw it; he saw that she saw
t. "You make too much of trifles, ma'am—"
"*Aë!*"
"Nothing but a bull-drag. Southward in
Belroze Woods. His epithalamion. I didn't seem
o recognize his cry. That's all."
An expression which was not relief, quite, but
which yet relaxed the look of tense concern,
assed across her lovely face. It did not linger
ong. Her long fingers left the instrument, came
ogether before her throat, and clasped.
"I do not like it," she said, almost as if to
erself. "No. No. No . . . I do not like it. . . ."

II

ALTHOUGH THE 3D scoping equipment here on
Prime World was as good as anywhere in the
multi-world Confederation ("the lands of the
Starry Compact," as Por-Paulo had called it in a
speech—inwardly wincing, so he confided in
Jon-Joras, at the purple phrase), the local econo-
my did not run to any viewing system: the Hunt
scenes could be shown off-world, not there.
Communications were non-visual. Some faint reflection that 2D was surely at least possible had
engaged Jon-Joras's mind, but not for long.
Prime World was, as far as the Hunt Company
was concerned, chiefly a game preserve; had
been little more for centuries. The hand of the
Confederation rested lightly, very lightly here.
What was good enough for the Hunt Company
in this now remote and passed-by globe seemed
good enough for the Confederation.

The face of the communicator was nothing
but an instrument board, and Jetro Yi, when he
called in as directed next morning, was nothing
but a voice.

"I'm lining up one of the best Hunters for
your principal, P. M.," he said, in his usual important tones. "A Gentleman by the name of
Thuëmorix. One of the *best*—"

"That's good, Company."

"He's promised to draw us a prime bull. A five."

"How's that?"

"A *five*. Dragons are at prime at five years. After that, well, they begin to go downhill. And before that, too green. I mean, huh-huh, literally as well as figuratively, huh-huh. How would it look for your king to come back with a skin that anyone who *knows* anything, well, they could at one glance just tell by the color that he hadn't had a first-class hunt? Wouldn't look good at all. You take some of these pot-bellied parvenus, come here in a hurry, all *they* want is the prestige, well, huh-huh, if they draw a hen-dragon or an old crone, who's going to know the difference, the circles *they* move in; skin could be pea-green or rusty-black. But not for your principal, no sir, nothing to worry about."

And he pumbled on and on There was nothing immediately requiring Jon-Joras's attention. In a few days he expected to have a lodge lined up for him to look at, to be let with staff while the owners went south on a long visit. "But nothing immediate. So just enjoy your stay with His High Nascence."

"All right, Company."

"And I'll report tomorrow morning."

"All right, Company." He flicked off before Jetro Yi could give a résumé of all the face-to-face conversations he had had with Jetro Yi. When you had heard him once you had heard him forevermore—unless you had a boundless appetite for the commerce of the hunt.

Leaving the communicator, he strolled at ease

through the charming, rambling house out toward the by-buildings in which he knew he
would find his host inspecting the livestock.
Aëlorix was in the deer-sheds, greeted him with
a wave of his hand towards a fat gray doe that
was being washed around the udders prior to
milking.

"Beauty, isn't she? Won two prizes."

"I must accept that judgment, sir. We have
none like this out my way, on M. M. *beta*."

"No, I suppose not. . . . This your king's first
hunt?"

Jon-Joras tentatively stroked the doe's soft
muzzle. It was Por-Paulo's first *dragon* hunt, yes.
("That's the only kind that counts," his host
said firmly, with the self-contained assurance of
an untraveled provincial.) Jon-Joras described
Por-Paulo's three quests for sundi in the swamps
of Nor, before his first election—the absolute
protective coloration of the sund—how (so the
king had described it) it seems as if a triangular
piece of swamp suddenly hurtles through the air.
"It's not a game for the slow, sir. Instant reflexes, or death."

"Mmm . . ."

"He's gone five or six times for fire-falcons,
too, out of the aeries of Gare. A thousand, two
thousand feet up, if you miss—"

"Mmm . . ." Insecurely mounted on one
winged creature and aiming at another, fiercer
one, as it swoops and spins and dives, hooked
beak and razor talons. But all Aëlorix said was,
"Mmmm . . . I don't deny there seems to be an
element of danger. But you can get *that,* you
know, from all I hear (oh, wouldn't go myself if

you paid me), just trying to cross a road in one of the populous planets. No. A hunt, you see—"

They left the deer-shed, host courteously leading guest by the wrist, and crossed a wide place of beaten earth. "—is not a mere matter of *danger*. Not a dragon hunt, at any rate. It's a matter of ritual, art, music, skill, color, tradition. There's more to it than just exposing yourself to a chunk of mud with teeth in it. And this is an acknowledged fact. Ask any Company man, 'What's your most popular, most sought-after, most expensive hunt?' One answer. 'Dragon.' " It was true, this last. Jon-Joras said nothing.

"Furthermore—" and here Aëlorix suddenly ceased looking rather pontifical, and exceedingly grim, "furthermore, these other items of game (if so you call them), what are they to those that hunt them? Nothing, really. Trophies. Mere sport. Nothing more. Whereas, the *dragons*," his mouth curled down, "we hate them. Don't be in any error about that. *We hate them!*"

This came as completely surprising to Jon-Joras, for nothing he had heard previously and nothing in Aëlorix's voice as he had discussed them earlier, had prepared him for this sudden emotion. It was as though the man had just remembered . . . and remembered a most unpleasant memory, too.

"Why?" he asked, astonished.

With a grimace and an abrupt gesture, the Master said, "It was the Kar-chee . . . They were the Kar-chee's dogs. They hunted us. Now we hunt them." Then the mask dropped again and he said, pleasantly, "Come and see how the training's coming on."

Jon-Joras, wondering mightily but saying nothing, yielded to the friendly hand upon his back, and walked on as desired.

On one side of the wide place a group of young, naked-chested archers were shooting at training targets. An elderly bowmaster with stained white moustachios walked up and down behind them, a switch in his hand. The targets hung high in the air and swayed in the wind; whenever a cadet made what was deemed too bad a shot—*whisshh!*—the switch came down across the lower part of the back. "Mm *hm,*" the Gentleman signified his approval. "Nothing better for the aim. Notice how careful old Faë is never to catch the shoulder-muscles. Ah . . . I see my boy's had one miss already this morning. Let's see if he has another."

They paused, Aëlorix's younger son, a chestnut-haired boy in his middle-teens, stood in his place at line, a thin red wheal marking his skin just above his belt. The old man barked, the boy whipped out an arrow, raised his bow, let fly. Jon-Joras could not even see where the shot landed, but his host made a satisfied noise. The bowmaster paced his slow way down the line, said not a word of praise.

On the other side of the field several squads of bannermen danced about with bare poles. A sudden thought entered Jon-Joras's mind, passed his lips before he had time to consider if it were polite to mention it. "Isn't this sort of an establishment expensive to maintain?"

"In my case, yes, because I like to see my people here at home, not hired out for Hunts all over the place. And I don't take Hunt contracts, myself. Don't have to. My older boy won't have to, either. But I suppose the younger will, unless I divide Aëlor' in my will, and I won't. Don't believe in it. Keep estates in one piece. I've got a smaller place up the river and he shall have that, and I'll start him off with a small establishment of his own. The Company will see that he gets a few good contracts until his reputation firms up. (That's where most of your best Hunt Masters come from: younger sons, you know.) The Company knows me, I know the Company. Hate to think if we had to depend on Confederation."

He did not elaborate, but added, a trifle defensively, "Not that we, not that I, have to depend on the Company, either. Far back as memory goes, this family has never had to buy a haunch of venison, a peck of potatoes, or an ell of common cloth. Show me a Gentleman that does and I'll show you a family going down hill," he rambled on, proudly. "That's how Roëdeskant got his estate, you know. Family that had it, never mind their name, extinct in the male line, anyway; they went *down* and he went *up*. Well, he earned it, I credit him, yes. Council of Syndics shall change his name to Roëdorix at the next Session, or I've lost all my influence and shall engage myself as a Doghunter."

They paused for him to watch the fletchers at work and to test a new batch of arrowheads with his thumbnail along the edges. He poked into a pile of potatoes and satisfied himself that the ones underneath were as good as those on top. He sampled the cheeses and sausages and the apples to see that they were being properly stored, and was en route to the armory to show

Jon-Joras his huntguns, when a party of several
coming towards them through a grove of trees
sighted them and called out.

"Chick-boys . . . what are they doing back so
soon?"

The boys—some of them actually *were* boys,
shock-headed imps with gaptoothed grins, never
having known a day's school or a pair of shoes;
others were all ages up to gray-beards who had
been *boys* forty years ago—beckoned their lord
and set down what they were carrying. These, as
Jon-Joras came up, proved to be wicker baskets,
covers tied on with ropes of grass; from within
them came a shrill twittering sound.

"What's up, boys."

All talking at once, they undid the baskets.
"Ah, now, Nasce', looka here at these beau-
ties—" "Isn't they a fine lot, Nasce'?" "Have a
eye on'm, won't y', Nasce'—" They held up
about a dozen young dragons, deep yellow with
just a faintest tinge of green along the upper
body in some of them.

"Very nice, very nice," Aëlorix said, brusque-
ly. "But if you've slacked off searching just to
show me a batch of chicks—No. You wouldn't.
What's up?"

They fell silent, eyes all turning to one man
who stood by the sole unopened basket. He
opened it now, reached in gingerly, winced,
lunged, and drew out something which brought
a roar from his lord. "What in blethers are you
dragging *that* back for? It's not a chick, it's a
cockerel—do you have six fingers and want
to lose one?—and a marked cockerel too!
What—?"

The man with the gawky dragon-child needed both of his hands to hold it, but another man pointed to the mark, the gray X on the underside which would grow whiter with age. Aëlorix bent over, silently, to examine it as the chick-boy nudged the scaly under-hide with his scarred thumb, and the dragon-cockerel chittered and snapped at him.

The Gentleman snapped up straight, his face red and ugly, criss-crossed with white lines Jon-Joras had not noticed before. "What son of a dirty crone marked that?" he cried. His rage did not surprise his men.

"Marky? Marky?"

An old—a shambling old chick-boy—whose incredibly acid-scarred hands testified to the contents of the ugly can he carried, shook his head slowly and sadly, eyes cast down. It might have been over the sorrow of a ruined grand-daughter.

"Not my stuff, Master Aë," he said. "Nope. That's a coarse, karchen stuff, very coarse, y'see." He prodded it with a caricature of a finger. "See how deep it's cut? I dunno a marky 'round here, 'r north, 'r south, who makes 'r uses stuff like such. And look where he put 'n, too, the dirty son of a kar-chee's egg—"

"Yes," his master said, bitterly, "Yes, look. Cut its throat," he ordered, abruptly, and stalked away with quick, angry steps. Suddenly he stopped and turned back. "Not a word to any one! The Ma'am is not to hear of this." It was a long few minutes before his breathing calmed enough for him to say to his mute guest, "Young man, you must amuse yourself for a while. I

must counsel with my neighbors on something.
Pray pardon and excuse."

But the Ma'am had already heard. Her weep-
ing was loud as Jon-Joras came into the house.
He thought it was best to make excuses of demanding duties, and to depart. It was not urged
that he change his mind.

Peramis was not much different from other of
the city-states of Prime World, that ancient
planet from which the race of Man had begun its
spread across the galaxies. It had stripped itself
bare, exhausting its peoples and minerals, in
launching and maintaining that spread. So it
was that, population dwindled and resources
next to nil, at a time when the son-and daughter-
worlds were occupied in their own burgeoning
imperialisms, old Earth had had to stand alone
when the Kar-chee—the black, gaunt, mantis-
like Kar-chee—came swooping down from their
lairs around the Ring Stars. Alone and almost
defenseless. And, defenseless (in all save their
native wit) and alone, what remained of her people had had to fight their way up. Small wonder
the very name of the conquerors had, in its cor-
rupted but still recognizable form, become a
common curse.

The establishment of Confederation, and a
belated recollection of and attention to the first
home of man, found scarcely a remnant of the
old status still remaining. Gone were the great
cities, gone the great states and leagues of states.
There might have remained even less than a little, had not the Kar-chee been perhaps more in-

terested in the sea than in the land. In response to impelling plans and reasons known only to themselves, masses of land had been blasted and submerged; others had been heaved up out of the primordial muck. Rivers had been changed in their courses, mountains laid low, mountains raised high.

The old maps were of limited use, where useful at all; and Jon-Joras, gazing at the slow-turning, giant model globe in the lobby of the Lodge, was obliged to forget his ancient history. That done, it was no great feat to locate Peramis, Sartor, Hathis and Drogue, the four city-states which—nominally, at least—divided between themselves the land-mass (more than a peninsula, less than a subcontinent) most frequented these days by those bound on dragon-hunts. And beyond was the uninhabited terra incognita called "The Bosky."

Aëlorix of Aëlorix had been right enough in his way. Dragon might perhaps not be the deadliest game, but they were the most prestigious. In ancient legends, preserved in richest form in the worlds of the Inner Circle, those first settled in the great wave of expansion, there were references to dragons. They did not seem to fit the present-day creatures at all. One theory had it that the dragons of the mythic cycles had retreated deep into forests and jungles (or, perhaps, the depths of the seas) and so escaped the attention of reputable historians, evolution . . . mutation . . . accounting for the apparant changes. Had the rupturing of the deeps, perhaps, brought them forth again? Jon-Joras wondered.

Others would insist that the Kar-chee brought the beasts with them, pointing to the existence in all their ruined "castles" of great sunken amphitheaters which the remnants of Man on Earth united in calling "dragon-pits."

One thing alone seemed fairly certain despite all the several theories: Before the Kar-chee came, if there were dragons on Prime World, no one knew of it. And by the time the Kar-chee ceased to trouble, the presence of the dragons was one of the great realities of Terrene life. Somewhere, somewhen during the Kar-chee Reign and the chaos, the mystique of the dragon-hunts had developed. And by now, centuries after, it was the only resource of the despoiled planet. Whatever the explanation, it was all very strange, indeed.

"Odd to think we all came from there," someone, pointing, said over Jon-Joras's shoulder as he stood musing before the circling globe.

He nodded, half-turned. It was the Confederation archaeologist, a certain Dr. Cannatin, whom he had, from time to time, heard lamenting in bar-lounge or Lodge-lobby the effort involved (and the money!) in dredging up a single artifact of the ancient days—or rejoicing on the latest one he had nevertheless managed to find.

"How is your new dig coming along?" Jon-Joras asked politely.

Cannatin, middle-aged, and fat, and depilated according to the custom of his native world (wherever it was), looked rather like an ambulatory egg. His round mouth made a grimace. "Hardly getting anywhere at all. The plebs . . .

that's not what they call them here, is it? No
matter. Dogrobbers? Dog*hunt*ers. Free farmers,
as they like to be called—hard people to deal
with. They would rather dig potatoes than build
sites. Hunt ruins? Rather hunt dogs. And I have
to pay through the nose when I can get them,
too." He sighed.

"I'm thinking of giving up around here, setting up a base camp on the far side of the river,
near Hathis."

Jon-Joras asked if the lower class in Hathis
was more amenable to archaeology, and Cannatin shook his naked head. "Not thinking of
them, I'm thinking of the nomads. The tribespeo-
ple. There's a few of their main trails converge
over that way. Now, these people going wandering in and out and all around. They must know
of sites nobody's even heard of. So I'm moving.
And *soon*—"

The sudden note of urgency surprised Jon-
Joras, but before he could inquire, Cannatin,
with a mumbled excuse, hurried away. Jetro Yi
was not at the Lodge, so Jon-Joras thought he
would look for him at the Hunt Company's of-
fices, seeing more of the "state" en route. A
number of ponytraps in the road outside the
spacious lodge grounds solicited his custom, but
he preferred to walk. Usually the streets in this
part of Peramis town were quiet, with few pedes-
trians; but scarcely had Jon-Joras crossed
through the park at the next crossroads when he
began to hear crowd noises.

A bend in the stately, tree-lined promenade
brought him in sight of the throng, moiling
around on the wide mall in front of an

important-looking building with a white plas-
tered portico. He had seen its picture in the
Company's travel brochures, reduced to min-
iature, clients not being much interested in the
local architecture; but for a moment he could
not recall what it was . . . the State Hall? . . . the
Chamber of the Board of Syndics?

A blind beggar squatting on the pave lifted his
head as Jon-Joras approached. "No room in the
Court, your Big," he croaked, raising his cupped
palms and asking a ·donation. Jon-Joras gave
him something and, wondering at the crowd,
asked what was going on in court. The beggar
canted his head as if to assure himself that no
one else was near, said, "Ah, your Big, it's that
dirty Doghunter what killed the Gentleman. For
why? Claims the Hunts people trampled his
'tato patch. Course they paid 'n for it, always
does. But them Doghunters is mean greedy, never gives nothing to a blind man, wanted more, he
done. Gentleman gives him a piece of stick to
bite on, they fights and he kills 'n. Terrible
thing, your Big . . ."

Jon-Joras left him whining and walked on to
the mall. A small group of Gentlemen were
standing close together in earnest talk; one of
them, with repeated angry gestures towards a
larger clot of plebs, seemed urging some sort of
action. Jon-Joras's path led him athwart the
larger group, and he paused a ways away to listen.

"—dirt, less than dirt," a burly man in a
greasy buckskin which left half his broad, hairy
chest exposed, was saying. "First comes their
own kind, then comes their bloody dragons, then

comes their damned servants what kisses their
backsides, and then comes their pishy customers
from outworlds. Outworlds! Did outworlds
help us when the Kar-chee come?" His hearers
growled and shifted. "And as for us, 'Less than
dirt,' I says. We is good enough to hunt the wild
dogs in the woods to keep things safe, but no
more'n that. 'Free farmers,' we call ourselfs.
Hah! How free c'n we be when our fields what
we plants with sweat is no more to them than a
path to run on or a wastegrounds to tromple
on?"

Times there are when the much goes slow and
the little, quick; but now it was that the much
went quick—and quicker yet. A cry echoed
down the mall, all heads turned, nearer, near,
from the Court: *"Guilty! Guilty! Death!"* A shout,
fiercely triumphant, from the Gentlemen—the
man in the buckskin hurled himself upon them
—in an instant the mall was a mass of bloody
turmoil into which Jon-Joras felt himself carried
away. He struck out, was struck back at.

The crowd, now become a mob, surged back
and forth. He fell on one knee, lifted his arms to
ward off being trampled on. But the mob had
swarmed elsewhere. For the moment he was
safe, and then, looking around as he began to
rise, he saw the girl on the ground on his right.
She was slender and slight and pale, a trickle of
blood upon her face.

He started to lift her up. She opened her eyes,
her face convulsed with rage; she struck at him,
leaped away free. In another moment she was
lost in the screaming crowd.

III

THE MOB DID not manage to free the convicted man but did manage to wreck the Court House thoroughly, and was in the act of burning it when the hastily summoned soldiery attacked. The standing army of the City-State of Peramis was small, but it was disciplined and the mob was not. Hence the battle, though nasty and brutish, was also short. The plebs, still roaring defiance, scattered, leaving their dead behind them.

The murderer, who had killed the Gentleman in a fight over more compensation for his hunt-trampled crops, was executed as scheduled; and in the usual manner: bound and gagged and hanged by his feet in the main square, he was filled with arrows by a squad of masked archers.

Whether this was a mistake or not, was much discussed at the Lodge. Chief Commissioner Narthy, killing time until the arrival of the weekly aerospace ferry for ConfedBase—the only area of Earth under direct Galactic rule, it was located on the landmass which the Kar-chee had created out of the Andaman Islands—"Hunter" Narthy treating the lounge-bar to a farewell round of drinks, insisted it was a mistake.

"Why, they've given the mob a martyr," he

said, sipping. "Everyone of those poor, down-trodden plebs that witnessed the execution is a potential rebel leader. No ... the execution should have been carried out privately, if at all. Then a program of education and land-reform, taking into cognizance the legitimate aspirations of the pleb-peoples—"

But an elegantly-dressed trader from the Blue Worlds shook his head. On the contrary, he said, to do in secret what had always been done in public would have been to admit to a fear of the mob. And nothing, he said, is more calculated to increase a mob's power.

"Besides," he went on, caressing his glass, "*what* legitimate aspirations of the pleb-peoples' exist? Every Doghunter would like to be a Gentleman, and who can blame him? But who can agree that this is a legitimate aspiration? An armada can't consist of all admirals, can it? As for the right of Hunts to go across plowed land—why, it's part of the age—old principal of eminent domain. This planet has no other resource but its Hunts, no other justification for Confederation being here—or for anyone from outside ever visiting the place."

A middle-aged Company PR man nodded. "And without us," he said, "the place would sink back into barbarism. You can't base a civilization on planting potatoes. No, we owe it to our ancient Mother World to continue our fructifying contact with it."

However convinced the lounge-bar was, much of the population of Peramis thought otherwise. The atmosphere in the streets was hostile, several visitors were jostled or stoned, and that night a Gentleman's country seat was attacked and burned and a number of its loyal servants slain. All in all, Jon-Joras thought he understood why Dr. Cannatin had decided to set up his base of operations elsewhere. He sought out Jetro Yi.

"What do you think of arranging my king's hunt in another city-state?" he asked. "Sartor or Hathis or Drogue? It would not do for his visit to be disturbed by all this unrest."

Jetro shook his head. "It would stir up jealousy, P. M. Utterly. We always try to avoid creating antagonisms of that sort."

Jon-Joras scanned the map. His finger pointed. "How about this area called The Bosky? Base the hunt in Peramis, officially, but have it there, in no-man's-land."

However, Jetro even more earnestly opposed this. He doubted that such arrangements could be completed in time—he was, in fact, certain that they could not. Jon-Joras afterwards concluded that Jetro was likely much more concerned with the loss of his commission if the Hunt was held in another district . . . but he felt himself ill-equipped to argue against those who held the local ground. He allowed himself to be persuaded that the trouble was dying down (indeed, it did seem to be), and set to work on his own task of preparing for Por-Paulo's visit.

The estate of Thuëmorix seemed quite satisfactory, despite its distance from the town—more than twice as far as Aëlorix, for instance. He hired a flyer, contracted for food, equipment, extra servants, entertainment, and all the thousand and two things needful. It was not only that he wanted his efforts to be successful from a

career point of view. He sincerely liked Por-
Paulo. The elective kingships of M. M. *beta* were
mankilling jobs. Por-Paulo needed the change.

Thuëmorix himself, a middle-aged man with a
wry sense of humor, had made the very
courteous gesture of sending his family on ahead
to Hathis-port, where they had close friends. He
stayed behind to offer his assistance to Jon-Joras. "I find that the warmth of affection is often in
inverse proportion to the distance between the
friends," he said. "As it is, they'll give me such
a hail-and-fare-well party in Hathis that we'll
never forget it. Between sea-sickness and the fact
that we'll have to spend at least four months
with my wife's aunt in Bachar, I'll be needing all
the pleasant memories I can get."

He brought out his best from the strong-rooms
and storerooms to furnish the quarters engaged
for Por-Paulo and his aides and guests, moving
furniture with his own hands to be sure it was
arranged right. Jon-Joras had been helping him,
and they were looking around them in sweaty
contentment, when the signal of a flyer brought
them out to the wide park-like lawn where the
vessel had put down.

"What's up, Röe?" the host called out as they
approached. "Don't tell me—an imprompt?"

Roëdeskant nodded while several Gentlemen
called greetings. "Yes, your High. Wish you'd
come along. A big drag's been sighted by the
river fallows what's part of the Lië lands, and as
its Gentleman's owed me a drag this two-three
years, why, he's kind enough to have give me the
hunt of it. Now, your High I will recollect that *I*
owes *you* a drag. So, if he don't mind taking it

now as an imprompt—?"

Thuëmorix didn't mind at all. His face lit up. "Just the thing for a send-off," he said, directing his servants to get his huntgun. "And one for my young guest, too. I don't think it improper for you to take a chance on a shot," he said to Jon-Joras, "before your liege arrives, since it's an imprompt, and hardly counts. Won't give you a title if you pierce your dragon, you see. We are so particular about the dragons, you see," he said, his manner suddenly becoming much more serious, "because the dragons used to be so particular about *us*. Do you know what I mean? The Kar-chee used them like dogs, to hunt us down. That's why, I suppose, that we never use dogs to hunt anymore. Fact. Only of course they are a bit bigger than dogs, a bit fiercer . . . and, leaving sarcasm aside, infinitely more intelligent. . . ."

Jon-Joras said, "I had really known nothing about all this—"

Thuëmorix nodded. "It's a wonder that there were any of us alive at the end, there, at all. . . . Well." He relaxed, smiled a bit, and with a wave of his hand invited the outworlder to admire the view below.

Over the forests, denser and denser as they proceeded upriver, the thick meadows and marshlands, the flyer made its way. The atmosphere was cheerful and relaxed. An impromptu hunt was evidently quite a different thing from a regular one. Many of those aboard were younger sons—some of them surprisingly young, including that son of Aëlorix whom Jon-Joras had seen at target practice. Evidently the archers today were all gentlemen amateurs.

"Drag's a monstrous big one, I hears," said Roëdeskant. "The tenant at Lië village sent word down by boat. Don't know his call, they says."

"A wanderer, I suppose. Seems to me that there've been rather a few more of those than usual, wouldn't you say, Roë?"

A shadow seemed to fall over the Master Huntsman's face. "P'raps so, your High," he muttered. Young Aëlorix looked at him, suddenly somber. Then someone started a song, and, one by one, everyone joined in.

> *The dragon I met in the morning,*
> *I followed him all the day.*
> *I'd waited since my borning,*
> *My dragon for to slay.*

"Getting there," someone said. "There's the island—"

> *The musics they grew tired.*
> *Their horns they sounded hoarse.*
> *But I with zeal was fired*
> *As I paced my dragon's course.*
> *The archers fired a volley,*
> *My dragon for to turn.*
> *When I saw him turn in folly,*
> *My heart with joy did burn.*

It was hardly great music or good poetry, Jon-Joras thought, wryly. In fact, it was rather dreadful. But it had a swing and a beat to it. The Aëlorix cadet was singing lustily, beating his fists on his naked knees.

My dragon rushed on towards me.
His talons ripped the air.
My bosom swelled with wonder
To see this sight so rare.
My dragon roared like thunder,
His mighty teeth all bare.
My life cannot afford me
More joy than I had there.
I sighted on his crux-mark,
His vital part to pierce—

The rest of the words were lost to Jon-Joras in
the babble of voices as the flyer put down in a
clearing in the woods, not a great distance from
the river. A small group of men was waiting for
them; one of them, a tall stalwart fellow in his
thirties, dressed in fine-spun, proved to be the
tenant—the others were his sub-tenants. By his
manner of speech he might almost have been a
Gentleman himself, and, indeed, Jon-Joras had
learned from the casual comments of the company, that he was the natural son of one.

The bannermen were in the acts of fastening
the colored wefts to the ends of their long poles
when the low, rather mournful cry broke upon
their ears. All heads went up, turned this way
and that. They sniffed the wind like animals.
"Not too far off," Thuëmorix muttered. *"None*
too far off . . ."

Roëdeskant quickly got things in order; while
he was doing so, Thuëmorix repeated the in-
structions he had given Jon-Joras in the flyer.
"Don't fire until you're told to," he concluded,
"if you *are* told to. And aim *only* at the crux of the

X, remember that. If you hit it, you pierce the only nerve-ganglion that counts. Otherwise you can spend the rest of your life shooting into him, if he'd let you—Holy Father! *Already!*"

He shouted. Lights glinted onto faceted eyes. Thuëmorix shouted, Roëdeskant flashed his arms, cymbals sounded and shawms blared. The dragon came hurtling out of the woods. The bannermen danced and waved to draw him to the right. He ignored them. Cymbals clashed, arrows flew. He ignored them. Bannermen and archers closed in towards him, running. The dragon, running swiftly, too, ignored them. He reared up upon his hind legs and the archers filled the hide of his belly with their barbs and this time he did not ignore them.

Pivoting upon one great jointed column of a leg, he came pounding down upon the archers. "Oh, blood!" someone cried. "A rogue! A rogue! *Rogue dragon!*"

The bannermen flew like deer, teasing their bright flags under his very snout. He roared. They downed their poles and fell, hidden, to the grass. The dragon did not stop, came charging on. Screams and turmoil in the grass.

Blood upon the great clawed feet of the dragon.

"Shoot free, shoot free!" Roëdeskant shouted. "Any with a sight—*shoot free!*"

Jon-Joras saw three men raise their guns, fire almost together. The dragon came on, the dragon came on, two more shots, then three, then four, the dragon came on. The archers held their ranks, firing their useless shafts. Not one turned to run. And the dragon, hissing, screaming, flanks and chest and sides and stomach bristling with arrows, bleeding, eyes flashing dreadful beauty, the dragon stooped upon the archers. His talons swept to right and left, his head darted down, came up, jaws grinding, head tossing through the reddened air.

The son of Aëlorix fired his last shaft as the great bull-dragon's claws swept him off his feet. The boy's mouth was open, but no song now came from it.

The beast was everywhere, and so, at last, he was in the sights of Jon-Joras's gun. *Aim only at the crux of the X. . . .* He remembered Thuëmorix's voice (where was Thuëmorix now?) saying the words. But the crux of the X had been obliterated by all the shots poured into it, was a gaping and bloody chasm. Unthinking, automatically, into it he fired his own shot. And fired. And fired. And—

Someone ran into him full-tilt. His last shot before the gun fell went wild. The man, whoever he was, beat upon him with clenched fists, screaming in terror; at last threw him down and ran. Stunned, scarcely able to breath, Jon-Joras felt the concussion of the great beast's feet, saw out of the corner of his eye, something vast, something blood-stained go sweeping by. There were screams and screams. A voice cried out, shrill, thickened, ceased.

The sky darkened, wheeled, became a whirling concentric circle. Jon-Joras felt himself go sick and cold. And all was black.

Somewhere in between his fainting and his awakening he had heard what he now identified

as the sound of the flyer. A sudden tenseness of
his muscles warned him just in time to turn his
head. He vomited. Then, fearful, lay back for a
long moment. But there was nothing to be heard
except the drone of flies.

The sun was out and birds called. How many
people had come on the impromptu hunt? Jon-
Joras, numbed by the sickening sights that lay
all about, did not know. Nor could he guess how
many might have made their escape in the flyer
(if any but the pilot had) or into the woods. No
one answered his calls . . . at first. . . .

Only when he held the bloodied head on his
knees did he realize that he had never known the
boy's name. Aëlorix's boy stared blindly right into
the sun. "Tell . . . tell my mother . . ." he began.

"I will. I will," Jon-Joras said. And waited.
And waited. But the dead lips spoke no more.
Tell his mother! What could he tell her, he wondered, that she had not already guessed and
feared!

Numbly following the custom of his own people, he laid a clot of earth on each closed eye,
and straightened the arms at full length, folding
the hands together in a loose clasp. " *'Ended is
this scene and act,'* " he said. " *'May the curtain rise
upon a fairer one. . . .'* " He could not remember
the rest of it.

When you have no idea in which direction
anything is, it makes as much sense to go in one
direction as another. The river and the Lië village were not too far away, but he had no notion
where. The sensible thing was obviously to wait
right where he was until help came. But this was

the one thing he could not do—not at that field
of death, over which the dark birds had already
begun to circle.

He made a circle of his own around the clearing, and took the first path he found. The afternoon was late indeed before he dared admit that,
wherever the path led, it did not lead to the Lië
village. And then he heard the dogs. It should
not have come to him as the heart-swelling surprise it did. Where there were Doghunters, there
were bound to be dogs. Besides, had he not seen
their severed heads? Recalling the mottled teeth
in the bloody muzzle, he broke into an awkward,
stumbling run.

Someone was there; he saw the glimmer of
cloth off to one side on the slope. Instantly upon
his outcry, it vanished, and he left the path to
follow, leaping over fallen trees and little rivulets
running through the soft, mossy earth. Someone
was there ahead of him in the darkening
daylight. . . .

A girl.

"Please!" he called. "I won't hurt you! I
don't want—They're all dead, all the others—
the rogue dragon—"

She stopped at that; stopped and whirled
around. The shock of it stopped him, too. For a
moment they stood staring at one another. It
was the girl he had tried to help on the Court
House mall; the girl who had struck at him, run
away, as she was, in the next instant, running
now.

"Don't leave me here alone," he cried, de-
spairingly. "The dogs—! The dogs—!" They
were nearer now, and nearer and nearer; they

seemed to be all around him. He could no longer
see the girl. He snatched up a stick of thick wood
and looked to see a large tree that he could get
his back against—or, better, climb. But he was
passing through an area that had been burned
over not many years enough before; there were
no large trees at all.

"*Don't run!*" A man's voice. He whirled
around. The dogs had been on all sides of him
because the men who were leading them on thick
ropes of braided leather were on all sides of him.
He let out his relief in a gusty sigh and let the
stick drop.

"Oh, Lord . . . I'm so glad to see you. . . . I
was on the hunt, back there—" he gestured, in-
definitely; he no longer knew just how far or in
what direction "back there" was. The men were
dressed in hides and cloth; two of them handed
over their leashes to others and came towards
him.

"It was a rogue dragon, and it wouldn't die, it
wouldn't *die*—" The words caught and clicked in
his throat.

The two men looked at each other. Little
lights seemed to kindle in their eyes.

"*Was* it?" said one. ,

"*Wouldn't* it?" said the other.

They came up to him and he put out his hand.
With untroubled but with deft emphatic movements, one took that hand and one took the other and they swung them behind his back and
tied them fast with thongs.

"Walk on," said one. "Just walk. No tricks.
It's easier to let loose the dogs than to hold on to
them."

He picked up Jon-Joras's stick and thumped him in the ribs with it. *"Walk!"* he said, again. Jon-Joras walked.

IV

THERE HAD BEEN no ponies on MM *beta*. It seemed to Jon-Joras that there was no longer any skin on the inside of his thighs. His hands were now free, but his feet were bound instead, by a line passing under the pony's belly. The dogs loped alongside, from time to time looking up at him—hungrily, it seemed. Their eyes glowed red in the torch-light. He did not remember dozing off, but when he snapped awake, two men who had been holding his arms on either side withdrew.

The uncertain flaring light showed nothing that told him where he was. Not on the interminable path any more, for certain; it was not wide enough for three men to ride abreast. One of the riders grunted, pointed. Another, nodding, said something which vanished into a yawn. Jon-Joras, following the gesture, saw a great black block of rock canted at an angle. Vines grew over it. There was another. And another. The soft thudding of the ponies' hooves suddenly began to echo, the air was instantly closer. They were in a tunnel of some sort; a tunnel which wound around and around, always up-hill. The smell was faint, but it was an alien smell, and he shuddered at it.

A wave of cool air washed his face; the echo

vanished. Stars were overhead, but only overhead . . . not to the sides. He felt, rather than saw, the encircling wall which must be there. Where this place was, and *what* this place was, he had no idea. But he felt certain that it was never built by the men who held him captive.

The hunt itself had taken toll of him a drain of nervous energy equivalent to many days hard work; his long walk, his flight from the dogs, the ride . . . He fell from the pony, but the pain (as they loosed his bonds) seemed academic. His body was being hurt, but he—Jon-Joras—was not his body. Vaguely, he was aware of being half-carried down a long, winding ramp into a room where torches blazed in sockets on walls so high he did not see the tops. Food was set before him, he ate, nodded, slumped onto the tables. Men stripped him of his trousers, rubbed his sore skin with curiously-scented salve. He fell asleep again while this was being done.

But even in his sleep he heard the hissing, heard the low, almost melancholy call of the dragon.

He awoke on a pile of hides and rushes, sunlight streaming through a window very high up. He blinked. It was not a window, but a breach in the smooth black wall that went up and up and up. . . . The room he was in was not quite a wall, but a partition of planks which scarcely reached higher than his head. He began to get up, stopped, with a sharp cry of pain.

Every muscle seemed sore—including muscles the existence of which he had not known before. He thought that a hot bath might relieve the soreness in tendons and ligaments, as well as re-move the grime and dried sweat—but he feared what it might do to the raw skin on the inside of his upper legs. And, at any rate, where in this place—half improvised camp, half ancient ruin —could he expect to find a hot bath?

The answer came sooner than he expected. A fat, toothless old woman came bustling in with a bowl of hot water and a rag. "You'll have to get up now," she said. "I'm going to be needing this room to sort my potatoes. Wash up and get along."

If this were a prison, it was an odd and in-formal one. He winced, but was glad of the wash, such as it was. "I don't know where to get along *to*," he said, scrubbing gingerly. The old woman said that this wasn't her problem. So, carrying the trousers he didn't dare to try to put back on, he wandered out into the hall which sloped down between the partitions. Again the light coming through the hole far up caught his attention. He followed the shaft of sunlight to where it lit on the opposite wall, and it was there that something struck his attention.

It appeared to be a frieze; high up as it was, and at a bad angle, obscured by dirt and cobwebs in places, he could not clearly make it out. But one figure seemed to leap into focus. It was not a human figure. With a blink and a shudder, he understood. He was in one of the ruined and abandoned castles of the noisome and chitin-mantled Kar-chee.

But who the people were who had moved into it as a hermit-crab moves into an abandoned shell, he had yet to learn.

At any rate, they took a friendly enough interest in him as he hobbled slowly along. Someone offered him a fried egg, someone offered him a boiled potato. Someone offered him a finespun tunic that had seen better days. And someone offered to apply another dressing of salve to his saddle-sores, and to bandage them as well. He accepted all these offers.

After thanking the last donor, and finding that he could now walk much more comfortably, he said, "I am not complaining . . . but how is it that I'm not tied anymore?"

The bandager, a middle-aged man with a broken nose, said, matter-of factly, "Why, because you couldn't get out of here until we were ready to let you. Other than that, it's Liberty Hall." He chuckled briefly.

Jon-Joras said, "But I must get out of here. I have duties . . . outside."

The bandager gave a grim little nod. "We all have duties . . . outside. For the time being, though, some of us have our duties . . . inside . . . as well."

"Forgive me. But—you don't talk like a Gentleman *or* like a Doghunter. I'm an outworlder, and easily confused."

"I'll tell you. At one time I lived in the State. The town or city, I mean. Drogue. Never been there? Not much of anything. I liked it, though. I was a shopkeeper. Had a little house on the outskirts. A garden plot." His sentences got shorter and his face grew redder. "My land bordered a Gentleman's, you see. Oëgorix. Rot his blood . . . One day I came home. Tired. Sit in my garden. I thought.

"Garden? You see one here? That's what I saw there. His High——" —the word he uttered was not "Nascence"— "had decided to extend his training grounds. So, rather than take a chunk out of his own grass or garden, he merely appropriated mine. Not a flower, not a plant did he leave me. His bloody musics were tramping up and down and under my window where the rosebeds had been."

In the fight that followed, the shopkeeper had gotten his broken nose. He went from his house to find his shop wrecked, returned from his shop and saw the smoke of his burnt house. "So I went to Hathis. But things no better there I found. The Gentlemen do as they like in every place. Except here. Here, we do as *we* like. But we don't like it here, much. And sooner or later . . ."

His mouth twitched. Then he said, in a smothered voice, "You'll see. Go on, now."

In some ways it was as if a highly eccentric Gentleman had moved his estate, herds, followers chick-boys and all, into the black basalt ruin of the inhuman and forest-laired Kar-chee castle—and then mixed it all up, humble-tumble. Here a woman hung a cloth bag full of soft cheese to drip, there a fletcher picked through a pile of feather in his aproned lap. A young boy practiced scales on an old horn. A woman on a stool stitched colored cloths into banner wefts, from time to time giving her rather dirty baby's cradle a rock with her bare (and dirtier) foot.

But nowhere, anywhere, was there a hall windowed with oiled and painted paper, bright with flowers and gay with birdsong and the sound of water, where a dark woman in embroidered robes sat making crystal music.

A vision of the shattered face of the boy with chestnut hair rose before Jon-Joras's inner eyes. What connection there might be between that bloody death and this curious wild encampment, he did not know; only that he felt a stirring conviction within him that such a connection there was. And then, through the contented confusion of the courtyard, a man with a scarred face picked his way.

He did not see, or seem to see, the prisoner at large—or for that matter, anyone else—but everyone saw him and marked his passage. The man was tall, with little deep-set eyes under black brows like nests of snakes. The bones of his face seemed about to burst through the reddened skin, the mouth was an all but lipless slash between the grim nose and the almost impossibly long and heavy chin. The scar went from scalp to neck, interrupted only by the stump of one ear. His feet tramped the black slabs as if all his enemies lay upon them.

Almost automatically, Jon-Joras stopped still and drew in upon himself until the man passed; entirely automatically, he fell in behind—well behind—him. Only as he followed after the unnaturally stiff figure, hands clenched at sides, did the formed thought reveal itself to his upper mind: *where this man was, the answer was.*

And so, passing through the wake of whatever emotion lies between fear and awe, Jon-Joras followed on as if drawn by rope and held by magnet.

*   *   *

Perhaps it was only a dream dragon that he had heard in his sleep that night. But the one he heard now was no dream—unless this whole scene, Kar-chee castle and court and all, unless *it* was a dream, too. His ear-drums vibrated with the hiss that became a scream. But—*perhaps* it was a dream!—no one else so much as looked up. And still the man walked on and on.

He stopped only at a low wall and there he leaned over. Jon-Joras walked on a bit, then put his hands on the parapet and peered. The thick, dark odor of dragon caught him sharply between nose and throat, but he didn't turn away. Below him in an area partly ringed with seats, a dragon came rushing down the ground. His hide was thick with arrows and the stumps of arrows, and a smell Jon-Joras knew from other places, other times, came from the beast—the fishy stench of old, of rotten blood.

At first glance the scene below appeared to be a normal dragon hunt. Almost at once, though, Jon-Joras saw the differences. It was like seeing double. There, for instance, was the row of archers. But behind them was another row. The arms and hands and bows of the archers moved. The row behind them, clad in the same leaf green, moved not. And in front of the row of archers was a trench.

The dragon came beating down the ground. Another flight of arrows bored into his hide. He neither plucked at them nor slackened pace. The thought came into Jon-Joras's mind, *this one is no virgin!* At his near approach, the front row of bowmen seemed to vanish into the earth—one jump—the narrow trench, too narrow for a dragon-paw, received them. The row of dummies swayed slightly on the shaking ground. But the dragon ignored them. Unwavering, it rushed on and on.

From behind a low earthen wall directly in his path, up leaped a row of figures, bright banners waving on long poles. Jon-Joras had to squint and peer a moment before realizing that these, too, were dummies. The dragon plunged on through their midst. Jon-Joras flung his head around and his eyes flew down the arena to see what lay dead ahead of the plunging questing beast. He had not far to look.

There were the figures in huntsmen's clothes, guns in hands. Bellowing his hatred, pain and rage, the dragon came on and on and in great, maddened leaps, flung himself upon the group. Jon-Joras had not seen this one trench. He blinked as the figures vanished into it. All but one of the figures vanished into it—that one, a dummy fastened to a stake, flew first right, then left, then was lifted high into the air to be worried as a rat in the jaws of a dog.

Something splashed and spattered on Jon-Joras's face and chest. Thoughtlessly, he raised his hand, wiped at it. It was warm. It was blood. He looked, incredulous, at the figure which the dragon now held in its paws and tore into bits. And then he vomited again.

"*That,* you see," the tall man with the scar said, abruptly turning to him "is what happens to *traitors!*"

His voice had started out astonishingly soft

and smooth, the face as blank as ever; but on the last word the face convulsed, the voice rose into a shriek, cracked upon the last note. The hands leapt up from his sides. Jon-Joras fell back. Then the face struggled, the mask fell into place again. So did the hands.

The voice was soft again. "You outworlder—you're a boy. A pawn, a slavey. You don't know, does you? What's been going on here on our old Earth? Think about the worst enemy they's ever had in your world. Times it twice, add to it. And think what rotten things turns traitor, turns enemy. Is *that*—down *there*—too bad for it? Oh, no, boy. No . . . Too, good." The voice fell lower on the last word, and the effect was somehow more frightening than when it rose. The tiny eyes glinted. The thin mouth stretched.

Abruptly, he beckoned, turned his back, started down a ramp. And again Jon-Joras followed. Dimly he wondered if the Prime World, supposedly so old and so tired, might not be too much for him. Its unexpected vigor, wasted as it was in strange ways, was all too different from the tight and organized hegemonies of MM *beta* —where even the unexpected was predictable.

They came at last to a scene untouched by the turmoil and disorder of the rest of the place: a chamber immaculately clean, furnished with a trestle bed, a table consisting of a wide plank set on two more trestles, and a doorless cabinet lined with shelves. There were no chairs.

"My name is Huë," the tall man said. "Not Huëdeskant and not Huëlorix—just Huë. Never mind telling me yours, I know it since you come here. We been watching you. We watches everyone. First, naturally, I thought maybe you was a spy. Now I think you isn't. Probably . . ." His sentence ended on a significant pause.

"Where was the dragon hunt yesterday? Near the Lië village?" He went to a map on the wall and marked it with a piece of charcoal. "Tell me about it. *All* about it."

His gaunt, scarred face remained impassive, but his tiny eyes glittered under his Medusa's brows. Then he was silent a while.

"All right," he said, answering an unspoken question. "Here it is, see. What justifies the Gentlemen, that they lives on others' labor and does what they likes with others? Why—they hunts drags. Yes. And the drag is terrible big and terrible dangerous. Isn't he? Of course. You has to be out after him with beaters and musics and bannermen and archers and guns. Yes. And to make damned sure that you kills him, you takes him when he's a chick and marks him with acid —feels carefully for that certain spot and paints the X so the crux is right over it. Correct?"

Jon-Joras nodded.

"All right," said Huë. "Now. If the Gentlemen really had any interest in putting down dragons, they'd have the chick-boys kill 'em . . . and not mark 'em. Right?"

"Yes, of course—but you're making a point that no one needs to have made. Of course they preserve dragons, the whole place is nothing but one big game preserve."

Huë said, "Right. And they's the game wardens. And what're we? Poachers? We lives here, too. Haven't we got no rights? No. None. Once in ten years, maybe, one of us is lucky enough to get took on as a scrvant to a Gentleman. And once in, maybe a hundred years, some servant is lucky enough to get made a Gentleman—"

"Roëdeskant!"

"Yes . . . Roëdeskant . . . Does he remember what his grandser was? His stick is heavier against us than anyone's. Or *was*. Don't know, yet, if he got away alive. But, to go back. The drags, now—"

His flat voice droned on. But Jon-Joras was far from being bored at what Huë had to tell him, told him with the endless attention to and re-iteration of detail which only the monomaniac is capable of. Distilled, it amounted to a realization that the dragon, *if left alone,* was harmless; a sort of gigantic chicken, with no brain to speak of. No one needed beaters to go round up sundi so that they would come and be hunted; it was not nec-essary to tease and to confuse dire-falcon with banncrs and musics and archers.

The entire principle of the ritual murder which constituted a dragon hunt was *misdirection.* Anyone in good health and who could keep his head, could manage to stay out of a dragon's way—if the dragon was not goaded into frenzy. Such skill as there was in a hunt was mostly on the part of the bannermen. The function of the archers was only to goad the beast—and create a picturesque pattern of arrows on his hide—and make him rear upright, so that his X-mark was exposed. Anyone who could hit a moving target could kill a dragon.

And the dragon was thus always killed.

Wasn't it?

Pea-brained as the species was, the individual

members were still, like any creature, capable of learning something from experience. But no dragon was allowed to do so, under the Hunt system. All talk of small, feeble Man the Hunter pitting himself against the skill and cunning of the great dragon was cant and hypocrisy. The novice dragon had neither skill nor cunning, just his teeth, his talons and his weight. Now and then it had happened, over the years, that some trembling finger on the trigger did manage to miss. If the dragon then turned and ran from the guns, his one vulnerable spot no longer visible— if the same dragon, escaped, was unlucky enough to come across another hunt—and again escape—

"Why, then, boy, you got the one thing that every Gentleman fears more than anything in the world. You got a dragon that knows better. You got *a rogue dragon!*"

Light blazed in Jon-Joras's mind. His body, which had been drooping with stiffness and with pain, jerked straight upright. "And that's what you're doing here!" He cried. "In the dragon pit —you're training rogues!"

Hué's scarred head nodded, nodded slowly. "That's exactly what we're doing in the dragon pits. We're training rogues. We're training the drags so that they'll know better than to be distracted by banner-wefts and music. We're training them so that they won't waste time plucking at arrows. By the time we're done and he's ready to be released, you've got a dragon that's what the Master Huntsmen claim every drag really is." His voice sank and his thin, lipless mouth opened wide.

"And aren't they surprised . . ." he whispered.

Memories of that "surprise," the terror and the panic and the bloody slaughter, made Jon-Joras wince and shudder. But another memory, at first as small and nagging as a grain of sand under an eyelid, grew and grew and became large. "But a rogue dragon," he said, slowly, "is still only a dragon. It may have learned cunning, but, physically, it is the same. Training hasn't changed the fact that if you put a shot through a certain place, it dies. I pierced that rogue yesterday, myself. At least a hundred shots pierced it . . . the crux of the X-mark was obliterated, it was a bloody pulp . . . but the dragon didn't die. *Why not?*"

Huë looked at him, relishing the moment. "Why not? Why, because it's true the dragon's body hadn't changed. But something else was changed. Not *in* the body. *On* the body. We don't take drags that the Gentlemen have already fixed for themselves. Wouldn't be fools if we did. Oh, no. We got our own chick-boys. And we finds our own chicks . . ."

Faintly, faintly, conscious of the cold creeping over him, Jon-Joras saw Aëlorix looking at the dragon-cockerel, saw the acid-burned finger of the old marky pointing at the X-mark, heard the words, *"Look where he put it, too!"*

"It's only a matter of a few inches," Hue said. "A difference you can't see when you're looking up from below, and all excited with the hunt. Only a few inches, yes, boy, but it might as well be a few miles."

Everything else that Huë told him seemed an anticlimax, though he would have found it exciting enough if he had heard it without the other. There had always been outlaw bands of one sort or another in the forest. But previously, generally, they had been content to remain in the forest. The one now established in the old Kar-chee castle, however, had no such intentions.

And now a thought which had for some time not been far from the surface of Jon-Joras's mind rose to his lips as well. *The old Kar-chee castle . . .*

"But I don't see," he began slowly, then proceeded more rapidly; "I don't see how, if the dragons are as naturally stupid as you say—"

"They are! They are! I do say! No man alive knows more about they, boy, than I do. Dragons had been my science, boy, my library. I know what I tell you." His thin, almost invisible lips curled away from his teeth.

Jon-Joras, who had paused, brushed his black hair from his forehead, and went on, in part repeating himself in order to complete his question: "If the dragons are as naturally stupid as you say, how is that the Kar-chee could have used them as—so to speak—dogs, to hunt the people down with?"

Huë's fierceness was somewhat abated by his genuine puzzlement. His perplexity did not seem that of one who merely did not know an answer, rather it was the baffled attitude which comes from inability to understand the question. "What you mean, boy? That's what the drags *was*—Karches."

Now it was Jon-Joras's surprised incapacity to comprehend. "But the Kar-chee were not dragons—"

"Course they was! What else was they?"

Jon-Joras gestured. "Back down there, near where I slept last night, there's a frieze—"

"There's a *what?*"

"A frieze, a relief . . . Pictures! Carved into the wall, up above."

Huë shrugged, as he might shrug off a merely mildly-annoying insect. "Oh, them things. Not Karches, boy. Just big bugs. Karches is another name for dragons, just like 'drag' is another name for dragon." Questions, more questions, tugged at Jon-Joras's mind; he poured them out. How could the pea-brained dragons have ever conquered the Earth and transformed its land and sea—this was the burden of them. But it was clear that Huë knew nothing and cared nothing of all that. Whatever mass of legendry and ignorance his history consisted of, it was not the past which concerned him. So, in the face of his growing annoyance, the conversation changed from past to the future.

"What do you intend to do about the dragons, if you get into power," Jon-Joras had asked. And the answer was immediate.

"When we get into power? Drags? They shall all be killed, every one of them—in the egg, and out."

"And . . . the Gentlemen?"

"They shall all be killed, every one of them—in the egg, and out."

At first Jon-Joras thought that Huë had not fully heard nor understood the second question, was still replying to the first. But then he realized that both of the questions had the same answer.

V

AND IN THE night, the Kar-chee castle was penetrated.

He had slept but ill, his aches and pains contending with what he had heard from Huë, and what he could not forget of the rogue dragon in the wood and the rogue dragon in the pit, at keeping him at least half-awake. He had heard the noises, for quite some time before he even paid much attention to them—padding of feet, whispering, scuffling—and then, when he had begun to wonder vaguely what it was about—

He smelled the smoke and guessed the fire before a scream came, signalling chaos. As even a man whose house is rocked by an earthquake may pause to put on his shoes, so, now, Jon-Joras, while the castle exploded into uproar, slowly and painfully drew on his trousers. They were fighting in the corridor by the time he got there, men of the castle against men he did not know, men in fleecy capes.

Jon-Joras did not know them. But they seemed to know him. "There's the outworlder!" someone shouted. He turned to try and identify the voice, knowing only that the accent was strange.

Someone seized his arm. "Run! Run!" he cried. "Follow our line—follow our torches—when you see the last one, tell him, *'Pony and pride!'* You got that? Then, run!"

Jon-Joras ran. That is, he proceeded at a painful, agonized stagger. The torches of the strangers were made of reeds bound in bundles, easy to distinguish from the tarry sticks of the castle-folk; nor were the strangers hard to tell apart, either.

Stumbling and now and then crying out in sudden pain, he made his way through the confusion as best he could. It was only when he stumbled in the darkness that he realized the fighting was behind him. For a moment he stood still, listening to the echo of it. Ahead, in the distance a single torch flared, and by the uncertain light he saw, or thought he saw, a fleecy cape.

Slowly and fearfully, his hands groping out ahead of him, he made his away along. From the direction of the torch a voice cried, "Who's that? Speak out, or I'll arrow you—by my mother, I will!"

In a strangled voice Jon-Joras said, "Pony and pride!" Then he shouted it: *"Pony and pride! Pony and pride!"*

The man with the torch laughed. His hair and beard was the same light golden brown as his cape. "Come on, then . . . come on . . . Ah. The outworlder! How's the fight going, up there? Well enough, I suppose, if someone had time to give you the word. All right!" He stopped and selected a reed torch from a pile at his feet, lit it, handed it over.

"Now—" He gestured. "Straight along as you go, you come to a hole in the wall. Go through it. Wait! Take another light, slow as you're humping along, one might burn out on you. On with you!"

Actually, the torch did not burn out on him— quite. The hole led into a tunnel like the one through which he'd entered the castle, though smaller. Again, the faint and alien odor troubled him . . . he thought it must be the long lingering emanation of the Kar-chee themselves. The floor of the tunnel was thick and soft and dusty. The roof was hung with cobwebs. The small hairs of his flesh began to prickle. He could have cried with relief when he finally saw torchlight ahead, and the air freshened on his face.

Riding, curled up on his side, on the soft floor of the litter was better than riding astride a pony, or even than walking. The litter was not there for him, as the person for whom it *was* there had made and was making quite clear.

"Time was, me coney-boy, when I could stride a cob with the best of them, yesindeed, ride all day, frolic and dance and make love all night. But those days are gone, yesindeed. Gone before you were hatched, my chick. Or didn't they hatch on your world? Bear live, do they?"

A gust of laughter took the withered little creature in the corner of the litter. It was day, early day, now. But he could still be no more certain if it were very old man or very old woman there, buried in the mound of furs and fleeces; save that it had been addressed as *ma'am*.

"You listening, Jonny? Awake, are you?

Good. Not that it makes much difference at me age, there I was, babbling to myself for hours, thinking you were listening, all the while you were dreaming away, but I went on babbling, anyway. We'll stop by and by for a bite to eat and something hot and sweet to drink. Now, then, must mind me manners—

"Ma'am Anna, that's who I am. Call me Queen of the North People, if you like; call me the Tribe-Hag, if it likes you better. One way you look at it, I pays taxes to their nasty, priggy little Lordships the High-Born Syndics of Peramis, Hathor, Sartis and Drogue, for the pleasure of me folks' wandering through what the stiff-necks like to think is their territory. Look at it another way, they pays me tribute for not raiding into their borders. What it amounts to, nowadays, want to know: We exchange presents. Eee, the folly of folks!"

She winked, tittered, flung up her ancient paws. Then, with a mutter, drew a horn whistle from somewhere under her coverings, and blew on it. Almost at once a head thrust into the litter, and a hearty voice said, "Well, our ma'am, have you finished seducing this young cock-dragon? And can the rest of us, poor respectable nomads as we are, pause and rest?"

The old woman cackled and gestured. A horn blew, voices cried out, the litter (carried by two fat-bodied, short-legged animals that might have been small horses or large ponies) halted. And over the hot breakfast which presently made its way into the palanquin, to be divided between matriarch and guest, Jon-Joras reflected on what he had heard; for he had not been altogether

asleep all during the ride, merely too tired to reply or comment.

The raid had not been planned to free him,
although that had been part of it. The raid had
not been planned to pick up a dozen or so likely
young women, although *that* had been part of it,
too. (The women had shrieked and struck their
captors and engaged in some semi-ritual wailing
until cuffed into silence, but they seemed to have
accepted their change in fortune serenely enough
after not very long.)

"That Huë seems to think that nothing but
what *he* wants counts, me coney," old Ma'am
Anna had complained. "Well, now. How stupid
do he think the Gentlemen are? They know that
something doesn't smell right, yesindeed. Sooner
or later, they're bound to come looking. Now, we
North People, we mind our own business. And
we do not want any troops and armies coming
and poking around. Wars, you know, me boy,
wars are catchy things."

Boiled down, then, the raid had been intended
to re-establish the status-quo before the city-
states went to arms in order to re-establish it
themselves. And, the dragons, she had said, were
dead—dead in their enclosures behind the pit.
Pausing with a piece of wild honeycomb in his
fingers, Jon-Joras asked about that.

"How were the dragons killed, Ma'am Anna?
I heard no gunfire. No one could have gotten a
good shot by the torchlight, anyway. Besides,
they were all marked wrong."

She nodded, supped noisily from her bowl. After a moment, she wiped her toothless mouth,
said, "That's another thing, you see. Huë and

his rogues. Rogue drags can be as bothersome as
soldieries, yesindeed. I daresay he intends they
all go downriver, towards the hunting country. I
suppose he does his best to drive them so. But
they don't, me cockerel, no, they don't always
stay drove . . .

"How were they killed? Why, we poisoned
them. Never mind what poison. Leave at least
one of us be able to eat with an easy mind." She
bent over in a spasm of silent laughter.

Breakfast over, the day quite on its way and
the sun warmer, Ma'am Anna had the curtains
of the litter drawn back and relinquished a layer
or two of her coverings. The signal horn
sounded, and the nomads got on their way once
more. Far off in the bosky distance a faint
smudge showed in the air on the horizon. The
black stones of the sinister, alien Kar-chee castle
would not burn, but just about everything the
outlaw Doghunters had carried into it was flam-
mable.

"How did Huë get his scar, do you know?"

Her wrinkled lips came together in a pout. She
shook her head. "That was bad, yesindeed.
Someone with an -ix to the tail of his name—this
was when Huë was just small of size—decided
he didn't find him meek enough. Maybe was
drunk, too. However it was, he picked him up by
the scruff and tossed him in with a dragon-
cockerel that he happened to have around. The
cockerel was bigger than Huë was. . . . I don't
altogether blame the man. Things oughtn't to be
the way they are, altogether. But letting a mad-
man burn down the barn is no way to improve
them."

It was not a barn, exactly, which was burning back there. Her eyes followed his and, evidently, her thoughts, too. "Do they have dragons where you come from, coney? No. No, I suppose not. Because you never had no bloody Karches, did you, then? Lucky you. Did you know that they turn into Karches in the night-times? Yesindeed. So you be careful, hear me now, in wandering off in the dark. Particularly if we gets near unto The Bosky. Fierce, terribly fierce, is them Bosky drags."

Jon-Joras, torn between his desire to hear more of this new aspect of the legend—the dragon as were-Kar-chee—and his desire to hear more of the almost unknown land beyond the official territories of the city-states, decided that if he let her talk he might well hear of both. Which he did.

The nomads apparently knew very well that the dragons were not Kar-chee. How Hüe and Hüe's people had formed the notion that they were, Jon-Joras could not guess and didn't now try. The notion that at certain times and in certain places the dragons shifted their shapes into those of the long since departed Kar-chee was perhaps, however, not much more scientific. If at all.

". . . they even changes their smell, me cockerel," old Ma'am Anna hissed, wide-eyed in emphasis.

"I know how dragons smell, but how do . . . how did the—"

"The damned and bloody Karches? You knows that, too. You was in their castle for sure enough, yes indeed."

Was that faint and alien odor that he had noticed, then indeed that of the castle-keeping Karchee? Faint, faint, so very faint—yet still so distinct. The thought alone was capable of evoking it. Could it have lingered all these centuries? He could not say, could not begin, even, to conjecture. And, as for The Bosky—

Time and time again nomad bands had desired to graze their flocks on the rich and untouched grasses there. But the dragons were so incomparably fiercer in that region that it was long since any herdsmen had even thought of trying. Too, in times past, free farmers—individually and in groups and leagues—had endeavored either to settle in The Bosky or at least to pass through it in search of regions where the Syndics' writs did not run. Where farm land might stay farm land and not become a target-alley or a parade-ground, where potatoes might stay where planted until harvested and not be dug up and trampled into muck because they had impinged on dragon ground. That curious and strange loving hate existing between hunters and hunted . . . Off, then, their gear and baggage laden aboard crude wagons and on packhorses, did they have any; or bending beneath the weight themselves, did they have none, the free farmers had set off for finding places where they might be free indeed and farmers indeed and need nevermore be "dirty doghunters" save on their own account.

"Some come back quicker than they went, young outworlder. It made them content to suffer what they'd suffered in discontent but where the dragons don't fight unless they're coaxed or

goaded. I says, '*It* made them . . .' What did?
Why to see how terrible them awful Bosky drags
tore up them as went before them. In their blood
they saw them, yesindeed, mere bones and
shreds," Ma'am Anna sighed.

Jon-Joras caught at a word. " 'Some' came
back, you say—?"

"You mean, and what's of the others? Isn't it
clear? Them as was found torn and scattered,
was them that never come back."

He frowned and mused. There was nothing
utterly impossible in this account, nothing of the
historical absurdity of confusing Kar-chee with
dragon nor of the physical impossibility of the
one turning into the other and back again, so.
But there remained one considerable question
which alone put the whole matter into doubt.

"Are the dragons any bigger or any different
there than here?"

"Nope." Ma'am Anna smacked her gums.
"Just fiercer, like I say."

But . . ." And this was it: "Why should they *be*
fiercer there? I mean, with no one to hunt them
and bother them, you'd think they'd be *less*
fierce, wouldn't you?"

"No, I wouldn't," she said, with inflexible
logic; "because I knows they be *more* fierce. As to
why, hee hum, old as I am and not fit for much,
rather than go and maybe find out and be made
into salad meat, by your leave, me coney, I'll
stay over here and in ignorance."

And there the matter rested.

They were due to meet up with the main
horde at about noon; and, at about noon, they

did. The camp was, like a Gentleman's seat, a small city-state of its own. Tents and lean-tos dotted the area for about a mile, the small animals from which the fleeces evidently came milled and bleated, and ponies by the thousands —so it seemed—grazed in hobbles. And in the center was the great circular tent which was the Ma'am's capitol.

"Mutton!" she directed, as she was being lifted down.

"I want me fat mutton—grilled and crisp and chopped fine!"

"Yes, our Ma'am."

"And tomorrow I want the flocks taken up to the white stony brook—that was all burnt over a while back, should be nice, fresh grazing."

"Yes, our Ma'am."

"Tomorrow. Not today. Today I want the children to go up there instead. Have 'em bring all the buckets and baskets—they'll be good berrying there."

"Yes, our Ma'am."

They set her down on a pile of fleeces and blankets raised off the floor, propped her up with pillows.

"Did Cuthy beg Brun's pardon, publicly, like I said?"

"He did, our Ma'am."

"Paid him twelve goats, too?"

"Twelve goats, our Ma'am. He wanted to include a wether, and Brun wouldn't have it, but the Elders said a goat was a goat, so he took it, rather than do without."

She nodded. "That's right. There's many a buck with stones that does the nannies no good;

this way he won't have to wonder. . . . Teach
Cuthy to leave Brun's woman alone. All right!
All right! Get out, now! Stop vexing me old
head with all your questions. Bring enough mutton for the outworld boy, too. Come sit . . . of
whatever way is comfortable for you . . . over by
me. Now, then—"

She took his hand. "We'll be here long enough
for you to mend. What do you think on doing,
once you can ride again?" He said that he
thought he'd rather not ride again at all, asked if
she couldn't send a messenger for a flyer to take
him back to Peramis. "Ah, me cockerel, but isn't
that part of the question? What do you think on
doing, once you're back in Peramis?"

Seeing that he was still not understanding her,
she explained in detail. What did he plan to say
about things? The rogue dragon . . . the mysterious, secretive Kar-chee castle and what it
contained . . . the nomad raid . . . He began to
catch her drift; asked what she thought he
should say.

Slowly, the old head nodded.

"That's the point. Yes indeed, that's the
point. You see, me coney, few things are ever
simple. If you go back and talk free, then the
wasp's-nest is stirred up for sure. The armies
come out. We don't want that, for our own reasons. And when the armies are out of the States,
what's then? Riots, I hear, in Peramis. Put down
by the army. Maybe the Dogrobbers would just
as soon sacrifice their tricks off in the woods, for
a chance to burn things up."

He had to agree that it was not simple. Certainly, he could not forget what had been done to

the son of Aëlorix, his former host, to whose salt
he assuredly owed something. Certainly, he
could not deny that the outlaws had just grievances. More: they, too, had been his hosts. Finding him wandering near their secret place, they
had been justified in taking him prisoner; but
they had treated him with kindliness, once he
was safe inside.

"Is Huë still alive?" he asked.

She shrugged. "I don't know for sure. The
men told me they saw him go down, before they
had to withdraw. But they're not sure he wasn't
in shape to get up again. Why?"

He told her why. "*'They shall all be killed, every
one—in the egg, and out . . .'*"

"When things reach such a stage," Jon-Joras
said, "the right which is based on having been
wronged becomes a wrong in itself."

The old woman stooped her chin upon her
hands. She sighed. "Well . . . Well . . . We have
to think. Both of us. But not now. Here they are
with the mutton. If there is one thing I don't
have to puzzle about, it's mutton," she said, contentedly. "I like it fat. And I like it crisp."

From time to time in the next few days, Jon-
Joras thought about his forcibly neglected
duties. He knew that Por-Paulo would not blame
him or think less of him; besides, the Hunt Company was experienced enough to fill the gap well
enough in making arrangements. Meanwhile,
there lay open before him the life of the nomad
encampment, utterly strange to him except as a
half-forgotten paragraph in half-forgotten books.
In a way it was far freer than any life he had ever
known, but it was subject nonetheless to the

sway of law. The tribesmen elected their council of elders and over the elders was the old queen, Ma'am Anna, who ruled them all as the benevolent semi-despotic matriarch of a family. But even old Anna had to go where the grass was green and the water was sweet; even she could not prevent storm and snow and flood and disease.

She gave Jon-Joras a pony, as casually as she might give a child a sweet; the tribe had plenty of ponies, after all(she said), and she could not burden her litter with him forever. He thanked her for the gift—somewhat fearfully remembering how sore he had been from his first ride— and somewhat reluctantly, realizing that this probably meant he was not going back to Peramis in the immediate future. But there was nothing he could really do about it . . . except make the most of it.

He learned how to ride the shaggy little beast, gingerly at first, then with growing confidence and enjoyment, over the low swelling hills and flatlands fresh with new herbage; only a fleecy pad for a saddle, only a braided grass rope for a bridle, the sweetsmelling wind in his face instead of the strong musty odor of sheep which hung around the camp site.

Sheep and shepherds alike fell behind him as, food in his saddle-sack and water in his leather bottle, he set as his goal some distant landmark —a wooded hilltop, a pond glittering in the sun, a valley opening wide in welcome—and headed for it. No one, least of all Ma'am Anna, seemed concerned about his possibly not returning, any more than his earlier hosts, the outlaws, had been. He was after all as bound by his limited knowledge of the terrain as by the encircling high black walls around the castle of the swarming, conquering, and now-vanished Kar-chee.

Both Jon-Joras and the tribesmen, however, were in this guilty of one mutual mistake. Both realized that he did not know enough about the countryside to escape successfully. Neither realized that he knew little enough about it to get lost successfully. But he did.

Born and raised upon the infinitely controlled planet which was M. M. *beta,* where everything was so complex as to be simple, so controlled, so subdued, so organized, that even a blind man could hardly lose his way; Jon-Joras—despite theoretically knowing better—did not consider the possibility that one wooded hill, one pond, one valley, might well look just the same to him as another. He had always found his way back successfully before. If by nothing else, he guided himself automatically by the almost tidal regularity of the flocks and herds as they drifted back, campwards, as the day drew to a close.

He never thought to ask, and no one thought to inform him, that the lands towards which he rode that day had been so thoroughly grazed that the flocks and herds had been diverted from them, sent elsewhere. Once outside the perimeter of the camp Jon-Joras rode through empty fields—but this meant nothing to him. He noted the brook to leftwards, and headed in its general direction. But much broken land lay between them, and the source of the stream was in one of the many declivities he was bound to avoid. So when, at last, he finally saw a brook to his left, he did not realize that it was not the same brook but another and a farther one. Guiding himself by its course, eventually he turned the pony's head and began (so he thought) to ride back towards the encampment.

The cooling air and the still-empty landscape told him of his escape. But it was an escape as useless as it was inadvertent, one of which he could make no use. He had no idea of where he was, none of where he wanted to go, and (he realized with some surprise) little of even where he wanted to be. There on the hilltop in the sallow light of lowering day, M. M. *B* seemed infinitely far off in space and time and reality, Peramis was the mere thin fabric of a dream, and the encampment of the tribe little more than a setting from a 3D drama or travelogue.

He sighed. After a moment he began riding his mount in a slow circle on the rise of ground. He saw nothing and nothing and yet nothing. Sunshine and clouds wheeled in counter-circles, slotted shafts of light broke through the gathering dusk, and in one such thrust of brightness he saw three small figures riding along far away and below. He thumped the pony in the ribs and rode towards them.

They were long in hearing him, indeed, it was only after he ceased to call after them that they turned around, perhaps having heard the sound of the hooves . . . perhaps not even having precisely heard them . . . but become somehow aware of . . . something. However it was, they turned, drew reign, awaited him.

They were three in number—one was an older

man, one was a younger man, one was a woman.
To be more exact, a girl. To be even more exact,
the girl who had repulsed his assistance in the
mob scene before the Hall of Court . . . the girl
whom he had seen and who had fled from him in
the woods between the fatal coming of the great
rogue dragon and his capture by the outlaw
Doghunters.

She had said something upon seeing him now
and, obviously, recognizing him; something
swift and low-voiced to her companions. And
then for a long while, all four of them riding
through the long, slow twilight over the empty
plains, she said nothing, but slumped her chin
into the blue cloak whose folds enveloped her.

The older man was a swart, stocky, grizzle-
bearded fellow, his knees stuck out at angles
from the sides of his thin gaunt horse. He wore a
long cloak of the same blue as the girl, but, cast
half aside, it revealed a garb of greasy buckskin
beneath. Gold rings glittered in his hairy ears.
His male companion was something else altogether—young, slender, upright and trim . . .
elegant was the word which occurred to Jon-Joras. His tunic was Gentleman's white, his
trousers the elaborate embroidered affair worn
on festivals by tribesmen, and his cloak—arranged with elaborate neatness so as to leave his
arms free—was fastened across his chest with a
silver chain and clasp. A bracelet of gold chased-
work encircled a wrist held out as stiff and proud
as if it bore a hawk.

At length the elder cleared his throat and spat.
He scratched himself reflectively. "I've been

thinking on what you said before, Henners," he observed. "And I can't see that I agree, no, not one bit. There is nothing at all wrong with the triolet."

"Nonsense, Trond," Henners said, vigorously. "It is archaic, contrived, artificial, jejeune —and anything else you like. It altogether lacks the simplicity and directness of the couplet, neither does it lend itself to amplified assonance and alliteration."

Trond screwed his face up into a truely hideous squint, compounded with a frown. "But the couplet"—the last word exploded into an enormous eructation—"the couplet is so monotonous!"

And so they rode on, as the air turned blue and the sky went purple and the first tiny stars appeared, discussing different modes and meters of poetry; and finally the bright and dancing light of a fire shone before them. And another, and another. Voices haled them, figures rose and crowded around. The girl dismounted, someone took her horse, she vanished from Jon-Joras's sight.

"Fellow poets," said Henners, gesturing, "allow me to present our guest, one Jon-Joras by name, an outworlder and sometime semi-captive of those coarse persons, the Northern Tribe. I think we may be of some small assistance to him in the matter of getting him back to a state . . . and I think we will find him not ungenerous, hem, hem, in the matter of expenses. Well! Are we not to eat and drink before falling to the making of new verses and rhymes, the chief end of such portion of mankind as dare deem itself civilized?"

Invitations were at once shouted, the guest was assisted from his pony and led to a seat by the largest of the fires where a pair of lambs were grilling on a spit over a bed of coals. Someone thrust a goblet into his hand, of some drink which managed to taste both sweet and acid at the same time; and strong, and smelling of honey.

"First verse!" a voice close to him called. Others took it up. "First verse! Guest! Outworlder! First Verse!"

The realization that he was to compose, instant and impromptu, a short poem, found Jon-Joras with an empty mind. Empty, that is, of everything except the feeling that there was something odd about the lambs which were becoming supper. He held up his hand, the crowd became silent. He spoke:

> *"Three rode forth, and four returned*
> *When supper grilled and fire burned.*
> *A mystery they found, ere sleep:*
> *Whence came lambs, when there's no sheep?"*

The briefest of quiets followed the recitation. Then it was swallowed up in a burst of laughter. Someone pounded him on the back. Someone poured more drink into his golden goblet. And someone on the other side of the fire, whose face he could not distinguish, started a reply.

> *"Such miracles you find, our guest,*
> *Along with drink and food and rest.*
> *The truth we tell, although it grieves:*
> *The simple fact is—we are thieves!"*

VI

POETS THERE were on MM *beta,* though mostly
employing verse forms so involved and elaborate
as to make the triolet seem simpler than the
couplet. And there were thieves there, too, although even the apprentice ones would scarcely
bother with anything as small as a lamb. Poetic
thieves, however, or thieving poets—this was
something new to Jon-Joras. He suspected it
might be something new (or, at any rate, something different) to students of societal set-ups
throughout all the teeming galaxy.

And so, there by the leaping flames, he
learned and he listened—amused, amazed, dis-
approving, entranced—while Henners recited
(in couplets and quatrains) his exploits in re-
moving the jewels and gold and silver plate of
His Serene Supremacy the Chairman of the
Board of Syndics of Drogue, while the latter sat
at meat in his high chamber.

With guests.

He was mildly annoyed at the distraction of
having a voice break in on the recitation . . . at
first. But when the words sank in, he forgot
Henners and all his works.

"She's a mean one, that baggage . . . isn't
she?"

Jon-Joras, turning his head and seeing Trond, face reddened by the fire light, had somehow no doubt who was meant by "she."

"Who *is* she?" he asked, half-whispering. Trond jerked his head to the left, moved off, and Jon-Joras followed him. Henners' voice was still audible when they stopped at last, but the words could no longer be made out. A fat and gibbous moon rode the cloud-flecked skies and afforded plenty of light to the park-like glade where the thieves' jungle was set up.

"Who is she?" Trond repeated the question, sat himself on a moss-covered tree trunk lying where it had fallen in some long-ago storm. He did not answer the question, said, instead, "She claims you're following her. . . ."

Speechless indignation followed by indignant speech. She claimed that he was following *her?* If the truth was anything at all like that, it was strictly the other way around. He told the older man of finding her in the mob scene in Peramis when the Doghunter had been convicted of killing the Gentleman, of his own attempt to help her and how it had been repulsed—almost rabidly.

"That could have been an accident, our meeting the first time. She couldn't have known I was going to be there, I certainly didn't know she was going to be there. And as for the second time—" Abruptly, he stopped. Did Trond or any of his fellows know about the Kar-chee castle and what was being done there? And, assuming that he and they didn't, did Jon-Joras want them to? Quick reflection decided him that he didn't. He went on, a bit lamely, "—and the sec-

ond time I was just lost in the woods, I'd gotten
separated from the people I was with, and I was
picked up by some Doghunters.

"I had no notion she'd be wandering the same
woods. And this last time, I—"

"You got lost," said Trond, nodding, ex-
pressionlessly. "Again."

The night was warm, but the young man felt
his face go warm. "It may sound like an unlikely
coincidence," he said, defensively, "but you have
to remember that I'm an outworlder . . . a
stranger. . . . And besides—how could I have
known that she—and you—would be riding
along at just that time?"

Trond grunted. He produced an oddly-shaped
piece of wood, thrust it into a pouch and did
something to it, blew on the end of a stick he'd
brought with him from the fire, and, when it
glowed red, thrust the device into his mouth and
touched it with the ember end. Odd little noises,
then a cloud of smoke . . . and another . . . the
acrid odor made Jon-Joras cough a bit—and
then he remembered. Tobacco! Its use had not
followed mankind outward to the stars, and even
here on its native world it was suppose to be all
but extinct. Where had Trond gotten the ancient
herb? For surely the Poets cultivated no crops!
Most likely he had stolen it.

"Well," said Trond, on a prolonged note, with
a puff, "I'm just telling you what she says. I
could think of a lot of ways it might be true . . .
if I was minded to . . . but I'm not. Why not?
Because. Like I say. She's a mean one, that baggage. As the triolet says—"

But Jon-Joras did not at that moment want to

know what the triolet said. He grasped Trond's knee, and repeated, "Who is she? *Who?*"

Trond puffed at his pipe a moment more. "Her name," he said, "is Lora."

Lora. "No . . . It doesn't mean a thing to—"

"Maybe her father's name might mean a thing to you."

"Her father?"

Trond nodded. His pipe made a gurgling sound. "Yes. Tall, thin, *ukh*-looking man. Name of Huë."

Away in the night Henners' voice ceased. There were cheers and applause. Jon-Joras, feeling stunned, feeling stupid, said, "But *she* hates me. Her father doesn't hate me."

Trond made a noise which might have been a grunt or a chuckle. "Don't fool yourself. Of course he hates you. You're an outworlder, aren't you? Well, figure it out. According to him, according to her, if you—all of you—didn't come here to hunt, the whole system would collapse. It doesn't pay for itself, that's for sure. Not hate you? He's just older, has more control over his feelings, that's all."

In his mind's eye Jon-Joras saw once again that grim, gaunt figure, preternaturally rigid, stalking the halls and walls and ramparts of the great black stronghold of the cold-blooded, castle-keeping Kar-chee; heard the screams of the rogue dragon in the pit, trained by torment —dragons: Huë's enemy: prepared to fall upon Huë's other enemy. Once again he saw the figure of the dummy that was no dummy, trussed and tied, then tossed and toothed and torn to bleeding fragments; heard the outlaw's outraged cry, "That . . . is what happens to *traitors!*"

Huë hated him? Yes . . . it was clear enough now that he must. And what must he think of him now? What, but that he himself, Jon-Joras, freed by the nomad raiders, taking with him the castle's secret, was himself a traitor? And Jon-Joras imagined himself bound and fastened in the dragon-pit, watching and waiting and hearing and smelling the maddened creature come trampling down the pounded ground towards him. . . .

Nothing could save him from that, were Huë to take hold of him again. He felt his chin tremble and his skin grow cold and wet. If the daughter did not believe that he was accidentally present in the forest along the way to the outlaws' castle, would the father? Not likely.

"They mustn't take me," he muttered, his voice uneven. "Not again. Not again."

Trond pursed his wide mouth, waved his hand. "Not much danger of that," he said. "You're worth more to us by getting you back to one of the states. Provided, of course," he raised his eyebrows, "provided, of course, you meant what you said. About our, uh, expenses. . . ?"

Jon-Joras assured him that, of course, he meant it. "Jetro Yi, the Hunt Company representative, has an ample fund, sufficient to repay you. Generously. Generously!"

The other man rose, stretched. "That's all right, then," he said, yawning. "We'll get you back, all right. Oh—" A sudden thought seemed to occur to him. He put a hand on Jon-Joras's shoulder, leaned so close that the reek of his tobacco was strong in the cool night air.

"You know one of ours, by the name of Thorm? Kind of a bandy-legged fellow with bulging blue eyes and his verses don't scan? No? Well . . . Anyway . . . Watch out for him. Kind of carefully. Let's be getting back to the fire, it's growing cold."

The moon continued to wander up the sky and a light mist was settling in the glade. The effect was luminous and ghostly.

"Thorm," Jon-Joras repeated. "Why should I? I don't know him at all. Does he know me?"

Trond stopped to rap his pipe against the boll of a tree. "No," he said. "But he knows Lora."

Jon-Joras recognized Thorm at once when, as soon as they got back to the fire, the man stepped forward, gave him an ugly look, spat on the ground, then stooped, dug up the clot of earth with the spittle on it, and flung it into his face.

"Well, *well*," said Henners, in a tone of pleasant surprise. "This *is* an honor, young our guest. You may neither realize nor appreciate it, but it is truly very seldom that we accord the dignity of challenged combat, and all that it implies, to those not of our own select group. And certainly not as soon as this. Some might be inclined to disallow it. . . . Eh?" He looked around in a politely questioning manner.

Trond said, "It's not customary. It's what you might call an innovation."

There was a murmur of approbation. "Like free verse," someone added, disapprovingly. But another voice said, "I wouldn't be inclined to quibble. The guest's poesies were really quite acceptable, I thought, from a non-poet—wouldn't you agree? Voice vote! Voice vote!"

And the *Gos* outnumbered the *Nos*.

"Very well," Henners said, equitably. "It's *go,* then—Oh, if the guest accepts. Do you?" he asked. "Do you choose to accept the challenge and all that it implies?"

Jon-Joras felt that he would much rather not; much, much rather not. But he felt unable to say so. And he asked what other choice he had, instead.

Henners cleared his throat, frowned slightly. "I, well, really, the other choice is so very unpleasant, I would really rather not go into it. My word as a rhymer. Accept the challenge. Eh?"

And Jon-Joras nodded. And a cheer went up.

A space was cleared, two wicked looking knives produced, one given to Thorm and one to Jon-Joras. There were ritual preliminaries, but he did not hear them. A chill was on his heart, and with all his chill heart he cursed this the world of his race's birth and all its bloody ways. Knives! Duels! Combats! What did he know of such things? On his own home world nothing more dangerous than wrestling—

And, *"Go!"* cried a hundred throats.

Thorm came forward in a sort of dancing crouch that instantly put Jon-Joras in mind of a stance quite popular at the Collegium; finding that the knife in his hand not only felt unfamiliar but was likely to impede him, he thrust it between his teeth, and then, almost automatically, without a second's hesitation, leapt forward,

grasped Thorm by the right ankle, and pulled
him off his feet.

A cry of delight went up from the crowd, including one man who was casually whittling the
end of a long stick.

Thorm fell, Jon-Joras released the ankle and
reached for the shoulders. But Thorm, whose
knife was not between his teeth, slashed at him;
Jon-Joras swerved, missed the shoulders, felt the
knife tear his side. At the moment what he felt
was not pain, but a sort of sick surprise.

They broke and parted. Jon-Joras had
achieved the first fall, but Thorm, the first blood;
and as they were engaged, not in a wrestling
match but a duel to the death, progress so far
was definitely his. One thing was clear: Jon-Joras must henceforth concentrate, not on his
opponent's shoulders, but on the wrist of the
hand holding the knife.

What followed was a nightmare. The thud of
body against body, the smell of sweat, the fear,
the trembling, the scramble towards safety, the
eye ever on the bloody knife . . .

. . . the bloody knife which once more, then
twice more, then a third time more, grew blood-
ier yet from his own torn flesh.

It happened thus: Thorm had left himself
open and Jon-Joras jumped him, had—almost—
his fingers upon the wrist of the knife hand, felt
his foot turn upon a pebble, swerved without
meaning to or being able to prevent it, was
seized by Thorm and carried backward, downward, backward—Then he partly righted
himself, did, indeed, grasp the dangerous wrist.
And so they found themselves, half-crouching,

half-kneeling, unable to move one the other. But
it was Jon-Joras, held fast by Thorm's arms and
legs whose back was to the fire. And his back
was very close to the fire, and soon the smell of
his singed tunic came to his nostrils, and after
that began the pain. Pain unbearable.

He did not later remember doing what he
knew he must have done. All he remembered
was, suddenly, in the sudden silence, seeing—
over Thorm's shoulder—the handle of the knife
buried in Thorm's back. Thorm never said a
word nor made a sound as he slumped, sagged,
sank with all his weight into Jon-Joras's arms.
Who, his back seeming all afire, screamed, gave
a mighty thrust forward, felt himself staggering
backward—

—and was grasped by many willing hands
and pulled away. His smoking tunic was torn
from his bleeding body. Voices cried, *"Take!
Take!"* He stared at them, stupidly.

"Take what?" he asked.

For answer, someone seized the knife from
Thorm's hand (the body lay where it had fallen,
on its back, the prominent blue eyes staring at
the starry sky, mouth open on a note of unut-
terable surprise), someone ripped open tunic
and pulled up shirt, someone parted the pale
skin of the chest with the knife, reached in,
twisted, tugged, hand emerging with something
dark-red and dripping. It was in an instant
skewered on a long stick and someone handed
the stick to Jon-Joras.

He grasped hold of it automatically and un-
comprehendingly. "What . . . what do I do with
it?" he asked.

There was a *huh?* of astonishment; then the man who had whittled the sharp end to the stick, this man said, *"Do* with it? Why, what else would you do with your enemy's heart—except grill it and eat it?"

Body shuddering, face twitching, Jon-Joras held it at arm's length, as far away as he could, straining to be quit of it. But it didn't vanish, it stayed where it was, and it dripped. "No . . ." he said. "No . . . No . . . I can't . . ."

"You *can't?* But—why *not?"*

Neither could he vanish himself. He forced himself to answer. "It. Is. Against. My custom."

At length the puzzled silence was broken by Henners. He took the stick with the pierced heart out of Jon-Joras's clenched, stained hand. "Well, if you can't, you can't," he said. "Of course, one must keep one's custom. But . . . Still . . . Well, all I have to say is, in that case, you've wasted a damned good man."

Had Jon-Joras wisdom to know and freedom to choose, he could scarcely have selected anything better for him just at that time than that which was selected for him. No sooner was his back dressed with scented oil and his wounds medicated and bandaged, then Henners and Trond asked if he felt well enough to ride.

"It won't be very far," the older man said, a hint of constraint in his voice. "Then we'll take water."

Jon-Joras said that he did. "I'd appreciate it," he added, "if my pony could be returned, with my thanks, to Ma'am Anna. I don't want her to worry about where I am." She might worry

about other things connected with his leaving
her custody, but he could not help that.

Henners nodded, and they were on their way.
The campfires had died down and the camp was
sunk in sleep. Of Lora, there was no sign. The
moon was low on the horizon as they rode along
the trail—trail which must have begun to follow
water quite some while before Jon-Joras noticed
it—which was only when they suddenly swerved
and started to splash across the ford. The
splashing must have been signal enough to alert
the three men who came out of the moon-mist
and darkness to meet them on the other side.

In the low-voiced talk which followed, he took
no part until Henners broke off and spoke to
him. "That's right, isn't it—you'll pay the expenses of the boaters, the watermen, as well as
ours?"

"Yes."

He followed them along the narrow beach
south of the ford, trees and bluff overhanging
closely, the air very dark and cool and damp, the
water widening, the water mumbling and cooing
to itself in a low, slow, confident voice. "Best dis-
mount now," someone said. "Take my hand,"
someone said. There was a shoving and straining
in the darkness deep into the banks and suddenly there was a boat upon the water and they were
in the water and it rose over their feet and onto
their legs. "Take my hand . . . here . . . gently . . ." And they were in the boat.

For yet a little while the moon sent silver rip-
ples and silver mist to mark their passage as they
glided (with only now and then the plash of a
paddle, so it seemed) straight down the water

into the huge and ghostly moon. Then, slowly, then, rapidly, it sank into the water and was gone. For a while all seemed so black. Later, starshine showed them their way. And then the stream disembogued into a wider water which Jon-Joras knew must be the great river itself; it shook the long, low and narrow craft for a moment; then the boaters lifted their paddles in unison. *Ssss* . . . the paddles plunged in the bosom of the water . . . *ssss* . . . they rose again . . . And so, hissing the rhythm, the watermen guided their craft steadily out into the quiet water of the clear channel. And all of his sickness, his sorrow, his disquiet and his pain seemed to leave him, seemed to sink into the broad and watery plain he rode upon, seemed to wash away. And a cleanness and a quiet took ahold of him, and he floated off into a sleep.

He awoke into a misty, pearl-gray dawn. Henners sitting upright looked as trig and elegant as ever; Trond sprawled on a gunwhale, snoring loudly. Now for the first time Jon-Joras was able to get a clear look at the boaters—all of a family, seemingly, or perhaps their looks were all of a clan—race—caste—rufous, long-haired little men, with skinny legs tucked under them as they tirelessly plied their paddles.

Well before the sun had done its work of burning the concealing mist off the water, the watermen had taken the boat off the main stream and up a narrow inlet leading into a still narrower, winding creek; and moored her to a skeleton tree near a tiny clearing. Quickly, they cut brush for a lean-to, trimmed the short and springy-twiggy sprigs of an evergreen for bedding. Trond half-scrambled, was half-pulled ashore; like a sleep-walker, began to snore before he sank down again. And they with him.

Once, springing stiff and terror-stricken from the slackness of dreamless slumber, Jon-Joras heard a dragon sounding its deep and melancholy mating call. But it was not near, and when next it came it was farther yet away. And the fatigue, and the ability of his young and healthy body to respond to it, was strong upon him; and he slept again. Not always restfully, to be sure: for once he waked to think he smelled again the ancient reek of the castle, and once he dreamed he woke to see a great, gaunt Kar-chee shadow in the moonlight. . . .

When they were next all awake the boaters had speared fish and proceeded now to cook it. Trond smoked his pipe, Henners carefully made his toilet, the rivermen pretended to count their paddles lest the poets had stolen one of them . . . so, easily, the hours passed till dark came again and the voyage was resumed. Jon-Joras knew now what the plan was and what was expected him: a landing near the thickets by the shallows of northern Peramis, a riverman to go with message to Jetro Yi, the Company man to come with the money to pay the "expenses," and a point of honor to say nothing till time enough had passed for the guides (and guards) to be safely all away.

This was well enough with Jon-Joras. He felt slightly feverish, rather light of body and mind, day and night passed like gentle and unimportant dreams . . . in the background there were hints of hideous things . . . but only hints . . .

and only in the background. . . .

He was not quite sure how many of these days and nights there were (though surely not many). There was the hot smell of the grass and the resinous scent of the evergreen boughs, Trond and Henners now talking of Lora's attempts to urge the Poets into counter-action against the nomad Tribesmen, now reciting to each other old verses or new or once again comparing couplets and quatrains and sonnets and triolets; the ruddly little rivermen squinting at them and him good-naturedly and not understanding or caring about a word of it. There was the river at night, throbbing with its own great pulse in the incredibly yellow moonlight, golden buttery reflections rippling and melting and coalescing; and on a night like that a wedge of boats advanced towards them from downstream and another had spread out behind them from upstream, and—

"Yield! *Yield!*" cried voices all around, Trond swore, Henners wordlessly slipped from his clothes and was pale as moonlight as he dove into the stream, the boaters pulled their vessel around and darted for the nigher shore, but then a bow twanged and one of the watermen cried out and caught at the shaft in his shoulder.

VII

"THAT WAS just for formality," said a voice from the now hostile night. "We have guns, too. *Yield!*"

And added, for further formality, "—in the name of His Serene Supremacy, the Chairman of Drogue, who keeps the peace of The River."

"We yield," said Trond, sullenly. And the dark, swift craft were all about them.

"Go forward, boaters," the voice directed. Two of the three played their paddles in silence, a silence broken by occasional calls from those guard-boats that had gone in search of Henners . . . evidently without success, for they by and by rejoined the formation.

They landed at a wharf bright with lamplight, and Jon-Joras, finally and completely emerged from the doze or daze which engaged him through most of the trip, now observed the men who were surrounding them—after having emerged with precision from the flotilla. Challenges were evidently not the only things done with formality in Drogue; its armed force, in form-fitting black with adornments of crimson and gold, made a considerable contrast to that of Peramis, which (he remembered) was clad in loose greendrab.

"You are now under charge of arrest," said a

tall and grim-faced officer. "My report will note
that you yielded on the second challenge." He
asked and received their names, proceeded:
"The man Henners—who has succeeded in
evading us for now—was indicted in absentia for
grand robbery, *lèse majesté,* and sedition of conduct. *You,* the man Trond—"

"I can produce a hundred witnesses that I was
nowhere near Drogue when Henners—"

"—by your presence with the man Henners
tonight, have become guilty of consorting with
criminals."

Trond shrugged. "The outworlder has nothing to do with all that," he said. "He was lost
and were guiding him back down to Peramis—
that's all."

As if Trond had not spoken, the officer continued, *"You,* the man Jon-Joras, by your presence
with the man Trond, have become guilty of consorting with criminals."

Aghast, Jon-Joras cried, "But how far can you
carry that?"

The officer, who had turned away with a
gesture, now half-turned his head. "Infection
never ceases," he said. And continued on his
way. Even before he had spoken, the black-clad
river troops had closed in on Trond and Jon-Joras, bound their arms at wrists and elbows. No
sooner had he uttered his last sibilant and
turned his head away, than the two prisoners
were led off at a fast half-march, half-trot that
left no moment for anything but compliance.

The boaters had not been mentioned in the
charges of arrest, had stood by with mournful
faces and drooping heads, as if they knew what

was coming. What came was a brusque grunt of a command from a petty officer. A pair of axes glinted, raised in the air. The rivermen broke out into a wail. The stove boat burned slowly. But it burned.

Jon-Joras, well aware that he was unlikely to find here any faintest reflection of the enlightened penal policies of his homeworld, had conjectured vision of cells dank and narrow and festooned with fetters set into dripping walls. The reality was rather different.

They passed through a series of bleak and empty rooms whose desks and cabinets hinted at some activity during daylight hours. They passed through a room full of bustle and smells of food and drink—a sort of canteen for the troops—where a few score men in black and red and gold glanced at the prisoners and then returned to their eating and guzzling and gaming. Someone of them did indeed fling a question at the convoy's guards—

"What's ye got, Blue?"

"Candidates for Archie," was the curious answer. The questioner looked at them with briefly quickened interest and pursed his lips. Then he bent to his meat and turnips as if nothing else concerned him.

They passed then through a series of apartments in each of which (so it seemed) a grumbling turnkey rose up from his pallet on the floor to let them into the next, wife and children sometimes opening a sleepy eye to peer a moment, sometimes—more often—continuing to snore on. And, finally, the last thick and barred door behind them, the guard in charge rasped a metal-tipped rod against a great reticulation of a grill-work gate.

And then, impatient, seized hold of a rope and began to toll a brass-voiced bell. And at least a hundred human voices broke into clamor.

Dim and tiny lights burned overhead at intervals in the vast room, filthy rushes scattered underfoot, and from heaps of these reeds prisoners were still rising as the two new ones were let in through a narrow door in the great grill.

"Fresh meat!"

"New blood!"

"Who's them?"

"What's ye charges?"

The warder, roused from a little wooden room like a dog-kennel, cursed ineffectually, produced (after some search) a grubby and grimy little tattered book, signed in his new charges with his tongue protruding from the corner of his mouth. By the time he was done the other troopers were gone and many of the prisoners had returned to their sleep. Others, however, still crowded around and still put their questions.

The place—it was not so much a room or a hall or keep as simply a large leftover space inside the building—the place stank abominably, and many of those now thrusting forward their eager, open mouths, stank worse.

Trond, wincing, shoved them away—not gently. He peered through the rancid gloom, demanded, "Where's the Poets' Corner? Any poet here?"

The crowd muttered, milled around a bit, parted, finally, for a tall and thin and stooped

old man who came blinking forward to be identified by Trond before he had focused his own
blear old eyes.

"Serm. Still here, poor ancient?"

"Still here . . . Who's that? Trond; don't tell
me; it's Trond. Well . . . I don't know this young
sprig. Give me a rhyme, my sib, with your name
in acrostic."

But Jon-Joras, depressed, made no answer.
He breathed through his mouth. Trond and
Serm mumbled, low-voiced in each other's ears.
The warder had meanwhile simply returned to
his shed. Most of the other prisoners went back
to their heaps of rushes and committed them-
selves, sighingly, to sleep. Serm shuffled away,
Trond beckoned, Jon-Joras followed.

Followed to a corner by a narrow, slitted window, with its own lamp, and—actually—a
cleaner heap of rushes than were elsewhere, a
crude table, rickety chair, jug of water, and a
very worn blue riding cloak. Only the three of
them shared it. "This is what's called 'Poets'
Corner,'" Trond said, with a gesture and a
quirk of his mouth. "It don't look like much—
but compare it to the rest of this rat-trap: it's
palatial. And it's ours by right of tradition."

Old Serm nodded. "Used to be a flower in a
pot and a little bird in a cage. Died, both of
them." He drew in his breath with a gusty noise.

"Sure, living and dying
Is sorrow and sighing—"

With an abrupt change of manner, he said
"Young outworlder, tomorrow you must see the
Chairman. Insist on it. Do you hear? Insist on
it!" Then, with groans and creaks, he settled

down on his heap of reeds, took a corner of the cloak, and invited the two other occupants of Poets' Corner to share the rest between them.

Jon-Joras, when the sun had finally penetrated the prison-room, did insist on it. He insisted on it the next morning . . . and the next . . . and the next. . . . It became a ritual.

"Want to see The Man With The Hairy Nose, do y'?" asked the warder, with a small smile. Long years of constant communication with criminals had give him a complete command of their argot.

"I am informed that it's my right to petition the Puissant Chair for attention to grievance," said Jon-Joras.

The warder grunted, scratched his naval. "Your right, hey?"

"And I insist upon it."

Yawn. Stretch. Scratch again. The warder craned his neck to watch the progress of a nearby dice game. "Well . . ." after a long moment, "I'll pass the word along, sib. I'll pass the word along. . . ."

And so, eventually, the word was passed back.

"You, there. Archie-bait," said the warder one afternoon. "Strip down and wash your crummy rags and ribs. I'll open the water-room for y', there's wood for fire and pots to boil the fleas in."

"Good!" said Jon-Joras, peeling off his clothes and taking the little shovel of embers from the man. And—"What? *Soap?* Why—"

"Mustn't smell bad when you're up before The Man," the warder said. So Jon-Joras heated

water and boiled his clothes and enjoyed the lux-
ury of soap for the first time in—how long?—as
he scrubbed himself down in the dank and
seldom-used water-room. He wrapped himself in
the riding-cloak and waited for the garments to
dry.

Serm said: "Tell him you'll pay any fine
within reason. That dragon-cod can't even read
his own name unless it's written in gold ink."

And Trond said: "Your line has to be, that
you realize it's been all a mistake, in fact, it's
kind of amusing, and you're not mad at all. But
High King Pung-Pickle, or whatever his name is,
will be getting ready to tear the states apart,
board by board, if you don't show up—and
soon."

Serm said: "You must get word to our band.
To the Poets."

And Trond said: "You were lost in the woods
and we offered to guide you back for a fee. That's
all. It's a true word, isn't it? So—that's *all*. Huë?
You never even heard of Huë."

And at last the clothes were dry and Jon-Joras
followed the guards who held his tether, out into
the starlit, sweet-smelling night. A pony-wagon
was waiting, its sides enveloped in black curtains. They did not bother to explain or
apologize for binding his feet and gagging him.
The conclusion came to Jon-Joras, not for the
first time, that the exercise of civil rights in the
City-State of Drogue left a good deal to be desired.

Facing them at the other end of the long hall
was The Chair itself—so far, an unoccupied
piece of furniture. It was, however, the most

elaborate piece of furniture he had seen anywhere at anytime: high, enormous, carved pro-
fusely, polished, gilded, cushioned in velvet and
damask. He thought of the noisome and ver-
minous rushes on the hard, stinking, sodden
floor of the prison room. A bitter taste was in his
mouth.

The guards jerked him to a stop, removed his
gag. He, familiar, after all, with the intensely so-
phisticated court of King Por-Paulo, watched
with the interested eye of a connoisseur the cere-
monies which accompanied the entrance of His
Serene Supremacy, the Chairman, as the latter
took his seat on The Chair. Roëlorix III was a
swift and slender man in his late thirties; tucking
his purple-slippered feet under him, he made
slight movements of head and hand. The guards
nudged Jon-Joras.

Who identified himself as a Private Man of his
king, stated his reason for being here on Prime
World . . . "Earth," he corrected himself . . . and
went on to say, "I address The Puissant Chair
for attention to grievances."

The Puissant Chair, looking a little weary, a
little cynical, invited him—by the smallest
change of expression, to continue his address.
He explained his being present at the impromptu dragon hunt, described that melancholy scene. The Chairman at once became intent, and more and more so as Jon-Joras proceeded with his description of the Kar-chee Castle and what went on therein. He had only
hesitated an instant, recalling Trond's advice to
say nothing of it; then decided that it was best to
tell the whole truth.

Indeed, he spoke freely of everything . . . omitting only the matter of his duel to the death with Thorm. It did not seem to him to be pertinent, and, besides, he could not bring himself to dwell upon those still horrifying memories.

"The two men of the People called Poets agreed to guide me back to Peramis," he said, concluding, "and therefore I went with them."

"And therefore," said the Chairman, speaking for the first time; "and therefore you traveled at night and concealed yourself during the day."

"I—I never considered the implications of that," Jon-Joras stammered. It was true; he never had. "It was night when we decided to leave, and it seemed natural to rest during the day. . . . Conceal? I didn't . . . I suppose I took it for granted that it was the local customary way—"

The Chairman, in a movement so swift—yet completely unhurried—that Jon-Joras scarcely observed the details of it, rose to his feet. Pointing his finger at Jon-Joras, he said, in a clear, quick voice, "You lie. You have consorted not only with thieves but with outlaws, and with rebels—the worst, the most dangerous kind of outlaws—at that. You have condemned yourself by the imprecations of your own mouth, and this is the verdict which we have reached in Our capacity as Chief Magistrate: that at a time to be decided upon you be taken to a place to be decided upon and there bound hand and foot and hanged by the heels and shot to death by archery."

Dumbfounded, and too incredulous to feel either anger or fear, Jon-Joras watched the chairman walk out with quick, concise strides.

He barely felt the gag forced back into his mouth. And then the guards led him away.

Trond winced, grunted, shook his head. Serm was remorseful, full of self-reproach. "I should never have put that notion in your ear," he moaned, "about asking to see the Nose. Who'd have thought it? It passes understanding—doesn't it. Trond? *Never* heard of such a thing—arching an outworlder! Did you, Trond?"

"No! And I'm not going to hear about it now, either," Trond said, vigorously. "Don't you let your cullions crawl, young fellow—this is a time for desperate measures, and I'm going to take them, too!"

The warder looked at them, as they approached, with melancholy satisfaction. "Sometimes, don't pay, to insist," he observed.

Trond shrugged. "Well, like I tell him, no one lives forever, anyway. Right?"

"Right."

" 'Don't wiggle,' I tell him; 'hang still, give the archies a clear target, soon be over.' Right?"

"That's what *I* always tell 'em. Right."

"So, what we want to do, we want to give him a big good-by party—drinks, eats—the works."

The warder slowly drooped his right eyelid and his lower lip in understanding and assent. Then he rubbed a thumb and a forefinger together. Trond slipped a ring from off one of his own fingers, placed it in his palm. Instantly, the warder said, "That bandy won't bring much." But he didn't stop looking at it. A glint of light reflected in his eye. He didn't stop looking at it.

"It'll bring enough. What do you says,

Wards? Sell it and keep half for yourself and buy
booze and bites with the rest."

He held out the palm. The warder took the
band with restrained eagerness, sighed with
hypocritical regret. "Too bad . . . too bad . . . a
nice ring . . . a nice fellow . . . Sure. Sure. Glad
to do what I can. *Glad* to. Never mind *my* cut. I
won't take a thing. Depend on me. I'll see you
get what you need."

The ring vanished into a pocket inside his
greasy old shirt. Trond thanked him, led Jon-
Joras away. "There's a rogue, if you like," he
muttered. " 'Won't take a thing'! He won't take
more than two thirds of it, is what he means."

Only now did the fear of death enter the
younger man's heart. He felt it chill and swell.
"Listen," he said, uncertainly, "I don't want to
have any parties, I want to—"

"Want to get out. Right." Trond took his
hand and patted it. "Have no fear, friend. Wards
can't dispose of that bandy in any regular jewels
shop. One look at him, they'd call the guards.
No . . . Only a fence will buy it from him, and
there's only one fence in Drogue that handles
bandies of that value: Old Boke: Old Boke will
have the whole story out of him before he pays
him a penny.

"*And*—" he gave Jon-Joras's cold and sweating hand a final pat-pat, "Old Boke will pass the
word along where it will do the most good. The
Poets have their friends in town. Have no fear, I
tell you again. And sleep light tonight. You listening? *Sleep light. . . .*"

In fact, of course, Jon-Joras didn't really sleep

at all. As, one by one, the scant oils in the tiny slut-lamps of the prison room were used up and the smoldering wicks vanished into winking red little eyes in the darkness and then were gone, he sank into a kind of feverish phantasmagora. He felt ill and dizzy; the vertigo helped persuade him that he could feel what it was like to be upside down; the ankle-bands of his shoes became the bonds fastening his feet; and every rough rush penetrating his loosened clothes became the shaft of an arrow penetrating his frightened flesh.

Then, suddenly, the illusion changed. All, all had been a dream: the raid on the great, gaunt Kar-chee castle, the time spent with the nomad tribes, the duel with Thorm, the long trip down the great river, capture and imprisonment: all a dream. He was still in the Kar-chee castle and none of the rest had happened. But—and this he knew with frightening and absolute certainty—it was all *going* to happen, every bit and detail of it. And he could not prevent it, it had already begun, and the proof of this was that once again he smelled the smoke of burning torches.

With a stifled groan and a sigh, chiefly of relief —for even the uncertainty of life with Huë was better than lying under sentence of death—he raised his head in order to see the light of the flambeaux he was sure he smelled. He wondered, as he did so, if he must follow the predestined pattern of events indeed . . . or if there were not some possibility of escape. And then his mind became suddenly as wide-wake as his body.

There was a curious scuffling sound faintly

over his head. A change in the rhythm of their
breathing told him that both Trond and Serm
were also now aware of something unusual going
on. They rose cautiously in the darkness without
speaking. Someone took Jon-Joras's arm, felt
along it to the hand, guided the hand, unresisting, through the darkness. He felt rope . . . a
stick of wood . . . more rope. Trond—it must be
Trond, those sturdy arms—pushed him upwards. He seized hold of the rope ladder and
began to climb.

The door from which the ladder depended
had probably once been intended to open onto a
corridor in an upper floor which had never been
built. For uncounted years it had opened onto
nothingness, onto air—except, of course, that it
had never been opened at all. Along with the rest
of the wall the door had once been whitewashed,
along with the rest of the wall it had long since
been covered with dust and dirt and soot. Jon-
Joras, below, had never even noticed it.

The torch which he had smelled burned at the
end of the corridor above. At first he did not
know any of the faces belonging to those who
held the other end of the rope-ladder. Gradually,
in the darkness, as, first Serm, then Trond,
mounted to join him, his eyes accustomed themselves to the dim light. And when one face
turned, having carefully seen to the careful closing of the door behind it, he recognized it at
once.

Henners!

VIII

EVEN IN A darkness dispelled only by the sullen glare of the single torch, the halls and rooms through which they now soon passed had the naked and unresisting look of things long concealed. The bricked-up windows gazed blindly, sagging and dust-covered shards of furniture lay in limp tangles all about. Once, Jon-Joras stepped on the dry bones of a rat, and they crunched and snapped. He shuddered, pressed on ahead.

At length they left narrow confines behind them and came to a wide hold emptying on one side down a broad cascade of steps into a vast pool of darkness. Following a gesture by Henners, all advanced to the carven balustrade, paused to fling down the torch and extinguish it by a method as primitive as it was effectual (and easier on bare feet than stamping). Then, in utter blackness, felt their way down the board steps, each holding onto the shoulder of the man in front in a sort of shuffling lock-step.

The stairs seemed endless, and the floor they finally led onto, even more; and here and hereafter they hugged a wall. Once, by sudden, unspoken and common consent, they stopped and held their breaths. Far, far off, someone crossed at right angles to their own path, a slut-lamp held unsteadily in hand, and either moaned or sang . . . something . . . in an inhuman, crooning sort of voice which froze Jon-Joras's blood. Voice and light and sound died away at last. They moved on.

They moved on.

After endless black years (and the ground grew rough, and the ground grew damp) he saw, like a fabled wanderer ages uncountable before him, overhead, the beauteous stars.

"But I would feel easier in my mind," Jon-Joras explained, not for the first time, "if I were with my friends."

The old man nodded, gently and carefully applied another coat of sticky liquid to the oddly-shaped wooden box. "I know . . . I know . . ." Absently, he wiped his fingers on his tangled beard. "But, as I have explained to you—I think —before—it makes much sense to divide you up. If the troopers get wind of something and make a raid, why should they get all of you at once?

"No, no . . . Let them swoop down just once, and, *poof,*" he blew out a breath which scattered his long, untidy mustaches; "we scatter you again. See?"

Jon-Joras did not take as much encouragement as his host intended. "But what if *I*'m the one gets taken? Eh? A lot of good your *poof* will do, then," he said.

The old man pursed his hairy lips. "You won't be," he said. "None of you will."

"What makes you so sure?"

"Within wheels—" he plied his small brush with absorption; "—there are also sometimes

wheels. So. The Chairman is supreme; true;
may he burn like a moth fallen into a slut-lamp;
but even if he is too strong to be gainsaid, he isn't
too strong to be envied. Do you believe, young
outworlding, for one moment, that it was a crim-
inal underground alone which managed your escape?"

Jon-Joras, who had indeed imagined that very
thing, paused in his pacing up and down the
crowded and rather pungent little loft (wood,
paint, varnish, breakfast, dinner, supper),
looked at the old man in surprise.

"Ha!" Enjoying and prolonging the moment,
the old man ignored him, sighted down his work,
murmured, "Ah, what a beauty fiddle this will
be. No one in Drogue can make them like I make
them, mmmmm, no. . . ."

"Explain, please, sir. Explain."

And the violin-maker explained that, while
there existed at present no active movement to
overthrow the Puissant Chair and replace its oc-
cupant with another, the ranks of the Gentlemen
of Drogue were by no means without those who
would like to see the Chair shaken. Each shake
diminished the present Chairman's influence,
and even the Board of Syndics was not entirely
averse to that.

"I name no names," said the violin-maker;
"for a good reason: I don't know any. But I
know this: Your friends' friends, they wouldn't
have gotten, not one inch, not one foot, inside the
building without certain persons of influence
and authority had helped them: enough said."

"But . . . How does helping us escape shake
the Chair?"

" 'How?' Tchk! You get back to Peramis, you

tell how the cruel Chairman · arrests you on trumped-up charge, convicts you in fake trial held *in camera,* throws you in rotten prison, almost kills you—You—important outworlder! What, my guest, you think the Hunt Company will like that? You think the Galactic Delegatic will like it? Of *course* the Chair will shake. Tchk!''

As for plans to get Jon-Joras back to Peramis, he, the old violin-maker, knew nothing.

The loft lay at the top of a teetering old tenement deep in the festering slums of Old Drogue. Below, illicit wine was made from wild grapes, and unlicensed tobacco cured and sold; there was an inn—*de facto,* not *de jure*—which kept no register of those who found cheap if uncertain slumber on the rag beds of its frousty floor; an entire establishment of ladies officially if not all actually young, who failing any gainful skills above a certain level, got their living by the use of such passive skills as lay beneath it; and a number of seamstresses and tailors who lacked time and place and perhaps inclination to weave the cloths they cut and sewed, depending instead on the activities of those who preferred not to vex the original owners with the tiresome bookkeeping inseparable from purchase.

Jon-Joras had been told something of all of this. It had perhaps not sunk in sufficiently. He was perhaps too centered on his own concerns and person. At any rate, it did not occur to him, in lifting up the tattered rag of a window-blind when clamor arose in house and street, and seeing the narrow and noisome way below crowded with black uniforms decorated in red

and gold, that those who wore them were present for any reason other than to affect his own
capture and semi-judicial murder.

He gave an exclamation of fear and, without
even waiting to discuss the matter with the old
violin-maker, ran from the loft and scurried up
the ladder to the rooftop. The troopers, as it happened, were only engaging in a more-or-less
quarterly round-up of unlicensed trulls, in hopes
of bribes and free fornication. But when they observed someone fleeing across the roof and en-
dangering life and legs by dropping heavily to
the adjacent housetop, they immediately assumed that he was not merely taking exercise.

They pursued after him, he fought back, they
kicked him and beat him and, as they con-
siderably outnumbered him, in a very few
minutes had him trussed up like a bird ready for
the roasting-spit.

Meanwhile, the other inhabitants of the alley,
faithful to tradition, had turned out for their own
share in the sport, and from windows and roof-
tops showered the troopers with abuse, refuse,
and, as they warmed up to it, more solid tokens
of social criticism.

"Look at the poor barster, tied up like that!"
"Tried to help the poor girlies, I s'pose—"
"Leave him go, you—"

A rotten bulk of timber came hurtling down,
followed by bricks, chunks of plaster ripped from
decrepit walls, pots the tinkers had given up long
ago, mugs, jugs, coping-stones, firewood—

"Get the crows! Get the woodpeckers! Get
'em!"

The troops, half-leading, half-dragging their

quarry, turned to head through another way. But the whole quarter was now aroused; it was astonishing how swiftly barricades had been erected—

"Take the kid! The kid! The kid! Take the kid!"

The heavy rain had begun to draw blood, black-red-gold troopers were down, now, on all sides of him. Jon-Joras felt the hands slip from his arms, started to stagger away, felt something hit his shoulder a sickening, numbing blow. Once again he seemed to hear the pounding of great, inhuman feet . . . once again the dark circle whirled, closed in, bore him away down a roaring tunnel. Then all sound as well as sight was gone, and he floated, cold, on the waves of an unknown sea.

The down-river packetboat wallowed heavily in the main channel. Now and then the tattered and dirty sail gave a petulant slap and the sweating passengers took brief pleasure in the sudden breath of wind. But it never lasted long enough to bring much relief. A market woman sat on her crated jars of wild honey, voluminous thighs and skirts spread out for coolness as she ate soft fruit. A smeary-faced little girl tugged at her sleeveless arm.

"Mar, Mar," the child screamed, companionably, "what for is that man got that thing on him, Mar?"

" 'That thing,' " the mother chuckled juicily at her daughter's clever turn of phrase. "That's what you call it a straight-jacket, dearyme. He's a nut-head, the poor poke."

"But what for is he got that *thing* on him, Mar?"

"I *told* you, dearyme: he's a *nut*-head. Look what he's got his head shaved all off, huh? Because what for, otherwise he'd pull out his hair and *eat* it." She shoved her neighbor, another market woman whose head had dipped in a midday doze, waking her abruptly. "Look a nut-head," the first honeywife said, gesturing with her dripping morsel.

The second looked, loose, toothless mouth agape with interest and concern. "Ah, tut, the poor poke," she observed. "I suppose somebody, what, stole his spirit, huh?"

Her neighbor shrugged. "What can you do?" she asked, rhetorically. "Some people, what they're like."

The child looked and looked. Then she came to a decision. "He's a nut-head," she screamed. The two women laughed at this perceptive remark, urged each other to eat more fruit before it spoiled. There was no telling how long the trip would take, but it was not likely that they would be bored.

There was an old man with his left leg gone at the knee, who had used up all his conversation on his near neighbors, then used up his near neighbors by running through his conversation two or three times over again. As he sat alone on the cover of the cargo hatch his attention was caught by the shrill exchange between the honey-women and the child. He looked up brightly, hoping to catch their eyes and a fresh chance at conversation, but they never looked his way. It didn't seem as if they were ever going to,

so, after a while, he sighed, dragged up his
crutches, stumped down towards a niche in the
bulkhead which had once held a water-barrel
and now held the lunatic and a young boy.

"Going downstream?" was his first, idiot
question. The boy nodded. "Thought you
weres," said the gaffer. "I say to myself, 'They're
going downstream,' I say . . . I'm going downstream myself."

No answer was returned to these confidences.
"I'm going in that direction myself. I'm going to
Peramy, you may have heard of such a place,
Peramy? I'm going there. My grandson's boy, he
lives in Peramy, sells fish in the market there, he
sends word to me, come down and help. What
for? An old bate like me, with only one hind
paw? What for is that I've got both forepaws,"
he gaped and chuckled, "so I can sit on my stool
and scrape the fish, the scales, you know, scrape
the scales off of them . . .

"What for . . ." he concluded, slightly dis-
couraged at the lack of interest.

The brown waters gurgled slowly past the
packet's hull, the forest slid by on either side,
league after league, all the same, all the same.

"Mighty hot," the old man said. The lunatic
groaned and mumbled. The old man's eyes
rolled a bit uneasily.

For the first time the young boy spoke, saying,
"He won't hurt you, granther."

The old man leaped to his comment like a fish
to a fly. "What for he's like that, boy? Huh?"

Rather wearily, as though tired of giving the
same reply so often, the boy said, "He slept outdoors one night in the black of the moon. So."

Wide-eyed, but utterly believing, the old man gave a long, drawn out *Ooooo;* nodded rapidly. "Poor poke. He must've let his mouth open when he slept, what for some dirty person stole his soul." And he proceded to tell an interminable anecdote incorporating several others equally interminable, about people he knew or had heard of who had suffered the same outrage. The boy's head drooped, snapped back up, drooped again. The old man droned on. He told the story of his life, including the loss of his leg ("An afternoon, hot as this one") to a rogue dragon long, long ago.

The boy's sleepy eyes lit up and his lips parted. Then he closed them both again. And the old man droned on. And the lunatic drooled and moaned.

There was some discussion at the land-stage in Peramis as to whether the boy had to pay head-tax for one person or two. A reference to the dirty, dog-eared book of regulations, however, soon provided the answer.

"No . . . Boy's right. Nut-heads and little kids, no head-taxes . . ." Absently, the official took the boy's money.

"*Estates* of nut-heads got to pay land-taxes," another official pointed out, unwilling to lose the argument absolutely.

" 'Estates,' 'land,' " the first one said, testily. "Estates and lands got nothing to do with us . . . Honey, huh. How many jars you got, woman?"

They began to count and squabble. The boy and his keeper drifted away through the crowd and out into the streets.

Presently they wandered along a refuse-strewn alley backing on a row of cookshops, entered a gaping doorway. Time passed; not much. The boy emerged again, a man with him, arm in a sling, head covered with what might have been ill-trimmed hair . . . or . . . if one looked quite closely . . . a wig. The man's gaze was blank. Now and then he made a faint mewing sound.

The alley led into another which emptied onto a court, the doors and windows of its rotting tenements boarded shut. The boy studied the crude grafitti, scrawled in charcoal, mostly obscene; rapped softly on one, in an irregular rhythm.

Silence.

He rapped again. The man began to move away, was jerked back, whimpered.

There was a screech of seldom-used wooden hinges and a door opened, narrowly, boards and all, the entire frame moving in. After a second or so, it opened wider. Man and boy entered. The door closed behind him.

A bitter-faced woman said, in a harsh voice, "You've been long in coming." Then, looking at the man: "He's had black brew to drink." He looked at her, blankly. The boy nodded. "I'll make some white," the woman said.

In the sole clean room of the cluttered warren she set charcoal to burning in a small brick stove, put herbs into a pot, added something fine and powdered, and water, fanned the fire with a shingle.

"I can make something to eat," she said after a while.

"No."

The white brew boiled, was poured off, strained, diluted with tepid water in a mug. The woman put it to his lips, he drew his face away, she jerked his chin down and poured the drink into his mouth. Much ran out but his throat bobbed and he swallowed.

"Now we'll see," the woman said. They both looked at him, expectantly.

He winced, shuddered. His face, his limbs, his body, began to twitch. This soon stopped. The man looked around him, confused. He licked his lips, frowned at the silent woman with the bitter face. His head turned slowly. At sight of the boy he cried out, jumped, then gave a groan of pain. He subsided in his chair.

"How did I get here?" he muttered.

Then he asked, "Why are you dressed as a boy, Lora?"

IX

NOW IT WAS her turn to frown. Perhaps it was his use of her name—although there was no reason for him not to know it by now—or not to use it.

Her voice was low, restrained, husky. She gave her head the immemorially conventional toss, forgetful that her hair was now cropped short. "We picked you up when your shoulder was hurt," she said. "And brought you here."

"We?"

She hesitated. "*I* brought you here."

"Using the riot for your own purpose . . ."

Her laugh was brief, scornful. "Who do you think began the riot? Or why?"

He considered this. His shoulder and arm were throbbing. "I can't remember . . . anything . . ."

"You were drugged. It was easier to get you out that way. Everyone thought you were a lunatic."

"Mmm . . . And now I'm here. . . . Where *is* 'here'? Peramis? At last. Well . . . What's to prevent my talking freely?"

He blinked when she told him; nothing prevented it. He had in fact been brought here for that reason, not any other one. There was no longer any purpose in keeping, or trying to keep secret, the work at the Kar-chee castle. It was disrupted, it was known. Another training place would have to be set up in another location, there to teach the dragons how to kill their hunters. But this could not be done in a day and a night—indeed, it was impossible to say how long it would take.

And Hüe's purpose could not be delayed, whatever advantage so far gained dared not be lost—

"You tried to have me killed," he interrupted her.

She waved this away with her hand. "That was before we realized that there was no point in silencing you. No, we almost made a mistake there. Now we want you to talk, tell everyone, let the whole Galaxy know what we've been doing, why we've been doing it. And why we intend to keep right on doing it until we win. Maybe it will help us. It's clear it can't hurt us any more.

"The only thing we ask you not to talk about is this place here. It's useful to us, and we think you owe us that."

For a moment he reflected. Then he nodded. "All right. But answer me this: Has your father anything to do with the dragons in the Bosky? No? Curious. Well. Take me as near to Company House as you can. I won't say a word about your hide-out here."

Nor did he. He wasn't even asked. Jetro Yi's effusive and almost incredulous pleasure at seeing Jon-Joras return soon vanished on hearing what he had to say.

"Then it's true? It *is* true! We've heard rumors, we were naturally, P. M., you under-

stand, we were unwilling to credit them. But—
Oh, that's horrible! That's unbelievable! But
. . . I mean . . . actually training them to become
rogues! That's worse than anything I could imagine!''

His rubbery features were distended, distorted
by shock. He took him to his superior, the Hunt
Company's Chief Agent in Peramis, one Wills
H'vor. H'vor was a man of full flesh, he began to
tremble, then to shake. Before Jon-Joras was
quite finished, the Chief Agent's heavy face and
pendulous cheeks, the slack muscles of his arms
revealed by the sleeveless shirt, were wobbling
and quivering. His teeth clattered. With a convulsive movement, he steadied himself enough to
speak.

"We—we-we-we—we might have all been
killed!" he burst out. Clearly, no conceivable detail of that dreadful death was escaping his imagination. "How can we be-be-be *sure?*" he
cried. "From now on—?"

"Whether the dragons are honestly marked or
not? And rogues or not? You can't," Jon-Joras
said. "I suppose that's part of their purpose, the
outlaw Doghunters, that is." He felt no desire,
now, to go into the morals of the matter, to
blame the raging hatred of the outlaws any more
than the cold, indifferent oppression of the Gentlemen. His injured arm was giving him infinite
pain, he felt sick and hungry and weak. "My
king's hunt will have to be put off . . . canceled
. . . or held elsewhere. It may *have* to be in The
Bosky, Company Yi—still no? Well—" Jon-Joras shrugged, sighed.

"Please get me ConfedBase on the com-

municator," he said. "And then . . . then . . . I
think I'd better see a physician. . . ."

Wills H'vor waved a trembling fat flipper of a
hand. Jetro Yi's instinctive and obsequious reaction lacked much of its usual fulsomeness, but he
hastened to comply. Voices came and went behind the blind face of the comspeaker, Jon-Joras
wearied of repeating himself over and over again
only to be switched on to somone higher up—
and then having to begin yet again. Finally—

"Delegate Anse on. *Who* is this?"

It might have been imagination, but it seemed
to Jon-Joras that on his mentioned (for the tenth
time, perhaps) the phrase, ". . . Private Man of
King Por-Paulo of M. M. *beta* . . ." he heard the
voice of the Galactic Delegate undergo a clear
but subtle change. But he did not pause to question this, went on with what he had to say. He
stumbled, repeated himself, but he kept on talking.

"All right . . . No more for just now," Anse's
voice instructed, interrupting him. "We'll finish
this up together. When. Mmmm. See . . . Today
is Thirday . . . You missed the ferry, won't be
another till next Firsday. I can't take the time off
just now, or I'd come up by special. Should I
send a special to bring you here?"

It was decided, finally, that Jon-Joras should
rest, under medical care, until the regular weekly ferry trip the following Firsday. There were
special facilities at the Lodge; he should take advantage of them.

"Meanwhile," concluded Delegate Anse,
"this information had best remain uncirculated.
Does anyone else . . . Companymen Yi and

H'vor? I'll get on to them. And you, P. M., take
it soothly. Heal well.''

Under the ministrations of Physician Tu,
graduate therapist of the famous schools of
Planet Maimon, Jon-Joras's injuries soon ceased
to vex him. In his quiet room at the far end of
one wing of the Lodge, he lay on his couch looking out the transparent wall. Dark and green
rose the wooded hills afar off, the great river
flowing silvery as it bent in the middle distance.
Dimly, like a picture scroll slowly unwinding,
images, images passed before his eyes.

The hall at Aëlorix . . . the young archers at
practice . . . the singing passengers flying to the
impromptu dragon hunt . . . the incredible moments while the great bull-dragon failed to be
diverted . . . the stumbling through the forest . . .
barking dogs . . . musty tunnel . . . cyclopean
and secret-keeping Kar-chee castle . . . training
the rogue . . . blood spattering . . . midnight raid
and smoke . . . free and open, life in the nomad
camp . . . the heat of the fire and Thorm straining to place his knife . . . gliding down the broad
moonlit river . . . the stinking prison room, the
cold, impassive face of the Drogue Chairman,
the mob raging . . .

But gradually these images faded and were
gone, were replaced by others: the central lawn
at the Collegium, like blue-green velvet . . . a
crowd of boys taunting one of their number,
black-haired and white-faced and defiant . . .

Then, slowly, slowly, this too vanished. He
continued to lie on his couch, increasingly tran-
quil, and the afternoon sank beneath the weight
of night. Only when the great red sun hesitated

on the horizon he arose. And it was then that the shot pierced the transparent wall and shattered the panel lamp no more than an inch or two over his head.

He gazed at it, more curious than disturbed. It was the second shot which convinced him that while he was visible he was in danger. Unbothered but obedient, he lay down on the thick, soft rug. The vibration of the floor reminded him of what his ears had failed to convince his mind: the thick, unceasing clamor of alarm bells.

The door burst open and many men rushed into his room.

Physician Tu insisted that the health of his patient was paramount; questions, he said, could wait. And over the protests of Senoëorix, Commander of the Peramisian force, he had Jon-Jor-as removed to a room within the lodge's central core. The wall was turned to opaque, guards posted, the sick man placed under drugs intended to counteract the shock of his attempted murder.

Senoëorix, claiming that the physician's interference made his task impossible, engaged in no search of the countryside. But the lodge staff responded to the claim, next day, of a free farmer whose name no one bothered to learn, that he had seen someone fleeing in the dusk a few leagues off at about the time of the attempt. They followed his directions. And there in the woods they found a huntgun and two spent capsules.

"Off hand," Physician Tu said, reflectively, "I'd say that there's a huntsman who doesn't like you."

Jon-Joras nodded equitably. "Affection cannot be forced," he said, the last word echoing in
his drug-happy mind: *forced, forced, forced*. His lips
moved, obedient to the echo.

The therapist threw him a sharp, appraising
look. "I may have given you too much. I'm not
certain I've ever treated anyone from your world
with it before, and, while there appears to be no
morphological difference, well . . . diet . . . en-
vironment . . . it's difficult to tell. I—Well." He
dispelled his doubts with brisk directions. Go to
bed. Eat your dinner when they bring it. Don't
go out of your room. Don't go out.

Jon-Joras nodded with a dim smile. *Out. Out.
Out.*

He went back to bed, ate his dinner, didn't go
out. Nevertheless, as he lay back after the tray
had gone, he had a definite impression that he
was losing consciousness. It was not with the
suddenness of shock nor the slower procession of
a faint, but he was (slowly, slowly) fading away
from the world of the senses.

The opaque wall showed a dim forest scene. If
he looked carefully, he thought, he might see
what was lurking behind the trees, before the
scene ebbed away—might see the mysterious,
slouching, chitinous Kar-chees themselves. *I will
grasp the rail of this bed,* he thought, *with all my
might, and hold on tightly, tightly; if I find my hands
anywhere else I will know that I've been unconscious.
. . .*

It seemed, somehow, important that he should
know. And so, he did know, when he found his
hands clasped on the coverlet, that he had
slipped away. It must have been then that the

man had entered his room.

"Now, please, Big," the man said, in a hoarse whisper; "don't make no noises. Listen to what I got to tell ya, huh."

Jon-Joras nodded. "Doghunter," he said, pleased with himself at having made this out.

The man didn't bother to affirm or deny his class. "They want to kill ya," he said. "You know who I mean. The bigs. The gents. Before the king gets here. *Your*—"

"*My* king?" He struggled against the sweet mists of indifference to undestand.

"King . . . King Paul? He gets here tomorrow. And I can tell you—they're not going to wait. You stay here, you'll be dead by then, huh."

Jon-Joras swung his legs over the side, feeling the railings cold to his flesh. "I won't wait," he said. "I have to see him. I'll go . . ."

He paused. Go *where?* Where would he be safe. The man in the darkness thumped his chest. "Go with me," he offered. "We'll see you safe. I won't mention no name, but you know who I mean. Him: tall. Her: young. With *me.*"

Jon-Joras nodded. Huë and Lora. Naturally they'd want him kept safe—now. If he were to be killed before he could talk, tell of what he knew, they'd have to begin from scratch, find some other safe and far-off den to bring their dragons to and train them there. "I'll go with you. Just lead me. Just lead."

The corridors were filled with soft darkness here and there spotted with tiny small lights. A thin thread of very quiet music seeped from hidden speakers. The man was a big man, but he moved silently. It could have been no more than a pair of minutes before he had found a stairwell which led them soon to the cool and safety of the darkness without.

A long while afterwards he reached to grasp the man's shoulder. "Someone's behind us," he whispered.

The man mumbled something, Jon-Joras could not clearly hear the words, but clearly he was neither surprised nor concerned. They kept on going. And by and by a door opened so suddenly that his eyes received the unexpected light almost like a blow. A voice inside was muttering, "—still say the Bosky would be—" It fell suddenly silent. His guide turned and took him by the hand to draw him in. Perhaps Jon-Joras's light-struck eyes made him hesitate, perhaps they noted nonethless a sudden change in the man's expression. However it was, he hesitated, drew back. The hand on his wrist tightened, pulled.

There was not one person who had been behind them in the night, there were three. Jon-Joras not only went in, he went down. The door closed upon his astonished cries.

"I should have killed you when you were on my own grounds," Aëlorix said. "And buried you beneath the dung of the deer-barn." His mouth arched like a bow, down at the corners.

Feeling dazed, dull, stupid, Jon-Joras said, "But I saw your son die. He died in my arms. He —"

"He died, at least, with honor. Sooner or later one way or the other, every man meets his dragon. *His* was a dirty one—a rogue. A man-made-rogue!" The aristocrat's voice clicked in his throat, his face showed a disgust greater than grief or rage.

Protesting, bewildered, "But I had nothing to do with that," Jon-Joras cried. "I might have been killed there myself. I don't understand. I don't understand!" His anguished gaze took in the rough-looking man who had brought him there and his rougher-looking fellows. "And I certainly don't—You! You are not of the Gentlemen! Why are you doing this?"

The guide gave a short laugh. "Ah, you thought you was so clever, huh. 'Doghunter,' you said to me. That's just one of your mistakes. I'm not a Doghunter, huh, any more than I'm a Gentleman. Maybe you don't know everything about this place after all. So I'll tell a few things, make it all clear. What's it that the old nut-head who digs in ruins calls us? 'Plebs'? So we're plebs, huh. *But that don't make us Doghunters!* Or what's it they like to call themselves, 'free farmers,' we don't want no farms, dig potatoes, all that. Nah . . ."

In small mood to appreciate the rude logic of what he heard, Jon-Joras listened nevertheless. It did make sense. Many of the plebs gave full approval to the Hunt system. They did so because of the employment it gave, the trade it brought, the color it afforded their otherwise drab days; they did so from simple habit, too, and also because they held themselves to be superior to the Doghunters—who opposed it. And because it allied them, thus, to the Gentlemen, whom they envied—and with whom, thus, they identified.

It was that complex. And that simple.

In vain Jon-Joras pointed out that to expose the outlaws' program of mis-marking dragon-chicks and of training some of those thus disfigured to be rogues, must inevitably result—one way or another—in the destruction of the outlaws' program. Uselessly he declared that he himself was taking no sides, that Huë's people had captured him once and subsequently tried to have him murdered.

To the first plea Aëlorix said only, grimly, "We know how to take care of that ourselves." And to the second, "Too bad they didn't succeed." Adding, "But *we* will. . . ."

Why? *Why?*

But the questions were based on the assumption that reason and fair-play prevailed, and in this situation neither did. The outlaws now wished their outlawry revealed and Jon-Joras had agreed to reveal it. Therefore he was doing their bidding. Therefore he was on their side. Therefore he had made himself the target of the full rage of the Gentlemen and their jackals.

More— When Aëlorix said that he was no dependent on the Hunt Company, he spoke only in the most economic, limited sense. Every single Gentleman was dependent on the Company because the Hunt System was dependent on the outworld trade and the Gentlemen, as a class, were dependent on the System. Even such finite freedom as Aëlorix himself possessed was the exception.

"Do you think I don't know you for what you are?" he asked, scornfully. "Outworlders?—cowards—the lot of you. One hint of danger,

you'd never show yourselves on Earth again.
And then what? Grub in the dirt—*us?*—like
Doghunters' brats?"

Then, as he paused, over the sound of his
heavy breathing, another sound came in from
the night . . . low. Low, troubled, melancholy
. . . the cry of a questing dragon. Almost for the
first time there came to Jon-Joras's mind, preoc-
cupied as it was with his own fears and his trou-
bles, some thought of dragon *qua* dragon—poor
beast! predestined to torture, agony, death for
another species' sport—when all it wanted was
to find a mate, to couple as nature intended it,
off there in the cool and ferny darkness.

The eyes of master and men swung in the
direction of the cry, then; rested briefly, swung
back to the prisoner; met each other. Whatever
thoughts were theirs, pity was not one of them.
The erstwhile guide began to grin.

"There it is," he said.

Aëlorix nodded. Jon-Joras felt his flesh
prickle. "What—" he began.

" 'Sooner or later,' " Aëlorix quoted himself,
" 'one way or the other, every man meets his
dragon.'

"Hear it? That's yours."

X

AËLORIX'S FINAL words to his prisoner and former guest were never finished, but did not need to be. "Why *you* should live, and *he* be dead —" the man said; his face twisted with grief and hate and he turned away. It was the age-old cry of *Why me and not another?* and in his bitterness and his rage, fed from a hundred springs, somehow he blamed Jon-Joras for his own son's death.

It was the time between dawn and earliest morning. Mostly the sky was gray, but the mist to eastwards had begun to show pink. All was quiet, all was cool, as they took him from the small house in the woods. The Gentleman himself said nothing more after that, but his low-born thugs cursed and muttered and hawked and spat and complained of the chill. Dew still trickled and fell upon them, going down the barely visible path.

"Give it a blow, Big?" one of the men asked. Aëlorix nodded. The man fumbled in a kit by his side, took out a small bottle, swore, put it back, fumbled again, this time came up with something made of wood and bark, and put it to his lips. His cheeks inflated. Had Jon-Joras not been watching he would never believed that what he now heard came from anything but the mouth of a dragon.

The soft sad notes faded away on the dim air. All listened, all were still. For a while, nothing. Then, from off to the right and a distance (to Jon-Joras, incalculable) came what almost seemed a deeper echo of the same cry. The men nodded.

"That's him," they said. "Hasn't moved much in the night." The man behind him poked Jon-Joras with the huntgun. "Get flapping," he instructed.

They came by and by to an end of the woods and entered onto a wide and flat park-like place covered with waist high grass and here and there a low tree. Again they sounded the dragon-call, and again and again. And the dragon responded and the voice of the real dragon came nearer.

Halfway across the great clearing all stopped. "As far as we go," one of the thugs said. He gave Jon-Joras one last, painful prod in the kidneys with the squat muzzle of the huntgun. "You better not move away from right here," he warned, "until the drag comes in. You *do,* and—" He imitated the sound of the capsule being fired.

"*After* the drag comes in, why, you can move all you like. Maybe—if you're lucky—if you move fast enough . . ." He shrugged.

Jon-Joras half-turned, watched them walking back at a brisk pace in the direction they'd come from. Then he swung back to watch the woods ahead of him. His legs twitched, but he beat down the impulse to flee. After a long while, or so it seemed, the cow-call came again from behind him, was answered by the bull in the forest ahead.

A tree moved in the wind that blew from the west, from behind, then another. His heart

swelled and his head snapped as he saw that the
second moving thing was no tree. The long neck
swung from side to side, the faceted eyes
gleamed yellow and green. And then the body
moved out into the open. The great mouth
parted, sounded its immemorial question.

And then the utterly unexpected happened. A
dragon call from behind . . . but not the sub-
missive one of a cow-dragon as before. This was
a bull, another bull, a defiant and challenging
bull; instantly, along with it, came the strong
and bitter reek of bull-scent. Jon-Joras felt his
bowels turn. Trapped! Before and behind him!
Trapped—

The visible dragon bellowed its vexation. And
Jon-Joras saw it all.

There was no bull-dragon behind him, just as
there was no cow-dragon behind him. The call
came from the same source—a small instrument
of bark and wood. And the odor of dragon-suint
had come from the bottle in the same kit-bag.
Trapped? Tricked! He and the dragon, both.
Only—

Only the dragon would not know that, could
not know that. His tiny and now-troubled brain
served chiefly as a clearinghouse for instinctual
responses. Female dragon: Go to her. Male
dragon: Will want her, too: Slay him.

The bull in the woods now left the woods behind him and began to cross down the clearing
at a lumbering trot, shooting forth his bifurcated
tongue, tasting the air . . . air in which Jon-
Joras's own scent was mingled with that of the
"other" . . . man-scent now inextricably identified in the brute mind with that of its sexual rival
and enemy.

The dragon did not know the trick, but the man did. And the man reasoned and the man remembered, the man remembered what Huë had told him in the Kar-chee castle—that the dull brain of the great beast was mastered by misdirection alone. Aëlorix and his toadies now had none of the apparatus of the hunt except the single huntgun. They had no beaters, no musics, no archers, no bannermen. They were making up for all that now by using the artificial call-horn and the scent drawn from the musk-glands of some dead bull-dragon. These they had.

Jon-Joras had nothing but his mind.

Again the wind from behind brought the ugly reek and the male call. The dragon ahead paused for a slow second, a shiver of rage moving the powerful muscles beneath the green-black hide. His cheek-nodules began to puff with mindless rage. He bellowed, he hissed, he began to run. Run?

That was what they hoped Jon-Joras would do: panic. Run. *"Maybe, if you're lucky—if you move fast enough—"*

But no man could move fast enough against a frenzied dragon. Long before he would have a chance to make the dubious safety of the woods (and behind, the great engine of the pounding dragon-body crashing the trees aside like reeds), the dragon would have seen him running, would have known him by his scent for enemy, and would have run him down, seized him, worried him, torn and trampled him.

Thus, the trick. And, thus, the game.

But Jon-Joras wasn't playing according to those rules. His legs still twitched and trembled and he let them. His arms, it was, that moved

now, moved swiftly. Arms and upper body
slipped out of the loose hospital shirt which was
still his only garment; arms reached up to the
lowbranches of the low tree, little more, really,
than a large sapling, and tied the shirt to them
by its sleeves. The innocent wind at once caught
at it and it flapped and flew about and danced.

If the shining eyes saw it, facets flashing yellow, flashing green, Jon-Joras could not say for
certain sure. But the dragon roared at the same
second, and at that same second Jon-Joras
stooped into the grass which had been as high as
his naked breast and now closed over his naked
head. He still did not run.

He walked. Knees trembling, body sweating,
he folded his arms upon his swift and fearful
heart and walked away into the grass at right
angles to the dragon's path. He did not look up
even when the earth shook and the noise grew
nearer, grew louder. Dependent on the meager-
ness of the animal's mind, hopeful of its not
swerving from its path, trusting to its being for
the moment intent upon the tell-tale shirt, Jon-
Joras walked on.

To the men hiding in the woods it might have
seemed that he had fainted after tying the shirt
to the tree. Would they realize why he had tied
it there? Or suspect in which direction he had
gone if he had not fainted? Likely they would
imagine that, if he were not now huddled at the
foot of the tree, he would be surely taking the
shortest way out of the clearing—the one he was,
in fact, now taking.

In which case, they might well divide their
numbers and, by circling around, try to head
him off. They could not move fast, for they

would not dare to expose themselves in the clearing, and it would be slow going in the woods.

The sun was now high enough for him to feel its rays on the side exposed to it. Without lifting his head or shoulders or increasing his pace, he began to turn, turned, and walked in towards the sun. He could not see, he could feel the dragon as it passed, bellowing, to his left. He kept on walking.

It had not noticed him! *It had not noticed him!*

That it had noticed the shirt was almost certain, for it had paused in its rushing and he could hear the snapping of the tree and (so he thought) the ripping and the tearing of the cloth.

He kept on walking, the sun warmed his naked shoulders, and presently the sun ceased to do so and the grass fell away from him and underneath it was mossy and overhead it was shady. Slowly and cautiously, but still stooping, he turned around. He saw that he had entered the forest . . . and safety.

Farther off a dragon called and sounded, but he could not tell if it were real or false.

Once he had been lost in the woods after a dragon had been busy in a clearing, and he was worse off now than then in that he was now naked. But in everything else he was, he reflected, hopefully, better off. For one thing, he was only a foot-journey away from the town instead of a flight-journey. For another, should he find himself again among Doghunters, he could count on aid instead of capture.

But most of all he was better off now because he had already had the experience. And he was where he now was—and *how* he now was—not because he had fled in numbness from a scene in no way of his own making, but because he had brought himself out of danger into safety. He was mother-naked and alone, there was a wild beast to one side of him and men who sought his life to another.

But—he found to his astonished and his marveling delight—he was no longer afraid.

The clean sweet smell of the woods was all around him. A tiny gray creature for which he had no name paused on its way up the side of a leaning tree and regarded him curiously.

"When in doubt," Jon-Joras said aloud, "do as the natives do."

He followed the gray one up the tree and looked all around him.

The trees here on Prime World—at least, in this particular area of Prime World—were not as tall as he had seen elsewhere. On Dondonoluc, for one example, or on its mirror-twin-world, Tiran-lou, with their incredible depths of topsoil, the mastadonic trees towered several hundred feet high. But, as though in keeping with the foliage, if Prime World's trees were not tall, neither were Prime World's buildings. How far he might be from the nearest settlement, Jon-Joras did not know. The oozy green gum of this one, rank and odorous but by no means offensive, ebbed out onto his flesh as he pressed against the bole and craned, and mingled with the hair. A breeze met his inquiring face, a little wind rich with the smell of sap and earth and plants. But all he could see, whichever way he looked, were more trees, and yet trees.

Not altogether realizing what he was doing

(and, afterwards, somewhat surprised that he had in any way thought of doing it), Jon-Joras let his eyes go out of focus. The trees blurred, trunks and crowns and branches. And, in the corner of his eye, something which had not been there before . . . or which had not appeared to be there before . . . took shape . . . a wide, shallow concave arc . . . a tall, abrupt and flaring fin . . .

Slowly and carefully, as though fearful that the new shapes had newly materialized from the ambient ether and might, if he were incautious, take fright and vanish away again, he turned his head so that he might see clearly where they were and mark their location. He did, and they stayed where they were and then he climbed down the tree.

Despite his having taken a careful sight on it he still had a hard time finding the flyer. There were not many around, that he had seen; this depleted world could afford neither materials nor fuel, and the cost of importing made it impossible there should be many. He had seen them, silver and gold and several other colors; no where on Prime World had he seen another one camouflaged. In fact, nowhere did he know of this being done at all . . . except, of course, on the so-called War Worlds, which did not form part of Confederation.

But he found the flyer at last.

The door was open, as though someone on guard had just slipped out, but if there had actually been someone on guard, and where or what he slipped out to, Jon-Joras never learned. It is only in fiction that all loose ends are always neatly tied up. A tiny nameless creature with stripes along its little back looked up with bright, blank eyes to see the naked man flitting from tree to tree all around the clearing and then dash across it and up and into something for which the small creature had no familiar image. It blinked, instantly forgot, and scurried on, looking for nuts.

There were many things on Jon-Joras's mind, but one of them was a firm resolution that first things had now to come first. He padded quickly to the controls and he took the flyer up and up until he saw nothing but a green blur beneath him. Then he put her on *Hover* and locked her so. Then he sat down to consider things.

There was food and drink in the proper compartment and the greedy way he ate informed him that, for one thing, he had been quite hungry, and that, for another, he seemed now to be all better. He thought about this as he gobbled and gulped and picked at something which proved to be a bolus of sticky tree-sap entangled in the hair of his leg. This, in turn, reminded him that he was still naked. He stood up and patted his stomach and stretched and gave vent to an enormous and enormously satisfying eructation. Then he started rummaging around. He found clothes and those items which weren't clean were clean enough to suit him now. He had a dim recollection of the fastidious Jon-Joras of M. M. *beta*-world who shifted himself from head to foot three times a day and tossed the discarded items in the incinerator; but he did not pause even to smile. He suddenly had something else on his mind. The under-tunic stayed for a moment just where it was on his arms about to slip over his shaven head. For in that moment everything stayed where it was. Then he lowered his

arms and slipped the under-tunic off and held it
in his hands, staring, staring at it. Then he
brought his face close to, next to it. He did not
really think that he was mistaken, but he
thought that he might perhaps . . . just possibly
. . . perhaps . . . be. So, slowly, one by one, he
picked up the other articles of clothing and one,
by one, he smelt them.

They smelled, every one of them, faintly, faintly, but definitely perceptively, of that ancient
musty odor of the Kar-chee Castle.

But it had burned—had it not? It had. And he
had seen it burning. Had . . . whomever these
clothes belonged to . . . had he been there then
or since, it was inconceivable that his clothes
should not be smelling of smoke. *Reeking* of
smoke. But it reeked of nothing, had merely the
normal smells of man and of flyer fuel and (not,
hardly normal, this—) the alien and shadowy
scent of the old ruin's ill-frequented lower pas-
sageways. Therefore—

Therefore the man who had worn these
clothes there had worn them there and had been
himself there *before* it had burned. And not too
very long ago, either, or they would not still re-
tain the scent.

Which made no sense at all.

Huë might not be there now, in the black
basalt shell of a ruin, but he . . . and his people
. . . had been there, steadily, for at least some
period of years before. And Aëlorix . . . and *his*
people . . . were Huë's enemies. Jon-Joras
stopped here and carefully considered all his
thoughts. For one thing, what made him so certain that this flyer belonged to or had at least
been used by Aëlorix? Its mere proximity?

Once again he explored the small cabin, this time not looking for anything in particular and therefore looking for everything in particular. The chart-cabinet, the gear-locker, the food compartment, the spaces under the seats, the boot—all yielded nothing in the way of information. Certainly, it was not certain that Aëlorix or any of his men had been the ones who brought the flyer here into the woods. But, if not them, who then? Who else had reason to camouflage the craft and secrete it here, so far from anything? He had no answer, and yet he would not accept that there should be no answer, and yet he would not accept that there should be no answer. So once again he began looking slowly through everything. And this time he found something.

It was only a small something which might turn out to be a nothing. The pile of charts was neatly stacked, perhaps a trifle too neatly. For the regularity of the pile disclosed one tiny irregularity which he would have failed to notice if the charts had been shuffled up in a disorderly manner—and this was the fact that one corner of one chart protruded just the slightest from the neat arrangement of the rest. As if the stack above it had been removed very carefully and then the one chart extracted and subsequently replaced with an elaborate care which had not quite come off. Was it so? Jon-Joras lifted up the charts above and removed this single one.

It was a map of The Bosky.

Or, to be precise, of one sector of it.

There were no notes or markings, no arrows, no circles—nothing of that sort. But he looked at the chart carefully, very carefully, scrutinizing it very closely, and it did seem to him that on one portion of it the paper was just a trifle smudged, as though it had been often traced by ascertaining fingers. Fingers intent on indicating the terminus of a secret route, perhaps . . . If one paid visits to The Bosky it certainly made sense to go there by air; it certainly wasn't safe to go there by land if one could believe the stories. But . . . still unanswered . . . why should anyone want to go to The Bosky at all? That is—not to settle there or to pass through it in order to settle elsewhere, but to go there to one particular place and then return? And just once, either.

The Bosky . . .

What did he know about it? It was the terra incognita, the land unknown, the land without people, and it lay beyond the farthest boundary of the land claimed by Sartor, Hathis, Peramis and Drogue. The land where hunts could not be held. No-man's-land. Where, according to old Ma'am Anna, queen of the Northern Horde of nomads, the dragons were fiercer than elsewhere —so fierce that they needn't be provoked into charging—so fierce that, time after time, they had prevented human penetration of the area by either herdsmen or farmers. Dragons with which Huë, so his daughter said, had nothing to do. That was The Bosky. And it was also the place where the unknown crew (unless the crew was, after all, composed of Aëlorix and his gang) of the mysterious flyer had gone, and gone again and again, on their even more mysterious errand.

Thus, the strange Bosky, and was it the strangest thing of all on this strange planet believed by most of humankind to be their own ancestral world? With all its peculiar features, known and unknown, hidden and revealed: no. Not stranger, certainly, than the whole antique structure of Prime World society. Certainly not stranger than the brutal-sophisticated customs of the Hunts. Gentlemen-Huntsmen hating their dragon-prey, Doghunters hating dragons even more than the Gentlemen did and simultaneously hating the Gentlemen and being hated by them; this was strange enough, but this was not all. Nomads hating nobody and trusting nobody, working against the Doghunters who were working against the Gentlemen, but sure that they the Nomads were in all this working only for their own selves and opposing the Doghunters because in doing so they were also opposing the Gentlemen. And the band of thieves whose code of battle was perhaps more brutal than that of the Hunts they ignored and scorned, delighting —it seemed so—equally in the most elaborate forms of poetry and in murderous wrestling matches which ended or which were supposed to end in an elaborate and attenuated form of ritual cannibalism. The urban mobs and the rural sycophants. The dragons roused to fury in the woods and the dragons goaded to frenzy in the pit. The beautiful, involved, involuted, convoluted, contrived and bloody ballet of the dragon hunt, which brought to Prime World the wealth and questing zealousness of men from a score of hundreds of other worlds . . . though Prime World grew no richer, its aristocrats deepening into moral decay, its poor either flinging themselves in murderous fury against the adamantine wall of their oppressors' scorn or taking the slow road to sudden death in distant fields or submitting to the yoke in ignorance or in silence . . . or kissing the bloody hand and fawning at the bloody boot.

Jon-Joras sighed, shook his head. What was behind it all? Was anything? Was there a pattern? There did seem to be hints and shadows and he wanted to know and he had to know if there was more. The ancient saying of ancient Charles Ford or Fort, curious chronicler of curious occurrences in the history of pre-Expansion Prime World, arose in his mind. *One measures a circle beginning anywhere . . .*

He got to his feet and went to the controls, took the craft off *Hover,* placed the chart on its scan-sight alongside the drive-seat, and set himself a course for The Bosky.

Below, far, far below were the waters of the Gulf, the land lying to the south of it, and— beyond the land—partly obscured by a mass of cloud like fleecy smoke, were the yonder waters of the Bay. Behind him lay the Main Sea, before him the Main Continent. The original, or at least the natural contours of the Gulf floor lay revealed to him like some great relief map: shelves and shallows and banks and basins and deeps. And, flashing over and through and across all, like some jagged submarine lightning-bolt, was the deep-scored trench which the Kar-chee had made—one of thousands and of hundreds of thousands such in this one body of water alone. Like an ill-healed scar it showed there, and told its tale of how, floating down upon the planet from their lairs around the Ring Stars and finding a world whose land had been almost scraped bare of metals in making multitudes of ships to fling its children out across the

galaxy, the invaders had delved into the seas
themselves for metals of their own.

He wondered what ores they had sucked up
from the hidden treasures of the sands there, beneath the water. Black sands, they looked to be,
and had probably been rich in rare earths and
heavy metals such as zircon, rutile, ilmenite and
others. He wondered—

The flyer's speaker broke into voice.

It was a meaningless jumble of phonemes to
him. Helplessly, he looked at the decoding cams
under the speaker. But unless he knew the com-
ination, he might press on them forever without
result. The voice, having made its unintelligible
announcement calmly, paused. Then it repeated
it a second and then a third time, calmly. Then
it waited. It spoke again in its broken syllables,
and it seemed to Jon-Joras that there was now a
touch of impatience . . . a fifth time . . . annoyance . . . pause . . . a sixth time . . . concern
. . .

The voice barked its scrambled syllables at
him now, abruptly ceased, abruptly spoke in
plain speech, softly, so softly, that Jon-Joras
jumped.

"Who has this boat up?" He made no answer.
He could hear the man's troubled breath. "Listen, now—Put the controls onto *Receive* and lock
her so. We'll guide her back and in. Do you understand? Or you'll be in trouble. Answer. Answer.

"Answer—"

But Jon-Joras said nothing. And then, softer
yet, sickening in its implications, the voice said,
slowly, *"Oh . . . you . . . karching . . . thief—"*
and clicked off on the closing fricative.

And the thief looked behind him in dismay, as if he expected pursuit to burst immediately from the nearest cloud. He laughed at himself, but not for long. What should he do now? Put her on *All Speed?* If he did, he would leave a trail along the sky. Head for clouds and hope to hide the trail? The clouds were too far away, and not where he wanted to go, anyway. He put her into a diagonal descent as fast as she'd go without making marks, and leveled off at about a hundred feet above the water, and locked her so. Then he swiveled the seat around and looked up and waited.

He had not much long to wait.

The pursuers seemed to come bursting out of the fabric of the firmament, their trails thick and heavy and angry. He shot down at forty-five degrees, surged forward against his safety-belt as she hit the surface and watched the sudden surge of frothy water close over the dome and bubble like a dying whale. He put her onto full descent; descend far she could not, of course not, but if it were only hold here where she was as she was— And if the seams and shell proved leak-proof— And if they, the ones so way up high, did not see him—He looked at the chronomoter and tried to calculate how long it would take for them to pass over and be gone.

The small craft surged slowly back and forth and slowly up and down. A dull, grinding nausea which seemed to go down to the very marrow of his spine began to afflict him. Finally, he could not go on standing it, tried to surface slowly, shot up like a cork in a spume, fell back and wallowed and rocked again. Hastily, he looked up, but through the moisture running down the dome he could see nothing. And when, finally, he could, he saw only the fading trails of vapor, vanishing into the Gulf.

And now at last he came to the end of that more-than peninsula and not-quite-subcontinent where it joined the main landmass. He looked at the chart a moment, magnified in the sight-scan, then looked again below. Those rounded hummocks (from above they seemed little more than that) must be the Sixteen Hills; those sudden sparkles of light, the sun reflecting on the Sweet and Bitter Lakes. And there, there, shadowy and sere, was the abrupt descent of the Great Dry Valley. All the landmarks.

Beyond lay The Bosky.

He dropped lower. He looked up and around again. And still no signs of recurrent pursuit. The speaker was, as it had remained, silent. Whom had it been? Who *were* they? Again, Aëlorix? Or—his mind raced and tumbled about a bit—the Chairman of Drogue? Was there perhaps some force on Prime World of which he had never heard? After all, there was a lot more to it than this part which lay behind him and which was about all that he had ever known. Were there not thriving cities, so it was said, on that great archipelago which formerly formed part of Australia and ringed round that shallow sea once called Lake Eyre? It was possible that the flyers might have come from down there. But bound upon what mystic errands which required them to camouflage their craft, hide in woods, speak in code, and pursue him as though he were himself a rogue dragon—? He could conceive of nothing, in answer. And turned again to chart and to controls.

Meanwhile, let him pursue some answers to some previous questions. And follow his course to the nameless, numberless hill which seemed to have been the locus or focus of the unknown fingers whose tracery had left, faintly, the only clue there was. He went lower. He went lower. And there he saw where it was and what it was. His breath hissed in between his teeth. His decision was immediate, neither to stop nor even—there—to slow down. He went on as though he had not seen it at all. He had certain qualms as to whether or not it had seen him, though. But these did not preoccupy him long.

They came down on him like stooping falcons while he was still thinking of what he had seen. *Them,* he had not seen. The warning he had was cast by shadows and was a matter of seconds, but it was enough, and he did what the weaker birds do (if they can) when the falcon stoops: He hid in the thickets.

Not precisely, of course. What he did, precisely, was to dart down into a glade of great-boled trees with low and widespreading branches; he simultaneously turned obliquely and shoved her speed as low as it would go and still keep him aloft. She wobbled and wavered, but she bore it wonderfully, and he floated in between the sunshine and the shadow, between the branches and the ground, turning round and round the tree-trunks as close to them as he could in a sinuous figure-of-eight movement.

But the nigh pursuer was not as fluent of flight as a falcon. One convulsive effort he made to break—then he crashed. The off one did manage to break, escaping by the breadth of a cry. Up and up he went, hovered and darted and

swooped. Time and time again he made as
though to dash down into the glade, but his flyer
was three times the size of the one Jon-Joras was
in, and so, every time, he withdrew. But even
while Jon-Joras played at his little game in safety
below—in and out, in and out, around, around,
around—at every tiny clearing and across every
beam of light, he saw the great, dark, heavy, hov-
ering shadow.

Once, skimming round the bole of a vine-en-
crusted tree, Jon-Joras caught a glimpse of the
smoke and fire of the wrecked plane. Then, turning and twisting, he saw the end of the glade up
ahead, and the rough and broken ground which
ran for a good wide way until ended abruptly by
the gaunt escarpment of a tumbled cliff. He
made to go back the way he had come and keep
up the game until his fuel ran out or until the
other's fuel ran out or until . . . until . . . he
scarcely knew what, until.

The idea came to him more suddenly than its
execution followed. It might work, it might not
work, it was infinitely risky, foolhardy, it was all
those things—but he could not go on flitting up
and down the glade like a butterfly. So he took
his flyer deeper and deeper back into the thickest
of the glade, slower and slower, and lower and
lower. He put the controls on *Circle,* and locked
her so. Then he stepped to the door and stepped
out. It was just a short jump. Slowly and ponderously, like a fat woman who has had just a
shade too much to eat and drink, the flyer went
wobbling around and around. He turned and
looked back after a minute. But, so well had she
been painted, he could no longer see her at all.

He paused a moment to calculate his bearings

by the angle of a pencil-thin sunbeam. Then he slipped away through and into the woods. Later, looking back again, he saw the other craft still patrolling.

The trail, when he came upon it, puzzled him. There should by right be no trail here, in fact, how could there be, when there were no people? There were no people, but other things lived in the forests here beside birds (and, for that matter, dragons) and had to move about. Often he saw the rough patches of rougher hair upon the sides of the tree, two or three times he saw the small neat heaps of dung, and once he saw (but passed along as though he did not see) the twin spotted fawns lying so securely in the shady covert of the glen.

But of dragon he saw none. Nor did he hear any.

"Dragon? Dragon? Are you a dragon-chick?" he stooped to ask and to pick up a tiny, delicate orange lizard. It pattered cleanly and delicately along his hand and paused at the cushion of his upturned palm and looked at him so bravely, gravely, carefully he put it down upon the mossy rocks a foot or two in and off the trail where (he hoped) not even the dark hoof of a deer would menace it. He moved on.

Finally, as the sun commenced its decline, he saw what he had come to see, though of course by no means at first knowing that it was *this* that was here, had been here, waiting for him all alone. He had the notion of his having come full-circle, and of the thing there saying to him that he should Look—See?—You cannot escape. Not from me. Not from us. Not from them. It was though he saw now as a whole the same place he'd seen before as a collection of fragments. But still all he saw was now an outside, looming and staring and gathering in its black stiff folds about it, head and snout thrust foreward darkly from the green over-mantle—

A Kar-chee castle . . .

And what was in it?

More men like monomaniac Huë and all his crew? More dragons being tormented into murderous patterns of behavior? More plots and plans to overthrow the status quo? He crouched and stared and thought that all the sweet waters of the Earth must be stained with blood; he saw them welling and spreading like a great scarlet stain across all the face of this aged and afflicted world.

But from within the black basalt walls came neither signs nor sounds nor movement.

His own movements, as he backed off, lips bared, were—though he did not know it, did not have the image, even, in his subliminal memory —for all the world like those of a dog in the presence of something known to be deadly and dangerous but otherwise all unknown. And, like a dog, he began to circle about the thing of menace. And it was while so doing that he observed for the first time a dragon.

With its green-black, black-green, green and black skin, its deepset and faceted eyes flashing yellow and green and blue and red, long neck and huge body, it looked no different than any other dragon. In form and body, no different, that is. But immediately and immensely and frighteningly obviously it looked very different than any dragon he had ever seen, and the difference lay in its manner. It did not move in a mindless rush capable of being instantly diverted by a waving flag or the sound of a horn. And neither did it move in the relentless fashion of one intent upon its prey and knowing just what and just where that prey was. Least of all did it move along like some great, grazing pea-brained cow.

The word (it came to him in a moment that seemed to chill his skin) the word for this dragon was *alert*. And the other word for it (the echo after the shot) was *intelligent*.

It came slowly along, slowly and carefully, head turning from side to side, tongue tasting the air. Now and then it paused and it raised its head, slowly and deliberately, gathering in the details of sight and sound and scent at all levels. Then it proceeded in its careful, one might almost say its measured, pace. Then, too, in a third terrifying flash of understanding, Jon-Joras understood what now in retrospect seemed blazingly obvious to him: that the paths which he had been treading through the forest were too wide by far to have been made entirely by the narrow slots of deer's hooves. He had been walking, careless—almost—and certainly all unknowing, in the dragons' walk! He had been treading in the dragons' tracks! And now he had at once to retreat and to vanish, otherwise this careful questing beast of a dragon would certainly, soon, be treading in his, Jon-Joras's, tracks—!

But even as his tendons tensed to move him back and away, the dragon, as though in obedient command to his, the man's own fears, turned aside and moved away and in another moment was hidden in the woods and in the

towering thicket. Jon-Joras did not relax, grate-
fully or gracefully; he slumped and almost fell
over his own sweating legs. He had come here in
response to a stupid bravado, and now he was
trapped—at least twice-trapped. The patrolling
flyer kept him captive here in one way. And now,
it would seem, the patroling dragon might (if he
were not exceedingly careful) keep him captive
in another. If it didn't kill him first. The strange
thing (*the* strange thing? and was all else com-
monplace?) was that the dragon had not looked
fierce. Its fear and its terror came from other at-
tributes entirely. This beast might not charge
him upright upon its hind legs ... neither,
though, was it likely to be diverted by a rag of a
shirt fluttering in the breeze, or some other trick
of the sort.

Time enough some other time to wonder why
this one dragon was so different. Time now all
but screamed aloud to be used to go as far and as
fast away from here as might be possible. He
would head back as silent-swift as ever he could
to the general area where he had left the stolen
flyer. The patrolling vessel might have gone
away. Or its pilot might have landed it and come
out himself to investigate. Or Jon-Joras might
simply regain the one he'd used before and continue a terrain-hugging, tree-hiding tactic until
some better notion or occasion offered itself.

Then he looked up and saw that, although he
had moved and the dragon had moved, the
dragon was in front of him once again. He
crouched. He slunk off to the left. The dragon,
moving slowly and without undue concern,
moved in the same direction. He moved more
quickly. So did the dragon. And now, from a

great distance, overlaid with a multitude of memories, he heard the voice of Aëlorix speaking to him at the estate, back when all was well and all was amity and peace. *They were the Kar-chee's dogs . . . They hunted us . . .* Was that what this one was doing now? Hunting him? With deliberate speed and awful majesty? No . . . No . . . Not quite, not quite. Jon-Joras crept here and crept over there, crawled, dodged, twisted, retreated, retreated . . . The dragon followed, followed, followed. But actually it was not at all that Jon-Joras was going where he wanted and the dragon merely following.

Actually, Jon-Joras was going where the dragon wanted him to go, the way the dragon wanted him to go. He wasn't being hunted. He was being herded.

And so, through the great, crouching, vine-heavy gate of the castle, Jon-Joras walked with slouching shoulders and with hanging head, and the dragon walked watchfully behind him.

The dragon had ceased to be a surprise and, when he saw it at last, the Kar-chee really came as no surprise. It was not just that he had smelled it, the scent not faint and old and musty as it had been in the other, in the abandoned castle, but strong and fresh. But scent and, subsequently, sight, were but confirmations of what logic—without either—had already revealed. For if the dragons had been the Kar-chee's dogs and if here and if now a dragon was acting like a dog, then—

It was the man who was the surprise.

—then there had to be Kar-chee to direct them.

But he did not expect to see the man and the Kar-chee together; he did not expect to see the man at all. Any man at all.

One picture only had he ever seen, and then the carven figure in the frieze, dusty and webby and observed from a bad angle; but there wasn't and couldn't be a second's question or doubt. The dull black and ten-feet tall form, the comparatively tiny head, the huge anterior arms bent so that the hands or paws were folded loosely together upwards, the upper body slanted and canted forward, seemingly under the weight of its limbs: unmistakably, the Kar-chee.

The man was colorless, ageless, dirty, face and figure loose where one would think to find them tight, tight where they should have been loose. He sagged, blinked, mumbled his mouth and smacked his lips and he said nothing. In his hands, hands held up hieratically as a Pharoah's with crook and flail, he the man held some curious arrangement of fans or fronds and sticks.

The dragon composed itself for rest and observation on the mossy, grassy terrace, ran its tongue out once more, hissed a bit and made a slight coughing, barking, grunting sound.

The Kar-chee snapped its head up and began to move itself in an odd way and made an odd sort of rustling, clicking noise. And the man, in turn, cocked *his* head and looked away and the Kar-chee stopped and the man looked at Jon-Joras, and, in a curious sing-song voice he said, "Oh, mmmm, message, mmmm, so, It appears that he this man has not come here-place in, mmm, a proper, an authorized, mmm, orderly fashion, purpose, mmm." Click, click, rustle, rustle, click-clack. "Does-has he the man a correct mmm intent, mmm in coming here-place, so, or is it mere, mmm, intrusion; what reply is conveyed? Mmm, so."

Jon-Joras, astonished, allowed his mouth to fall open, said nothing. The Kar-chee clicked and rustled and the interpreter, allowing his dull and uninterested eyes to slide over the newcomer, said, "Communicate with, mmm, he the man and obtain, mmm, mmm, the reply. So." The voice changed a trifle in tone and timbre and the empty eyes appeared to try to concentrate. "Why did he the—No. Why did you come?"

Thinking rapidly and fearfully for what might be an acceptable answer, even a lie which—if not too outrageous—might be carried off—Jon-Joras said, "The overlords have sent me."

The interpreter clicked and rustled his stick and his fan or frond. The Kar-chee rustled and clicked, and Jon-Joras stared at its gaunt, chitinous body.

" 'What overlords?' "

"The overlords of all the stars of men."

" 'Why approached in furtive manner?' "

"Desired not to be seen by the other men who sometimes approach."

" 'Why desired not?' "

"Lest they prevent the consultation."

" 'Purpose of consultation?' "

Here it was, and Jon-Joras could think of nothing safe to put forwad. So he decided to leave this to the other, and so he said, "To discuss and discover what it is that the Kar-chee most want, with a view to adjusting matters."

Silence fell. After a moment the Kar-chee clicked, then stopped, then rustled, and stopped.

The interpreter coughed a bit and cleared his throat. Then the Kar-chee "spoke" rapidly and abruptly turned and made off in its eerie, stalking, waddling gait. The interpreter spat on the ground and rubbed his spittle into it with his foot. He glanced up, grimaced, shrugged, seemed to hang and dangle on invisible wires which, if cut, would let him collapse into a huddle of puppet-cloth.

"What did he—What did it—What did the Kar-chee say?"

"Mmm? Say? Said to give you food, take care of what you, mmm, will want. . . . What will you want?" the old man asked, almost querulously. And added, "Come, then. Come. Come on."

The rank odor of the Kar-chee was thicker down below, but it was largely replaced in the old man's quarters, away off in a distant chamber down long and dusty echoing empty corridors, by the at least equally rank odor of the old man himself and his quite indifferent housekeeping. New clothes were piled in a niche in the wall and old clothes mouldered on a heap in the corner and one nasty garment hung over the sill of the high slit-window as though the effort of tossing it there precluded any attempt to correct the poor aim and shove it on through. The old man sat down on his frowsty bed and coughed and rumbled and spat. Then he stared blankly at his sudden guest, a long while. From time to time a flicker of something passed over his dehumanized face and it twitched and made movements as though it were about to express interest or another emotion. But before ever this was done, the face sagged into the same blankness as before. Was he drugged, perhaps, Jon-Joras wondered.

"What's your name?" he asked.

This did produce reaction; after all, the old man's function was to serve as a channel for questions and answers to pass through and to repass through; he had to employ his own mouth and tongue and vocal cords for one of these passages, and his mind, no matter how mechanically, for both. "What's . . ." the question seemed to sink into the sands of stupor and there be lost, but after a moment it welled up again, a bit diminished: ". . . *name?*" Blear eyes looked up, slack mouth pursed and twisted, lips blubbered in a short, abrupt sound which might have retained the ghost of scorn or pain or laughter: the scornful, painful laughter which ends in a little bubble of blood, seen or unseen: the hands fluttered in the briefest, slightest gesture of pushing things away; then fell back and down.

There was a not-quite-mutter, a more-than-whisper, which might have been, "Never mind . . ."

"Well, but . . . Where do you come from?"

No. Not drugs. The old man's mind had simply rusted away. Who could say how long he had been here, a prisoner? A prisoner-at-large, but still a prisoner. He licked his thin lips with a bluish tongue, stirred on his dusty couch and looked about him. "Food," he said. Sighed. Pointed. There was a small pile of camp-rations, and empty and part-empty containers lay where they had fallen or had been dropped, adding the rotten-sweet tainted smell of garbage to the other ill smells of the room. "Food," he said again.

Jon-Joras got up and helped himself, paused with a bit of something almost at his mouth. "They bring it here for you?" he asked. And, answering his own question, said, "Yes. They bring you the food and the clothes, too. The other men who come here—the ones who approach in a proper order. Who are they? Who are they? And what is this all ab—"

Now the old man leaped up and scuttled across the dirty floor and sort of crouched before him, looking up and breathing into his face a fetid breath and now his face was distorted with feeling and he grasped Jon-Joras's arms and he said to him in a whisper like a scream, "Oluc? Oluc? You know Dondon-oluc?"

Remembrance sprang into the young man's mind and must have instantly been reflected on his face, for the old one tightened his timid grip and made anguished little noises.

"Dondon-oluc and Tiran-lou," said Jon-Joras. "And the huge old trees—"

"And Lou! And Lou!" the old man cried, in a jerky voice. "Oluc and Lou, ah! And the trees, the trees! The trees . . ."

He fell into a heap of smeared and smattered clothes that cried and twitched and made dreadful, sobbing noises. Jon-Joras was torn between pity and dismay and hope, and then the old man scuttled backwards away from him and rose to a slouch and stared at him with his awful crumpled face askew and then turned and ran, tottering, out of his nasty room and down the dim, black corridors and whimpered and flapped his wrinkled, dirty hands.

Jon-Joras stared after him. Run after him? No, no, he might get lost, and he had no desire to get lost here in this place where the Kar-chee scent was forever strong, forever fresh. Was the old interpreter off to reveal something to his alien masters? It seemed not likely. Likelier only that he had been all unsettled by having some of the rust and dust of decades fall in scales and flakes from his poor withered mind and memory. The young man put the bit of food into his mouth and looked out the tall slit-window. Outside, downside, between the castle and the woods, the dragon patrolled. Alert, watchful, and with deliberate leisure.

"I'm afraid, I'm afraid," the old man said. "I'm so afraid." He spoke in halting, stifled tones, again his face so close to Jon-Joras's.

"Of what, Old Man?"

"I could be punished. Back there. Ah, back home. Why I came away. Ran. Left me here. Didn't dare, don't dare. Afraid," he wept.

"Confederation has a twenty-five year statute of limitations," Jon-Joras reminded him. "And Dondon-oluc and Tiran-lou, both, are confederate-worlds. Surely it must be longer than that, you've been here?"

Bit by bit and scale by flake, he was trying to do a work of repair. Vast holes had been hopelessly eaten away. The Old Man was either determined to have no name or had simply lost that intensely important part of his *persona*. Nor would he, or, perhaps, nor could he, describe how or when he had come here or who had taken him here—the *who* being certainly those still supplying, the those in contact with the Kar-chee. It seemed obvious, though, that whoever they were they had taken advantage of his fugitive status. An interpreter was certainly always needed here, the Kar-chee being incapable of articulate human speech. There had been an interpreter here, of course, when the Old Man had first arrived. "The Poor Woman," he called her. However awful this life-in-death must be to a man, how much more so must it have been to her!—whoever she was or had been. Poor woman, indeed. For some while at any rate they had been some company for each other, she teaching him to understand the Kar-chee "speech" and to reproduce it; and then she had died.

Longer than twenty-five years that he'd been here? Closer, probably, to fifty!

"Afraid all changed, on Oluc. Oh, terrible—!"

"I was there just two years ago. It didn't seem to be a place of the sort which changes fast. And the soil was still as thick and rich and the trees were still gigantic." He reached into his memory for such names as he could recall, trees, rivers, towns . . . the Old Man made dreadful attempts to smile.

"Afraid of them, still, always. Here."

"The Kar-chee?"

"Of them, too. But most afraid of this?" And again the dreadful terror-whisper. "Suppose they go? The Kar-chee. *And take me with them!*"

Enough, indeed, to make the mind of any man, even if young and even if strong and sound, freeze with fear: the Kar-chee departing at long and ancient last for their lairs around the Ring Stars, black and cold and devoid of man and the things which stood between man and madness: this was indeed just cause for fear, to be taken along and to tarry there forever.

Slowly, simply, repetitiously, firmly, Jon-Joras told the Old Man that he was in close contact with the Confederation Delegate on Prime World, that he was also the Private Man of an important out world ruler. That, whoever had brought him, the Old Man, here and kept him here, it was not Confederation. And therefore it and they by definition were of lesser power and hence unable to withstand the wishes and directives of Confederation . . . once Confederation knew.

"So the thing that must be done is this: I must get to ConfedBase or at least make contact with Delegate Anse, if I can get away from here in time to meet him when he comes to Peramis. In either case, you see, *I must get out of here.*"

It was not to be done, it could not be done. The guardian dragons would not allow him to make an escape. They would tear him in pieces. "But," Jon-Joras protested to the protesting Old Man, "the dragons here obey the Kar-chee, so—"

Now he was to see the other side of the mirror, and its image was at first to be as obscure as its obverse; for the interpreter knew only of the dragons "here" and of none other. "The dragons," he said, shaking his head, *"are* the Kar-chee . . ."

Jon-Joras stared. "But that's what Huë said!"
" 'Huë'?"

"Old Man, I don't understand. I saw a dragon. I saw a Kar-chee. *They were not the same.* How can you say that they are?" Explanations, though, were not forthcoming. Merely he repeated, They were the same. So another ques-

tion was asked. "What is the set-up between the
Kar-chee—and these other men? The other men
do something for the Kar-chee, that is, they do
something for you. They bring you food and
clothing. *But what do the Kar-chee do for the other
men?*"

They kept guard. They let no other men
through. They—the Kar-chee who were also
dragons—destroyed any others who attempted
to enter this territory. Why? Ah. Mmm. The
muttered, fragmented pieces of comment scarcely deserved to be called information. But here
and there and finally some pieces fell into place.
The Old Man was terrified to approach the Kar-
chee unsummoned. He had never done so, dared
not do so now. Did not even know where, in the
maze below his level, it laired. But his will-
power, positive or negative, had so long ago
fallen into complete desuetude that he could not
resist Jon-Joras's mild but insistent pressures.

They came out blinking into the sunlight and
went to the rampart. The dragon presently came
into view, glanced at them, paced onward. With
hands which trembled at first, but soon fell into
habitual and pacifying actions, the Old Man fell
to rattling and clicking and rustling his artificial
but quite intelligible reproduction of the Kar-
chee language. And the dragon paused and
looked and it was plain that the dragon listened.

And then, up from where? No matter. Up
from wherever it had been, the Kar-chee came.

" 'Message. If he the man inquires if we the
Kar-chee desire to depart, then he the man un-
derstands that we the Kar-chee desire to depart
and his the man's question is no proper
question.' "

" 'Always they the proper men offer future-when to depart we the Kar-chee to the proper place of we the Kar-chee but never from first-when to present-when have they the proper men done so.' "

" 'If the message of he the man is properly communicated and properly understood, is it that he the man declares that the proper men are not the proper men, but that he the man and his fellows are the proper proper men and that the never-kept promise will in present-when be kept? These the before-when declared being the Overlords?' "

And Jon-Joras reiterated that those selected by all the worlds and stars of men to run their common affairs were indeed, through him, offering to return the Kar-chee to their Ring Star lairs; and this to be done as near to immediately as could be managed. "Only," he said, firmly, and reassuringly, "that this man who communicates messages is not to depart with the Kar-chee but is to remain here with us his fellows." And he emphasized this with gestures and at length he put his arm around the Old Man's trembling shoulders, and added, "For when the Kar-chee are in their own and proper places they need never and will never communicate with men again, and so will have no need of him."

The Kar-chee's dull eyes showed nothing. And then, in an abrupt and shocking change of pronoun and of phrase, it said, "I must consult with my other self. Await."

There was a silence, and a long silence. The Kar-chee above did not move and the dragon below did not move. The Old Man trembled and trembled. The dragon hissed. The Kar-chee lifted its tiny head. Overhead a flyer shot into view. Jon-Joras started, stared.

" 'He the man is at this present-when to go below and there remain.' "

Jon-Joras moved as quickly as his legs would let him, and as he ran he called out, "Don't tell them anything and don't worry. Don't worry!"

He made his way towards the Old Man's room, but recollection of its dirt and disorder dissuaded him, so he went to wandering in an off-corridor. A wink of light caught his eye as he passed one of the chambers, and he turned to look. It was a mirror, of the quaint hour-glass shape once so popular . . . how long ago? On his own distant and orderly world, the *beta*-planet of Moussorgsky Minor, perhaps more than a century ago. Allowing for the lag in time and transport and fashion . . . here? . . . who could say how less long ago. Fashionable, yes. But only among women. He entered the room.

Dust had almost deprived the old mirror of reflective capacity, and dust cloaked and choked everything in here. Yet, despite and underneath the dust, things were all arranged in order. A bed was neatly made. Clothes hung in orderly rows. An antique desk still bore a scripter set with all as it had been left, well-readied to use. It came to Jon-Joras with a shock and pang of pity that here had been the room of the previous interpreter, "the Poor Woman." He opened the scripter, slowly, delicately, with even a slight touch of fear.

it should make no difference to me how things will go here, for well or ill, but as this unfortunate young man must probably remain here for his own

*forever, it's well that he has learned as much as I
can teach him. And now there is no more reason I
should delay Death, that importunate suitor, any
longer. He does but carry me across this dim
horizon, and I hope it will be brighter there.*

He had no time to reflect on this. Somewhere
up above someone was calling his name. It
sounded vaguely familiar, and a wild surge of
hope brought him almost to the door—Delegate
Anse?—Delegate Anse's voice would not sound
familiar, he had heard it only twice and was sure
this wasn't it—Por-Paulo? It was not *that* voice
at all, the thought made a wave of longing for his
still-absent king sweep over him, but it was not
his voice—a prickle of unease slowed him up and
kept him inside. Who had been in the flyer and
knew that he was Jon-Joras and knew that he
was here? Aëlorix? It was not the Gentleman's
voice, but it might still be that of one of his associates. But why did it sound so familiar?

Perhaps, though, whoever it was did not know
that he was here at all. He might be guessing,
trying . . . trapping. Well. If friend he was, then
some delay would little matter. And if he were
no friend . . .

Jon-Joras flitted through the back of the room
and into the next one and thence to the next.
The voice seemed to be rather nearer, but he was
sure it was still in the main corridor. His intention was to get behind it and have a look at
whomever it belonged to.

"Jon-Joras?"

"Jon-Jo-o-o-r-as . . ."

"Jon-*Jor-as* . . . .?"

If it were a friend, why did he not announce
and identify himself?

He was about to peer with considerable caution out into the corridor, when a voice, and not that voice, said, close by and with disgust, "It sure stinks in here." Jon-Joras hugged the webby wall.

" 'Money never stinks,' " a second voice quoted.

"Freaky vermin," the first one commented, unappeased. And then, "I always hate coming here. . . . Where *is* that son of a karche's egg?"

The voices ebbed away. Now Jon-Joras did peer out. The two men met the third one, presumably the first one, the one who had been calling, at the turn of the corridor. They shook their heads. There seemed, certainly, something familiar about his stance and movement, as there had been about his voice. But he was friend to these other two, and they were no friends to Jon-Joras. Friends do not come seeking friends with drawn weapons in their hands. And besides—*I always hate coming here,* one had said. So. These were the "proper men," the men whose coming was regular and by arrangement, and who had been coming here for decades. At least for decades. Who had provided at least two wretched devils of interpreters. Had allied themselves with the alien Kar-chees and with their murderous dragons. Who?

I must consult with my other self. What of that, for a conundrum?

Nothing of that, for now. For now there was only the matter of keeping out of the way. Had the Kar-chee, after consulting with its "other self," decided not to trust Jon-Joras? Decided to turn the matter over to the familiar, the "proper men"? Certainly it did seem so.

He came to another slit-window and looked out. There was no one and nothing to be seen. From the slant rays of the declining sun it appeared that he was now on the other side of the castle from where the Kar-chee (was there only one Kar-chee? Did not its curious reference to the "other self" plainly indicate there was at least one other?) and its domestic dragon were. Jon-Joras sighed. Let him but once get off this troubled world, he would take good care never to return to it. Now, how wide was this window?

It was wide enough.

There were foot-holds enough, too, and a conveniently canting, slanting tree. He made his way to the ground with no more difficulty than that provided by the constant fear of death, and then he crept into the underbrush like a lizard. He had gotten a good ways off and had raised himself from all fours to that same crouching or rather, stooped, walk, which had stood him in such good stead so early this morning, when a shout came from behind him and a tussock beside him exploded into a gout of dust and earth.

They had seen him.

XI

THEY KEPT on coming after him.

And, after them, came the dragon.

It was probably futile to try to escape them on foot. They were fresh, he was weary. They were armed, he was not. And even if he could outrun them, there was still the dragon to contend with . . . not the chicken-witted wittold of the settled regions, but the murderously intelligent great beast of The Bosky. Various old bywords went rushing through his mind. *If you can't go across, you must go around. If you can't go across, you* must *go across*. No, not those. He tried to bring his buttocks even lower than they were, and dragged himself, face first, through something nasty. *If you can't go across, you must go up*. Probably there was no such byword at all. Or hadn't been . . . till now.

He went up and he went up the far side of the twisted old tree. Something had built a nest or a den there once, and it still smelled rotten. Not matter. Such things had ceased to count long ago. He pulled his legs up after him and used the stinging twig-work as a blind to peer through. The men had not seen him, yet. Neither, apparently, had the dragon. It came running along as he had never before seen dragons run: lightly, and on all fours, but as though it ran on its toes and not upon the pads of its feet at all. It made no sound. It made no sound at all that Jon-Joras could hear.

But the men below had heard something. Or had felt or scented or sensed something. One of them whirled around and cried out. The others on the instant did the same. They scattered. And Jon-Joras in the tree realized a few sudden things. For one, the dragon was not hunting him. For another, the dragon was not hunting for or with the men. And for a third and last, it was hunting *against* them. It was clear that they knew it, too.

This hunt was short-lived, for the weapons the men were carrying were not the local model huntguns. They had not come loaded for dragon; at least, he knew of no reason why they should have. And in any event this one was not marked and was not even running erect so that they might guess at where its vital spot, where the fatal shot, might be and might be placed. So far as Jon-Joras knew, they had only come loaded for Jon-Joras, and his body rattled in a sudden spasm of fear when he saw one of them level the thick and snub death-weapon and blow the dragon's head into a mash of blood and brain and bone and pulp that flew all about. And then, then, oh, how horrible! to see the dying dragon, the dragon that should have been dead, still stumbling along, and groping and clutching for its prey while all the while fountains of blood spurted from its broken arteries and torrents of blood poured from its severed veins. It was as though the headless body still remembered what its eyes had seen and still knew where to go and what to do.

Pounding, now, pawing the stained grasses, it came on, came onward, still came on, while the man it approached scrambled backwards and stumbled backwards as though not daring to turn his head; and the other two retreated, took their stances again, and blew great chasms and abysses into it. Off in the woods another dragon called, briefly, abruptly, cut off in mid-cry. Were all the dragons of The Bosky being massacred? ". . . in the egg, and out . . ."? as, even now, this one, its spine exposed and smashed, fell at last to the ground, which shook to receive it. A short moment more the fore-limbs tore at the bloody turf and tried to pull the bleeding mountain of flesh further. There was a spasm, a flurry, and the ravaged hulk lay still.

The three, shaking their heads, came cautiously together and surveyed their kill. And the other dragon, walking fully erect—*walking fully erect!*—and again with that curious stride upon the tips of its toes—passed beneath Jon-Joras as he clung to the tree and peered in numbed more-than-fright through the soiled integuments of the abandoned nest. Beneath him, beyond him, nodules swollen in silent rage, and then it bellowed the rage that made the forest quake as it fell upon them. And ripped and tore.

One died where he stood, one fired upwards and vanished into the giant, trap-like mouth even as the limb his shot had shattered dangled and spurted blood; and one fled, shrilling as he ran, and was almost immediately followed down and dragged and torn and trampled. And so ended the last dragon hunt that Jon-Joras was ever to see.

What happened next was less terrifying, but

no less amazing. For the great beast, pushing aside the corpse at its feet, with one of its forepaws seized hold of a branch and transferred it to the wounded limb which grasped it convulsively but held it firm. Then it rooted out another. Then, turning around and around, and looking up and looking down and looking all about it, it began that beating together, that clicking and rustling, which could only have been a deliberate attempt at imitating the methods of the Old Man interpreter. It was capable of no other meaning than a desire to locate Jon-Joras. And a desire to indicate that its desire was not hostile.

Quaking and trembling, he came down from the tree. The faceted eyes flashed at him. It moved off, he followed, it turned and saw that he followed, and so it turned no more until at last they reached the castle. But he had not followed until, forcing his quivering stomach into obedience, he turned over one of the mangled bodies on the bloody forest floor. Only one, but that one was enough. Jetro Yi. No wonder his voice, his manner, had seemed familiar. Flunky Jetro. He would bow and scrape no more.

Thus far, the door onto the mysteries had opened. But up there in the castle, it had swung shut in a manner forbidding it should or could ever be opened in any near time again. The Old Man, his poor grimy forehead battered and blue where, presumably, the butt of a gun had struck it, lay face upwards and mouth open. He had been afraid and he had been rightfully afraid, but Jon-Joras was very glad that he did not seem to be afraid any longer. It was simply too bad that his release had been so long in coming.

The Kar-chee looked at him with huge dull eyes. It seemed, somehow, to be crooked. Jon-Joras looked more closely and saw that it, too, was hurt. The three "proper men," with Jetro Yi one of them, had done a fine day's work. It was possible to reconstruct it, almost as though the gaunt, hurt creature was able to tell him of it. They had appeared and spoken to the castle's keeper. They knew that Jon-Joras must be here, or—perhaps—they had only guessed that he might. Perhaps the timorous Old Man had somehow given it away. They had demanded him, the one who stole their flyer, had caused the death of the crew of the other, the crashed flyer. Of course it was not that alone or even mostly that which brought them after him. But—

Almost certainly the Kar-chee had confronted them with their perpetually broken promise. Had, likely enough, demanded that it be immediately fulfilled. Had refused to surrender someone else who had promised that promise to fulfil. Blows were struck. They left the castle looking still for Jon-Joras and certainly it had never been their intention to allow him to escape. He had a quick, over-vivid picture of his own head struck by the same shot which had killed the first dragon out there in the woods. The first dragon, the first and second dragons. Like minor players in an archaic play-drama . . . but their roles had not been minor, but their roles had been and still were things of the mystery. He thought that, finally, finally, he was beginning to understand. But with the Old Man dead (and perhaps, with his ruined mind, even if he had not been dead), he could never be fully sure that he had understood or ever would, entirely.

As for the Kar-chee—and he found it not hard to pity it now, wounded and alone, despite all that its kind had done so long ago to this the home of all man's race—it understood this much, at any rate: that only in and through Jon-Joras it had hopes of survival and escape. Therefore it had sent the dragon, not only to save him, but to bring him back.

Therefore *it had sent its other self!*

The flyer in which Jetro Yi and his two fellows had come was in the clearing where it had landed and which smelled of the stale fuel of its many prior comings. Perhaps forewarned against leaving it alone by Jon-Joras's theft of the other one that morning, they'd left a man on armed guard. But he was dead now, too, and from the shape (or shapelessness) of him, it would have been neither grace nor favor to him if he were still alive. Jon-Joras, infinitely weary, glad of the excuse given him by the slow and limping Kar-chee, slowed his own walk. It was almost dark when they reached the craft. He put its lights on and the two of them entered. Fortunately it was a larger craft than the one he'd made off with this morning, but even so the alien had to crouch, looking not less fearful because he was huddled instead of erect. But there was no longer, so it seemed, fear between them. And Jon-Joras made a wry smile at the thought that perhaps the Kar-chee was even now reminding itself that the fact that Jon-Joras had a bad smell did not mean that Jon-Joras was therefore bad!

He settled into the drive-seat with a grateful

groan of relief. He took the craft up and then he
radioed in to ConfedBase, down on the underside of the Earth in a small continent which the
Kar-chees had raised up around what had once
been the Andaman Islands, and had ConfedBase
connect him to Delegate Anse.

"How are you? Where are you? How have you
been? Why did you go away from the hospital?"
the questions came pouring out.

Jon-Joras said, "I'm in a stolen flyer up at
30,000 feet. I am very tired, but otherwise well.
One group of men tried to kill me early this
morning. Another group of them—or maybe just
another group—tried to kill me late this afternoon. I have a Kar-chee with me, and—"

"You have a what?" Anse interrupted, in a
low voice.

"A Kar-chee, he's injured, but I don't know
how much or how seriously. Where should we
meet you? Sir? Delegate? Are you—"

"I'm here, yes. I'm just thinking. I'm afraid
that you're still quite ill. The best thing would be
for you to put down in the nearest place you can.
Would that be Peramis?"

Jon-Joras later found it easier to see things as
Anse had seen them, but at that exact moment
he saw nothing incredible in his own report. He
did not make things any better by shouting that
nothing would persuade him to go anywhere
near any of the four city-states or, for that matter, anywhere near any place where dragon
hunts were conducted. "Think fast," he wound
up. "They may be monitoring this call right
now. They may try to bring me down."

"Oh, dear," said Anse. "Oh, oh, oh . . . Hold
on. Hold on."

Later, too, Jon-Joras realized that the anxiety was not at all occasioned by belief, but entirely by disbelief. At the moment, though, he found it somewhat gratifying. Anse came back in a moment, asked him how his fuel was, gave him a course to set, and informed him that a special fast-flyer was being sent out and would pick him up in as little time as possible and bring him down to ConfedBase. And this it did. That is, it did not so much pick him up as scoop him up. Then it went down a great ways and leveled out to allow him to transfer. Part of the crew were Prime Worlders, and promptly went into something approaching hysteria when they saw the Kar-chee. But the others had seen enough of aliens even more uncanny-looking than the Kar-chee, and, moreover, had no backlog of almost hereditary fear and hatred concerning Prime World's former conquerors. They even made educated guesses as to what it would eat and drink, and although it did not do much of either, it did enough of both to relieve Jon-Joras's mind. He reproached himself for not having thought of this, and was engaged in formulating a useless and incomprehensible apology when he fell asleep sitting up.

The sun was shining when he awoke, and, not reflecting that it was in the nature of things suntime at ConfedBase when it was night-time on the other side of the world, he thought he had had a good night's rest. He nodded amiably at the immense avenues of gorgeous flowering trees through which they passed, and, his memory of having seen them at the time of his arrival here on Prime World becoming confused with his seeing them now, he passed into a state where he

was not very far from dreaming, and thought of
what he recalled having been through as being
but singularly vivid visions seen along the roads
of sleep. He was in fact thoroughly asleep in a
very few minutes, and so he remained for hours
yet to come. At one point or at several points he
heard familiar voices and this comforted him
and it was of no matter to him at the moment if
they were dream-voices or real-voices or what
they were.

"I was certain that he was feverish or hallu-
cinating or something of that sort—result, you
know, Confidential Chief, of his previous illness."

"Were you?" said the other voice, the voice
which pleased him most to hear, although the
voice itself seemed not pleased at all.

There was a short pause; the first voice said,
"You know that we have little investigatory apparatus here. There has never been any need for
it. I saw him briefly when he came through here
to make arrangements for you and he said nothing of your special status then—"

"He didn't know anything about it. Go on—'

"I heard nothing further from him. Then your
communication arrived, and I wondered that I'd
heard nothing. I sent word out and was told of
his being missing after attending an impromptu
hunt which had evidently been attacked by a
rogue dragon. So many had been killed . . . I offered a reward . . . But still nothing turned up.
Then came his radio message and his, well, rather wild-sounding story. The physician said he
was certainly ill. Then he vanished, as you know,
from the physician's care. And when he said that
he had been attacked twice yesterday and had

stolen a flyer and had a Kar-chee on board with him—Now, would you not, in my place, have thought—"

And the second voice said, "I am not in your place, Delegate. Nor are you in mine." Then it asked, "What do you think of his story now? Of all of it, I mean?"

"A living Kar-chee? Here? After all these centuries? A living dodo or dinosaur would be less of a marvel. Much less. If that much of his story is true—and it obviously is!—then all the rest of it could be true, too. And what it all means, is more than I can guess.—You?"

"Me? I have neither need to nor intention of guessing. When my boy wakes up he will tell me. He looks so thin and worn. And so young, so young, so very young . . ."

The voices fell away. And the young, young, very young man slept on and on. Now it seemed to him that he was aware that he was sleeping and this was pleasant. Somewhere outside was danger. Inside all was safe. The Kar-chee was at the head of his bed and the dragon was at the foot of it and Por-Paulo sat beside it, on the right, the side of honor, which was proper. For he was the proper man, the *proper* proper man. It was a pity that no one could tell this to the Kar-chee. But perhaps he knew it anyway.

"In a way, old Ma'am Anna was right," Jon-Joras explained over a long and leisurely breakfast, after having slept the clock around. "Because, in a way, the dragons *did* turn into Kar-chees. And, in another way, Huë was also right. Because, in a way, the dragons *were* Kar-chee. Neither was altogether right nor altogether wrong. I think that the truth—as nearly as we can arrive at it—lies somewhere in between. And I think that it goes a long way towards explaining the whole history and mystique of the dragon hunts. Where to start?"

Well-rested, well-washed, well- and cleanly-clothed once again, in slow contented process of becoming well-fed, and two exceedingly important older men listening intently to his every spoken word—Jon-Joras had reason to be as well-pleased with his present situation as, indeed, he was. He had surprises to spring . . . but then, surprises had been sprung on him as well. And on an empty stomach, too.

Delegate Anse, a small, thin and precise man whose pale hair was cut in the tonsure customary to his native continent, had registered a very mild note of complaint on one of these latter matters. "I don't recall your telling me," he had said, "that besides being the private man of Elected King Por-Paulo, you were also his freeborn son."

"He didn't know it, Delegate," Por-Paulo said. He was a big man, grayhaired, prominent of nose and jaw. "I very much wanted to marry his mother, but she had—and has—her own ideas on this, as on many subjects. She not only refused me, she chose to reserve the information. And according to our hegemonial laws I could not reveal it myself. But—" his eyes, uplifted for a brief, gleaming instant, "they don't apply here . . ."

Unspoken but understood was the intimation that this was at the least one of the reasons for his sending Jon-Joras to Prime World. And following after him. And Jon-Joras had only repeated, bewildered, but never in the least displeased, "I didn't know. I didn't know. I always wondered. But I didn't know. . . ."

The delegate dismissed the matter, as far as he himself was concerned, with a brisk nod, and, "He being free-born, the Nepotism Acts do not apply . . ." then continued, "You seem to have really done a quite good job, Private Man. I commend you for it—and I commend you, Confidential Chief, for your choice."

Por-Paulo nodded rather absently, and continued to regard his natural son with the affection he had previously been unable to express openly in his closely, intensely regulated native hegemony. For Jon-Joras, however, it had been another by no means unpleasant shock. *Confidential Chief!* Not only was Por-Paulo his father— and it might be years before he could fully adjust to this: in the past, though father had been inhibited, son had been totally ignorant—but he was one of the one hundred "shadow rulers" of the Confederation, chosen by lot from among the thousands of paramount executives!

Jon-Joras hoped, and rather expected that he would be able to digest both surprises as well as his breakfast. "Where to begin?" he repeated, now. "I wish the Old Man were still alive. Then we'd be able to speak to the Kar-chee, and check my guesses against its own knowledge."

Anse said, "It might just be possible. It seems to me that Dr. Cannatin has arrived. Let's have him in."

The egg-round, egg-bald archaeologist was not in the best of humors at having been abruptly removed from his dig and flown down to ConfedBase. "Three pot-shards and half a glass medicine-bottle may not seem like much to you," he protested, "considering the time I've spent. But I can assure you of the value and significance of the—"

"I have no doubt—" Anse had begun.

"Not that the medicine-bottle is of a particularly rare type," Cannatin swept on along. "No, on the contrary, it's found with sufficient frequency to justify dating other artifacts by its presence in a given stratum. We are, however, still not certain what the name of the medicine was. Hrospard Uu—you've of course read his monumental *Tentative Glot-tochronology of the Ichthyopophagous Peoples of Alghol*—"

"Dr. Cannatin, we—"

"—Uu claims it was called *colacola*. Dr. Pix, the labial surd chap, on the other hand, insists that *cococo* is the proper form. I should like an explanation of why I was bundled up and hustled down here, if you please. Well?"

His annoyance vanished quickly enough on hearing the explanation. For, like all archaeologists of his time, Cannatin was also a linguist. And, as Delegate Anse, who had examined his records on his arrival on Prime World, knew, the scholar had at one time done excavations on the non-affiliated world of Laralpersis, Off in the Lace Pattern.

"Wasn't there—isn't there—" Anse asked, "a colony of Kar-chee in that place?"

Cannatin nodded, then at once shook his head. "Kar-chee-*like*," he corrected. "Smaller. Gray. Not the same. Similar. I did some work among—Why do you ask? Dare I hope that at last I'm to be allowed to try my hand on Kar-chee sites? I've always wanted to, but there were always obstructions put in my way. Nothing can really be done here, as I'm sure you know, without the cooperation of the Hunt Company. And the Hunt Company, for some reason . . . Well, I suppose they're not interested in anything but hunting. Eh?''

He was incredulous when they told him that a living Kar-chee was present there at Confed-Base, that the physicians were doing their best to treat its injuries, and that anything he knew or could surmise about its morphology or habits or language—in short, anything about it—based on his knowledge of a kindred species, would probably be of considerable help.

"In-*cred*-ible!'' he exclaimed. "W*on*derful! Yes. Yes, yes, of course. I do know something of the subject. We used a little mechanical device to communicate with them, electronic, similar—or, at least, not grossly dissimilar—to the ancient telegraph instrument. And not utterly, remote, either, to various drum-systems of reproducing certain languages. I'm sure I could rig one up with a little help. Mind you, it's no magical-tele-pathic gadget, it won't teach me their talkee-talkee. But . . . on the basis of what I know about a presumably cognate type of language, plus what we all know, all we linguists, I mean, on the question of general communications between intelligent species: I should be able to manage something. It will be fine fun to try, and, mean-while, well, my pot-shards and medicine-bottles will stay and wait for me. Nobody else wants them.

"Take me to your Kar-chee,'' he wound up. "And,'' to Jon-Joras, "I'll be sure to mention you, with full credits, young man, in the paper I mean to write about this.''

Jon-Joras, mouth full of marmalade, gestured to him to stay a second more. Hastily swallowed. Asked, "Did the ones on Laralpersis give the appearance of living in symbiosis with another form of life?"

Cannatin frowned. "Hadn't thought of it in those terms," he said, after a moment. "Symbiosis, commensality . . . There was a fuzzy little nothing of a creature that all the Kish-chefs seemed fond of—in fact, we were told it was as much as our life was worth to tamper with one of those fuzz-balls. Why? Well, I'll ask you later. Duty, duty."

It fit in, it all fit in. *I must consult with my other self*. In the past, among men, the possession by one entity of more than one ego had been regarded with, generally, fear and terror. They had spoken of demoniac indwelling, of satanic possession, multiple personality. Victims had been exorcized, lobotomized, mulcted, hospitalized, incarcerated—If the Kar-chees, and their cognates, the Kish-chefs, had ever in an earlier stage or age of their species, undergone similar experiences, could not be said. What could be said, though—and Jon-Joras said it clearly—was this:

"There seems to me to be three things certain. One, is that every member of this species has at least two egos . . . selves . . . personalities. Maybe some have more, I don't know; the only one I spoke to mentioned only one other self. Two, that they solved the problem, if indeed it ever was a problem to them, by finding another life-form to serve as host to the other personality. This other life-form was, had to be, one whose own intelligence—or should I say, intelligence-

ego?—was sufficiently feeble to present no obsta-
cle. In the case of the Kish-chefs, this 'mount'
was what he calls the 'fuzzy balls of nothing.'
And this brings us to number three: The 'mount'
used by the Kar-chee was the creature we call *the
dragon*.

"No wonder it seemed 'that the dragons were
the Kar-chee's dogs.' The Kar-chee could be in
one place and one of his selves in the Kar-chee
body in that place; meanwhile, the other self was
in the dragon body, hunting down the comparatively feeble human. As long as the dragon
body was being 'mounted' by a Kar-chee ego, it
was capable of acting intelligently. The moment
it ceased to be occupied, or, as I've been saying,
'mounted', by a Kar-chee ego, it had nothing in
charge of it but its own low-grade, feeble intelligence. Which wasn't interested in humans,
generally speaking. See how all the fragments fit
together. Before the era of the Kar-chee: no
dragons. After the Kar-chee reign: lots of
dragons. And a tradition which absolutely as-
sociated the dragons with the Kar-chee but
which, through ignorance, was utterly confused
as to what that relationship was.

"I see no other possibility but that the Kar-
chee did bring the dragons with them. And in
their campaign of conquest they fought the humans here in both their sets of bodies. But the
ones which the humans saw the most of was the
dragon set. The Kar-chee sets would have been
mostly inside the walls of their outposts—the
castles, as we call them—planning, directing,
moving land and sea. All that. With no humans
around to observe. The humans were all outside,
being pursued by the dragons. So some of them

thought that the dragons were a sort of were-Kar-chee, or vice-versa, changing their shapes back and forth. And some of them . . . and I take this to be a later tradition . . . fused their memories and assumed that the dragon-shape was the only shape. The dragons, then, to them, *were* the Kar-chee! And of course, in a way they were, only in a mental rather than a physical way, don't you see?"

It seemed odd that they were not bothered by the fact that the Kar-chee had certainly been at least the equal of humanity in intelligence, while the dragons had the intellectual ability of a barnyard fowl. But this was beside the point. Which was, that the human race on Prime World had waged war upon a hideous and hated enemy which had (although not exclusively) the form of the dragon. And right down to the present day, the human race on Prime World was still waging war upon that enemy! It was a war which had never ceased, stylized, ritualized, former 'enemy' reduced to an animal, goaded into battle, preserved chiefly that it might be destroyed: but war, nonetheless. Revenge, it could be called revenge. Racial sadism, it could be called that, too. And it would be equally correct to call it a symbolic re-enactment of the liberation of Prime World. But in the end it still returned to the same point.

War.

The dragon hunt was war.

"It does," Delegate Anse said, reflectively, running his thin hands over his thin, pale hair, when Jon-Joras stopped; "it does seem to make sense. Much sense."

Por-Paulo thrust out his chin, as he did when

he was displeased, and pushed his lower lip out after it. "Well . . ." he said. "I suppose it could be argued that it serves a useful purpose and function of sorts. There are plenty of parallels. I believe that even up to the First Expansion Period here on Prime World there were such ritual combats. 'Combats' I say. They weren't really. They never are, these sort of things. It's always fixed, always rigged. The beast is always doomed. It's better to face the fact honestly and not pretty it up with a lot of lies about blowing off steam and reducing tensions and getting rid of this and that, acting out anxieties, moment of truth. Piddle. There's an ancient word, I don't know what language it is. *Bazazz*. All those arguments are a lot of bazazz. Unless you're wiping out vermin or hunting for meat to eat, the man who kills animals does so because he likes to kill. And people who like to watch do so because they like to see things being killed.

"I hunt. But I know my own motives. And I know what keeps the Hunt Company in business. And, speaking of which—"

"Yes—" said Anse.

"Yes—" said Jon-Joras. "The Hunt Company as business. Which it is by definition. But whereas, in places like Gare or Sundi, it fits its purposes into the local scene without interfering, here it has in effect taken over the whole continent and frozen it solid and made everything and everyone else fit into *its* purpose. The Gentlemen as a caste are ideally suited for that, they make admirable instruments. They want to live without creative toil, and the Hunt Company is delighted to help them do so. So decorative! It means nothing that most of the population has been turned into helotry and that some of them —Huë, I mean, and his followers—have even been driven into functioning insanity as a revulsion against the Hunt System and the Gentlemen caste. Hang them up by the heels and shoot them full of arrows . . . *that's* decorative, too for that matter.

"Of course not all the Gentlemen are deliberately base. But I've seen what absolute devotion to the principle can do to a man of the caliber of Aëlorix. I've seen what it can do in the way of corrupting official justice, and I almost died of it. But it never was quite clear to me that the Hunt Company wasn't just riding the wave, that it was in fact *creating* the wave. I did wonder that Jetro Yi always put me off whenever I wanted to come over into The Bosky, but I thought he was just worrying about perhaps losing a commission on one single hunt, or perhaps that he had caught a kind of superstitious fear of the place as a result of all the stories told about it."

Delegate Anse was unhappy, and Delegate Anse had good cause to be. This had been going on under his eyes and he had never seen it. Others, elsewhere, had suspected something of it— wherefore Jon-Joras arriving in all innocence to make arrangements for Por-Paulo's hunt; Por-Paulo all the while acting on behalf of the Confidential Chiefs and their suspicions—but Anse had had no suspicions. It was well enough to say that this had all been going on for a long, long time before he had arrived to take up his residence on ConfedBase. This was true, and it was also true that in adhering to the policy of "non-interference in local ways, rules, and customs" he had only been carrying out Confederation practice. The truth is not always an absolute defense. Anse had been ignorant of what had been going on, and he ought not to have been ignorant. It is one thing to avoid gross interference and it was another thing entirely not even to know that something was going on which he might (and, then, might not) have been justified in not interfering with.

Anse had a problem. But in this particular respect it was all Anse's problem.

"Companies have become corrupt before," Por-Paulo said, in a sort of growl. "The temptation is always there, and when the place it operates in is both distant and primitive, the temptation is even greater. I don't know if we can stick the whole Hunt outfit with responsibility for this rotten local scene. It may really be that the rest of it knows nothing about the local branch working hand and glove with the Kar-chee in keeping people out of The Bosky. Not much doubt as to why they were doing it, I suppose?"

Anse, still musing over his personal problem, had nothing to say. But Jon-Joras had. "Not much doubt in my mind," he said. "If The Bosky had been wide open, the plebs—Doghunters or Free Farmers, call them what you like—the poor; there—they'd have abandoned the city-states in large numbers. And rightly so. Now, of course, the Gentlemen don't want that. Nor does the Hunt Company. They want the rotten, picturesque pattern preserved, never mind at what terrible cost to the majority of the population. They want the Gentlemen on their estates and the archers and the bannermen and the musics and the beaters and the whole archaic and hypo-

critical rest of it. And they want it cheap, too.
Package deals for rich offical and executives.
They couldn't have it at the price they want,
which is the current price—the current price as
paid by the Hunt Company, that is; if they raise
their mark-up, that's the Hunt Company's business—but they couldn't have it at the present
price if the population dropped because of a migration into The Bosky. Sooner or later, those
who'd be left would realize that there are no
longer a hundred men eager and waiting and
ready to step into their shoes. And they'd set a
better sort of price on themselves and their services. They might even say, The Hell with it!
and dispense with offering their services altogether."

He pushed away his breakfast. His appetite
was dulled, and he thought of the gray-haired
"chick-boys" and the old "marky" with his fingers eaten into twisted stumps from decades of
smearing acid into X-marks so that rich men
could murder dragons and go and boast of it;
this thought did nothing to restore his appetite.
"I don't know how long this blockade of The
Bosky has been going on. I don't know who it
was who first got in touch with the Kar-chee and
started it going. Or if there were more Kar-chee
then and this is the last, or—well, any of that. It
brings up a thousand questions. Was there a colony of them left behind? Do they live long, very,
very long? I don't know. Maybe with Dr. Cannatin working on the communications, we'll be
able to find out. Ohh, and—I did promise, while
the Old Man was still alive (and there's another
strike against the Hunt Company, another

black, black mark: giving those interpreters over to a life-long exile and a living death there. Locked up with beings so alien that gradually they became all but de-humanized. Why! This last one, Old Man, I mean, he had been brought all the way from Dondon-oluc! So someone there must have known about what was going on here . . .).

"But, as I say, I did promise that the Kar-chee would be taken back to the Kar-chee worlds, to the Ring Stars. I hope that my promise will be kept, sir?"

Por-Paulo shifted in his seat and nodded. Then he blew out his cheeks. "I don't at the moment know how, boy. And its dragon, too? But I'm sure that it can be done. And so it will. Because—What—?"

"Oh," said Jon-Joras, "the thought just came to me. It's that the Hunt Company is the biggest rogue dragon of them all. What's to be done about that?"

He had some notions, and he expressed them, about annulling its charters and disqualifying its officials. Por-Paulo grunted, muttered something about *baby* and *bath-water*. The best thing, he thought, was to do nothing and allow nothing to be done. Just let the word get around that the dragons in The Bosky were harmless, and nature —human nature—would take its course. "You just stated rather clearly what it was that the Hunt Company didn't want to happen. Well, then. We've drawn their teeth. The mere fact that we *know* and that they'll know that we know will see to that. And all those things will just go ahead and happen. And we'll just let them. The

Company and their gentlemanly allies will hurt.
All right. Let them. They'll adjust. It won't happen overnight.''

The flower-scented, salt-scented breeze came
in through the screens. Jon-Joras moved and
stretched. He had a quick picture of sandy
beaches and surfy waters and perhaps, probably, why not? female company. But first. "And
meanwhile, sir? What of all those mismarked
dragons wandering around? And all the trained
rogues? Are we to allow the hunts to go on when
they might turn into massacres? In a way, I suppose, we could say, if any over-ripe Commissioners get smeared all over Belroze Wood
that it serves them right. Eh?''

His father pulled his nose and pulled his chin
and said *Mmph* a few times. "Well, what do you
suggest, damn it?" he demanded, after a while.

Promptly, Jon-Joras said, "That we not do
nothing. That we do *something*. A ten-year
moratorium, at least, on hunting. That will not
only allow the marked and mis-marked dragons
to die off, it will let the Company and the Gentlemen do their hurting *now*. That way the pain
will fall on those who deserve it and not on their
children and successors. In fact, I'm not sure
that it might not be a bad idea to send trained
crews to comb the woods and blow the heads off
everything over hatchling size. That way would
make *sure*. And I certainly wouldn't let the movement into The Bosky and beyond go on
haphazardly. What's to stop some Gentleman
who's shrewd enough to see the handwriting on
the wall from moving in there himself? With his
servants and his little private army, I mean, and
carving himself out another little feudal empire

and getting ready to start the whole thing all over again?"

Again Por-Paulo grunted and fingered his face. And now Delegate Anse unexpectedly had something to say. Confederation, he suggested, could do more than continue its passive role. This was after all, *Prime* World, the birthworld of mankind. Confederation had many debts to pay here, and this was an excellent place to begin. "We have ample experience in helping settlements get started in proper fashion," he pointed out. "We needn't let this one go higgledy-piggeldy, root-hog-or-die, and devil-take-the-hindmost. We can help those who want to move to help themselves in the most efficient fashion. And the same goes for those who want to stay. In fact, I rather think we'd better. There must be lots of the Huë sort around . . . men whose sufferings have unhinged them to the point where they'd rather burn the house down than see it cleaned up. I rather think we'd all rather see it cleaned up."

The answer of Por-Paulo to this was oblique. "But I want to have a personal talk with Gentleman Aëlorix," he said. "And as for that puissant poop, the Chairman of Drogue . . ." He thrust out his chin and his lip and he growled. Then he turned to Jon-Joras. "Finish your breakfast," he said.

Jon-Joras pushed the tray away. "I don't want any more," he said.